FREE AS A BIRD

FREE AS A BIRD

Ken McCoy

This first world edition published in Great Britain 2007 by
SEVERN HOUSE PUBLISHERS LTD of
9–15 High Street, Sutton, Surrey SM1 1DF.
This first world edition published in the USA 2008 by
SEVERN HOUSE PUBLISHERS INC of
595 Madison Avenue, New York, N.Y. 10022.

British Library Cataloguing in Publication Data

McCoy, Ken, 1940-
  Free as a bird
  1. Sisters - Fiction 2. Great Britain - Social life and
  customs - Fiction
  I. Title
  823.9'2[F]

ISBN-13: 978-0-7278-6583-0   (cased)

All Severn House titles are printed on acid-free paper.

Typeset by Palimpsest Book Production Ltd.,
Grangemouth, Stirlingshire, Scotland.
Printed and bound in Great Britain by
MPG Books Ltd., Bodmin, Cornwall.

To Isabelle Katherine and Ava Mae

With thanks to my wife, Valerie, who has an unusual knowledge of things way beyond my fairly wide range of interests. In all of my books she has made many and varied contributions and offered valuable advice and valid criticism. Especially this book.

Prologue

Leeds Register Office, March 1944

Lola looked up at the man who was to take her father's place and what she saw didn't impress her one bit. He was a big man with an empty face that told her nothing; it could have been carved out of a lump of old wood. In the brief time she'd known him he'd never done anything to particularly offend or hurt her; but then again, he'd never done anything to particularly please her. Her mother had said that, after the war was over, this man would come back and look after them, but Lola knew for certain that he'd never replace her daddy. Her memories of her father were patchy, but she did remember a certain look in his eyes that said he loved her without him having to open his mouth and tell her so. He had been a genuine war hero, killed in action. She knew the only reason her mam was marrying this po-faced man was because she was going to have a baby. Lola liked the idea of a baby sister or brother but she couldn't, for the life of her, figure out why it meant her mam had to marry this man. She might only have had a vague idea about where babies came from, but there was one thing she knew for certain – they didn't come from men. Only last year Mrs Pickles from next-door-but-one had had a baby all on her own while Mr Pickles had been in a Japanese prisoner of war camp since the beginning of the war. So why should Mam involve Ezra Lawless? There were things grown-ups did that made no sense at all.

She wasn't too struck on the names he'd chosen for the child. And how come he chose the names? It was Mam's baby. Some weeks ago she'd discussed it with her mam, but she hadn't got far.

'Mam,' she had said, 'why are you going to call it Adam

or Eve? I thought you said you'd call your next baby Carol if it was a girl or Harry it was a boy. That's what you told Daddy when he was alive.'

'These are proper biblical names, Lola.'

'Oh,' Lola had said. She went off to find the family bible and came back. 'We could call it Esau or Moses or Caleb or Delilah or Mahlah or Hoglah—'

'You're being difficult, Lola. The baby's going to be called Adam or Eve.'

'If it's a boy we could call him Lucifer.'

'Lucifer's the devil's name.'

'Daddy said they call matches Lucifers,' said Lola. She began to sing:

'Pack up your troubles in your old kit bag and smile, smile, smile.

'While you've a Lucifer to light your fag, smile boy that's the style.

'What the use of worr—'

Her mother had cut her off mid-song. 'Mr Lawless is very fussy about names.'

Lola was nothing if not persistent. 'Daddy wasn't fussy about names. Daddy would have let you choose. Daddy said he didn't care what you called him so long as you didn't call him late for his dinner . . . sorry, Mam.'

Too much mention of her daddy was making her mam cry so Lola had shut up and put an arm around her. Rachel hugged her back and wondered what the hell she was letting herself in for.

Lola's proper name was Dolores Drinkwater, which was quite modern, if not grand. She didn't mind being called Lola, which, she'd been told, was a bit exotic – although she wasn't quite sure what exotic meant. But she wasn't looking forward to becoming Dolores Lawless.

Ezra wore his army uniform and her mam had had her hair permed. Lola's hair was dark and glossy. Her eyes too were dark and shone out of an unusually pretty face, which was destined to be beautiful. A beauty that would require an inner strength or it might well be her downfall.

She had been given confetti to throw but, with her only being seven, she couldn't reach high enough to tip it over their heads as they walked out into the street into the drizzle. Anyway, damp confetti doesn't flutter as it's supposed to. She made an unenthusiastic effort, which ended with her tipping the confetti on to the pavement. Her new stepfather leaned down and whispered in her ear, 'Don't expect life to be a bed of roses, girl, just because yer've got a new father.'

He was more than true to his word; but there would be one day, eleven years in the future, which would turn everyone's lives upside down.

One

'I'd like a pair of wooden clogs, please, size nine and a half. I wish to pursue a lucrative career as a door-to-door clog dancer.'

'Keith Penfold, shouldn't you be in class or something?' Lola replied without looking up from her work, which entailed squeezing a pair of shoes on to the reluctant feet of a four-year-old boy.

'Teacher let me off early because I got me sums right.'

The bemused four-year-old looked up at the young man who had just entered the shoe shop. Keith smiled down at him.

'Let me see you walk up and down,' said Lola to the boy.

Keith began to walk up and down the shop.

'Not you, you fool.'

The boy's mother chuckled, so did Lola. If nothing else Keith made her laugh. She smiled at the boy and asked, 'Are they comfy?' She squeezed the toes to make sure he had room to grow.

'They grow so fast at his age,' said the mother.

'Can you wiggle your toes?' asked Lola.

The boy confirmed that he could wiggle his toes, as did Keith, much to the boy's amusement.

'They're not all locked up,' said the mother.

'He wants locking up,' said Lola. 'He's supposed to be up at Durham University, studying history. He's going to be a teacher. Why aren't you at university studying history?'

'There's no future in it. Clog dancing's the thing for me.'

'They let him go early cos he got his sums right,' said the boy.

'This boy will go far,' said Keith, patting the boy's head. 'So I thought I'd pop down here and propose to you.'

'Propose?' said Lola. 'Are you insane?'

'Ah, now that was never officially proved. I propose you take me out tomorrow night to the Mecca Locarno, on account of me being skint. We can wine and dine and clog dance the night away. After that we can talk about marriage, but only if you must.'

'Keith, I've only known you a fortnight.'

'Really? It seems like years.'

'My marriage is a bit like that,' said the mother. 'Who do I pay?'

'Could you pay Mr Jessop behind the counter?'

'Thanks, love.' She inclined her head towards Keith. 'By the way, if he does ask I should snap him up. He might not be much ter look at but he'll make yer laugh. There's not too many good uns about nowadays.'

'True,' said Lola.

She was thinking about Ezra Lawless.

29 Atkinson Terrace, Leeds. 6 p.m.

'Please don't play with your food, Evie!'

The miserable weather matched the mood inside the house. Rachel was trying to scold her youngest daughter but her heart wasn't really in it. Her heart was rarely in anything.

Evie pushed a few beans around the plate with her fork. Lola looked from her mother to her sister and recognized something in Evie's demeanour that disturbed her.

'Are you OK, kid?'

Recently Evie had become withdrawn and cheerless, especially when he was in the house. The telephone rang. Rachel got up from the table and went into the hallway to answer it. Lola reached out and ran her hand through Evie's mousy hair, comfortingly. Rachel came back in the room.

'Who was it?' Lola asked her.

Her mother shrugged. 'Oh, someone for your father – he sounded a bit posh.'

'He's not my father, my father was a good man.'

'All right, Lola, so he's not your father. You don't make things any easier by your attitude towards him.'

'Mam, I detest him – he's a brute and we all know it.'

'What time's he coming home?' Evie sounded nervous.

'I don't know, love. He's on the same shift as your uncle Seth so they might call in for a drink on the way home.'

Lola pulled a face. 'That means he'll be worse than ever, fists flying and filth pouring from his mouth.'

'Come on, Lola, he's many things but he's not a drunkard.' Rachel wondered why the hell she was defending her husband. 'I just wish I was . . .'

Her voice tailed off before she admitted her weakness to her girls. But she scarcely needed to admit what they already knew. She got up from the table, walked to the window and opened the curtains a few inches to stare out at the rain, wishing, for the thousandth time, that she had never met Ezra Lawless, much less got pregnant to him on their first date.

She'd met him when she was still deeply depressed and grieving for her first husband and wasn't thinking straight. Ezra Lawless hadn't really been a shoulder to cry on, he'd simply been a bit of company for her. She'd taken a job as a waitress in Collinson's Café to supplement her war widow's pension. Ezra had been a customer – a soldier on leave – and Rachel had been impressed by him. Why the hell she'd been impressed she couldn't, in later years, explain to anyone, not even to herself, other than that her senses had been dulled by her grief over losing her beloved Daniel.

Apart from anything else she felt she'd betrayed her dead husband by allowing Ezra to take advantage of her vulnerability.

She'd become pregnant on a forty-eight-hour pass, married on a week's home leave and had given birth to Evie a month after the Normandy landings, which Ezra had regrettably survived.

At the time, she'd actually been grateful to him for having the decency to marry her – but at the time she didn't realize what his motives were. Once she got to know him she thought it would have been far better if, like Daniel, he'd died a hero's death in Germany and made her a war widow for the second time around.

'I think I'll go up straight after tea.' Rachel closed the curtains and turned back to her daughters. 'I've got one of me headaches coming on.' It was her way of dealing with this life.

Lola put on a cheerful face. 'You go up, Mam, we'll do the washing-up.'

Evie went over and gave her mam a kiss. 'A good rest will do you good, Mam.'

Millgarth Police Station, Leeds. 6.10 p.m.

'Ezra? It's Clive Campion. Sorry to ring you at work but the desk sergeant told me you were on a break.'

'Mr Campion, how are yer?'

'I'm well, Ezra, and you?'

'Fair to middling. What can I do yer for?'

'Well, I'm up in Leeds on constituency business and I was thinking about that favour your brother asked me for.'

'Our Seth asked yer for a favour, did he?'

'I believe he wants a move to plain clothes. I feel I might be able to help.'

'Well, I'm sure our Seth will be ever so grateful, Mr Campion. No doubt yer'll be wantin' a special favour in return?'

'Favours are what makes the world go round, Ezra.'

'So I've heard, Mr Campion.'

'Will you be out and about tonight?'

'Yer looking for a favour tonight are yer, Mr Campion?'

'If possible, yes.'

Ezra didn't bother to disguise a sigh of exasperation. 'Right – our Seth's on the same shift as me. I'll go with him on the Crown Point beat before we finish. I suppose four eyes are better than two. Are yer staying at the Queens?'

'I am, but I don't particularly want to come back here.'

'I see – so, yer'll want me to give yer a ring at your hotel when we find something suitable.'

'That would be ideal.'

'Mr Campion.'

'Yes?'

'Yer might owe me a favour before the night's over.'

'I've already done you many favours, Ezra.'

Ezra put the phone down and shook his head. He was getting a bit fed up of this bloody man. He'd tell him where to go but he knew, deep down, that Campion pulled his strings. He was his social superior and he had power and influence.

He had first met Clive Campion in Germany; a fellow Yorkshireman who was then a captain in Ezra's regiment. There was a base, animal cunning in Ezra that enabled him to see in Campion something that he thought might be to his advantage. Campion, although a married man, seemed, to Ezra, something of a nancy boy – a term he'd got from his father.

He introduced Captain Campion to a young private who was of the same persuasion, and from then on Ezra and Campion formed a relationship that they carried back to Yorkshire after the war, founded on a quid pro quo basis.

On his demob in 1946, Campion stood as a candidate in the general election and won a seat in North Leeds. When Ezra's demob came through he went back to his old job with the Leeds City Police and moved into Rachel and Daniel's marital home.

After the next election, in 1951, Campion was given a job at the Home Office as junior minister. This enabled him to reward Ezra for his many introductions, over the intervening five years, to young men with criminal connections who were far too scared of Ezra's retribution to protest. So Ezra was promoted to sergeant, a promotion that was inexplicable – to anyone but Ezra.

It was then just a question of time before Ezra, with Campion's reciprocal help, brought his younger brother, Seth, into the police. Seth soon became an eager participant in this arrangement and saw it as a way of advancing his own career. His primary ambition was to join the CID.

29 Atkinson Terrace, 7 p.m.

Rachel had gone upstairs and the girls were doing the dishes. Lola said, 'You don't look well, kid.'

Evie had a slight cast in her left eye that got worse when she was stressed. She shrugged and carried on with her work, but Lola was one to get to the bottom of things.

'You remind me of me when I was ten. You were just two, and dear old Ezra had just come home from the war – alive, worse luck.'

Another shrug from Evie. Lola pressed on, she needed to know the truth. 'I wish the Germans had killed him like they killed my daddy. Evie, do you wish the Germans had killed him?'

Evie stopped what she was doing and stared out of the

window at the grey drizzle. The rain running down the glass mirrored the tears running down her cheeks.

'If it were just us three we'd get by all right,' Lola went on, trying to push her weeping sister into some kind of verbal reaction. 'Wouldn't it be great if it were just us three? Me, you and Mam. No vile rectum to ruin our lives. Wouldn't that be great, Evie? Wouldn't that be just the best thing ever?'

She put down her tea towel and placed an arm around her younger sister. Then she saw Evie's reflection in the window.

'Has he been hitting you, Evie?'

'He hits all of us.'

'I mean, really hurting you, especially when no one else is around?'

Evie nodded. 'This morning – he hit me with a stick on my bare bum because I was late leaving for school. He's clattered me loads of times, but he's never hit me on my bare bum before – it was awful. I was only late because he made me clean the fireplace out and I had to get washed again. Then he kicked me out of the door and said he'd finish off my punishment when he got back from work – I'm not looking forward to that.'

'He'll forget,' Lola assured her.

'Promise?'

Lola mimed a cross over her heart. 'Cross my heart and hope to die. He used to say the same to me. Never remembered once. Not once. The only good thing about the rectum is that he's as a dim as a Toc H lamp.'

'What's a Toc H lamp?'

'No idea – my daddy used to say it.'

'Thick as pigshit and twice as nasty, that's what I'd say.'

Lola feigned shock. 'Evie Lawless – wash your mouth out with soap!' Then she grinned. 'Hey, it pretty much describes him though, where'd you get it from?'

'Arthur Cracknell, he's in our class.' Evie rubbed her backside. 'It really hurt, Lola. Did he ever hit you on the bum?'

'Yeah, he did it to me for years – never when anyone was looking – such as you or Mam. It was as if he knew he was doing something shameful – which he was.'

'Did you ever tell Mam?'

'Once, but it was as if she wished I hadn't told her. I think it made her feel bad about not being able to stick up for me. So I never bothered telling her again. Then one day I got really mad and told him I'd go to the police and report him for indecent assault if he ever tried it again.'

'You didn't, did you? What did he say?'

'He didn't say anything,' Lola told her. 'But I've never seen so much hate in anyone's eyes. It didn't stop him hitting me, but never on the bare bum, and never anywhere where it might show. Never the face and never the bare bum, not after I told him what I'd do – I'd have done it as well. He knew that – maybe I should have reported him.' She looked at Evie and shook her head. 'I always thought you'd get away without having to put up with the really bad stuff – you being his own flesh and blood. I always thought he took it out on me because I wasn't his real daughter.'

'Well, I wish I wasn't his real daughter,' Evie muttered. 'I'd swap you dads any day of the week. It used to be the odd crack around the ear, but now this is a lot worse. I feel like running away, but I don't know where I'd go.'

'I ran away,' remembered Lola. 'I don't suppose you remember that.'

'I didn't know,' Evie said, quietly. 'Where did you go?'

'Not sure where I ended up, really. I just got on a bus out of Leeds and went as far as my money would take me, then I got off and walked. I was young, skinny and scared – just like you.'

'Is that what I am – skinny?'

'Better than being fat.'

Evie examined her reflection in the window. 'Skinny girl with a squint, I'll never be a film star.'

'You'll be a late developer. Prob'ly end up looking like Doris Day.'

Evie grimaced. 'I look more like a Boris than a Doris – anyway, what happened?'

'The coppers found me asleep in a shop doorway and brought me home. I wanted to tell them why I'd run away, but with him being one of them I didn't think it would do any good.'

'What happened when you got home?'

Lola felt tears of her own arriving now as she remembered. 'He told Mam to take you up to the bedroom while he dealt with me.'

'Did he hit you?'

'Hit me? He went absolutely potty – like a mad dog. I honestly thought he was going to kill me. He punched me, kicked me, hit me with his belt, swore at me, spat at me. I just curled up on the floor and waited for him to kill me – I ended up unconscious. That's when I should have reported him but I was in no fit state to go anywhere. Thinking back I should have gone to hospital but he just kept me off school for a week until the bruises had more or less gone.'

'What did Mam do?' Evie asked.

'Nothing, she never came down. I suppose she was too scared to. I thought she didn't love me. I should blame her for not sticking up for me, but I don't. He's set everyone against her. Told everyone how useless she is without him. They all think he's husband of the year. Do you know why I think he married her?'

'Why?'

'Because he's a bully and Mam's weak. Bullies need someone they can control.'

'Was she always weak?'

'I don't think so,' said Lola. 'In fact I'm sure she wasn't. I reckon all the stuffing was knocked out of her when my daddy died. The rectum's worn her down, taken advantage of her. It's not her fault.'

7.10 p.m.

The brothers strode out of the Victorian police station in Millgarth and headed for Crown Point Bridge. It was an area run down to the point of dismal squalor, populated mainly by drunks, vagrants, prostitutes, rats and feral dogs. The weather was damp and they both wore rain capes, which conveniently covered their police numbers. In their opinion having identification on open display didn't help with effective policing, which often involved their own methods of dispensing rough justice. PC Seth Lawless was even bigger than his older brother and they were both firm believers in the law of the fist, the boot and the truncheon. To them it was a shame that British police officers weren't armed. With a gun apiece they could cull the local scum to manageable proportions – and enjoy the sport. The uniform helped their sport enormously, especially on this patch, Central Leeds. But this evening they had a different mission in mind. It was a mission that had Ezra feeling decidedly ratty, mainly because there was nothing in it for him.

'I'm getting a bit fed up o' doin' favours for that bloody nancy boy.'

'That bloody nancy boy's promised to get me my transfer to CID. Yer'll not begrudge me that, surely.'

'It's him I begrudge,' Ezra muttered. 'I begrudge him bein' a queer.'

'He's done you a few favours,' Seth pointed out.

'He's got me three stripes that I'd have probably got for meself anyway.'

'And he pays yer telephone bill, and he's got you outa the shit more than once. Anyway, I need a transfer. The wife's been givin' me earache about not betterin' meself.'

'I don't know why yer don't just give her a bit of earache, with the flat of yer hand. I know I bloody would. I don't know why yer married that moanin' cow. I allus thought yer liked 'em a lot younger. Liberty bodice and gymslips – that's more in your line.'

Seth's mouth tightened at his brother's implication, but he said nothing. Saying something might lead to an argument he might well lose. The gusting wind blew a shower of harsh rain into their faces so they diverted through the bus station.

'If I gave the wife another belt the bitch'd leave me,' Seth said. They sat down on a wooden bench to wait for the rain to pass. 'Like Mam left our dad.'

'The owd bastard,' remembered Ezra, 'beat me black an' blue quite regular.'

'And me – while he were spoutin' quotes from the Bible,' Seth reminded him. 'Let's not forget the Bible.'

'I'll not forget it,' Ezra said. 'He hit me with it often enough. Weighed a bloody ton did that Bible. I'd liked to have kicked the owd bastard's head in before he died. Still, he taught us discipline.'

The rain abated, they continued on their way. As they approached the bridge a prostitute, well known to the brothers, swung round a corner right in front of them. She had a client on her arm.

Seth wished her a good evening and added, 'Would you like to contribute towards our Rid the Streets of Indecency campaign?' To the client he said, 'Fancied a bit o' rough did you, sir? If you do, you've hit the jackpot with Marlene. Rough as a bear's arse is our Marlene.'

Marlene cursed and fumbled in her handbag. She offered them a coin. 'Here, half a crown should cover it.'

Seth shook his head and sniggered. 'From what I hear, a teacake wouldn't cover it. Maybe yer gentleman friend would like to contribute. A crisp ten bob note would do nicely.'

The man meekly handed over a ten shilling note and hurried on, with Marlene clinging to his arm. The brothers turned to watch them go. A youth of around sixteen approached. Seth gave a grin.

'Kevin Weatherall, the walking tobacconist. Just what the doctor ordered.'

Kevin wore a trilby hat and belted raincoat, which, Seth rightly suspected, would be carrying contraband cigarettes. The youth spotted them and made to cross the road.

'A word, Weatherall!'

Seth's shout stopped Kevin in his tracks. He slouched, spiv-like, towards them.

'I haven't done nowt.'

'Rumour has it, lad,' said Seth, taking hold of Kevin's lapel, 'that yer've been selling dodgy fags around the pubs. Is that true, Kevin?'

'No, Mr Lawless, I wouldn't do nowt like that.'

'That's just as well, lad,' said Ezra, with ice in both his voice and his eyes – he still hadn't got his dad out of his thoughts, 'because yer underage and have no business on licensed premises. Open yer coat, lad.'

'What?'

Ezra cuffed him to the ground, then looked around to see if anyone was watching him. No one was.

'I said open yer bloody coat!'

Kevin, got to his feet and, reluctantly, opened his coat. It had six large pockets on the inside, each one bulging. Ezra stuck a hand in one and brought out a packet of foreign cigarettes.

'Where are these from? France or somewhere?'

'Russia,' muttered Kevin.

'Russia? They're smuggled in from bloody Russia? That's a couple of years in Borstal, lad.'

Kevin appealed to Seth, whom he knew better. 'Aw, come

on, Mr Lawless, just take the fags. I don't want another stretch in Borstal. Me mam'll go mad.'

'Oh dear, well, we wouldn't want yer mam goin' mad, would we now?' said Seth. 'But the thing is, Weatherall, I don't think either of us like Russian fags. It's like smokin' dried dogshit.'

'Is that what yer doin' Weatherall?' Ezra chipped in, looking round to check he wasn't being watched as he repeatedly slapped Kevin around his ears. 'Tryin' ter fob us off with a load o' Russian rubbish? Do we look like idiots?'

'No – I don't think you're idiots. I just thought—'

'Yer just thought?' snarled Ezra. 'Well, yer know what thought did, don't yer?'

'No,' moaned Kevin.

'It followed a muck cart an' thought it were a wedding – that's what thought did. Is that what yer do, Weatherall? D'yer go round following muck carts thinkin' they're weddings?'

'No, I don't Mr Lawless. Is there some way yer can let us off? I'll do owt yer want.'

Seth rubbed his chin, pensively. 'Maybe there's a way round this, Kevin, lad.' He looked at Ezra. 'What d'yer think, Sergeant? D'yer think there's a way round this?'

Ezra nodded, pretending to size the youth up. 'He might fit the bill. Tell yer what,' he said, 'do as yer told and keep yer trap shut and in less than an hour from now yer could be off the hook. How does that sound?'

'Sounds all right to me, Sergeant.' Kevin said it with a mixture of gratitude and apprehension at what he was letting himself in for. 'What, er, what is it yer want me ter do?'

'Some lads might find this job a bit unpleasant,' said Seth, then he sniggered. 'Then again, some lads might really enjoy it. Are you up for it, lad?'

'I'll do it, Mr Lawless. Whatever it is I'll do it. I'll not let yer down, I promise.'

'Right,' said Seth, 'I have to give our friend, Mr Green, a call. In the meantime, I think the nice sergeant might want yer ter take a little walk with him.'

Ezra took Kevin's arm and took him down a street that led to the river as Seth went to a phone box to ring Campion.

7.20 p.m.

Rachel lay in her bed, listening to the buzz of conversation coming from downstairs and she knew what her daughters were talking about. It wasn't about young girl things, as it should be – the older giving advice to the younger, telling her stories about boys and school and stuff – general giggling and fun. This wasn't a house of fun. They were talking about Ezra.

He was a man of meticulous personal habits. He shaved twice a day, had his hair cut every two weeks, changed his shirt, socks and underwear every day without fail and sometimes more often if the circumstances so dictated. He demanded that Rachel, Evie and Lola were always well turned out. On the rare occasions that he took Rachel to a police function he was always attentive and polite to her. But behind the closed doors of 29 Atkinson Terrace it was a different story.

Over the years she'd been married to Ezra he had isolated Rachel from family and friends, and crushed her with his constant scorn at her general uselessness as a wife and mother. It was an attitude that had been instilled into him by his fanatical Calvinist father, who died before the war, having scared off his wife and beaten and twisted his two sons into self-righteous, amoral monsters.

Rachel slid up a window and lit a cigarette. Smoking in the bedroom was strictly forbidden and would be punished with a beating, as would slack housework and insubordination. It was brainless and irrational and cruel but she couldn't fight it. She hadn't the strength. The conversation downstairs continued. Lola was grumbling.

'This isn't even his house. This was Mam and Dad's home, not his.'

A cuckoo clock on the wall announced it was eight o'clock. Lola glared at it. 'The only thing he's brought into this house is that flipping clock!'

Both girls looked at the clock that Ezra had brought home from Germany.

'I hate that clock!' Lola snorted. 'He thinks more about that clock than he does about us – that's because he's a cuckoo himself, in another man's nest. I wouldn't care, but it sounds more like a goose farting than a cuckoo!'

'Lola Lawless, wash your mouth out with soap!' Evie was smiling for the first time that day. Then her face suddenly crumpled and she burst into tears.

'I can't stand living here, Lola, if he's gonna keep knocking me about, I just can't.'

Evie sounded so wretched that her big sister took her in her arms and hugged her until the sobbing had stopped. Lola came to a decision.

'You won't have to. I'm going to tell Mam that we all need to leave him. There's no point just us two leaving, we all have to do it. If necessary I'll tell his pals at the police station how he's beating us all up. I'll keep shouting about it until someone listens. They must know what he's like down there.'

Evie burst into tears again. 'You can't do that, Lola! You mustn't do that. He'll go mad.'

'It'll be OK, Evie. I'll make sure he doesn't hurt you.'

'Promise?'

'I promise.'

'Cross your heart and hope to die?'

Lola crossed her heart and hoped to die, although she hadn't a clue how she could protect Evie from Ezra. She only knew that if that time ever came she'd do whatever was necessary. Evie's shoulders seemed to straighten, as if a heavy burden had been lifted from them.

'I'm glad you haven't left home, Lola. I was really scared you might leave home when you left school.'

Lola gave a dry laugh. 'I thought about it often enough.'

'Oh please don't, Lola, not without us.'

Lola had only stayed at home because of Evie and their mother. She knew she mustn't let them down. She thought about her daddy and how he'd have made mincemeat of Lawless for doing this to his daughter. But her daddy had been shot down over France in 1942 when Lola was six. He'd been awarded a posthumous DFM, which had been pinned to Lola's best frock when she went with her mother to Cranwell to be presented with it. There had been a band playing and Lola had almost burst with pride at being the only daughter of Flight Sergeant Daniel Drinkwater DFM. She'd been introduced to the air commodore as Dolores Elizabeth Drinkwater, which, she thought, sounded ever so grand – much better than Dolores Lawless, which was a bit of a tongue-twister. In three years' time she'd be twenty-one – old enough to change her name back to Drinkwater. In the meantime she had responsibilities. She took Evie in her arms.

'I'm not going anywhere without you and Mam. We need to sit down and think about what to do, how to get away from him. I'll tell her tomorrow, when she's feeling a bit better.'

'Will she be on our side?'

'Why shouldn't she? She hates him as much as we do. With a bit of luck she'll divorce him.'

'She won't do that, Lola. It's against the faith.'

'Ah, the faith,' said Lola, bitterly. But she knew that Evie had a point.

It beat Lola how her mam could cling to a God that had let her down so badly – Evie as well, for that matter. Ezra, with his strange sense of morality, allowed them to go to church. They both went to regular confession and communion and neither of them missed Mass on a Sunday. The latter was something they had in common with Lola – she didn't miss it much either. The faith had left her long ago. Ezra Lawless had seen to that. He had denied her every advantage that he himself had been denied. She had left school at fifteen despite being one of the brighter girls in the fourth form at Notre Dame. It had been at Ezra's insistence.

'Women don't need no education. A woman's place is ter provide a man with his needs, in the kitchen and in the bed. That doesn't take O Levels.'

So Lola had got a job in a shoe shop.

7.30 p.m.

Seth led Clive Campion down an alley leading to the River Aire where Kevin, naked and blindfolded, was standing beside Ezra. Campion looked the bruised and bloodied youth up and down, and was unable to keep the excitement from his voice.

'Dear, oh dear! What happened to him?'

'He's what yer might call, reluctant,' growled Ezra. 'I don't like reluctance in a lad – it shows weakness of character.'

Kevin wasn't sure what to expect. All he knew was that

he'd been knocked around, then ordered to strip by Ezra. From behind his blindfold he recognized Seth's voice and screamed.

'What's happening, Mr Lawless?'

'Calm down, lad,' said Seth. 'A few minutes and it'll all be over. Just keep yer bloody voice down.'

'Best put a gag on him,' decided Ezra. 'We don't want the whining little sod scriking all through it.'

'All through wha—' was all Kevin managed to get out before Seth put a gag in his mouth. He began to struggle. Ezra cursed and knocked him unconscious with half a dozen heavy blows, then he looked at Campion.

'It might be best all round if he knows nowt about it. Yer don't want him struggling, putting you off yer stroke.'

'I'll be fine,' said Campion, gazing down at the unconscious youth and taking off his coat. 'I'd like a bit of privacy if you don't mind.'

Seth and Ezra walked away to have a smoke and a chat about Leeds United, who were doing well for a change, periodically glancing across at Campion, then turning away in disgust. Fifteen minutes later the MP walked over to them, breathing heavily and adjusting his clothing.

'Have yer finished with him?' asked Seth.

'Er, yes. Will he want any money or anything?'

'Don't you worry about that,' said Seth. 'So long as yer return the favour.'

'What favour?'

Seth took him by the scruff of the neck. 'Yer know what favour. Don't piss us about!'

'Oh yes, sorry. My mind was on other things. I'll er – that's not a problem.'

Campion extricated himself from Seth's grip and walked, quickly, away. The brothers strolled over to where the youth was just beginning to regain consciousness.

'He's in no fit state to be going back home to his mam,' Ezra commented, out of the side of his mouth. 'I think our right honourable bloody friend got a bit carried away.'

'It's you what got bloody carried away,' grumbled Seth. 'What the hell's got into yer ternight? A bit of a slap was all he needed.'

They had procured several youths for Campion, but had

never damaged one as badly as this. Kevin needed hospital
treatment. The minute he went home his mother would be
ringing for an ambulance, probably the police as well.

'We could be in deep trouble,' said Seth, 'and I'm talking
deep, custodial trouble.'

'Oh yeah?' snarled Ezra. 'I go to all this trouble an' what's
Campion gonna do for me? Bugger all – that's what he's gonna
do for me.'

'Campion, who's Campion?' moaned Kevin, wondering
why every part of his body, inside and out, was in so much
pain.

Seth glared at his brother for mentioning Campion's name.
'Well bloody done, bonehead! That really puts the bloody tin
hat on it, that does!'

Just for a second the brothers squared up to each other,
then they saw sense and turned their attention to the youth
as they weighed up the various pros and cons of allowing
him to go home – and they couldn't see too many pros. They
walked around him, looking at him, then at each other, shaking
their heads as they realized there was only one safe solution.
Kevin's eyes followed them, dark and scared. He was naked
and shivering in the winter air. His teeth were chattering, his
hands covering his genitals, and he was hoping that whatever had happened to him was all over.

'Can I go now, Mr Lawless?'

His plea was ignored.

'Are we agreed, then?' said Seth.

Ezra nodded, reluctantly. He would have been happier were
he to benefit from this night's work, but the only beneficiary
was Seth.

'There'll be some chains in Murgatroyd's yard,' Seth said.
'I'll nip over the wall.'

Within a minute he was back, lugging a heavy chain behind
him. Kevin was moaning and sobbing as they wrapped the
chain around his trembling body. The youth hadn't an ounce
of fight in him.

'What are you doing? I thought you said I could go?' His
voice was little more than a squeak.

'Just one last thing, Kevin lad,' said Seth, gruffly. 'It's for
yer own good, then it's finished.'

Kevin didn't question why wrapping a heavy chain around

him was for his own good. His senses were numbed by fear
and shock and pain. But when this was done it was finished.
That's all he wanted to hear.

'I can go home after this, then?'

'Course yer can, Kevin.'

With the chain knotted tightly around him they picked him
up and threw him into the river, where he disappeared with
barely a splash. Then they picked up his clothes and the
contraband cigarettes and stuffed them into a dustbin much
further along their beat, taking great care to cover them with
rubbish.

'That never happened,' said Seth.

'What never happened?'

They completed their beat in silence.

Two

8.30 p.m.

Rachel was smoking a Capstan Full Strength by her
bedroom window when she heard Evie saying goodnight
to Lola and coming up the stairs to bed. Rachel called out
'Goodnight' herself. Evie opened her mother's bedroom door
a couple of inches.

'Goodnight, God bless, Mam.'

'Goodnight, God bless, Evie.'

Rachel flicked her cigarette end out of the window. She'd
been contemplating suicide once again but that brief goodnight to Evie had told her not to be so stupid. She couldn't
leave her girls at his mercy. At least while she was there she
took the brunt of it.

His cruelty was as much verbal as physical, a sudden
memory of this made her cringe. It had been three years ago
that Ezra had suddenly forbidden Rachel to go out of the
house on her own without his permission.

'But why, Ezra?'

'Because yer likely to consort with dirty men.'

Her daughters had been listening, and wondering. Evie was seven and Lola was fifteen.

'But, I wouldn't do such a thing.'

'Yer a dirty, filthy woman. Yer seduced me on our first date and got yerself pregnant, why wouldn't yer do the same with other men?'

He had pointed at Evie. 'That child is a product of yer filthy ways. I bring her up because it's my duty.'

Evie had burst into tears. Lola's eyes had blazed with defiance of Ezra. 'Wasn't it six of one, half a dozen of the other?' She hated it when her mother wouldn't stand up for herself. 'If Mam was filthy, you must be filthy as well!'

She had braced herself for his venom. His eyes went as cold as a mortician's slab as he turned to look at her. Rachel pleaded with him not to hurt her, but to no avail. He punched Lola so hard in the stomach she thought she'd never breathe again. Then he stood over her as she lay on the floor, gasping.

'Men are the weak victims of filthy women.' He spat the words out. 'Women like yer mother know that man's flesh is weak and they take advantage.'

And so their lives went on. Ezra had a fetish about tidiness, a legacy of his childhood and his time in the King's Own Yorkshire Light Infantry. He would carry out frequent and unannounced house inspections, with his wife and the two girls walking behind him to take the full force of his criticism. His fat finger would wipe surfaces and pick up dust that had settled there only that day; in that part of Leeds dust didn't take long to gather. He would rearrange furniture and cushions and ornaments from the position he himself last put them in and if he returned and found them in a different place he would fly into a rage, deliberately smashing things that he knew were of sentimental value to Rachel. Failure to pass these inspections resulted in physical punishment, as would his wife's failure to come up to expectations with her cooking and housekeeping and general behaviour.

Rachel lit another Capstan and wondered just how much worse things would get if she stood up to him for once. If only she could summon up the guts. The very thought of standing up to him gave her the shakes. But why? The worst he could do was kill her – and that wouldn't be so bad, would it? If he killed her they'd have to lock him up and the girls would be free of him. This was a much more practical idea than suicide. The more she thought about it the more attractive this sounded.

8.59 p.m.

Lola's anger had been mounting since Evie had gone to bed. She was remembering the beatings she'd suffered at the hands of Ezra; and the times she'd watch him humiliate her mam – humiliate her and beat her and laugh at her. And now he'd started on Evie. It had to stop here. She glared at the clock, armed herself with a cup and waited until the minute hand clicked round to the top of the hour. The cuckoo popped its head out, but it would never get back to safety quickly enough. Before the brief echo of the goose fart had died away the flying cup detached the bird from its spring and sent it spinning across the room. It was a good aim and a good result. But it wasn't enough to calm Lola down.

Twice she'd been to the door with her coat on, armed with sufficient rage and a determination to march down to the police station and barge into the superintendent's office and tell him what sort of man Ezra was and that if they didn't do something she'd go to the Sunday papers. Then she'd stopped and thought of the consequences of dragging Evie and their mother into this without forewarning them. No, let them sleep, tomorrow would be soon enough. Tonight she'd make do with telling Ezra Lawless just what a cowardly pig he was, without telling him what was in store for him.

She was sitting in a chair, half listening to the wireless, half trying to read, when he arrived home at half past nine. His shouting started outside in the street, as if he was building up steam in readiness for the ear-bashing he was going to give his wife – literally and metaphorically. He didn't often get drunk but when he did it didn't take much to get him loud and angry.

Lola didn't take her eyes off her book as he stood in the

living room doorway. She wanted him to think he wasn't worth her looking up for.

'Where's yer mam?'

No answer.

'Hey, snobby bitch – I'm talkin' ter you!'

'Mam's gone to bed to get away from you.'

'What? Who the bloody hell d'yer think yer talkin' to?'

'To a coward who beats people up who are a lot smaller than him. That's why you joined the police isn't it? To beat up people for fun – maybe even kill a few.' She looked up at him and sneered. 'Who have you killed today, Ezra?' She was goading him but the look of fear in his eyes was something she hadn't expected.

'You're a bloody idiot, girl.'

'And you're a coward who beats up his own daughter when no one else is looking – just like you did with me!'

The fear dropped from his eyes. 'What the hell's that squinty-eyed little bitch been tellin' yer? She'll feel me belt across her bare arse, tellin' lies about me like that!'

Then, as if he knew that all was not as it should be, his eyes swivelled around the room. He gaze passed the clock, stopped, stared at nothing as if his addled brain was late in registering what his eyes had just seen, and then went back again to where the clock was hanging off the wall. The cuckoo's door was wide open and, dangling from it, the spring that usually held the annoying bird. But no bird.

'Where's me bastard cuckoo?'

His lips drew back across his nicotine-brown teeth, the veins in his neck stuck out and his eyes bulged in unbalanced rage. His words came out in a strange half snarl, half petulant whine.

Lola saw the comedy in his ludicrous question. It sent her into a fit of manic laughter. 'It was getting on my nerves, so I shut the squawking little sod up!'

Ezra roared with anger. 'Yer bust me clock?'

'You beat up your own daughter, you cowardly bully!'

'Yer mouthy little shit!'

He reached down, grabbed her by the front of her cardigan and spat at her. She screamed at him with a rage equal to his and hammered her fists into his face.

'She's your daughter, your flesh and blood, but that doesn't matter to you. You get a kick out of beating up women and children. You're not a man, you're a rotten, stinking coward!'

He punched her in the mouth, sending her crashing backwards, over a chair and banging her head on the floor, then he stood over her and kicked her in her ribs.

Blood was pouring from her mouth and nose as he yanked her to her feet and dragged her to the door, roaring at her, with spit spraying into her face. 'Gerrout and never, ever come back, yer little bitch!'

He slung her into the street. Lola lay on the pavement in agony. Curtains twitched but no one came to help. Lawless's reputation was such that helping her would make an enemy of him. No one round here wanted him as an enemy. She pushed herself to her feet and spat out a mouthful of blood. Her ribs hurt, her lip was split, her nose was bleeding profusely and, as if to deliberately add to her sorrows, the drizzle turned to heavy rain. It crossed her mind to go to Keith's house but she'd never met his mother and these were hardly the right circumstances. Besides, whatever relationship they had was pretty much in its infancy and this was serious stuff to drop on a casual boyfriend. Her best friend, Theresa, lived two streets away. She'd be welcome there – well, for one night at least. Tonight she would gather her thoughts and her courage. Tomorrow she'd round up Evie and their mam and go to the police station to set the ball rolling. They'd tell the police all about his savagery to them over the years, and definitely go to the Sunday papers, whatever the cops did. Her pain eased as she envisaged the headline in the *News of the World*:

Dead War Hero's Daughter Savagely Beaten by
Cruel Cop Stepfather

Oh, yes. The evidence of his cruelty was all over her bruised and bleeding face and body. She would put this beating to good use. What was that saying – 'hoist with his own petard'? He'd regret this night's work. Somebody would have to do something about him. And why should they move away? Let him move away – it had never been his house.

Evie was watching through the window as her sister walked, painfully, across the road. She knocked on the glass. Lola turned around and looked up as Evie mouthed, 'Are you OK?'

Lola stuck a thumb-up and gave a bloodied smile. Evie tried to smile back but failed.

Lola twirled a finger around her temple then, with the same finger, pushed up the front of her nose to imitate a pig, then she held her nose between finger and thumb and mimed the pulling of a lavatory chain. Evie managed a proper smile as she recognized Arthur Cracknell's insulting description which so aptly described her father. She stuck up a thumb to confirm her understanding of Lola's mime.

'I'll be back tomorrow,' Lola shouted. 'Tell Mam. Everything will be OK. I promise.'

Evie waved to her sister then turned away as she heard more sounds of violence coming from downstairs.

Rachel heard the door slam and went downstairs to see what the noise was all about. She looked around the room.

'Where's our Lola?'

'I gave the mouthy bitch a slap. She's gone and she won't be comin' back.'

Rachel saw blood on the floor. 'For God's sake, Ezra! What have you done to her?'

'I've done nowt to her, except kick her arse out of that door – she bust me cuckoo clock.'

His eyes were bloodshot but there was a mad light in there as well. Watching what Campion was doing to the youth had disgusted him, but the murder had left him excited. That night he'd had power over someone's life and death. And he'd chosen death.

Rachel couldn't take her eyes off her daughter's blood and she remembered the time he'd beaten Lola senseless after she had run away. That time she'd done nothing, even though she listened from her bedroom, thinking he was killing her daughter. She'd been too terrified to come to Lola's aid. It had left her with a sense of shame and self-loathing. What kind of useless mother was she? She looked up at Ezra. There was an astonished look on his face as his wife screamed at him.

'Where is she, you pig?'

Her concern for Lola had overcome her fear of her husband.

'Never you mind where she is.'

There was defiance in Rachel's eyes, something he'd never

seen before. 'You've hurt her, haven't you, you bloody pig! I can see it on your face.'

Ezra's eyes bulged. This wasn't how it should be – wives talking back to husbands. If he knew nothing else he knew that. The rage that had begun burning at the memory of his father's brutality was still on a low light and it wasn't going to take much to make it flare up. Kevin Weatherall had suffered because of it and if this bitch thought she could talk to him like that she had another think coming. The rage was fuelled by the six pints of Tetley's bitter he'd drunk with Seth on the way home. Pints drunk in complete silence. His words came out in a low growl.

'Who the hell d'yer think you're talking to, woman?'

'I'm talking to you, Ezra Lawless. You've hurt my girl, haven't you? Where is she? I want to see her.'

She made for the door but Ezra blocked her way. 'You go nowhere, woman, without my say-so.'

'Let me past. I want to see Lola. You've hurt her, you bastard. I know you have!'

There was a frightening madness in his eyes. 'Oh yeah, and would yer like some o' the same, yer whinin' cow?'

He grabbed her and slapped her, twice, across the face before she pushed him away and tried to kick him. Ezra's rage now exploded. He punched her in the chest, knocking her to the floor.

Upstairs, Evie could hear him effing and blinding and kicking furniture. As she crept out on to the landing she could hear her mam sobbing and begging him to stop. His terrifying violence had subdued Rachel's fragile defiance of him.

'Please, Ezra, you've had too much to drink. I just want to make sure Lola's all right.'

Ezra replied by delivering a flurry of obscenities and blows and kicks that had his wife curling up to protect herself. He was completely out of control, more so than when he'd beaten up Kevin – Kevin hadn't given him any backchat. Kevin hadn't called him a pig and a bastard.

Evie made her way downstairs. Her heart was beating louder with every step. Her father was cursing, drunkenly and obscenely, and Evie could hear heavy blows being struck. She listened at the living room door. Her mother's squeals of anguish sounded so bad that she could almost feel the pain

herself. She needed to stop her mam being hurt but didn't
have a clue how to do it. Evie pushed the door open and her
face streamed with tears at the sight that confronted her.

Her mother had stopped screaming, blood was running
from her nose, one of her eyes was swollen and destined to
be a real shiner. She was on the floor and he was kneeling
astride her with his hands around her throat. The Bush radio
on the dresser was tuned in to Radio Luxembourg. Her mam
was being throttled by her dad to the accompaniment of Eddie
Calvert playing 'Oh Mein Papa' on his golden trumpet.

The look on Rachel's face scared her daughter. It was the
look of someone who had given up the fight and was allowing
death to take her away from the horror of her life, but content
in the knowledge that this was a worthwhile death. One that
would see her husband hanged and her daughters freed from
his brutality.

As Evie entered the room and approached her father from
behind her heart was thumping as loud as a Sally Army drum,
causing her to clutch her hand to her breast to suppress the
noise she was sure she was making. The ironing board was
still up from where her mother had been ironing Evie's school
clothes and her husband's uniform. Rachel was now semi-
conscious and dripping with sweat and blood. The sobbing
had subsided to a weak grunting noise, like a dreaming dog.

There was an intense horror about the scene that clutched
Evie in a grip of fear and revulsion. She could scarcely catch a
breath, much less move a muscle to help her mother. She would
simply have to watch her die and maybe she would be next.

Then, suddenly, she gave a violent shudder and saw her
father with a complete and startling clarity. He was a bully
and a coward and if her mother died he might as well kill
Evie too. Her fear caused her brain to send a signal to her
renal glands to start pumping very large amounts of adren-
alin into her bloodstream, resulting in a feral rage that few
people will ever experience. Every ounce of strength at her
disposal now concentrated itself into protecting her mam. She
leapt on his back. Her fingers clawed at his eyes, digging
into them until he roared with pain and rage. He grabbed her
wrists and somehow spun around without letting her go. She
yanked herself free and stepped away from him. His eyes
were wild, saliva was running down his chin, but she knew

that the worst thing he could do was kill her, and what was
so bad about that?

'Yer little bitch!'

He lunged towards her but stumbled over Rachel's
outstretched legs and went crashing to the floor. Evie grabbed
the iron from the ironing board. It was a heavy iron but she
managed to hold it high above her head. There shouldn't have
been enough strength in her scrawny arms for her to do such
a thing and no one would ever believe her true account of
this night.

The iron's own weight brought it down, all she had to do
was guide it to its target – her father's head. The force of the
blow brought a swift end to his brutality, and her strength
subsided as quickly as it had come. She let the heavy iron drop
to the floor, then she stepped back as he slumped over on to
his side with his eyes half open but seeing nothing. Once more
Evie went rigid with shock. She could do nothing, only stand
there and look down on him. Nothing about him was moving.
There was a film of perspiration on his face; he stank of cigarettes, sweat and alcohol; and he was stiller than anyone she'd
ever seen before. He used to have a twitch under his left eye
when he was angry, but the twitch had gone. His anger had
also gone and, deep down, Evie knew his life had gone and
that she had ended it. She turned her back to him and vomited.

Her mother was now gasping and choking and wondering
what miracle had kept her alive. She adjusted her disarranged
clothing and held out her arms to her daughter, who was now
retching on an empty stomach. Evie wiped her mouth with
the sleeve of her nightie and knelt down beside her mam,
happy that she was alive but stunned at the price they'd had
to pay. A good life for a bad life. Maybe they'd got a bargain,
but what next? Was there more to pay?

They clung to each other in silence as the clock on the
mantelpiece ticked away the first ten minutes of Ezra Lawless's
dubious afterlife. Evie was wondering how long it would take
him to get to Hell – maybe he was there already, cursing at
the Devil. Her mam got her breath and some of her strength
back. She managed to croak through her damaged throat:

'What happened, love? Last thing I knew was your dad stran-
gling me and . . . and I thought I were gone, then this. What
the hell happened?'

'I hit him with the iron, Mam. I gave him a right old crack.'

'Thank God you did, that's all I've got to say. Thank God you did. You saved your mam's life love, there's nothin' more certain. Where the hell you got the strength and courage to do that, God only knows.'

'I don't know myself, Mam, I just clocked him with the iron.'

Rachel let go of her daughter and knelt down beside her husband. Evie had already seen too much of him; she averted her gaze.

'He's dead, isn't he, Mam?'

'I think he is, love – and may God forgive me for saying this, but the world's a better place without him.'

'Will I get into bother?'

'No, love.' Her mother stroked her hair. 'I'll tell 'em I did it – and I'll tell 'em why. Don't you dare tell 'em any different. I'll say you were in bed when all this happened. Don't make me out to be a liar.'

'Will they believe you, Mam?'

'Why wouldn't they? I'm allowed to defend myself when I'm being attacked, even if he is me husband.'

'I don't know – maybe with him being a police sergeant.'

'Well, I suppose it might be a bit awkward. But if you hadn't clocked him one it'd have been a damned sight more awkward for me. I thought he'd done fer me, as God is my judge.'

'Why did he hit our Lola?'

'Oh, God – Lola!'

The events had pushed Lola to the back of Rachel's thoughts. 'He did something to her. Please God let her be all right.' She staggered to the door, pulled it open and shouted into the street.

'Lola . . . *Lola!*'

Rachel turned to Evie with panic on her face. 'Oh God, she could be anywhere!'

Evie took her arm. 'Mam, she's OK. I saw her through the window. I expect she's gone to Theresa's.'

'Oh, thank God for that – are you sure?'

'Dead sure. I think he'd knocked her about a bit but she was OK. Do you want me to fetch her?'

'What?' Rachel thought for a few seconds, then went back inside the front room. 'No, love – leave her out of this for now. I need to think.' She looked down at her dead husband with no sense of bereavement. Then she picked up his coat from the floor and covered his head to hide him from the eyes of her daughter, who was trying to make sense of what had just happened.

'He was trying to kill you, wasn't he, Mam?'

'He was a very bad man, Evie.'

'I know, Mam. I never loved him, never.'

'Nor me, love. He wasn't a lovable man. I blame meself. I should never have married him.'

'It's a proper bugger is this, isn't it, Mam?'

'Yes, love, it's a proper bugger.' Rachel's mind was racing. 'Look, love,' she said, 'until I say different I don't want you telling anyone you were in the room when this happened. Lola weren't here and neither were you. You heard the racket, you came downstairs and found all this. If they think you did it they might take you off me – send you to one of them horrible homes what yer never come out of.'

'Shall I tell our Lola what really happened, Mam?'

'No, love. She's better off not knowing.'

'Have I murdered him, Mam?'

Rachel held her daughter close to her. 'No, love, you just saved my life.'

Three

HM Prison Long Munckton, West Yorkshire, 15 February 1955

They had the room to themselves. The remand wing governor had allowed them a private mother/daughter visit. Lola was to be allowed one as well, but Rachel had asked to see Evie first.

'I'm told you're living with someone called Mrs Parkinson – how are you going on?'

Evie shrugged. 'She's OK – she brought me here. She's

got five of us to look after. Some of the other kids are a bit
bonkers, but she's OK.'

'What about Lola, is she coping OK?'

'She's been to see me every day. She's moved into lodgings, you know.'

'So I've been told. Is she OK?'

'Yeah, she's OK.'

'So, everything's OK?'

'Yeah.'

Rachel reached across the table and grasped Evie's hand.
Her voice dropped to what was little more than a whisper
and didn't carry to the female officer sitting beneath the barred
window, reading the *Daily Herald*.

'Evie, have you told anyone what happened?'

Following her mam's lead, Evie gave a whispered reply.
'No, Mam, you told me not to.'

There was relief in Rachel's eyes, then guarded concern.
'Not even Lola?'

Evie shook her head. 'No, Mam. I think she ought to know,
though. I don't like telling her lies. It's not right, Mam.'

'It's the only safe way, Evie. You know what Lola's like.
If she finds out the truth she'll go round kicking up a stink
and then where will we be? This way's better, love.'

'I know if she were in my shoes she wouldn't keep quiet,
Mam, no matter what you said to her. She'd have gone round
telling everyone the truth and to hell with it.'

'That's exactly what I mean, Evie. Sometimes the truth
does nobody any good. Not this kind of truth, anyroad.'

'What's going to happen, Mam?'

Rachel gave her daughter a reassuring smile. In many ways
she looked better than Evie had seen her in a long time. Free
of Ezra's brutality, probably.

'Well . . . I'm going to plead not guilty to murder but guilty
to manslaughter. I'll get Lola to testify about how she was
beaten up that night.'

Evie raised her voice. 'But, Mam, you said they wouldn't
even arrest you for it, with it being self-defence. You've got
to let me tell them what happened.'

Rachel held on to Evie's hand and shushed her into silence.
They both glanced up at the officer, who was more interested
in the newspaper than their conversation.

'Evie, they were always going to arrest me for it. I'm going to jail, there's no question of that. It's just a question of for how long. Ezra was a copper. You can't go round killing coppers and expect to get away with it.'

'Mam, I don't want you to go to jail. Please, let me tell them what happened.'

Rachel held Evie's hand tighter. Her voice was now stern. 'Evie, we've just been through all that. You weren't even in the room. It was just me and your dad.' Evie looked forlorn. Her mother stroked her face and smiled. 'Look, Evie, if the worst comes to the worst, according to my barrister, even if I'm found guilty of murder I can always plead mitigating circumstances.'

'What are they?'

'It's just a way of telling the court that it wasn't all my fault. It means I'll be released early no matter what they find me guilty of.'

'Mam, you shouldn't be going to jail at all.'

Rachel now took both of her daughter's hands. She regarded her, gravely, leaned forward and spoke in a low, modulated voice.

'Evie, just listen to me. You saved my life once and I don't need you to save it again. You're just a kid who's been forced to kill your dad to save your mam's life – that, on its own, is a hell of a lot for you to cope with. The very least I can do is take the blame. If I don't, you'll have to live out your whole life as some sort of freak kid who killed her own father. They'll lock you away somewhere awful for years, then, when they eventually do let you out, you'll have to have a new name and a new identity. Either that or you'll have to live with newspapers writing stories about you when they've got nothing better to fill their pages, which means people pointing and calling you names, and you not being able to get a decent job or have proper friends because of it all.

'I know this, Evie. I've been speaking to people. All the time you're locked up I'll be on the outside knowing this is happening to my own daughter, who did this to save my life and I couldn't stand that, Evie, I honestly couldn't stand that. It'd be ten times worse than being in jail. Wives and husbands kill each other all the time – it's the most common type of murder in the world. But children killing parents is a different kettle of fish altogether. When I get out I'll be OK. I promise you, I'll be OK. I might even get married again to some decent bloke who loves me and doesn't bully me. Besides, being a cop killer's not a bad thing to be, in here. I get more respect in here than I ever did on the outside.'

'We respect you, Mam.'

'I know you do, love. But let me do this – please, Evie. I want you to promise.'

Evie pulled a face.

'Evie.'

'OK, Mam, I promise.'

Four

Mrs Parkinson's house was a Victorian end-of-terrace in an area of Leeds that had seen more salubrious days. Evie was sitting on a wall outside, huddled inside a double-breasted, gaberdine mackintosh that she would grow into one day. It was dusk, cold and foggy. She was waiting for Lola, who called round most evenings on her way home from work. Sometimes with Keith. Evie wasn't certain about Keith. She was hoping that Lola would be on her own because what she had to tell her wasn't for Keith's ears. Lola appeared out of the gloom, her smile appeared first. That'll soon disappear, Evie thought.

'How're you doing, kid?' asked Lola.

'OK.'

Evie got down from the wall, determined to get it off her chest right away. 'Lola, there's something I've got to tell you.'

'OK, spit it out.'

Evie wavered. Her eyes searched her sister's face, wondering if she had any inkling of Evie's secret. Something that might make it easier.

Lola could see her sister was struggling. 'Have you had your tea?' she asked.

'Yeah,' said Evie, 'if you can call it that. Two spam sand-wiches and water biscuit. She doesn't overfeed us doesn't Mrs Parkinson.'

'Right, there's a place a few streets away called the Cosy Café, we'll go there.'

Evie linked arms with her big sister and they strolled through the evening rain. When they got to the café she'd tell Lola, and Lola would know what to do.

'Could we have two teas please, and two slices of choc-olate cake?'

Normally this might have brought a smile to Evie's face. Chocolate cake was her favourite. She hadn't had chocolate cake since she'd been at Mrs Parkinson's. But this time she didn't smile. She had an unpleasant duty to perform, the repercussions of which she couldn't imagine. Lola picked up the two teas, Evie picked up the cake and followed her sister to a table near the window, grateful that the café was almost empty. Evie was forming the words in her mind. Lola slapped her head with a hand.

'Completely forgot. We both got letters from Mam. Mine says the usual stuff. She'll be out before we know it and to look out for you and not to be nosey and to give you yours without me reading it. Spoilsport.' She took an envelope out of her bag and gave it to Evie. On the back of it was stamped HMP Leeds. Lola saw her looking at it.

'I know,' she remarked. 'Not very good for the ego when a postman who looks like Tony Curtis hands you a letter from a prison.'

Evie opened her letter.

My Dear Evie,
I hope you are well. Make sure you eat properly, espe-cially your school dinners. Do well at school. I'll be home before you know it and I don't want to come home and find you've been neglecting yourself. Important thing, Evie. Remember your promise to me and never break it. A promise to a mother is the most important promise in the world.
 See you soon,
 Your loving mam
 xxxx

'Well?' asked Lola.

'Well what?'

'What does it say?'

'It's a private letter to me.'

'Fair enough.' Lola picked up her tea and took a sip. 'So, what was it you wanted to ask me?'

Evie stared. 'What?'

'You wanted to tell me something. That's why we've come here.'

'Oh, right.'

'Well?' said Lola, sitting back. 'So far this has cost me a shilling. It had better be good.'

'It's Keith,' she said.

'Keith? What about Keith?'

'I don't think he's good enough for you.'

'What?' Lola burst out laughing. 'Evie, he's a boyfriend, we're not engaged or anything. And he's great company is Keith.'

'Well, you never know what it might lead to,' Evie said, smiling back. Deep down she was relieved her mam had got her off the hook.

Five

London, March 1955

Clive Campion MP bought a *Daily Mail* from the news vendor outside King's Cross Station. He read it as he stood in the taxi queue. The sports pages included an item about Leeds United winning promotion to the First Division. He wasn't much interested in football but it did no harm to be able to talk knowledgeably about things to do with the city he represented in parliament. The front page was all about the death of Sir Alexander Fleming, the man who discovered penicillin. His funeral was to be at St Paul's this coming Friday. Clive wondered if he'd be expected to attend and wished they wouldn't have bloody funerals on Fridays when people had trains to catch. It was an item on page two that stopped him in his tracks.

Body of Missing Leeds Youth Found in River Aire

Normally he would have paid it no attention. The brothers hadn't mentioned the youth's fate to him; in fact he hadn't spoken to them since that night. He'd bent someone's ear about PC Seth Lawless's move and when Campion bent someone's ear it didn't straighten until he got a favourable result. Many people down the Home Office ladder wished to curry favour with him and he'd no doubts that the awful man would be in CID before much longer. It was the photograph that made him shudder. He had only been there once and that was in the dark, but he remembered seeing the silhouette of a huge warehouse. Although the photograph was taken in daylight the outline of the building was the same and he knew the dead youth was the one he had raped. Despite the chill morning, sweat ran down his face as he read the story.

A shoe had been found and identified by the youth's mother as belonging to her son, who had gone missing a month ago. Campion ran the date of his disappearance through his memory and it tallied. The river had subsequently been dragged and the lad's body found. Campion had gone abroad on business the day after the attack and hadn't read about any missing youth. As far as he had known the lad was alive and had been paid for his inconvenience. The stupid idiots had thrown him in the river. Jesus! Well, one of them had already got his comeuppance, courtesy of his wife by the sound of it; but one of them was still alive and if he was caught he would no doubt tell all. Campion would end up inside as an accessory at least – if not charged with murder.

A busker twanged his guitar and strode the length of the queue, singing Dickie Valentine's current hit song, 'Finger of Suspicion'. Campion looked around, half expecting to see pointing fingers. The man behind him said something about the bloody busker making more money in a week than he

did in a month. A cab had pulled up alongside and the driver
looked at Campion, expectantly. The MP stepped out of the
queue and the man behind took his place.

Campion needed to get to Leeds and speak to the surviving
idiot. He walked back inside the station where he rang his
office to say he'd been called back to Leeds on an emer-
gency.

Six

Court Number One, Leeds Assizes, Tuesday, 5 April 1955

Lola was the only witness called by Mr Ormerod, Rachel's
defence counsel. She told of how Ezra had come home
drunk and had beaten her for no reason and thrown her out
into the street.

'And, considering his drunken state, did it surprise you to
learn that your stepfather had subsequently attacked your
mother?'

The prosecuting barrister stood up. 'Objection, M'lud. The
defence have yet to prove that Mr Lawless was the aggressor.'

'Sustained . . . rephrase the question, if you please, Mr
Ormerod.'

'If it please, M'lud,' protested Ormerod, 'Mrs Lawless is
a woman of five feet three inches and seven stones in weight.
Her supposed victim was severely inebriated, six feet two
inches tall and weighing more than fifteen stones. I scarcely
think the accused could be reasonably considered to be the
initial aggressor.'

The judge frowned. 'Mr Ormerod, if the victim was severely
inebriated he might well have been in no fit state to defend
himself against an unprovoked attack by a much smaller
person.'

Ormerod raised an eyebrow at this obvious bias. He felt
like pointing out that the judge was doing the prosecution's

job for them. He settled for irony, which often went down
well with a jury.

'I thank M'lud for offering the court his even-handed
advice on the matter.' The judge scowled as Ormerod
continued: 'I will of course rephrase the question. Miss
Lawless, did you give your stepfather any cause to injure
you so seriously?'

'None at all. I was sitting in a chair, listening to the wireless, he came in from the pub and started punching me – and
you can rephrase the question all you like, it didn't surprise
me at all that he did the same to Mam.'

Ormerod suppressed a smile. The prosecuting counsel
looked at the judge, expectantly. The judge looked fiercely
at Lola then said to the jury, 'The jury will disregard that
last remark. The only proven aggressive blow struck that night
was the one admitted by the accused that ended the life of
Ezra Lawless. Everything else is a matter of conjecture.'

'No further questions, M'lud,' said Ormerod, who sat down,
reasonably happy that things had gone as well as could be
expected. The prosecuting counsel, Mr Forbes-Brooke, got
to his feet.

'Miss Lawless, did your mother see you being beaten by
your stepfather?'

'No, she was upstairs. When he beat us he always liked
to do it in private.'

'I see. What about your younger sister?'

'She was upstairs as well.'

'So, no one saw Ezra Lawless attack you and, of course,
he's not around to defend himself.'

'I had the bruises to prove it,' said Lola. 'The police took
photographs.'

'Are these photographs being used in evidence?' sniffed
the judge.

'Yes, I have them here, My Lord,' said the clerk.

The judge examined the photographs briefly then handed
them back before turning his attention to Lola. 'Bruises on
their own prove nothing, Miss Lawless. Bruises can't speak.
Bruises can't tell us how they came to be.'

Ormerod looked up in surprise from his copies of the photographs. This was all getting very one-sided. Did this judge
fully understand the word impartial?

Forbes-Brooke got to his feet. 'Exactly, My Lord. For all we know the bruises might have been self-inflicted.'

'Self-inflicted?' said Lola, amazed. 'Why would I do that?'

'I'm not saying you did –' Forbes-Brooke waved a demonstrative hand – 'I'm simply illustrating to the jury an alternative way of how these bruises might have come about. You may well have acquired these bruises without Ezra Lawless being involved. Someone else might have attacked you. You might have had an accident, fallen down the stairs, who knows how you got those bruises.'

'Ezra beat me up,' said Lola, quietly. 'That's how I got the bruises. It's not the first time he's beaten me up either.'

'Did you hate Ezra Lawless?'

Lola hesitated, wondering if the truth might do more harm than good. She looked across at her mother, who looked dwarfed and vulnerable between two large WPCs. Her mother nodded at her.

'Of course I hated him. He was an evil bully.'

'And do you love your mother?'

'Yes, I do.'

'Are you glad your stepfather is dead?'

'Objection,' said Ormerod.

'Overruled.'

'Are you glad your stepfather is dead, Miss Lawless?' repeated Forbes-Brooke.

Lola couldn't stop herself. 'The world is a much better place without him.'

'Hmm, we have had character witnesses who say otherwise. What are we to believe?' He looked at the judge. 'Might I suggest an alternative and quite probable scenario, My Lord?'

'You may.'

'Might I suggest, Miss Lawless, that you witnessed your mother kill Ezra Lawless and in your desperation you contrived somehow to acquire convenient bruises to try and blacken his character and thus mitigate your mother's brutal action against a man you hated.'

'That's not true.'

'Of course I can't prove this any more than you can prove how you say you got the bruises.' He turned to the jury. 'Which is why this witness's testimony is completely worthless. No more questions, My Lord.'

Some of the jury were nodding in agreement as he sat down.

Seven

Friday, 13 May 1955. 8.30 a.m.

Mr Barraclough came out of his newsagent's shop and slid a poster into the newsboard. Which announced in brief the dramatic events of that day.

MURDERESS RACHEL LAWLESS TO BE
HANGED TODAY

It was his bad luck that he did it right under the nose of Evie Lawless, who was on her way to church with Mrs Parkinson, with whom she now lodged. It was considered that church might be the best place for a child to be while the state hanged her mother. Mrs Parkinson looked from the girl to the headlines and back. Evie's face had blanched; her eyes had narrowed beneath furrowed brows. She shook herself from Mrs Parkinson's grip and flew across the street; her tiny fists were flailing as she crashed into the newsagent, knocking him off his balance despite his considerable size. He staggered backwards and crashed through his own shop window. Two passing women stopped, in horror at first, then ran to the man's assistance. Mrs Parkinson followed in their wake and took hold of Evie, whose rage had now gone and was replaced by an uncontrollable sobbing as she took out the poster and ripped it to shreds.

'You keep a tight hold of her while t'police come!' ordered one of the women. 'She's a flamin' lunatic!'

Mr Barraclough lay moaning among the shattered glass. There was blood all over his shocked face and the other woman was trying to help him up. More people arrived. Fingers were pointed at Evie and a man joined Mrs Parkinson in holding her captive.

Lola took a deep drag on her cigarette and gazed out of the window. Maybe she should have been with Evie today of all days, shared her sorrow, but she couldn't bring herself to do that. Not just yet.

Outside in the street everything looked normal, as if nothing had happened. A grocer's delivery boy was riding along on his bike, whistling. Two women had stopped for a chat and they were laughing – today of all days when there was nothing to laugh at. The sun was shining, as if it didn't care.

She had rented a bedsit on the first floor of a large Victorian terraced house not far from her mother's old home. It contained the basics: a bed; a table; two dining chairs; a two-seater settee with dodgy springs; a dresser with a cracked mirror; a wardrobe; a sink; a gas cooker and a couple of wall cupboards. On the dresser was a photo of her daddy that she'd been hiding, on her mam's advice, ever since Ezra Lawless had come on the scene. He looked so handsome in his RAF uniform and Lola wished he could be here to put things right for her.

She thought back to the day the news of her daddy's death came through. She remembered seeing the men in uniform come to the door and how her mam had exclaimed, 'Oh, no!' when she saw them through the window. They were getting out of a car with solemn looks on their faces. It was taking Mam ages to answer the knock. She kept walking round and round, putting off the moment. Eventually Lola had opened it and had smiled up at the men, introducing herself. Under other circumstances the men would have been charmed by her, instead they just asked if her mother was in. Lola was sent upstairs, which she thought very unfair. When she came down later the men had gone and there were two neighbours in the house. Mam was sobbing quietly and one of the neighbours said, 'Would you like me to tell her, Rachel, love?'

Her mam shook her head and took Lola in her arms. She stroked her hair and Lola hadn't a clue what was going on.

'Your daddy won't be coming home, love,' she said, very quietly.

'I know, Mam, he's away fighting Hitler.'

'Hitler killed him, sweetheart. He won't be coming home.'

'Oh,' Lola had said. But the gravity of the moment had yet to sink in.

She had very intermittent memories of her daddy. He was big and warm and sometimes smelled of pipe tobacco, which she loved. They had a piano which he played, and sang songs that she didn't really understand but they must have been funny because they made her mam laugh. She could never remember her mam laughing after that.

After he died her mam became very morose, not her old self at all. She couldn't have been, or she wouldn't have married that foul creature, Lawless. Lola had hated him from the first time she saw him, and he had proved himself well worthy of her hatred.

Her thoughts turned to Evie, who had killed that pig of a man. Evie had been a brave kid by the sound of it. Their mother had nothing but praise for her. Lola had been to visit her mam two days before she was due to be hanged. Rachel had just been told by the governor that a reprieve had been refused that morning by the Home Office. Lola had been amazed at the calmness with which her mother was accepting her fate.

'Don't blame Evie, she saved my life, love. I had to take the blame. Once I'd done that there was no turning back. If I'd said it was her who killed him they'd have thought I were just trying to blame her to save me own skin.'

'But it's the truth, Mam.'

'Lola, I've been through it all with me lawyer. In the end it's our word against the reputation of a dead copper. Someone has to suffer. They were never going to let us both walk away from it.'

'But Evie's confessed to it, Mam.'

'I'd already told them I'd done it. Good job I beat her to it, eh?'

'But she—'

Rachel stopped her with a raised hand and a quiet smile. 'It's what any daughter would have done to save her mam from the gallows – that's what they said. They don't hang kids but they can destroy their lives. If I'd let Evie take the blame it would have destroyed her life all right. They'd have locked her up somewhere for God knows how long and even if they let her out she'd be left with the stigma that would have clung to her like a disease for the rest of her life. I couldn't do that to Evie.'

There were two female prison officers in the condemned cell. One of them was writing down everything Rachel said to her daughter. Rachel turned to the officer doing the writing.

'Why do yer do that, Maggie?'

'We do it with every condemned prisoner, Rachel. The real villains sometimes give away valuable information.'

'Am I a real villain?'

'No, Rachel. None of us think you're a villain at all.'

Lola exploded. 'Then why didn't she get a bloody reprieve?'

'I don't know the answer to that, love,' said Maggie, apologetically. 'None of us do.'

Rachel squeezed Lola's hand. 'I should never have brought him into your life, Lola. I never got on with him from the word go. Whatever you do, Lola, don't marry a man you don't get on with.'

'What about love?'

'I've known love, Lola, but it died in 1942 over Germany – at least that's what I'm told by them who sent him there. I'm told his plane was shot down and I have to believe them because he didn't come back. There's thousands of wives who are left with no body to bury, just a piece of paper saying their man was killed in action – as if it's something to be proud of.'

'Aren't you proud of Daddy?'

Rachel shrugged. 'Proud? What good's being proud? All I know is that I worshipped the man. I wasn't bothered about being proud. I just wanted him here for me to love. I never expected to get that sort of love back ever again, but I should at least have picked someone I got on with. What's this boyfriend of yours like?'

'Keith?'

'Yes, how come I never met him?'

'I'd only been going out with him a couple of weeks before – you know.'

'Do you get on with him?'

'Yes, he's really nice. He's taking his finals at university at the moment.'

'That's where you should have gone. I should have ignored Ezra and insisted you stay on at school. It's me being weak that's got us in this fix. I should have stood up to him when he hit you, but I didn't. I should have stood up to him when he treated us all like dirt but I didn't. I should have been there for you both and I wasn't. My weakness caused you girls a lot of misery.'

'It was Ezra's cruelty that caused us a lot of misery.'

Rachel shook her head. 'You must have thought I didn't love you, but I did. This is the one strong thing I can do to prove how much I love you both.'

'Mam, you're doing this for Evie, not for me.'

Rachel looked at her with reproachful eyes. 'Lola, do you honestly think Evie would cope with a millstone like this hanging around her neck for the rest of her life?'

Lola shrugged. 'I can't see what difference it makes. She's going round telling everyone she did it, anyway.'

'Ah, but no one believes her – that's the difference. They think it's just her way of coping with me being sentenced to hang. Anyway, what's done's done and can't be undone. I've made me confession – and much to the priest's amazement I didn't include murder in me sins.' She turned to Maggie. 'Are yer gettin' all this, Maggie? The worst thing I could think of to confess was fiddling the Thrift Stores out of three penn'orth of change. Some hangin' offence.'

Maggie wrote it down. Lola asked. 'Are you scared?'

'I might still get a reprieve.'

Lola clutched at the straw her mother was offering. 'You will, Mam. I'm sure of that.'

Rachel took her daughter's hand and squeezed it. 'I'm not holding out any real hope, Lola. Last-minute reprieves are things you only see in films. I'm a bit numb about it all, actually. I must admit I really didn't see this one coming, but Pierrepoint's booked ter do the job and I'm told he's the best. They've weighed me to make sure they know how far I need to drop, and I'm told it's completely painless – isn't that right, Maggie?'

'There'll be no pain, Rachel. It'll be like turning the light off. No more painful than that.'

Rachel smiled at her daughter. 'See, I won't feel a thing. One minute I'm down here, miserable as sin, the next minute I'm up in heaven, free as a bird.'

'You still believe in all that?'

'I never had any doubts, Lola, neither should you.'

* * *

Lola stubbed out her cigarette and lit another. Yesterday she'd never smoked in her life; today she'd smoked a whole pack; tomorrow she'd stop. She had to do something. Yesterday she'd told her boss at Jessop's Footwear to stuff his job where the sun doesn't shine. Last night she'd had a blazing row with Keith who had simply been trying to comfort her.

God knows what time it was, she hadn't slept a wink. As the clock in the bedroom had ticked away the last night of her mam's life Lola had wept until the pillow was damp. Then, at 8 a.m. – an hour before the time – she had stuffed the clock in a drawer, so she wouldn't be aware of the exact moment. Lola paced up and down her cramped room, smoked cigarette after cigarette, prayed, cursed, wept, prayed again, looked at the drawer containing the clock but couldn't bring herself to open it. The clock would tell her her mam was dead. While ever she didn't look at the clock her mam could still be alive. Looking at the clock was somehow an act of betrayal.

She opened the curtains and saw the sun was high in the sky, and she knew the time was well past. She knew her mam must now be dead, but still she didn't look at the clock. There were voices in the hallway outside her door. One of them was a voice she recognized and hated. Seth opened the door and grinned at her.

'Just thought I'd pop in and offer my condolences, Lola.'

'Oh,' she said, not quite knowing how to react.

'I'm told she squealed like a stuck pig when they hanged the bitch.'

Lola looked at him with the loathing she used to reserve for his brother.

'You know nothing of the sort, you sick liar.'

'I hope she rots in hell.'

'It's your sick brother who'll be rotting in hell,' she retorted, 'and we both know why – no doubt that's where you'll end up. Like bad peas in a pod, you two.'

She had no reason to say this, other than to get back at him, so she was surprised when he blanched. Wondering, as his brother had, if she knew about the murder.

'Touched a nerve, have I?' she snapped. 'Go away, you're polluting the place.'

She slammed the door on him. He stood there for a few

troubled seconds, wondering just how much she knew. Should he have a word with Campion? This bitch seemed to know more than was good for her.

Lola took the clock out of the drawer. It was half past eleven; her mam had been dead for two and a half hours but Lola had no tears left to weep. She felt completely empty inside, as if her life had been drained out of her, just as it had her mam.

She thought about Evie and how their mother would have wanted them to be together today. Evie must be having it tough. She'd killed her dad and their mam had been hanged for it. That was tough to handle – especially for a ten-year-old kid.

But, ten years old or not, despite what her mother had said, Lola was struggling to forgive Evie for not coming out with the truth straight away, before their mam had the chance to condemn herself to death. Because that's what she'd done. Maybe she didn't know she was doing it, but that's what she'd done all right – condemned herself to death with a false confession. Once the words were out of her mouth her fate was sealed. Would she have been so ready to carry the can if she'd known, right from the start, that she'd hang for it? Lola very much doubted it.

When Lola had gone back home the morning after Ezra's death the police were swarming all over the place and everyone was talking about how Ezra Lawless had been murdered. She had been taken to the police station for questioning and all she could do was tell the story up to the minute her stepfather kicked her out of the house. She didn't know the truth of what had happened after that, even when she was allowed to see Evie, who was still sticking to the lie their mother had insisted on her telling. It wasn't until after the trial that Evie told her the truth . . .

Lola had left the court in shock after hearing the death sentence passed on her mother. She had run, pale faced, up the Headrow and jumped on a tram heading for where Evie was living. Her younger sister was sitting alone in the front room when Lola arrived. Evie looked up. Lola couldn't get the words out; all that came out were tears. She sat down and sobbed out her news.

'They're . . . they're going to . . . going to hang Mam.'

Evie let out a howl of anguish. Mrs Parkinson rushed in. Evie charged at her and hammered her small fists into the woman's chest. Mrs Parkinson put her arms around the girl and hugged her tight.

'She said she'd be all right!' Evie screamed. 'She told me she'd be all right!'

Lola was still sobbing but Evie's words were coming out in torrents. 'She told me not to tell them! She said she'd be all right! She said they'd lock me up if I told them! She made me promise!'

Lola looked up. 'Promise? . . . Promise what?' she asked, through her tears.

'Not to tell. She made me promise not to tell. I said I should tell you, but she said not to.'

Lola was on her feet now. Mrs Parkinson, also curious, relaxed her grip. With a not-too-gentle hand Lola turned her sister's face towards her.

'Evie, what are you talking about?'

Evie was shivering quite violently and was now having difficulty getting her words out. 'Mam didn't . . . didn't do it.'

Lola shook her head in disbelief. 'Evie, what are you saying?'

'I hit him . . . he was hitting Mam . . . so I hit him. Mam said I saved her life and I mustn't tell them.'

Lola took her by the lapels of her dress and started shaking her, violently. '*Why?* Why did you let her die? You've made her die! You did this. This all your fault. You've made our mam die!'

Mrs Parkinson got between them and made them both sit down. 'Look,' she said, 'if this is what really happened then your mam's going to be OK.'

Lola was now shaking with shock and rage. 'Only if she tells them the truth!'

'I will,' howled Evie. 'I'll tell them now.'

Evie's confession was dismissed as inconceivable. How was anyone supposed to believe that a skinny little kid like her could wield a heavy iron with sufficient power to kill a fifteen-stone man? The kid was obviously doing her best for her mother and fair play to her for trying. She was warned not to persist in such lies or they might land her in deep trouble.

Lola had struggled not to blame her sister. If she'd confessed straight away their mam would still be alive. Maybe she was being unfair on Evie. But it wasn't as unfair as their mam being hanged. It couldn't stay like this, absolutely not. This was something that needed sorting out. One way or another she'd prove to the world that her mother was no murderer.

Instead of a church Evie spent the day of her mother's execution, and all the following night, in a police cell. Her future looked bleak and she wished she could somehow join her mother in the trouble-free world of non-existence. But she was a Catholic and suicide was a mortal sin which would send her to Hell where her dad was. So, bugger that for an idea.

Eight

Waking up in a cell came as no great shock to Evie. It takes more than a jail cell to shock a kid whose mother's just been hanged. She'd been carried there after she'd fallen asleep in the interview room with her not having slept a wink for two nights. It was 2 a.m. The cell was eerily lit from an outside street lamp and from the partially open cell door.

She inspected her surroundings and wasn't impressed. There were quarry tiles on the floor, the walls were bare bricks painted a bilious green, the high window had five bars across its two-foot width and in the corner was a suspicious looking galvanized bucket with a lid on it. If it was what Evie thought

it was she hoped it was empty. She sniffed the air. There was
a faint smell of disinfectant but no evidence of anything else,
which was something. She hated the smell of other people's
pee. There was plenty of that in Mrs Parkinson's place where
there was a po under every bed. She thought of her mam and
she burst into tears. A policeman appeared, alerted by her
sobbing.

'Ah, you're awake.' He looked at his watch. 'You've slept
for a solid thirteen hours; we thought you'd never wake up.
I, er, I gather you're Ezra Lawless's girl.' He was young
enough to still have the remnants of teenage acne but, on the
whole, Evie thought he was very handsome. 'My name's PC
Bruce – you can call me Alfie. Look, everyone knows what's
happened to you, love. They'll be fair to you.'

Evie wiped her eyes. 'Did you know my father?'

'Well, yes – he worked here.'

'He was drunk and he attacked my mam. He was trying
to kill her so I hit him on his head to stop him so they hanged
her. Do you think that's fair?'

'I'll bring you a cup of tea.'

'I don't want a cup of tea, thank you. I want my mam.'

The constable sat on the bed beside her. 'The woman who
came with you, er . . .'

'Mrs Parkinson?'

He nodded. 'Yeah, Mrs Parkinson.'

'What about her?'

'Well, after what happened I don't think she wants to take
you in any more. She says you're too much of a handful.'

'Oh.'

Evie wasn't sure what to make of this. The time she'd
spent at Mrs Parkinson's had been time spent in a state of
limbo. It had been a time spent just on the edge of reality,
when she refused to believe that anyone would dare hang her
mother. Even now she could scarcely believe it.

'Where will I live then? Will I be sent to reform school?'

Alfie smiled at her. 'I doubt if they'll put you anywhere
like that, but you'll get a right telling off, that's for sure. The
man you knocked through the shop window had to have two
dozen stitches – half of them in his bottom – so he's not in
a very forgiving mood.'

'I'm very sorry about that,' said Evie. 'I didn't mean to do

that to him. Should I write him a letter telling him I'm sorry
and I hope his bottom gets better soon?'

'Well, I wouldn't word it quite like that.'

'Did you like my father?'

The constable hesitated before saying, 'No, I didn't.'

'He was a bully, wasn't he?'

Another long pause as Alfie remembered Ezra always refer-
ring to him as PC Spotty Clock. 'Yes, he was a bully.'

'So, why did they hang my mother? Was it because he
was a policeman? Was it because my uncle Seth was mad
at her?'

'Uncle Seth? Oh, right. No, of course it wasn't.'

'Why then?'

'I don't know, love.'

'Neither do I. Is he in, Uncle Seth?'

'No, he's not on duty at the moment.'

'Good. I don't like him.'

You're not on your own there, thought Alfie. He put his
arm around her shoulder and gave her a hug. Just at that
moment it was one of the two things she needed, the other
was a bit more urgent. She nodded towards the bucket.

'Is that the lavvie?'

'It is, I'm afraid.'

'I need to go.'

'I'll, er, I'll wait outside.'

He stepped out of the door and partially closed it as Evie
gingerly positioned herself over the bucket. It echoed inside
the tin receptacle, embarrassing her, so she stopped and called
out, 'Can you shut the door, please?'

The door clunked shut. Evie finished, and examined, with
some distaste, the 'Bronco' toilet roll standing on a shelf
beside the bucket. According to her mam it was handy for
wrapping up margarine but much too shiny for wiping the
bum. A tin bucket and a Bronco toilet roll; was that all she
had to look forward to in life? On a shelf next to the toilet
roll was a tin bowl and a tin mug full of water, presumably
either for washing or drinking. She took a tentative drink,
rubbed a finger across her teeth, poured the rest into the bowl
and washed her face and hands as best she could. There was
no towel so she dried herself on the bed sheet. Then she
tidied her hair with her hands and sat, demurely, on the bed.

'You can come in now.'

The constable came back in, this time accompanied by a sergeant. Evie looked at his stripes and asked, 'Am I a criminal, Sergeant?'

The sergeant looked down at her pale, pinched face. She wasn't a looker wasn't this kid, but she had something really appealing about her; the sort of thing it was hard to put your finger on. Just for a second he wished she looked like one of the mean-eyed, mouthy young wasters who passed through their doors all too often, and not the most beguiling kid he'd seen in a while. He looked away.

'No, well, yes – I mean, not as such, but you have to be dealt with.'

'Oh,' said Evie.

Alfie looked at his sergeant. 'It's not right isn't this, Sarge. Ezra's still causing misery, even after he's dead.'

The sergeant gave a helpless shrug. 'It's not up to us to decide what's right and what's not. It's up to us to produce the lass at juvenile court and let them decide what to do with her.'

'You mean she's having her future decided by the butcher, the baker and the bloody candlestick-maker, all playing at being judges?' snorted the constable. 'This kid needs looking after, not dealing with.'

'And just what am I supposed to do about that, Alfie?' snapped the sergeant. 'We don't make the rules, we just enforce 'em.'

The conversation was going pretty much over Evie's head, but she could tell her prospects weren't good. She turned her tearful gaze on the sergeant. 'They hung my mam yesterday. She didn't do it, you know. It was me who did it. If they were going to hang anyone they should have hung me.'

The sergeant stared down at Evie and shuddered at a sudden vision of her ten-year-old body dangling on the end of a rope. 'You mustn't talk like that, love,' he muttered. 'It'll not do anyone a ha'porth of good you talking like that.'

He ushered Alfie out of the cell, but not out of Eve's earshot as they'd left the door open. 'It's never bloody ending, this Lawless business. I hate to speak ill of the dead but he were as thick as two short planks were Lawless. He might have been a big bugger physically but he were what's known as a mental midget – beats me how he managed to tie his own shoelaces, never mind be made bloody sergeant. And now they've given that nasty bloody brother of his a CID job. What's going on, Alfie?'

'I've no idea, Sarge. I never thought for one minute they'd find Rachel Lawless guilty of murder,' muttered Alfie. 'I reckon it were probably self-defence.'

'No doubt about it, lad. That barrister they got her were worse than useless – couldn't win a raffle if he bought all the bloody tickets. And that bloody judge! He had her guilty the minute he sat down on the first day. When he summed up he practically ordered the jury to find her guilty of murder. I've never seen nowt so blatant. There's something stinks about this whole business. Do you know, this century, ninety per cent of women sentenced to death for murder have been reprieved? Ninety bloody per cent. Did you know that, Alfie?'

'No, I didn't, Sarge. How come Rachel didn't get a reprieve?'

'Well, that's just it – it's a mystery, lad. I mean, four weeks after sentencing and Albert bloody Pierrepoint's putting a noose around her neck. What was that all about?'

'Well, I hope young Eve's going to be all right, Sarge.'

The sergeant shook his head, confidently. 'Under the circumstances she'll be let off with a slapped wrist.'

Nine

Leeds Juvenile Court, 20 May 1955

'Eve Marie Lawless, you are a girl in unfortunate circumstances who is in urgent need of care and control before you get completely out of hand. It is the decision of this court that you be placed in a suitable secure home for a period to be determined by your behaviour, but not less than one year.'

The sentence meant little to Evie, who had learned to prepare for the worst. Her eyes scanned the court as she was being led out by Alfie. She was more concerned that Lola hadn't turned up.

Clive Campion read about Evie's case in the *Yorkshire Post*. He noted, with some satisfaction, that his wishes had been carried out. Prior to the execution of their mother, both Evie and her half-sister had denounced the late Sergeant Lawless as a man who had cruelly and systematically beaten them. The younger sister had even tried to carry the blame for her father's death, saying she had killed him because he was attacking her mother. This had disturbed the MP because it sounded a likely scenario, knowing what he knew about Ezra Lawless. Fortunately their accusations had been dismissed as the hysterical rantings one would expect from the daughters of a condemned woman, but there would be those who might give their story some credence. No smoke without fire, they might have said. Not any more, with one of the daughters now locked up for being out of control and her credibility therefore in tatters. This unprovoked attack proved that she was obviously a child who needed strong discipline and without her father's guiding hand her behaviour had gone from bad to worse. It had been important to Campion that the Rachel Lawless case came to a close with no loose ends – such as reprieved murderers with mouthy daughters – and he had the ear of the Home Secretary when it came to refusing this particular reprieve. The victim was a policeman and a clear message had to be sent out that anyone who murders a copper can expect no mercy. Even if the killer is the copper's wife.

His dash back to Leeds that day hadn't been necessary, except to give him peace of mind. Seth Lawless had swiftly arrested a local miscreant and held him for just long enough to deflect whatever suspicions might be headed his own way. Seth was now a detective constable and Campion had made it known that, because of the officer's keenness in this matter, he wanted DC Lawless to stay on the case of the murdered youth.

All in all, Campion was beginning to breathe easier.

Ten

West Moor Girls' Home housed forty-seven girls aged from ten to sixteen. Evie was the youngest occupant and within a day she acquired the nick name 'Squint' from Movita Lumsden, who was two years older than Evie and a good three stones heavier.

'Yer me slave from now on, d'yer hear that, Squint?'

'My name's Evie.'

Movita gave her a slap that sent her reeling to the floor. 'If I want ter call yer Squint that's what yer name is. My name's Lummy; your name's Squint, cos that what yer do.'

'It's not a squint it's a lazy eye – and I can't help it.'

Movita got her in a headlock that had Evie gasping for breath. 'Did I say yer could bleedin' help it? If yer could help it yer wouldn't squint, yer dozy mare. Anyroad, yer me slave.'

'Will you let me go, please?'

'Are yer gonna be me slave or not?'

'What do I have to do?'

'My bidding – that's what slaves do.'

Evie agreed to be Movita's slave as it seemed the only way to get free of the headlock, but it soon occurred to her that being Movita's slave might not be the worst way to cope with West Moor. She did the big girl's bidding as there wasn't a lot of scope for slaving at the home and the benefits outweighed the work insofar as Movita protected her assets with her fat fists.

Evie had been there a week when Lola came to see her.

Evie came into the day room wearing a maroon jumper, black pleated skirt, grey ankle socks and heavy, black shoes. She smiled, uncertainly, at her big sister.

'Thanks for coming, Lola.'

'You're my sister,' said Lola. 'Mam would have wanted

me to look out for you.' There were alone in the room apart
from a noisy canary and a goldfish in a bowl. 'How are you
coping?' Lola looked around the room. 'I don't suppose it's
a picnic living in this place.'

'I'd rather cope with this place than cope with Dad. Anyroad,
I'm a murderer, so it's only right I should be locked up.'

'Mam wouldn't have wanted this,' Lola said, 'and you're
no more a murderer than my daddy was when he killed
Germans. It's not murder when you kill bad people.'

'I hoped you'd have come to court.' There was a note of
censure in Evie's voice.

'I hoped you wouldn't have ended up in court,' countered
Lola. 'I certainly hoped you wouldn't have ended up in
here.'

'I didn't think I would. Everyone said I'd just be told off.
Alfie – the copper who looked after me – was disgusted with
what they did to me. He told me to my face.'

Lola shook her head. 'I'm disgusted as well, Evie. You do
stuff like you did, they're bound to lock you up. You can't just
hope they'll go easy on you because your mam's just been
hanged.'

This wasn't what Evie had expected. She expected Lola to
be on her side and as mad as hell that she'd been locked up
after everything that had happened to her. Lola was as mad
as hell all right – mad at Evie.

'I don't know why you're mad at me, Lola. It's bad enough
in this place without you being mad at me.'

Lola sighed. She didn't want to add to Evie's problems,
but it had to be said.

'Evie, our mam let herself be hanged so you wouldn't get
locked up in a place like this. That's why she confessed. She
didn't want you ending up in a reformatory. It's as if she did
it all for nothing. Here you are anyway – and our mam's
gone.'

Evie was instantly in floods. She hadn't seen it like this.
Lola couldn't help but take pity on her. She took her sister's
hand.

'She wasn't just your mam, Evie, she was my mam as well.
She was my mam before you were born. I loved her just as
much as you did. I'm sorry, Evie, but you ending up in here

anyway makes me think she made the ultimate sacrifice and it was all for nothing.'

Evie was sobbing. 'All I did . . . was push . . . push a bloke who was putting up a notice saying our mam was . . . a murderer.'

'It must have been more than that, Evie. They don't lock you up just for pushing people.'

'Well, he fell through a window and ended up in hospital,' Evie conceded, 'but that part of it was an accident.' She looked at her elder sister with tear-filled eyes. 'I'm sorry I let Mam down. I tried to tell everyone I did it but it was too late.'

'I know, kid. But losing Mam – especially like that – hit me really hard – and you ending up in here anyway made it all seem so pointless.'

'It hit me hard as well, Lola. Being in here's hitting me really hard if you must know.'

'OK, kid, I'm sorry for being rough on you – Mam wouldn't have wanted that. It's as if the whole world wants to give us a hard time. On the day Mam died Seth came round to my lodgings and told me he hoped she rotted in hell.' She remembered their confrontation. 'I told him he was just as evil as Dad had been. You should have seen his face. He looked scared, Evie. I swear he looked scared.'

Evie shuddered. 'Do you think he's as bad as Dad?'

'I don't know, kid. There's something about this whole business that doesn't fit.'

'The sergeant at the police station thinks it all stinks,' Evie told her. 'I heard him talking to Alfie. He says the barrister they got Mam was worse than useless and they couldn't believe she didn't get a reprieve.'

'And he said you shouldn't have been locked up?'

Evie nodded. 'Honest, Lola. I wouldn't say it if it wasn't true.'

'I think I'll go see him. What's his full name?'

Evie thought, then shook her head. 'Can't remember – he's really tall and good-looking. Black hair, same colour as yours.'

Evie looked at Lola and, not for the first time, hoped that her sister's spectacular beauty ran in the family and that it was just a case of waiting until she herself blossomed. She checked the mirror regularly, but the signs weren't looking too promising. She made mental comparisons. Where Lola's hair was dark and fell in silken tresses on her shoulders, Evie's hair was mousy and stuck out like a lavatory brush; where Lola's skin was smooth and unblemished, Evie's was covered in freckles, even in the middle of winter; where Lola's eyes were dark, alluring and full of mystery, Evie had a grey-green squint. Lola broke into her thoughts.

'I can't live with Mam being branded a murderer. It'll hang round us like a bad smell for the rest of our lives. It's started already – "There goes one of the Lawless sisters. Their mam killed their dad – what a family."'

Evie gave a glum nod. 'They've already made up a rhyme about it.'

'I know, I've heard it.' Lola paused before saying, 'Evie, it'd mean that everyone would have to believe your story – that you killed him, not Mam. I don't know what the outcome of that will be.'

'I want them to believe that,' Evie said. 'But how do we do it? I'm the only one who was there who's left alive, and they're even less likely to believe me after this.'

'Which is very convenient for them,' said Lola, trying to make sense of it all. 'It's as if no one in authority wanted to believe that Ezra was a bad man. If they believe you, they've got to believe that Dad was capable of doing the stuff he did to us. So, the more they can blacken your character the better it is for them.'

'Who's them?' Evie was baffled by her sister's reasoning.

'That's what we've got to find out,' Lola said. 'It could be that dear old Uncle Seth's one of them; maybe that magistrate who put you in here; maybe the judge who sentenced Mam to hang – and maybe none of them. One thing I do know – that sergeant's right; this thing stinks to high heaven. I'm off to see your policeman pal as soon as I can.' She checked Evie's description. 'Alfie, tall and good-looking, dark hair. How good-looking?'

'Better looking than Keith,' said Evie, 'and he's got a lovely smile.'

Eleven

'Is is just me, or am I fighting a losing battle with your Catholic conscience?'

It was a warm June day and they were out walking in Adel Woods. Lola summoned up a smile. 'It's not you, Keith. It's something I just can't shake off. It's probably something to do with Ezra.'

'Ezra?'

Her mother's first date with Ezra had had a disastrous effect on all their lives. She could picture him now, calling her mother a dirty woman, and Evie a dirty mistake. For reasons that didn't make any sense, such a memory was more of a sexual deterrent than any Catholic sermon on the sins of the flesh. But Keith was no Ezra. So far he'd made no serious attempt to relieve her of her virginity, which was still intact. She might well have been proud of that, had it not been kept intact by the spectre of Ezra.

'I'd never do anything to hurt you,' he said.

'Oh, Keith, I know that.'

'It's just that we've been going out for a few months now and all we've ever done is kiss.'

'Actually, it's all we're supposed to do, Keith.'

'Come off it, Lola, the chief rabbi's a more devout Catholic than you.'

Lola laughed and turned to him. He was no Cary Grant but he was pleasant looking, twenty-two, very tall, with floppy brown hair. He had just finished his history degree.

'You'll make a good teacher,' she said. 'All the girls will fall in love with you.'

'I'm not interested in all the girls, only you.'

He took her in his arms and kissed her. His hands wandered, briefly, over her breasts and Ezra returned to haunt her but this time she would fight him. She took Keith's hand and led him, determinedly, to a nearby beauty spot called Adel Crag where many a girl had happily lost her virginity. She was breathing heavily and squeezing Keith to her as they walked. Ezra had done enough damage to her family. Beneath the shadow of the large granite rocks they tore at each other's clothes, Keith with pent-up desire, Lola with the need to beat Ezra's poisonous legacy. She had a beautiful body and had never used it to make love.

Now she was naked with a man for the first time in her life and Ezra could go to hell. The sight of her was almost too much for Keith. It took him several awkward attempts before he entered her. He grunted with pleasure and Lola wept because this wasn't how it was supposed to be. She knew she was doing this simply to spite a dead man. It took away all the joy and ecstasy and therefore there was no triumph over Ezra. He'd won. He'd taken this away from her as well.

Keith lasted barely a minute before he collapsed in a spent heap on top of her. She pushed him off and wriggled out from under him. By the time he recovered she was almost dressed.

'Sorry about that,' he said. 'I didn't use much self-control.'

'It was OK.'

'I doubt it was for you. It was a bit wham, bang, thank you, ma'am. To be honest, I've never seen anything quite so beautiful as when you were lying there. Took my breath away a bit.'

'You're a nice man, Keith.'

'Nice? Please don't call me nice.'

'Sorry, you're a good man.'

'You could try exciting, dangerous, thrilling . . .'

'I don't want anyone exciting, dangerous or thrilling.'

'Ah, well, I'm your man then.'

They were both dressed and ready for home when he blurted, 'Lola, will you marry me?'

'What?'

'I want to marry you.'

Lola raised her eyebrows and smiled. 'Marry me? Keith, are you sure you're thinking clearly?'

'You've had a rough time, Lola. I can give you a good life.

I'm fairly sure I'll get a good degree and I've got a couple of jobs lined up. You did say you didn't want your life to be exciting or dangerous or thrilling – I can promise you all that and less.'

He'd made her smile, he could do that. But Lola wasn't at all sure she simply wanted a husband who could give her a good life and make her smile now and again. But she also wasn't at all sure she'd ever be able to do better than Keith Penfold.

'I need time to think about it.'

'At least you didn't say no. How much time?'

'As long as it takes.'

Although they had never met, Keith's mother didn't approve of Lola and had decided to make her feelings clear to him.

'I mean, you can tell by the name they've given her – Lola. Whoever heard of a decent girl called Lola? It's a prostitute's name, Keith, and she's got a prostitute's look about her.'

Mrs Penfold was a divorcee who would have resented any woman trying to take her son away from her.

'Mother, you've never met her. How do you know what she looks like?'

'I've seen her photograph in the paper.'

'Oh, that.'

'And I don't want to meet her – ever.'

'Her name's short for Dolores.'

'She looks a fast cat to me. Fast cats like her can trap boys into marriage – you know what I'm talking about?' She held him with an accusing gaze. 'Has she lured you into her bed yet, Keith?'

He turned away to hide his blushes. 'No, Mother, we haven't been to bed. Anyway you're jumping the gun, she hasn't said she'll marry me, yet. If she was trying to trap me she'd hardly be thinking things over.'

His mother shook her head, despairingly. 'Oh, you've a lot to learn about the wiles of women. Can't you see she's toying with you? Making you think she'd be doing you a favour by marrying her?'

Keith sighed. 'Mother, she's very respectable. Lawless wasn't her real dad, you do know that, don't you? Her real dad was killed in the war. He was awarded the DFM, which was more than my dad got. Dad said he spent the war writing out prescriptions for malingerers – he should have written himself one.'

'Your father was in a reserved occupation, Keith. During the war, being a doctor was more important than being a soldier.'

'Why do you defend him, Mother? He ran off with his receptionist.'

'Did you think I'd forgotten, Keith? Do you think I don't know what it's like to be hurt? Your father married me for money, I should have known that. He admitted it, you know. You marry the wrong person they hurt you. I don't want that to happen to you. I mean, where does this girl work? In a shoe shop. Doesn't that tell you anything about her? You can do better than a shop girl, Keith.'

'A minute ago she was a prostitute; at least she's coming up in the world. Why don't you just admit why you don't like her, Mother?'

'All right. Just think of your career, Keith. She'll always be Rachel Lawless's daughter and if you marry her you'll be Rachel Lawless's son-in-law.'

Keith sighed. Deep down he knew that his father had left home because he couldn't stand to live with his mother a minute longer. If it hadn't been his receptionist it would have been someone else. His mother was a difficult woman to live with and he just couldn't wait to marry Lola, if only to get away from his mother's constant carping.

'That Rachel Lawless's marked her youngest daughter with the curse. Lola will be next, and then you, if you take her as a wife.'

'What are you talking about, Mother?'

'I'm telling you the truth, Keith – having a murderess for a mother-in-law's no life for a young man with a future. It's a lifelong curse.'

It was the first time she'd brought this out into the open and he knew she had a point. He'd already heard the whispers and seen the nudges at work. Everyone in the country knew who Rachel Lawless was. He'd stuck by Lola throughout the trial and it hadn't been easy for him.

His mother, not wishing to be denied the ghoulish pleasure

she had got from her son's first-hand accounts of the family's suffering, had not expressed her disapproval during this time, which helped. But now the business was over, the woman was hanged, and her son had to get on with his life. And his life must not include an infamous murderess, whose name featured in newspaper articles, sick jokes, rhymes, graffiti – you name it.

Lola had been given her job back in the shoe shop. Her boss, Mr Jessop, had made allowances for her outburst, on top of which she brought in business from people who liked to boast that they'd been fitted with shoes by Rachel Lawless's daughter. Some of them were openly unpleasant and Lola knew it was only a question of time before she exploded at a customer who overstepped the mark. Her boss had warned her not to react.

'It'll blow over, Lola. Just weather the storm until it blows over.'

Mr Jessop had been in the navy so his metaphor carried some weight. He was a decent man and he also fancied her like mad, but he was in his late thirties and married, so Lola wasn't interested. She was still patiently weathering what seemed like a gathering storm. Only a couple of days ago there had been a photo of her in the *News of the World*, kneeling in front of a man, with an apologetic look on her face, under the heading:

MURDERESS'S DAUGHTER KNEELS IN FORGIVENESS

The photographer's accomplice had deliberately given her the wrong shoe size. Lola was photographed kneeling down as she helped the bogus customer on with his ill-fitting shoe. She was just saying, 'Sorry about this, sir,' as the camera flashed. The accompanying article gave an entirely different version of the story, giving the impression that Lola was constantly begging forgiveness for her mother's crime.

A female customer came in the following Tuesday and made a beeline for her – putting Lola immediately on her guard. The woman wore expensive looking clothes and had recently permed hair. She seemed pleasant enough at first, but Lola had learned to be wary of the pleasant-at-first ones.

'You have a court shoe in the window in light brown – 25s/11d.'

Lola forced a smile. 'I know the one, madam, what size are you?'

'Six.'

'Would you care to take a seat?'

The woman sat down as Lola went for the shoes. She returned and her hackles rose as she heard the woman talking, in a loud voice, to an elderly man being fitted with a pair of black boots.

'I recognize her now. If I'd known she worked here I'd have gone somewhere else. These people shouldn't have jobs working with the public.'

The old man didn't seem to have a clue what the woman was talking about. Mr Jessop caught Lola's eye and saw the anger there. He shook his head, warning her. Lola nodded to him and plastered the smile back on.

'Are these the ones, madam?' She took one out of its box.

'Yes, that's the one.'

'Would you like any help with it?'

'I know how to put a shoe on, thank you very much.'

Lola took a breath and said, calmly, 'I thought madam might need a shoe horn.'

'No thank you. I'd be grateful if you could stand away from me.'

'Madam?'

'I know who you are. The next thing you know you'll be apologizing for having a vicious killer for a mother. I read the papers.'

She gave a contemptuous smile and looked around the shop, trying to enlist support from the other customers. They looked away from her, embarrassed. Lola bit her tongue and looked towards the doorway, counting to ten. Keith was due to take her for lunch and to find out if she'd come to a decision. It had been over a week since his proposal and she hadn't made up her mind yet. Although as the days went by she was getting more and more fed up with the crap she was getting from the general public. If Keith could get a job in another town where her face wasn't so well known, maybe . . . It was a tempting prospect that was becoming more tempting by the second. The woman tried one shoe on, then took it off and threw it at Lola.

'Are you stupid, girl? Do I look as if I've got feet like a navvy?'

That's it, her mind was made up. Her answer was yes. He should be here any second. The instant he turned up she'd hand this bloody woman over to Jessop to deal with. She had a proposal to accept and this woman wasn't going to spoil things for her. Lola couldn't wait to see his face. She looked over to the doorway to see if he was there. A young man cleaning the windows gave her a large wink. He didn't know who she was but he knew she was the best-looking bird he'd seen all day. Lola composed herself and thought about how she'd go about telling him. Whatever you do, don't let this woman get to you. Don't let her spoil one of the magical moments of your life. She squeezed out a smile, much to Jessop's relief.

'They're a size six, madam, which is what you asked for.'

'A size five is what I asked for. Are you some sort of cretin?'

Lola stood her ground and said, evenly, 'You said size six, madam.' She looked to Jessop for support but got none. He shrugged as if to say he'd no idea what the woman had asked for.

'Are you calling me a liar, girl? What the hell is the world coming to when we have to put up with murderer's runts calling us liars?'

Suddenly Lola wasn't scared of the consequences of anything she did. She could see this woman for exactly what she was, and exactly what was needed to bring her down. The woman was sitting with her back to the window and was still ranting when Lola stepped away. She went out of the door and said, quietly, to the window cleaner, 'May I borrow this?'

The window cleaner followed her eyes down to a bucket of dirty water.

'Er, be my guest.'

'Thank you.'

Lola picked up the bucket, approached the ranting woman from behind and quickly plonked it over her head, drenching her and cutting off her rant in midstream. The window cleaner doubled up with laughter, as did the old man in his new boots. Jessop was frozen with horror; the other customers awaited the outcome with bated breath. Lola stood, with arms akimbo, until the woman had removed the bucket. Her hair was plastered to her head; her expensive clothes were soaked with filthy water that dripped from her on to the carpeted floor, and there was a look of intense shock on her face.

'Is that a better fit, madam?' Lola enquired.

The woman's mouth opened and shut like a goldfish, but no sound came out. Keith arrived at the door and gawped in dismay. Lola smiled at him.

'An awkward customer,' she explained, 'we get them now and again.' She turned to Jessop. 'I'll take my lunch break now, Mr Jessop.'

Her boss nodded, dumbly. Lola picked up her coat and linked arms with Keith, but Keith was still gawping.

'Mother?' he said.

'Keith?' said the woman.

'Oh, bugger,' said Lola.

Lola was sipping a beer in Whitelocks when Keith came in. She'd left him to it rather than make things worse by denouncing his mother as a harridan. The bar was busy, as it always was on a lunchtime. He made his way over to her table.

'I'm afraid Mother's rung the police about you,' he said. 'I tried to talk her out of it, but she's really cross.'

'Apart from tipping a bucket of water on her head, what on earth did I do wrong?'

'You tell me.'

'She called me a murderer's runt.'

Keith grimaced. 'Don't know what to say. There's no point me apologizing for her.'

'You could get me another beer.'

'Right, er – I suppose this has put a bit of a damper on my proposal, has it?'

'I don't know, Keith. I'd have thought it might be a bit awkward for you.'

'Mother's always been awkward – I'll, er, I'll get you that beer.'

Twelve

There was a sharp knock on her room door. Lola opened it to find a young policeman standing there.

'Dolores Lawless?'

'Well done, Constable. Not many people can say that.'

She hadn't gone back into work that afternoon. Jessop would understand. She'd ring him tomorrow and ask if she needed to work her notice. He'd say no and make up her pay packet. She wouldn't have minded asking him what the police had said, but that would wait until tomorrow as well. It wasn't a capital crime.

'My name's PC Bruce. We've had a complaint passed on from Leeds Central about you assaulting a Mrs Penfold. Would you mind if I come in?'

Lola stood back and allowed him through. 'I emptied a bucket of water over her head,' she said. 'Is that assault?'

'Technically, yes.'

'You'd better arrest me, then, seeing how I've just confessed. Do you want to know why I did it?'

'I think I already know. The lads at Leeds Central questioned both the manager of the shop and the owner of the bucket. Mrs Penfold wants to press charges but we won't do that unless we've got reasonable grounds. As far as I can see it was six of one, half a dozen of the other, but I need to get a statement from you.'

'She was verbally abusing me and it seemed a good way to shut her up.'

PC Bruce nodded as he wrote this down, then he looked up at her. 'When the call came through I volunteered to take it,' he said.

'Oh, why?'

'Because I've met your sister.'

'Evie?'

'I took her to court. Between you and me I thought she got a raw deal. It strikes me you're both getting a raw deal, so I thought I'd take the call to make sure things didn't get twisted.'

'Twisted?'

'Apparently, Mrs Penfold is a woman who makes a lot of noise in high circles. She's what we call a squeaky wheel, and you know what they say about squeaky wheels.'

'No.'

'They're the ones that get greased.'

'In Mrs Penfold's case the greasing would be at my expense?'

'Possibly.'

'So, I should be grateful, PC . . .?'

'Bruce, Alfie Bruce.'

'Pleased to meet you, Alfie Bruce.'

He was already infatuated with her. Never in his life had he seen anyone quite so gorgeous. What the hell was she doing working in a shoe shop?

Lola recognized the name; tall, dark hair, lovely smile, better looking than Keith. 'Alfie . . . yes, Evie told me about you. Won't you sit down, Alfie? My friends call me Lola, by the way.'

'Lola.'

He laid his helmet on the table and sat down in the settee. Lola sat opposite. 'She said you were kind to her.'

'Your sister's a nice kid. Doesn't deserve to be where she is.'

'She also told me you don't believe our mother should have been hanged.'

'Er, that's right. I suppose I came here because I didn't want another ton of bricks falling on your head. Off the record, your family's had a raw deal at the hands of the law.'

'Have you any idea why?'

He shook his head. 'Not a clue. But I'm not the only one who thinks there's something wrong with the way your mother and sister were treated.'

'And now it could be my turn?'

'Not if I can help it.'

'Mrs Penfold is my boyfriend's mother, if that's any help.'

'Boyfriend?'

Lola failed to suppress a grin. 'He would have been my fiancé by now if I hadn't emptied the bucket on her head.'

She wasn't oblivious to the effect she had on men. Alfie was obviously taken by her and she saw no reason not to take advantage of it. She held him in her gaze and said, 'So, you know about my mother, then?'

'Well, yes, she's, er . . . she was, quite a famous woman.'

'I think infamous is nearer the mark.'

He shrugged.

'One way or another,' Lola said, 'I'm going to clear her name. I know she didn't kill dad because Evie's admitted to it, and I believe her. I can't imagine, for the life of me, why anyone would want to see my mother dead, but it seems to me that someone did – and that someone saw to it that Evie got locked up too.'

'I find it hard to believe as well,' said Alfie. 'To quote my sergeant, "something stinks about the whole business".'

An idea struck her. 'Alfie, under normal circumstances would anyone take Mrs Penfold's charge seriously?'

He shook his head. 'Not a chance. We've got better things to do than waste our time on her.'

'So, if charges were pressed against me, you'd be surprised.'

'Very.'

'If I'm charged, then we'll know for certain that something does stink.'

Back at Millgarth, DC Seth Lawless was on the phone to Clive Campion.

'The big sister's in trouble now. A woman's accused her of assault.'

'Splendid! Has she been charged?'

'I'm afraid not. The victim wants ter press charges but I'm told there's not much ter go on.'

'Then somebody had better get something to go on. The family's obviously a menace to society. Send me details of the incident, Seth. I'll deal with it from this end.'

'Mrs Penfold?'

'Yes?'

'Good evening, Mrs Penfold. My name's Clive Campion, I'm the member of parliament for your constituency.'

Mrs Penfold was now gushing. 'Oh, I see. How can I help you, Mr Campion?'

'I'm ringing regarding your recent troubles.'

'Troubles?'

'I understand you were assaulted?'

'Oh, yes, that's right – in a shoe shop. All I did was complain about the service and the damned assistant poured a bucket of filthy water over my head. Ruined my clothes, and my hair. I said I wanted to press charges but the police say there's not much they can do about it.'

'This is exactly why I'm ringing, Mrs Penfold. It's the thin end of the wedge. There are too many people getting away with violent crime and it's part of my job to clamp down on it. Might I suggest that you insist on charges being brought and I'll bring some pressure to bear myself?'

Mrs Penfold was zinging with elation. 'I'd be delighted to do that, Mr Campion. The woman wants locking up.'

'I can't guarantee that, Mrs Penfold, but she mustn't be allowed to get away with it.'

Evie looked withdrawn when Lola went to see her a couple of weeks later. It was a warm day and they were strolling in the grounds of West Moor Girls Home. To the casual eye it looked like a nineteenth-century mansion until you looked closer and saw the bars at some of the windows. The perimeter walls were eight feet high and difficult to climb over, but not too difficult for a really determined escapee. Of which there were many.

'I saw the picture of you in the paper,' Evie commented.

'It was a set-up,' Lola told her.

'So, all that stuff about you begging forgiveness for our mam's crime was a lie?'

'Come off it, Evie. Don't tell me you believed that rubbish?'

Evie kicked at a stone and said, 'No.' But she wasn't very convincing. This annoyed Lola.

'You did, didn't you?'

'What was I supposed to believe, Lola? All the other kids made fun of me. They reckoned you were chicken. There's some awful girls in here, Lola. I don't like it.'

'I'll get you out as soon as I can.'

'Cross your heart and hope to die?'

'Cross my heart.' They strolled on in a silence eventually broken by Lola.

'Keith proposed.'

'Proposed what?'

'Asked me to marry him – don't you know what proposed means?'

'I do now. So, you're going to marry him, are you?'

'Well, there is a bit of a snag.'

'What's that?'

'His mother came to the shop and started insulting me. I didn't know who she was, so I emptied a bucket of dirty water over her head. I don't know – something just came over me. For a minute I just didn't care.'

Evie's grin broadened as Lola told her how she only found out it was Keith's mum just after she'd emptied the bucket over her head. Evie roared with delight at her sister's story, but Lola didn't join in with her merriment. It was obvious that she had other news to tell. She took Evie's hand.

'You mustn't tell anyone this.'

'About what?'

'Promise you won't tell?'

'Cross my heart and hope to die.'

'I'm pregnant.'

'What?'

'I'm going to have Keith's baby, so I'll have to marry him.'

Evie was stunned into silence. Then asked, 'How . . .?'

'It just happened,' said Lola.

'He didn't make you—'

'No, he didn't make me do anything. It just happened and that's that.'

'If you don't marry him it'll be a bastard, won't it?'

Lola was shocked that her sister knew such a thing. 'Yes,' she conceded. 'It'll be a bastard and I'll have a tough time.'

'Life's tough enough without being a bastard. You'll have to marry him, then. Can I come?'

'Course you can. It won't be a big do – probably a register office. I doubt if his mother will be coming and I haven't got any family except you. I'll probably ask Theresa as well.'

'Does Keith mind about you being pregnant?'

'He doesn't know yet. I think his mother might mind.'

Evie laughed again. This time Lola joined in. 'She'll throw

a right wonky wobbler!' shouted Evie. 'Bucket of water and a bastard, she'll wonder what you're going to throw at her next.'

'Sshh!' warned Lola, looking around. 'I don't want everyone knowing.' Then she became serious again. 'By the way, I'm being charged with common assault.'

'Oh, heck! Just for chucking water over someone's head?'

'The police didn't think it was worth bothering with; the next thing I know I've been arrested and charged. I'm due at magistrates' court on Monday morning.'

'Blimey, Lola, you might get locked up, like me.'

'If I plead guilty it'll probably be a five-pound fine, so I'm told – but it means I'll have a criminal record. Your pal Alfie thinks it stinks. There's someone trying to cause trouble for our family, Evie; first Mam, then you, then me.'

'Alfie – you mean the copper?'

'Yeah, he's the one who came to tell me about it – nice bloke for a copper.'

'Yeah,' agreed Evie. 'They're not all like Dad and Uncle Seth. Did you get the sack?'

'I thought I would, but Mr Jessop said what I did was wrong but understandable under the circumstances.'

'He's sounds a nice man. Why would anyone want to cause us trouble, Lola?'

'I don't know, kid, but I'm definitely going to find out. It could be something to do with the night it all happened.'

'How do you mean?' asked Evie.

'I don't know,' Lola said, 'but I've got a feeling that Dad did something really bad the night, and not just to Mam. I was goading him about maybe killing people for fun while he was at work. God, Evie! You should have seen the look in his eyes – just for a few seconds. He was scared, I swear to it. Scared I knew something about him.'

Alfie was waiting outside the magistrates' court in Leeds Town Hall when Lola came out.

'Twenty-pound fine,' she said, 'four times what it should have been – a month's wages for me – and bound over to keep the peace for twelve months. I got a feeling that they'd have given me ten years in jail if they could.'

'Did they give you time to pay?'

'Reluctantly. What is it, Alfie? Why do the courts have it in for us?'

'No idea, but you're right. They are being very hard on your family. If I can find out, I will.'

Thirteen

'My sister's getting married in September.'
Evie was reading the letter Lola had sent her. They were outside the home, around the back of the caretaker's hut, out of sight of prying eyes. Lola sent her sister at least two letters a week and managed to tell her interesting things each time. This letter told of how Keith had paid her twenty-pound fine for her and how she had agreed to marry him.

'Has she gorra bun in t'oven?' enquired Movita Lumsden as she chewed on an apple she had stolen from one of the other girls. Being in West Moor hadn't interrupted Movita's career as a thief. Every Saturday she went on a shop-lifting expedition into Leeds city centre and came back with pockets stuffed with cigarettes which she sold to the girls in the home. She never stole from Evie, as it wasn't done to steal from your slave. Evie fully agreed with this.

'Bun in the oven? How d'you mean?' said Evie

'Has he got her up the duff? Is she havin' a sprog?'

'If you mean a baby, yes.'

'Thought so.'

Movita continued chewing. She made more noise than any apple-eater Evie had ever come across. The big girl was sitting on an empty dustbin, kicking it with her heavy shoes to add to the noise of her eating. Movita was a walking noise, Evie thought. She was glad she didn't have to share a dormitory with her.

She didn't much like Movita, but then again she didn't much like any of the girls in the home. Movita afforded her an element of protection in exchange for Evie doing as she was told. But there were limits.

'We're off into Leeds on Sat'day ter nick some fags,' Movita said.

'What's new?' said Evie – who hadn't quite heard her properly. She was opening a packet of crisps and her head was more full of bridesmaid thoughts. Surely Lola would want a proper wedding in a church, with bridesmaids. 'You go every Saturday.'

'Not just me – me an' you. It's about time yer started workin' for all this protection what I give yer.'

'Me?' Evie paused in opening the twist of blue paper containing the salt. 'What will I be doing?'

'You'll be doin' the nickin'.'

'What? I can't steal. What if I get caught?'

'Yer won't get caught.' Movita tapped the side of her head. 'I've thought it all through. I'll keep 'em talkin' and you nick a few packets o' fags. Yer insignificant, yer see. D'yer know what insignificant means?'

'I think it means I don't stand out.'

'Correct – give that girl a lollipop. Me, I'm very significant.' She laughed. 'D'yer gerrit? *Sig*-nificant – that's why we're nickin' cigs.'

'I'm sorry, Movita,' Evie said, 'I can't do it.'

'Course yer can – d'yer know why?'

'No,' said Evie, innocently.

Movita's face turned vicious. She spat a mouthful of chewed apple at Evie then thrust the core into her mouth, forcing it down her throat until she was choking.

'Yer'll do it, cos I said yer'll do it!'

Evie was on her knees, choking and crying and spitting out lumps of apple. Movita drew back a fat arm and punched her on the side of her face, knocking her to the ground. Then she kicked her in the stomach.

'Sat'day mornin', ten o'clock, meet me here, else I'll get really mad wi' yer!'

Tommy Pearson had been working as a stringer for a couple of years, mainly selling stories to the local papers – *Yorkshire Post*, *Evening Post* and *Evening News* – but now and again he picked up a story that interested the nationals. The recent execution of Ruth Ellis had rekindled interest in the equally controversial Rachel Lawless hanging – and Tommy Pearson lived only a five-minute walk away from West Moor Girls'

Home where Rachel's youngest daughter was being held.
When he saw her standing at a bus stop right outside his
house he thought he'd try his luck and see if she was worth
a story.

'Evie Lawless?'

Evie and Movita turned to see a tall, young man walking
out of the gate of a nearby house.

'Say nowt,' warned Movita.

The man smiled and Evie thought his smile looked genuine,
unlike Movita's crocodile smile.

'Who wants ter know?' called out Movita.

'My name's Pearson, I'm a freelance newspaper reporter.
I wondered if I might have a word with you.'

'Not if you're going to write anything that might get me
in trouble,' said Evie. 'I'm pretty good at doing that all by
myself.'

Pearson laughed. He had a pale, intelligent face and nice
eyes behind his glasses. Evie decided she liked him. 'Will I
get any money?' she enquired.

'I get half,' muttered Movita.

'Depends,' said Pearson, 'on whether I can sell the story.'

'How much would I get if you sell the story?'

'Could be as much as ten pounds.'

'Fiver each,' muttered Movita.

'Will you write about my mam being hanged for a murder
she didn't do?'

'Maybe.'

'I was there when it happened,' Evie said. 'Is that a good
story?'

Pearson looked down at Evie and saw something in her
eyes he rarely, if ever, saw in a person so young. There was
a profundity there which made him know she would be worth
listening to. 'I'm sure it will be a good story,' he said.

'Do we get any money in advance?' asked Movita.

'Er, yes. I'll give you a pound; then, if the story sells, I'll
give you some more.'

'Ten bob each,' muttered Movita to Evie.

'OK, mister,' said Evie. 'What to do want me to do?'

'Well, if you and your, er, friend would like to come into
my house, my mother will make us all something nice to eat.'

'We're not allowed in people's houses,' said Evie.

'Oh, the garden, then. It's a nice day, we can all sit in the garden.'

A bus was heading towards them. 'I've got better things ter do than sit round in no bleedin' garden,' grumbled Movita. 'She can tell yer her story later. Just give us the money, we're off into town.'

Evie looked at Tommy, who looked OK. 'I'll stay here, mister,' she said, 'if you give Movita ten bob.' It seemed a fair compromise. Unfortunately Movita didn't understand compromises. Pearson took a ten-shilling note from his wallet and gave it to the surly girl, who climbed on the bus without a thank you or a goodbye.

A police car was parked outside the home when Evie got back. Some of the girls were gathered around it.

'What's happening?'

'They brought Lummy back,' one of the girls told her. 'Looks like she's got done fer summat – nickin' prob'ly. I thought you were s'pposed ter be goin' with her?'

'I was somewhere else.'

'It's to be hoped she dunt split on yer.'

'Split on me? What can she say? I wasn't doing anything wrong.'

The girl shrugged. 'Wouldn't trust that fat bugger as far as I can throw her.'

'Anyway,' said Evie, 'I thought you weren't supposed to split on your mates.'

'Mates?' The girl let out a hoot of laughter. 'Since when did Lummy have mates?'

Two policemen emerged, with Movita walking between them. She caught Evie's eye and glowered at her, as if this was all Evie's fault. Evie lowered her gaze and turned away as Movita's voice boomed out, 'Don't wet yerself, Evie, I'll not split on yer.'

There was a chorus of derisive laughter from the watching girls, one of whom called out, 'Yer just did, Lummy, yer barmy bugger!'

Clive Campion's fork froze in midair between breakfast plate and mouth.

'Bloody hell!'

His exclamation was because the story had made the front page. He had expected it to be no more than a few lines on page four. His wife remonstrated with him.

'Don't swear in front of the children. What the matter, anyway?'

'Oh, nothing.'

Pearson had done well to sell the article to the *Daily Herald* for fifty pounds. An exclusive such as this would elevate him above the lowly rank of stringer, selling reports of council meetings and flower shows to papers whose own reporters had better things to do. He'd give Evie an extra tenner on top of the pound he'd already given her. Tommy suspected this might spawn a few more stories.

Campion's eyes scanned the article as he chewed, angrily, on his bacon:

RACHEL LAWLESS'S DAUGHTER CLAIMS SHE KILLED HER FATHER

Evie Lawless, whose mother was hanged in May for the murder of Ezra Lawless, her police sergeant husband, insists that she killed her dad to stop him killing her mother.

Evie tells of how her father came home drunk on the night he died. He first attacked Lola, his stepdaughter, and kicked her out of the house, then went on to attack their mother. Lola confirms this, and her friend, Theresa Tomelty, tells of how a badly bruised Lola arrived at her house asking to be put up for the night, saying that her father had attacked her and kicked her out. Both Evie and her elder sister claim that their father was a violent and abusive parent. Evie described the scene she saw when she came downstairs after hearing all the noise:

'Mam was on the floor with Dad kneeling over her. I was scared. I thought she was dead but then I heard her moan. Dad was like a wild animal, hitting her. It was so awful. I just wanted him to stop hitting her. Mam had been doing some ironing and the board was still up. I picked up the iron and hit Dad with it. I just wanted to stop him hurting Mam.'

Rachel Lawless's hanging shocked the nation, as did the recent hanging of Ruth Ellis. The victim's brother,

Seth Lawless, also a police sergeant with Leeds City
Police, said in a statement today:

'You have to question why no one accused my brother
of abuse before he died. And I have to point out that
since he and his wife died the two girls have both been
found guilty in court of violent behaviour. I don't think
it's unnatural for children of parents who have died in
such a manner to act in an unbalanced way but I wish
they could do it without accusing my dead brother of
things he quite obviously didn't do.'

In order to cover his back, Tommy Pearson had rung Seth and
told him he was writing the article and that the girls had both
mentioned Ezra's cruelty to them, and did Seth wish to add
anything? Tommy had quite deliberately played down the
strength of the article as he wanted the readers to place their
own interpretation on it – and there was only one way to inter-
pret what he had written. Seth had immediately rung Campion.
Had the girl's story not been quite so comprehensive and
damning, Seth's rebuttal might have been enough, but, when
set alongside Evie's story, it sounded more like a politician's
answer than the words of an aggrieved brother; and no one
could see this more clearly than Campion, the author of the
rebuttal. It would set people thinking. Had a grave injustice
been done? Had Ezra Lawless got his just desserts at the hands
of his daughter? Had an innocent woman been hanged?

There was more than the one skeleton rattling around in
Ezra's coffin; it would only take one to get out for the tongues
to start wagging. Wagging tongues were dangerous things.
Wagging tongues might lead to a mysteriously murdered
youth. Murdered on Ezra Lawless's beat. Connections made
to brother Seth. Witnesses might come forward. Seth arrested.
Would brother Seth keep his mouth shut about Campion's
involvement? Can pigs fly?

All it needed, to start the ball rolling, was for someone to
come forward with an incriminating tale about the late,
heinous copper. There must be a few such people about.
Maybe a lot of people. The man had been a complete and
utter bastard. How the hell had he got mixed up with such a
man? All he wanted was a bit of young pleasure, the feel of
innocent, unspoiled flesh. Campion shuddered at the frisson

the thought gave him; then stole a guilty glance at his own son. He was of his own flesh – that was different.

Young as she was, Evie Lawless was a loose cannon, and she had to be discredited in a big way. Campion was now a junior minister and destined for stardom, maybe even a cabinet job. He was a man with nefarious influence over important people who had let their guard down long enough for him to take advantage of embarrassing situations. He had an eye and an ear for such things. Important people had much to lose and Campion had much to gain. A slip of a girl like Evie mustn't get in the way of his career. This would need thinking about.

His agile mind skipped through a few ideas, First of all he'd need indirect contact with one of the inmates at West Moor. Find out the inside story on young Evie Lawless. See if she lived up to her surname.

West Moor was a low classification reformatory, which came under the authority of the Home Office. People owed him favours; he always made sure of that. Favours would be called in. The girl must be heavily discredited. Her protests must become such a joke that newspapers wouldn't touch her with a bargepole. If her elder sister continued to kick up a fuss she'd be dealt with as well.

Fourteen

Evie was playing rounders with a group of the girls when Movita came back to the home. The big girl had been away over a week and no one expected to see her again. She was accompanied by a policewoman and she had a big grin on her face as she walked past the staring girls. Evie's summons to the warden's office came within minutes of Movita's return. Evie stood to attention in front of Mrs Thackley's desk.

'As you may know,' the warden began, 'Movita Lumsden has been away for a short time, due to her being caught stealing from a shop in town. She saved herself and everyone else a lot of trouble by owning up to everything, including your part in the thefts.'

'I never stole anything, Mrs Thackley.'

She looked through the window behind Mrs Thackley and saw a flock of geese flying along in an untidy V formation. It would be nice to be a bird, she thought. I bet birds don't lie about each other to get them into trouble. She returned her attention to the woman behind the desk, who was sitting back in her chair and glaring at Evie over the top of her spectacles.

'I don't appear to have your full attention, Lawless. Perhaps if I tell you I'm looking for a reason not to recommend you to be moved on to a more secure reformatory it might concentrate your mind.'

'I haven't done anything wrong, Miss.'

The warden looked down at a file in front of her. She turned over the top page and shook her head.

'Not done anything wrong? Are you not listening, girl? You've been stealing from shops and selling the stolen goods to girls at this home.'

'I haven't, Miss.

'So, you deny stealing from shops?'

'Yes, Miss. To be right honest, Miss, I'm fed up of being accused of things I haven't done. It was bad enough having my mam hanged for something she didn't do without me being accused of stealing when I never stole, Miss.'

'Yes, I've read the newspaper article, and if there's as much truth in that as there is in your ridiculous denial I doubt the article's worth the paper it's written on.'

'It was the truth, every word of it,' said Evie with a vehemence that took the warden by surprise. 'My mother didn't kill my father, I did. I killed him because he was trying to kill her.'

'Really? And it's also the truth that you never stole and sold off the proceeds?'

'That's Movita Lumsden telling lies, Miss.'

The warden cursed under her breath. Damn this girl! She needed something concrete that could be passed on to the newspapers. A tearful confession from a contrite girl would have done nicely. Mulish denial was no help at all. The reporter who had written the defamatory article would easily dismantle an accusation based purely on the word of Movita Lumsden and her cronies. True as that word might be.

'You are incorrigible, do you know that?'

'I don't know, Miss. I only know I wasn't with Movita when they caught her stealing.'

'I'm well aware of that – I suspect that's why she got caught. She's nowhere near as crafty as you are, Lawless.'

Evie's weak eye had wandered off track and gave her an odd look of innocence, but there was stubbornness written all over her face which told Mrs Thackley she was wasting her time arguing. The warden sighed with exasperation. The forces governing her career had made it clear that they would deem it a favour if she could prove the girl to be so dishonest that it would completely discredit the newspaper article which had caused so much disquiet. To hell with these people, you can't get blood out of a stone and she only had four years to go before retirement; it just wasn't worth the hassle. But it would do no harm to let them know she'd tried her best.

'You are gated for three months.'

It was the strongest sanction she could impose without recourse to the board of governors or the juvenile court.

'What does that mean, Miss?'

'It means you are not allowed out of the gates for three months. If you attempt to abscond I'll have you locked up in a secure reformatory before you can blink.'

'Will I be allowed to go to my sister's wedding on Saturday?'

'You will be allowed out on Sundays for you to attend your church. If you abuse that privilege it will be withdrawn. That will be all.'

Evie turned to go. She'd just been given the worst punishment she could imagine. And for nothing. As the door closed Mrs Thackley picked up the telephone and asked for a long distance number in London.

All Evie could think of as she went outside was how could she get to the wedding. There hadn't been any really big occasions in her life before, unless you counted her first holy communion and her confirmation. She saw Movita was standing talking to a group of girls and made a beeline towards her. Movita, alerted by one of her companions, turned to face Evie, who confronted her with a look of scorn on her face.

'I'm not allowed to go to our Lola's wedding because of you lying about me.'

'Do you want a thump in the face?' retorted Movita. She shook her fist at Evie, who didn't flinch.

'Why did you lie about me? I never went shoplifting with you, and you know it.'

There was a long silence, with all eyes on Movita, awaiting her explanation. Within minutes it would be all around the home that Movita had lied about someone to get them into trouble with the warden. Her voice, when she eventually spoke, was little more than a murmur. 'They told me if I didn't tell 'em what they wanted ter know I'd end up in Peterlee. I weren't gonna end up in there, fer you or nobody.'

Evie walked off. The other girls followed her, not wishing to be left in Movita's company.

She'd hidden the two five-pound notes that Tommy Pearson had given her between the pages of *Little Women*, which she kept in her drawer in the dormitory. It was as safe a place as any, with none of the girls being big readers; in fact half of them couldn't read at all. There was no point telling Lola she wasn't allowed out of the home to go to the wedding, her sister had enough to worry about, what with the wedding and the baby and that pig of a mother-in-law she was about to acquire.

Lola and Keith had decided on a register office wedding, which disappointed Evie. Mrs Penfold wouldn't be going; the rift between her and Lola was too wide to bridge. Because of this, many of Keith's family were staying away in sympathy. This suited Lola. There would be a small reception in the Victoria Hotel and a honeymoon in Whitby.

The ceremony was set for eleven o'clock and Evie needed to spend her tenner on a nice outfit. Lola had given her the rank of matron-of-honour and she intended doing the part some justice. All she had to do was sneak out without being seen, shin over the wall and make her way into town. She'd take her punishment later.

It was 7 a.m. and Seth Lawless's face cracked into a humourless smile as he watched the slight figure climb out of the window and scurry across the lawn to the safety of the bushes near the back wall. Seth had guessed correctly. He was sitting on top of the same wall, partially hidden by a tree. Swinging his leg around, he dropped, easily, to the roadside verge and loped to a car parked fifty yards up the deserted back road. He wasn't on duty; this little task was over and above the call of duty. The information passed to him by Campion had been good. This girl wasn't going to miss her sister's wedding simply because she'd been gated. She was making her escape bang on cue.

Walter watched Seth as he got into the car. He didn't know Seth but he instinctively didn't like him. In Walter's world people gave off good or bad auras, and Seth's aura was bad. Walter didn't know much but he knew good from bad. He was of uncertain age, probably too old to have been out all night, but it was summer and Walter knew he hadn't got too many summers left in him. He wanted to enjoy each one from dawn until dusk and then from dusk until dawn. He was a vagrant of sorts but, when the weather was bad, courtesy of kind people, he always had a home to go to, a warm place to sleep and food to eat. His secret was to make people smile. Make people smile and the world is yours. Walter didn't know much but he knew that.

Evie looked back at the home to see if anyone had spotted her. No one was there. She'd climbed out of the washroom window which was on the ground floor, and thus an easy escape route. Not that the home needed escape routes. The girls were all on their trust to come and go within certain hours. Most did because the penalties were severe. Evie wasn't thinking about penalties, she was only thinking about her sister's wedding and her role as matron-of-honour.

Seth was thinking of the satisfaction and relief he'd get from squashing the life out of this troublesome girl. Walter sensed there was a game afoot. This man was waiting for something to happen. Walter moved, silently, towards the car. Seth's eyes were fixed on the wall where Evie's head suddenly appeared. Walter spotted her as well. She gave off a good aura.

Evie looked around to check that the coast was clear. Seth slid down in his seat to give the impression that the car was empty. Walter noticed this and it confirmed his suspicions that this man meant Evie no good. Evie climbed over the wall and hung by her hands for a second before she dropped to the ground. Seth switched on the ignition and pressed the starter, hoping she wouldn't hear the engine. Evie was too concerned with a slightly twisted ankle to bother. She sat there and rubbed it for a while as Seth waited, with a beating heart, hoping against hope that no other traffic would appear.

Evie got to her feet and walked, gingerly, away from Seth. He slipped the car into gear and moved off. Evie was meandering down the middle of the road. Seth's excitement mounted. He put his foot to the floor and aimed the car straight at her. A dog hurtled over a fence and began to race alongside him, barking loudly. Had Evie turned round a second later she'd have been run down, crushed beneath the wheels of the heavy Standard Vanguard. As it was, she had time to fling herself to one side, landing in a ditch. The car roared on down the road with Seth, cursing, at the wheel.

The dog ran up to Evie and began to lick her face, panting and drooling all over her. She put her arms around it and hugged it to her. Her heart was hammering with shock and fear. What had just happened? Why hadn't the car hooted its horn to warn her? Why hadn't it stopped to see how she was? If it didn't sound so daft she'd have thought the driver was trying to kill her on purpose.

'Thanks, doggie,' she said. 'Thank you very much for saving my life.'

Walter wagged his tail and Evie vowed she'd get a dog just like him when she grew up.

She made her way to the main road where she knew there'd be a bus into town at seven fifteen. Seth was parked in a side street, watching. The streets were waking up and there was too much traffic on the main road for him to try another hit-and-run. He'd just have to see if anything else turned up.

By the time he followed her into Lewis's department store Seth was getting a bit past himself. He had always hated surveillance. He'd waited outside the bus station café while she had her breakfast; followed her down Briggate, where she looked in almost every shop window, and into Kirkgate market, where he almost lost her among the early shoppers.

Butcher's Row was busy with women buying the choicest cuts of meat for the Sunday dinner. Some were more concerned with getting a bargain than they were with looking after their bags. He spotted a known pick-pocket and took him by the arm.

'Got my eye on you, lad.'

The pick-pocket, who knew the policeman, blanched, took

a woman's purse from his pocket, thrust it at Seth and ran off. Any other day Seth would have followed him. But he had more important things to think about. He gave the purse to one of the butchers.

'Someone's dropped this.'

He didn't want to become more involved. He weaved his way through the crowds and eventually spotted her at a stall selling clothes for the pre-teens. She bought a pink, pleated skirt, a white blouse and a pair of white ankle socks. The whole lot set her back £3. 12s 10d. Then, at Rowley's discount shoes, for 25 shillings, she bought a pair of real leather, red sandals to compliment her skirt. All she needed was a nice hat, everybody wore hats at weddings. She'd seen a hat in the summer sale at Lewis's. It was a straw boater, with a hat band the colour of your choice, 17/6. She'd still have nearly a fiver left out of Tommy Pearson's money.

Evie walked through Lewis's jewellery department and headed for the escalator. Seth took a short diversion past the watch counter, having spotted that the assistant was busy chatting to a colleague. A minute later he followed Evie up to the first floor where she was trying on hats, watched, suspiciously, by a shop assistant. While Evie's back was turned Seth bumped into her and hurried on his way without looking round or apologizing. Evie was only distracted by him for a second, as the assistant was calling out to her.

'Don't play with them, if you're not going to buy.'

'I do want to buy one. I'm going to my sister's wedding this morning.'

She found the straw boaters, tried one on, and took it to the assistant. 'Can I have a pink hat band to match this?'

She took the skirt out of the carrier bag. The assistant was now interested in this young customer who was going to a wedding.

'Hmm – what colour shoes?'

Evie took the sandals from the bag; the assistant shook her head, thoughtfully. 'All pink and red can be a bit much – with it being the colour of your skin. I'd suggest a pale blue to compliment the pink – and maybe some brightly coloured beads around your neck.'

'Would you help me choose something?' Evie was delighted that a grown-up fashion expert, in Lewis's of all places, was giving her fashion advice. 'I've got some money left.'

The hat band had been chosen and the assistant was helping Evie try on a selection of bead necklaces when the store detective arrived.

'Excuse me, young lady, could you turn out your pockets?'

The assistant stepped away in dismay, no longer wanting to be involved.

'What?' said Evie.

'Someone's seen you take a watch from a display and put it in your pocket.'

'But I haven't—'

'Then you won't mind turning out your pockets.'

The store detective wasn't a very big man but he looked very nasty. Evie stuck her hand in her pocket and brought out a cheap purse containing the remnants of her money. In the other pocket she felt something unfamiliar. She took out a man's watch and stared at it in amazement. The man took it from her.

'I believe this came from this store. Do you have a receipt for it?'

'I don't know how it got there, mister,' Evie protested. 'I didn't put it there, honest.'

The man spoke to the assistant. 'I'll need you to come and verify that this watch came out of her pocket.'

The assistant nodded, unhappily. Evie looked to her for help. 'I didn't take it, honest, missis.'

The assistant wanted to believe this personable girl but to do so would make her look gullible.

'Butter wouldn't melt in her mouth,' commented the store detective. 'They're the worst kind. Ones like this get away with murder. Right, miss. You're coming with me. I've got somewhere you can wait while the police come. With it being Saturday it could be quite a while.'

Evie was in tears. 'I can't. I'm going to Lola's wedding.'

'Not until this is sorted out you're not.'

'Please, mister, I'm the matron-of-honour. It's at eleven o'clock and I've got to get changed.'

'You should have thought about that before you started stealing watches.'

Seth watched from a distance with a satisfied grin on his face. His work was done, maybe not as effectively as he would have liked, but there was always another day.

Fifteen

Evie never got to Lola's wedding. Lola didn't know why, but she wasn't going to let it spoil her day. Knowing Evie, there could be a thousand reasons why she hadn't made it. It wasn't until she got back from honeymoon and called in to West Moor that she found out her sister had been moved away to a home with a stricter and more secure regime. Caught shoplifting on the very day of her wedding. Lola found it hard to take. What the hell was going on?

'She's been sent to Askham Grange, near York,' Mrs Thackley told her. 'I'm afraid we're not equipped to cope with the likes of Eve Lawless.'

'The likes of Eve Lawless?' said Lola, annoyed. 'What do you mean, "the likes of Eve Lawless"? She's just a harmless kid. How well did you actually know her, Mrs Thackley?'

'She was one of over two hundred girls in this establishment. I didn't look after them all personally.'

'So, you didn't really know her and yet you say you're not equipped to cope with her. Shouldn't you have better acquainted yourself with her before passing such a damning judgement, Mrs Thackley?'

'She was caught shoplifting with the stolen item on her person.'

'No, no – there's something wrong here,' said Lola. 'Something stinks. Can't you smell it, Mrs Thackley?'

'I – I'm sure I don't know what you mean.'

The odd combination of Lola's beauty and incisiveness was putting the warden at a disadvantage. Lola held Mrs Thackley in her steady gaze as she asked the question: 'Mrs Thackley, was any pressure put on you to be hard on her?' There was a definite flicker of guilt. Before the warden could make her denial Lola got in first. 'I thought so – come on, what's going on, Mrs Thackley?'

'I'm not sure what you mean.'

'I mean you're keeping something from me. It's as though someone, somewhere, has had it in for our family ever since my vile stepfather died.'

'You shouldn't talk about the dead like that.'

'He was a thug, Mrs Thackley, and he used me as a punchbag for years. I think whoever's leaning on us knows something about him and doesn't want the truth to come out.'

As she spoke she watched the warden's eyes for more tell-tale signs of guilt. Mrs Thackley looked away.

'I'm right, aren't I?' Lola pressed. 'Someone's turning the screw on me and Evie and you know who it is.'

'That's not true. I've no idea who—'

She stopped mid-sentence. Lola finished it for her.

'No idea who it is. But you know it's someone. You know I'm right about pressure being put on us.'

Mrs Thackley remembered Evie's unlikely story about someone nearly running her down with a car on the morning she was arrested. *It was as if they were trying to kill me.*

At first she'd dismissed the story as a diversionary fantasy, designed to draw attention away from the simple facts – that Evie Lawless was a barefaced liar. But she couldn't, in all conscience, deny that pressure had been applied from above.

Was it just a coincidence that Evie had been caught red-handed on her sister's wedding day? A certain Home Office department had known it was Lola's wedding day because Mrs Thackley had rung and told them, in response to a request from them to be kept up to date on all matters relating to Eve Lawless. Not an unusual request considering the damning nature of Evie's newspaper story. But she had also told them that Evie was likely to abscond on that day to attend the wedding. That was a worry. Had they sent someone along to frame Ev—? No, the warden shook these thoughts from her mind. What rubbish. *I'm going soft in the head.* With girls like young Lawless, she thought, you have to fight fire with fire. The minute they think you're an easy target they'll take advantage. The only way to deal with unreasonable people is to be even more unreasonable to them.

'I have a job to do,' she said. 'And I believe I do it well.'

'You have responsibilities to the girls in your care,' countered Lola, scornfully. 'A responsibility to see they are treated fairly. If you treat them unjustly how will they learn respect for justice?'

'They have to learn discipline.'

'Do as I say, not as I do, is that what you're saying, Mrs Thackley? One rule for you and another for them?'

Mrs Thackley walked to the door and held it open for Lola. 'Your sister in no longer my responsibility. I suggest you make arrangements to visit her in Askham Grange.'

Lola walked towards the door then stopped beside the warden. 'I very much doubt if you ever regarded my sister as your responsibility. My sister will have been a name on a register – a name that became inconvenient to you. In my opinion, Mrs Thackley, you're not fit to lick my sister's boots.'

Sixteen

September 1956

K eith breezed in from work with his usual cheer. Lola was nursing Danny.

'I've wangled the day off tomorrow,' he said, 'so I can come with you to pick Evie up.'

She gave a slight frown. 'I might have to ask you to go on your own if that's OK. Danny's got a bit of a temperature. I've rung the doctor, he's says if he's no better tomorrow to take him in.'

'Fair enough. I think I can manage to collect one delinquent child without any help.'

He was joking and she knew it, but no way was he going to get away with it. 'She's no more a delinquent than you are.'

'My point exactly. We delinquents must stick together.'

Lola shook her head. He was incorrigible, but her life would have been a lot worse without him. It was difficult to be down when he was around. Still, it had been worse for Evie, who had spent the past year in Askham Grange for a crime Lola was sure she hadn't committed.

'There's an article in the *Herald* about her,' she said, handing him a newspaper.

Keith grinned and took it from her. 'Ah, the intrepid Tommy Pearson.'

Lola had mentioned Evie's impending release to Tommy, who'd jumped at the chance of doing another piece on her. His original story had been ridiculed in rival newspapers whose reporters didn't like being scooped by some backstreet chancer. But any stories concerning Rachel Lawless's controversial execution were always worth running and if the source of the original piece – Evie Lawless – was now to be released, it would do no harm to write a follow-up. The story was on page 2 under the heading:

LAWLESS GIRL TO BE RELEASED

The story went on to tell of how Evie was due to be released and how she had persistently claimed her innocence of the shoplifting charge and how odd it was that a girl with no previous record for theft should choose to start on her sister's wedding day by stealing a man's watch. What on earth would a ten-year-old girl want with a man's watch? It went on to query why Evie had been locked away in the first place, simply for losing control on the day her mother had been hanged, and why her mother had not been granted the reprieve which everyone expected – even the police – and how her sister had been fined £20 for a misdemeanour that normally wouldn't have even warranted a court appearance. The article went on to speculate what a terrible miscarriage of justice it would be if Evie had been telling the truth about her father's death. It would mean that her mother had been wrongly hanged and that Ezra Lawless was indeed the monster his daughters said he was.

Campion rang Seth from the privacy of a phone box in Parliament Square.

'Have you read the bloody thing?'

Seth hadn't read it. He'd been on nights and Campion had woken him up. Seth's wife had called him to the phone.

'Read what?'

'The *Daily* bloody *Herald*. They're letting the Lawless girl out and there's an article in the paper more or less saying the whole bloody family's been victimized by the state. I could really do without this crap.'

'Can't you put a stop to it?'

'How can I put a stop to it? The bloody thing's out on the news stands. Besides, it's all speculation. These bloody newspapers are allowed to speculate – it's called the freedom of the press. Has anyone said anything to you about it?'

'To me? Why would anyone say anything to me?'

'Because you're the one who set her up on the shoplifting business. Has someone found out what you did? If they have, you keep my name out of it, do you hear? I'll deny everything and make it worse for you. I can do that, you know.'

Big Ben was booming eleven o'clock. The sound easily penetrated the thick glass of the phone booth. 200 miles away in Leeds Seth could hear it almost as plainly as he could hear his wife shouting, 'Do you want two eggs or one?'

'Look, Mr Campion, I've just woken up. No one's said anything to me – two, and four rashers.'

'What?'

'I was talking to the wife. No one's said anything to me.'

'Haven't they? That's good. Are you sure they don't suspect you? There's talk about Ezra being a wife- and child-beater. If they follow up on that, they might start looking at you.'

'Will they now?' sneered Seth. 'And I'd say it was your job ter stop 'em lookin'.'

His wife's eyes were on him, questioning who it was. He growled at her, 'Just get on with me breakfast.'

'What?' said Campion.

'I was talking to the wife.'

'Listen,' Campion hissed, 'you need to deal with this from your end, properly this time. I don't want any comebacks. This thing is getting way beyond a joke. The girl is being released in the morning.'

'Oh yeah, and how am I supposed to deal with it?'

'Permanently.'

The pips went on the phone and Campion fished in his pocket for more change. There was none.

'Look, the pips have gone. Just deal with—'

The line went dead, signalling that he was out of time. He sighed and put the phone down, hoping that this lame-brained copper had enough about him to deal with the situation. Campion had gone out on a limb to thwart the blasted Lawless family, beginning with the execution of the mother. It would have been good if the two daughters had taken the drop with her.

He stepped out of the phone box and looked up at the Palace of Westminster. This was his life. It was the centre of his universe. How the hell had he put all this in jeopardy for the sake of a quick bout of lust with a scruffy backstreet youth?

The following morning Evie was standing at the front door of Askham Grange when Keith arrived in his mother's Austin 10. He got out and relieved her of the carrier bag full of her meagre belongings. She was looking in the car for Lola and Danny.

'I thought Lola might have come to get me.'

'Sorry, just me, I'm afraid. Lola's taken Danny to the doctor's.'

Her face showed instant concern. 'Danny? Is he OK?'

Keith smiled at her anxiety and Evie realized she probably liked him. This was the first time she'd seen him since before they locked her away.

'He's fine. Bit of a temperature, that's all, but you know what Lola's like. She'll never take a risk with Danny. The trouble is she could be hanging around for ages, so she sent me instead. Do I have to see the commandant or can we get straight off?'

'She wants a chat. I think you might have to sign something as well.'

He clicked his heels and gave a Nazi salute. 'Lead me to the führer.'

Seth sat at the wheel of his Standard Vanguard. He was a couple of hundred yards away from the gate to Askham Grange, having followed Keith's car from the house where the young teacher and Lola lived. Seth had formed a plan on the way there. There were many unknown factors that could damage his plan. It was a reckless and unwise plan, but it was its simplicity that appealed to Seth. A simple road accident with no witnesses would solve his problems. He wasn't interested in the whining MP. His only problem was that the older girl hadn't joined her husband in the car. Wiping both of them out at once would have been good. Still, maybe the death of her sister would make Lola back off. The thought brought a snigger to his lips.

Keith's Austin poked its bonnet out of the gate before turning left. Seth started his engine and moved off. The road wound through the countryside and headed towards the main

A64 Leeds to York road. A mile ahead was a bridge that spanned the River Wharfe where it ran through a deep gulley known as Appleton Ditch. As the road opened out into the long, straight stretch that led to the bridge a humourless smile creased Seth's face. The road was empty. He looked in his mirror. There was nothing behind.

The Austin was trundling along at a steady thirty with Keith chatting away to Evie. He'd had almost nothing to do with her in the past and he decided he liked this brave and feisty girl. She had Lola's tenacity, if not quite her beauty, but there was something bewitching about Evie's face.

'I was fitted up for the shoplifting,' she told him.

'Fitted up?'

'It's what they call it when someone makes it look as if you've done something you haven't done. The police sometimes fit people up when they can't get proper evidence.'

'Do they now?'

'Yes, they do it all the time.'

'I gather you've learned all this in there,' said Keith, jabbing his thumb back in the direction of Askham Grange.

'Yeah. Someone put that watch into my pocket, most prob'ly a copper . . . I remember a man bumping into me. It must have been him.'

'Why would they want to do that?'

'Dunno – why do they want to do anything to us?'

Keith shook his head. 'I don't know, Evie, I truly wish I did.'

It was obvious that he believed her, and was on her side. This made her feel that Lola had made a very wise choice of husband.

'Hey, did Lola tell you that someone tried to run me down the same day as I got nicked?'

'Yes, she mentioned it. Are you sure it wasn't simply a bad driver?'

Evie shook her head. 'Didn't seem like it. He didn't hoot his horn or anything, and he was going like the clappers.'

'So it was a man?'

'Well, dunno, really.'

There was a bang as Seth had rammed his car into the back of the Austin. Keith looked in his mirror.

'What the hell are you doing? You stupid sod!'

Seth changed down into third and put his foot to the floor

to give him the acceleration to overtake. His engine screamed as he forced the Vanguard into the side of the much lighter Austin, pushing it into the edge of the road. Evie looked through the window and screamed. 'That's him! That's the car that tried to run me down.'

Seth was wearing sunglasses, with his cap pulled down over his face. Keith was struggling to regain control of the Austin. The heavy, bulbous Vanguard had edged in front of him and was nosing him off the road. They were on the bridge. Keith slammed on the brakes but Seth's car had already pushed him into a low, parapet wall that crumbled beneath the combined weight of the two vehicles. Beyond the wall was Appleton Ditch. The Austin was now in midair, landing, nose first, in the river. Seth drove on, laughing loudly.

Just below the surface was a large rock. The force with which the car struck it pushed the engine back and trapped Keith's legs. The Austin sank, slowly, to the bed of the river. Water was finding its way in from all over the place. Keith was stunned, Evie was screaming.

'Keith, we've got to get out!'

Keith opened his eyes and assessed the situation. Then he tried to pull himself free.

'I can't move my legs,' he said. 'Jesus! What the hell happened?'

'Keith, you've got to get out.' She leaned across him and pulled at his legs. He screamed with pain. His right foot was wedged in behind the clutch and brake pedals and his leg was broken. He looked at her with tears streaming down his face.

'Jesus, Evie, I can't move, I can't get out.'

Water was up to their laps. In half a minute it would fill the whole car.

'You're going to have to leave me here.'

'Leave you? I can't leave you here. Please try, just once more.'

'I can't do it, my leg's broken. Evie, tell Lola I love her – and help her with Danny. Will you do that?'

'What? Course I will. I can't leave y—'

'You have to. Evie, for God's sake just get out!' He was screaming at her.

'I'm trying.' Evie was pushing at the door but the outside water pressure was too much for her. She panicked.

'Keith, it won't open!'

There was blood running down his face, mingling with his tears of fear and despair. 'Take a deep breath and wind the window down,' he said, as calmly as he could. 'When the car's full of water the pressure will be equalized. You'll be able to open the door. Can you swim?'

'No.' Evie was crying now. 'What about you, Keith?'

The water was up to Evie's neck, Keith was resigned to his fate. 'Evie, take off your shoes and kick with your legs as if you're riding a bike. Please, just take that deep breath. There's not much time left.'

He leaned across and kissed her on her cheek. 'Do as you're told, Evie,' he said. 'And do it *now*!'

She reached under the water and took off her shoes, Keith nodded his approval. She then took a deep breath and wound down the window. As she did it she knew she was hastening Keith's death. A couple of turns on the handle was enough for the water to flood the car. She pushed at the door. This time it opened. Keith, briefly, took hold of her hand, then let it go, as if giving her permission to leave. Her lungs were already bursting as she floated out of the car. There was no more than ten feet of water above her head but it seemed to take an age to break through to the surface. She gulped at the air, coughed out water and screamed for help.

The river was running quickly and there was no one to hear her shout. She pedalled with her feet as Keith had instructed, then she struck out for shore with an improvised doggie paddle, a stroke she'd vaguely mastered down at Cookridge Street Baths. At least she was keeping her head above water but she didn't know for how long. Her doggie paddle was inching her towards the bank. The river rounded a bend. There were over-hanging trees. An undercurrent swirled beneath her and sucked her below the surface just as she was about to grab a branch. She kicked wildly and paddled her arms up and down, her feet touched the riverbed and she kicked herself upwards with her last ounce of energy. Her head broke through the surface just as she was about to suck in a fatal lungful of water. Instead she sucked in life-giving air. A branch was just above her head, she reached up and clung to it like a limpet, coughing and spluttering until she thought she'd torn the lining of her throat. Then, with a supreme effort she pulled herself higher until she had the branch under her armpits and she could relax and get some strength back. It gave her time to think about Keith and she began to cry.

After a while she realized that she would probably need help to get from the branch to the bank. Her legs were still dangling in the water and she felt the strength draining from her arms. If she fell in now she'd never get out. She could hear birds singing, above the rush of the river. Birds that didn't have a thing to worry about. Apart from her predicament it was a nice day. The sun was flickering through the leaves and bouncing off the river beneath her. The river that might soon take her to the same watery grave that had taken Keith. She didn't want to drown. She'd just had a taste of nearly drowning and she didn't want that. Evie knew better than most about the fragility of life; how it could be taken away in the blink of an eye. From somewhere the strength arrived for her to slowly and painfully pull herself up on to the branch. She said the word, 'Mammy, Mammy, Mammy,' over and over to herself. It was the first word she'd ever spoken and a word that had always given her comfort and strength. 'Mammy, Mammy, I love you, Mammy.'

Now she was on the branch and inching towards safety, climbing out of the tree and lying on the riverbank in the morning sunshine, planning what to do next.

She felt in her pocket for her purse, and miraculously it was there, so she had bus fare if need be. No way was she going back to Askham Grange for help. She'd find Lola. She'd find Lola and tell her that Keith was dead but he'd been such a hero that she mustn't weep too much for him.

Seventeen

Seth was just walking into the CID room when his inspector called him into his office.

'Lawless, we've just had word from Tadcaster police. Your niece has been in a traffic accident.'

'Niece, sir? Which niece is that?'

'Evie – Ezra's daughter.'

'Young Evie. Oh dear, sir. Is she badly hurt?'

'She's all right, I'm happy to say. However, the chap in the car with her was drowned, poor beggar.'

Seth's disappointment upon hearing Evie was alive would have been quite visible on his face had the inspector been looking at him. But he was reading a note.

'According to this his name's Keith Penfold. I believe he was married to your other niece – Lola, is it?'

'Lola, that's right, sir.'

'Well, she needs to be told. Normally we'd send a WPC along but uniform are short-handed today and I thought with you being a relative, so to speak . . .'

'I'll tell her, sir.'

'And after you've done that I'd like you to interview Evie, who's saying the car was deliberately run off the road. They're keeping her in Jimmy's for observation. Apparently there's a witness confirming her story. Check it out. If there's any substance to it we'll pass it back to Taddy police. They might want to investigate. Probably some young idiot who thinks he's Stirling bloody Moss.'

Lola was breastfeeding Danny when the knock came at the door. She was beginning to wonder what was holding Keith up. He'd been gone over three hours – surely there hadn't been a last minute hitch? Evie would be mortified if they didn't let her out today. She looked through the window to see who was at the door and cursed to herself when she saw it was Seth.

'What the hell's he doing here?'

She kissed Danny, placed him back in his cot and went to the door. Seth had a big, smirky grin on his face. He was determined to make the best of a bad job.

'Well, well, well – if it's not the widow Penfold.'

'What?' said Lola. She was holding the door open just a few inches so that she could slam it in his face more easily.

'Widow Penfold. That's your official title, now your old man's popped his clogs.'

'What the hell are you talking about?'

'I'm talking about the late Mr Penfold, sadly deceased

due to waterlogged lungs. The last I heard he was sitting in his car at the bottom of a river. That's why I'm here – to officially inform you of his demise. You'll be needed to identify him later. That's if the fish have left enough to identify him with. There's some very big pike in that river, so I'm told.'

Lola opened the door wide, leapt on him and took him by his throat. The suddenness and viciousness of her attack gave her the advantage; he fell backwards with her on top of him, hitting him with flailing fists.

'You bloody liar! I'll report you for this, you sick bastard!'

Seth pushed her off him and stood up, still smirking. He waited until she got to her feet, then he thrust his face into hers. 'It's the truth, darlin'. Silly bugger ran off the road this mornin'. Splish splash, into the river. Dead as a dodo. If yer don't believe me, ask that squinty-eyed sister o' yours – hey, that's if she didn't drown with him.' He turned and walked off, thinking that the bit about Evie's uncertain fate was a stroke of genius.

Lola screamed at him. 'Where are you going? You can't do this to me. Where's Evie? Is she OK?'

'No idea,' he shouted back. 'I should check if I were you.'

Lola was weeping. 'But you must know if she's all right.'

Seth stuck two fingers up at her and got into his car. His day hadn't turned out too badly after all.

Evie was sitting up in bed in St James's Hospital when he walked into the ward.

'Uncle Seth?'

She hadn't seen him since before her dad's death, which was fine by her. Lola hated him and he was too much like her dad for Evie's liking, although she had no reason to believe he was as cruel as her dad. He gave her his version of a sympathetic smile.

'How are you, Evie?'

'OK. They're just keeping me in for observation. How's Lola?'

'I've just broken the sad news to her. She's taken it badly but she'll survive.' He sat down by her bed and did his best to appear caring to this girl who was blighting his life. 'Look, the reason I'm here is because I understand you were deliberately forced off the road.'

Evie nodded. 'It looked like the same car that nearly ran me down the day I was fitted up for shoplifting.'

Seth's compassion slipped for a second as her eyes bore into his. She was a strange kid, a bit unnerving at times.

'Did you get a look at the driver?'

'Not the first time, when he tried to run me down, but the second time it was definitely a man.'

'Just a man? No description?'

'Not really.'

Seth wrote it down, than asked, 'Did yer get a good look at the car?'

'It was a big grey car. I'd know one if I saw one.'

'No number or anything?'

'No, sorry – Uncle Seth,' she said, 'have you got a car?'

He stiffened. Where the hell was this leading? 'Why do you ask?' he said.

'Well, I've never been to Lola's house and I'm not sure where it is. If you've got a car, maybe you could give me a lift.'

He closed his eyes with relief. Then all the fake compassion dropped away and his expression became ugly. He pushed his face into hers and spoke in a low voice, laced with menaced.

'Listen, girl, I read all the lies yer told about me brother in that newspaper. Yer'll get no favours from me. Yer mother was a murderer and you're an evil little bitch!'

His whispered belligerence had Evie cowering. A nurse arrived and asked Seth, 'Are you a relative?'

'No, love. I'm a copper come to take a statement.' Then he walked up to the nurse and added, confidentially, 'I should take everything she tells yer with a pinch o' salt. Yer do know she's from a remand home. She's a bad lot I'm afraid.'

The nurse and Evie watched him leave. Evie called out. 'Excuse me. Do you know when I can go home?'

The nurse suddenly became preoccupied with things far more important than a twelve-year-old girl who had almost drowned.

'We can't discharge you until a doctor has seen you.'

'Do you know when that will be?'

'The doctor's a very busy man.'

This didn't seem much of an answer to Evie, but the nurse walked away, so it was the only answer she was likely to get.

She was the only girl in an adult women's ward. Most of the other patients were asleep or reading, apart from one elderly woman who was hugging herself and rocking backwards and forwards. She looked at Evie and gave her a smile that lacked humour and teeth.

'I'm not really potty, love. I just do this because it's summat ter do. There's bugger all ter do in this place. Once they've got yer they won't let yer go. I can't walk or I'd be on me toes in a minute. Can you walk?'

'Yes,' Evie said. 'Actually there's nothing wrong with me.'

The woman gave a cackle that reminded Evie of the wicked witch in *The Wizard of Oz*. 'They'll find summat wrong if yer give 'em half a chance. If I could walk I'd bugger off like a shot.'

Evie assessed her own situation. No one seemed to be falling over backwards to help her so she might as well help herself. Her clothes were in a bedside cabinet. She got dressed and checked that the 1s/10d she had in her purse was still there. It was – at least she had her bus fare. She knew roughly where Lola lived and she had a tongue in her head. It was all she needed.

Seth tapped on the inspector's door and went in.

'I informed Mrs Penfold of her husband's death. She took it quite badly I'm afraid – started hitting me, would you believe. You'd have thought it was me who killed him. I'm telling you this, sir, just in case she rings up to moan about me.'

'She's already done that,' the inspector said, sharply. 'I've just had to convince a hysterical woman over the phone that her husband was dead. A couple of WPCs have gone along to repair the damage you did.'

'I'm sorry, sir. But sometimes sending officers to break bad news to relatives isn't always a good idea. Maybe I should have asked you to send someone else – sir.'

The inspector shook his head. He didn't like Lawless, but the man had a point. 'Did you manage to interview the girl in hospital without causing a riot?'

'Yes, sir.' Seth read from his notebook. 'She thinks the driver of the car that ran them off the road did it on purpose.'

'Really? And does this story sound credible?'

Seth hesitated. 'Er, not to me, sir. She says it was the same car that tried to run her down on the day she was fitted up for shoplifting – her words not mine, sir.'

'I see. Pass what you've got on to Tadcaster.'

'Including my opinion, sir?'

'I should keep your opinions to yourself, DC Lawless. No doubt Tadcaster will form their own opinions.'

With a closed door between him and the inspector Seth rang Tadcaster police and was put through to the officer dealing with that morning's traffic accident.

'Hello, this is DC Lawless of Leeds CID. I've interviewed the girl in hospital.'

'You mean Eve Lawless?'

'Yes. She says it was deliberate but she has a history of telling lies, even to the papers.'

'I see. Unusual name, Lawless – are you related?'

'I'm her uncle, which means I know her better than most.'

Within half an hour of leaving the hospital Evie was knocking on the door of a neat, terrace house in Roundhay. She hoped it was Lola's door. It opened, slowly, to reveal her big sister's ashen face.

'Evie, I was coming to see you.' Lola's voice was empty as if drained of all emotion. 'Are you OK? I rang the police. They said you weren't hurt and they were just keeping you in for observ—'

She was rambling. Evie stopped her. 'Lola, I'm fine. Can I come in?'

'What? Oh, of course you can.' She took her young sister in her arms and hugged her tightly, weeping fiercely. 'Oh Evie, I feel so bloody guilty. I thought the world of Keith. He was a lovely, lovely man, but I feel so guilty.'

'It's OK, Lola. If it's anyone's fault it's mine. It's me he was after, not Keith.'

'After? How do you mean he was after you?'

'A car knocked us into the river on purpose. It wasn't an accident. Uncle Seth came to see me.'

'Did he really? He came to tell me Keith was dead. He was gloating, Evie. I could have killed him. I had to ring the police station to confirm his story. For all I knew you'd been killed as well.'

'He turned nasty on me,' Evie said. 'He was as nice as
pie at first, then he turned nasty when I told him I thought
it was the same car that tried to run me down the day you
got married.'

'What? Oh Evie, this is too much for me. So, you think
Keith was murdered?'

'Definitely.'

Lola sat down, rested her chin in her shaking hands and
heaved out a long sigh. She looked up at Evie and gave a
wintry smile. 'I feel so guilty because when I rang up and
they confirmed that Keith was dead but you were all right I
felt relieved. That's why I feel guilty. He thought the world
of me, but when it came down to it, I'd rather lose him than
my sister – and he's the father of my lovely baby.'

'You don't look as though you don't care,' observed Evie,
studying her sister's bereft face.

'Oh, I do care, Evie. I'm desperately sad. I'm not sure how
I'll cope without him. He was going to be my life –' she took
a Capstan from a packet and stuck it in her mouth – 'and
now he's not.'

She struck a match but her hand was shaking too much
for her to light the cigarette. Evie took it from her and held
it steady.

'Thanks, kid,' said Lola. She eyed her younger sister. 'Do
you want to tell me about what happened?'

Evie sat down opposite her sister. 'Keith was incredibly
brave. He was trapped, but all he was bothered about was
me getting out. I wouldn't have managed it if he hadn't told
me how.' She took Lola's hand. 'He told me to tell you he
loved you – and I've got to help you look after Danny.'

'I'm glad he was brave,' Lola said. 'I want to remember
him as a brave man, like my daddy.' She took a deep drag
on her cigarette. 'God knows how his mother's going to take
it. She detests me.'

'Can I see Danny?' asked Evie. She had never seen her
nephew. Visiting infants were barred from Askham Grange,
and seeing Danny was to be one of the highlights of this day.

'He's asleep,' said Lola, 'but I'm sure he won't mind his
auntie Evie waking him up.'

*   *   *

That evening Seth met with Campion in the Queen's Hotel in Leeds. The MP was distinctly uncomfortable with the meeting. 'What is it that can't be discussed over the phone?'

'I didn't want to talk over the phone because you never know who's earwigging,' Seth had explained.

'My Home Office line is secure,' countered Campion. 'I'm sure you didn't have to drag me up to Leeds.'

Seth leaned towards Campion and spoke into his ear. 'This is secure. I want to talk to you about a man I've just killed, following your instructions.'

'Ah, I assume it was you in the other car. I don't remember telling you to go round killing random people off.'

'You told me to deal with Ezra's girl – permanently. She's the one I was after. Our necks are on the line here. If I ever have to go down, you go down with me, you know that, don't you? This whole thing started when you went over the top with that youth. If you hadn't behaved like such an animal we could have scared him into keeping his trap shut and let him go.'

'Oh, so all this is my fault, is it? Nothing to do with you beating him senseless?'

'Yeah,' said Seth, 'all your fault, and it hasn't finished yet. These bloody Lawless girls have both got big mouths and they both need shutting up, once and for all.'

Campion took a gulp of his whisky and indicated for a waiter to bring him another.

'Make that two,' said Seth to the waiter, 'and mine's a double.'

They sat in an uncomfortable silence for a while, then the MP had a thought.

'This Evie Lawless girl is now in her half-sister's custody, isn't she?' He emphasized half-sister.

'Yeah, so what?'

'So what? So a woman with a record for criminal violence has custody of a minor who has severe behavioural problems. We can't allow that.'

'What are you thinking?' Seth asked.

A smirk cracked Campion's face. 'I'm thinking the solution to our problem is right under my nose.'

'I'm not with you.'

Campion jabbed a finger at Seth. 'You're the answer, don't you see? You're her uncle, her closest living relative – if you discount the dodgy half-sister. You're a respectable officer of the law, married, with no children of your own.'

'Still not with you.'

'I want you to apply for custody of the girl. I'll throw my weight behind it.'

'What? I can't do that!' Seth thought about it for a moment, and spotted additional advantages. 'Can I?'

'You can and you will,' said Campion. 'With her under your wing you can guide her along the path of righteousness and make sure she keeps her nose out of stuff that doesn't concern her.'

'Might even have to take her knickers down and smack her arse now and again,' sniggered Seth.

'Might have to come and watch,' giggled Campion.

Eighteen

K eith's mother hadn't seen Lola since the incident in the shoe shop. She had never visited Keith and Lola's home, nor had she ever clapped eyes on her grandson. Until the day of her son's funeral.

The grief she felt for the loss of her only son was matched only by the hatred she felt for Lola. Both emotions were etched darkly into her face as she watched Keith's coffin being lowered into his grave. The curate's words of comfort and assurance that Keith was now in a better place rose and fell with sing-song solemnity.

Mrs Penfold sprinkled a handful of earth on the coffin and gave Lola a look of intense distaste. Her voice cut through the silent air of the cemetery like a spiteful sword.

'I blame you for this. Had it not been for you he'd still be alive. You're not a fit person to carry the Penfold name.'

'I had your son's child,' said Lola in a quiet voice that the many mourners strained to hear. 'And I had his love.'

Mrs Penfold looked down at her grandson and the hatred in her eyes melted away as she saw the image of her own son looking back at her. Then her eyes travelled slowly back up to Lola's face and her expression hardened again.

'What chance has he got with you as a mother?'

Lola looked away. This wasn't the place to carry on a slanging match.

'He loved Lola,' said Evie. All eyes switched to her. 'It was the last thing Keith said.'

Mrs Penfold couldn't bear the thought of this young criminal being the only person with her darling son at the moment of his death. She glared at Evie, who met her gaze with an almost beatific smile, forcing the woman to look away. Evie hadn't finished.

'He told me to tell Lola he loved her. He was very brave. He saved my life.'

Watching and listening was Seth Lawless. He had arrived unnoticed and stood half hidden behind a nearby stone angel erected to the memory of Cecelia Undercliffe, who had gone to a better place in 1907.

The mourners left, leaving just Lola and Mrs Penfold by the graveside and Seth, reverently placing flowers on Mrs Undercliffe's grave; the first she'd had in over forty years. The hatred coming from Keith's mother was almost tangible. Lola didn't need this. She'd lost a good man, a man she'd grown to love. Her future was in tatters, the house was rented and she had Evie to look after.

'Look, if it offends you I'll give up calling myself Penfold.'

Mrs Penfold stiffened. 'Really? And you think that solves everything, do you? You'll lose more than the Penfold name when I've finished with you. You're nothing but a cheap, money-grabbing tart. You've taken away the only thing in my life of any value. Well, you won't get away with it. I'll see you won't.'

Lola saw no point in further discussion. She said a last goodbye to Keith and walked away.

Seth waited until Mrs Penfold had gone before making his way to the nearest telephone box.

Nineteen

Lola was dressed in funereal black but it didn't detract from the effect she had on Tommy Pearson as she opened the door to his knock. It was all he could do to stop himself saying, 'Wow!'

'Mrs Penfold?'

She looked around for accompanying photographers but saw none. He had a pleasant face and seemed rather shy if anything, but she still saw no reason not to be civil to him. Over the past two weeks she'd had several pushy reporters at her door, none of whom seemed to respect the fact that she was mourning a dead husband. Both she and Evie had studiously ignored every one of them.

'What is it you want?'

'Oh. I, er, my name's Pearson. I've done a couple pieces on your sister.'

'Pieces?'

'Yes, I'm a journalist, I'm afraid. Freelance, you understand. Evie knows me.'

'Tommy Pearson?'

'Yes.'

'Yes, I believe she does know you.' She paused for an uncomfortable moment before adding, 'Won't you come in, Mr Pearson? Evie's at school and I've just put my baby to sleep in the back room.' She pressed a finger to her lips and inclined her head towards a partially open door at the end of the hall. Tommy took the hint. He stepped inside, quietly, and followed her through to a comfortable living room. Nappies hung on a clothes horse by the fire, there was a rattle and a ball on the floor and a seasoned teddy bear sitting in pride of place in one of the easy chairs. Lola picked it up and held it to her as she sat down. She saw him looking and explained, 'It's mine really. My daddy gave me it when I was a girl.'

Tommy took the teddy bear's paw. 'Pleased to meet you ... er, what's his name?'

'Charlie.'

'Charlie,' he said, solemnly. Then he smiled. 'I've still got my rabbit – well, I've still got most of him. He's missing an ear and an eye. Mind if I sit down?'

'Oh, sorry, please do.'

Tommy sat down. Previously he'd only dealt with Evie, who had a certain precocious depth to her, but nothing he couldn't cope with. Lola, on the other hand, seemed like a woman who was way out of his league. The first thought that came into his head was, What the hell was she doing working in a shoe shop?

'Do you mind if I ask you why you worked in a shoe shop?' As a freelance he hadn't learned the art of disciplined questioning – the art of getting to the heart of the matter without appearing blunt. His question brought a smile to Lola's face.

'Why shouldn't I work in a shoe shop?'

'Well, look at you. You're the sort of woman I'd expect to see on the screen at the Odeon, not squeezing brogues on to sweaty feet.'

'Are you flattering me for a reason, Mr Pearson?'

'No – I'm just saying what's true.'

'I worked in a shoe shop because I needed to earn money from the day I was forced, by my ever-loving stepfather, to leave school with no qualifications. He didn't think a good education was necessary for a woman.'

'You don't sound like a woman with no qualifications.'

'You're flattering me again, Mr Pearson. As a matter of interest, how do I sound?'

'You sound more educated than I am, and I've got a first class honours degree in English.'

She smiled and hugged Charlie. 'If you must know, I got rid of my accent purely to spite my stepfather. I assume you know who I'm talking about?'

Tommy nodded. 'Ezra Lawless.'

'He was a foul, rough-tongued man. I rather hoped that my superior accent would make him realize how inferior he was.'

'And did it work?'

'Only enough for him to call me a snobby bitch. He wasn't intelligent enough to realize how stupid he was. And now I educate myself by means of books.' She waved an arm in the direction of a wall that had shelves of books from floor to ceiling. 'Most of them are Keith's, but quite a few are mine.'

'Oh, right, please accept my commiserations, Mrs Penfold. I was really sorry to hear about your loss.'

His sorrow seemed genuine, unlike the sanctimonious, professional condolences she'd had to endure since Keith's death. 'Commiserations accepted – I was thinking of going back to being Miss Lawless. I don't think there's room in this town for two Mrs Penfolds.'

'Ah, I gather she's a bit of a dragon.'

'She is. Trouble is there's not much honour in the name Lawless. Evie's stuck with it but she'll be able to change it one day.'

'What's it to be then, Miss Lawless or Mrs Penfold?'

'You can call me Lola if I can call you Tommy.'

'That sounds like a good deal to me, Lola.' He stood up and shook her hand.

'Why are you here, Tommy?' she asked him. 'Most of the stuff about us has already been written.'

'Stuff being the operative word,' said Tommy. 'I've read all that's been written and it's my guess that you haven't given any of the reporters the time of day.'

'I thought it wrong that they should bother me in a time of grief.'

'I agree,' Tommy said. 'It's probably why I'll never make Fleet Street.'

Lola laughed. 'A reporter with a conscience.'

'I prefer to call myself a journalist.'

'What's the difference?'

Tommy smiled. 'A reporter reports the facts; a journalist makes observations, writes articles. A journalist is allowed an opinion.'

'You mean you write factual stories.'

'That just about sums it up.'

'So, Mr Factual Story-Writer, why have you come?'

'Because I know there's a real story here. Maybe I'm being naïve but I believe every word that Evie tells me; she has a very convincing way with her. Things happen to you and your sister that don't happen to anyone else.'

Lola leaned towards him, still clutching Charlie. Her face grew serious and Tommy was mesmerized by her. 'Both Evie and I are scared, Tommy. The trouble is we don't know what we're scared of.'

Tommy suddenly wanted to hold her and tell her he'd make everything right. He'd known her only a few minutes and he wanted to take Keith's place – who on earth wouldn't? But he exercised self-control.

'The story you have to tell, about your fears and yours and Evie's experiences, will make a good article. Set against a background of your mother being wrongly executed I reckon it should have quite an edge to it. Might stir things up with the person or persons unknown who have it in for you. It might even make them back off and leave you alone.'

'I'm not sure I want them to back off and leave us alone,' Lola said. 'Maybe I want them to come out of the woodwork and tell me who they are and the real reason why my mother was hanged. I want her conviction quashed. I want her taken out of that unmarked grave inside the prison walls and given a decent burial. I want her to have a headstone telling of how she was unjustly killed by the state. And I want you to put that in the article.'

Twenty

Three weeks later an unwelcome letter arrived in the first post. Evie watched Lola's face twist into a frown as she read it at the breakfast table. Tears of anger bubbled up and Evie asked what was wrong.

'It's Keith's bloody mother. She's telling me she's applying for custody of Danny on the grounds that I'm not a fit parent.'

'She can't do that – can she?' said Evie.

Lola shook her head and twirled a forefinger around her temple. 'The woman's got a screw loose. It's just the thought of it that makes me mad. She knows I'm skint and she's loaded. Maybe that's her angle.' She screwed up the letter and threw it across the room. 'I don't know much about the law, but I know a mother's got ten times more rights than a nasty-minded old grandmother.'

She regained her composure and smiled at Evie. It would be OK with just the three of them. There was a bit of money left in the bank and a small pension would be due shortly, but she'd need to start earning a crust somehow, even if she had to resort to taking in washing. Jessop had already offered to take her back – yet again – but who would look after Danny?

'Anyway, never mind all this, you've got a test today. That's more important than some crabby old woman.'

Evie was due to sit a test to determine whether or not she might be considered for the thirteen-plus exam. It had taken a lot of persuasion by Lola to convince the head of Evie's school that she should take the test so soon after starting at the school – although it might have taken a lot more persuasion had the head not been a man. If she passed the test, and the February entrance exam, she'd be in the third form at Notre Dame Girls' High School in September 1957. Doors would open up for Evie that had been closed to Lola, and Lola knew her sister would walk it. She smiled down at Evie as the girl stuffed cornflakes into her mouth. It had been a bad time, but surely things could only get better? There was a knock on the door.

It was 8 a.m. that windy November morning and Seth tried to hide his glee behind a mask of false gravitas as he stood on Lola's step. She opened it and said, 'Go away, pig!' before closing it in his face. Then she stood behind the door with her heart pounding. Seth turned to his female companion, whom he dwarfed.

'Seems we're taking her away not a minute before time,' he called out.

The woman bent down and shouted through the letter box. 'Dolores Penfold, I have a court order to remove Eve Lawless from this house and take her to a place of care and safety. Please open the door.'

Lola opened the door a couple of inches. 'What did you say?'

'My name is Pritchard,' said the woman. 'I'm a juvenile probation officer and I have authorization to take your sister into my custody.'

Lola opened the door a few more inches and took the sheet of paper Miss Pritchard was holding out to her. She examined it then ran her hand through her hair. Evie's voice came from behind her.

'What's up, Lola?'

Lola handed her sister the court order. Evie read it, but didn't really understand it.

'They've come to take you away, kid,' Lola explained.

'Take me away? Where to?'

'To a place of care and protection,' Miss Pritchard called out, trying to get a glimpse of Evie. 'It's for your own good.'

'I want to stay with Lola,' shouted Evie. 'I'm OK here.'

Lola turned to face her unwanted visitors. 'She says she doesn't want to go with you. I'm her nearest relative and I want her to stay with me.'

'What you say counts for nothing,' said Seth, sharply. 'You have a criminal record and your sister has behavioural problems. The court has a duty to protect minors.'

'I'm not going!' Evie called out from behind Lola's back.

'You have no option,' retorted Seth.

'You should be grateful your uncle's offered to take you in,' snapped Miss Pritchard, frostily.

'*What?*' chorused Lola and Evie.

'Go with him?' Lola said. 'He's a vile lowlife. He's not fit to keep goldfish, never mind take care of my sister. He hates us, didn't he tell you that?'

'Now then,' said Seth, reasonably, 'I don't like the way you both carry on, but don't ever say I hate you. Evie's my flesh and blood, my own dead brother's girl, why should I hate her?'

'His dead brother was vile and brutal to both of us,' hissed Lola to Miss Pritchard. 'He was beating our mother the night he died. Did he mention that?'

Seth unleashed what he considered justifiable anger. 'How dare you speak of my brother like that? You and your sister are known liars. If you continue with this I – I'll sue you for slander!'

Lola stood firm and held the probation officer in a steady gaze. 'I'm telling you the truth, Miss Pritchard. His brother was a cruel bully who once almost beat me to death – and I've reasons to think he's the same.'

'Is this some sort of ploy,' said Seth, 'accusing innocent people of stuff you can't prove?'

'None of that was a lie,' Lola said, adamantly.

'I'd sooner go back to Askham Grange than live with him,' said Evie. 'He's a very bad man, miss. I don't like him. You mustn't make me go with him.'

The probation officer opened her mouth to speak and was beaten to it by Seth. 'Do you want me to arrest you both for obstructing the police? You've both got criminal records; another arrest won't sit well with the courts.'

'He's right,' confirmed Miss Pritchard, looking at Evie. 'I'm afraid you have no option other than to come with us, young lady.'

Evie burst into tears. Lola put an arm around her and glared at Seth. 'You really are the scum of the earth. I don't know what you're up to, but if you harm one hair of her head I'll kill you.'

The ice in her voice made Miss Pritchard shudder and she wondered what had gone on between DC Lawless and his nieces to provoke such a deep hatred. Despite their reputation the girls looked OK to her but she'd received instructions from on high and she had a job to do. 'Evie, you've got ten minutes to get your things together.'

'I'm supposed to be going to school,' muttered Evie, sullenly. 'I'm taking a test.'

'Not today,' said Miss Pritchard. 'Today you're coming with us. We'll be waiting in the car. Any funny business and there'll be a warrant out for your arrest.'

'And if there's any funny business with my sister there'll be a warrant out for your arrest,' Lola retorted, heatedly. 'If that pig doesn't treat her properly, the responsibility is yours. I'll put my fears in writing to your bosses, so there's no argument as to who's responsible.' Lola closed the door and turned to her weeping sister. 'You'd better go with them for the time being. I'll sort it out, don't worry. I'll get hold of Tommy Pearson, maybe he'll know what to do.'

Twenty-One

E vie knew little of her Auntie Pauline, Seth's wife. Seth and Ezra had rarely taken their wives out socially. The brothers would drink together but saw no reason why their wives should enjoy such conviviality. Wives had a place, which was in the kitchen and in the bed. Socializing was for men who did a hard job and needed to wind down, without a nagging woman by their side.

Pauline gave her niece a weak smile which Evie ignored. 'I've made the little bedroom up for you. It's very nice.'

Seth still had hold of Evie's arm. Miss Pritchard had gone. 'If yer try ter leg it, girl, I can make life very hard for yer,' he growled.

'There's no need to talk to the girl like that, Seth,' protested Pauline, releasing Evie from her husband's grip. She didn't seem quite as meek as Evie's mam but she was still the second-class citizen in the house.

'I'll talk to her how I bloody like,' Seth snapped. 'Accordin' to her, she killed our Ezra. I don't believe a word the lyin' little shit says but it's obvious she hated him.'

'With good reason, maybe,' said Pauline. 'Ezra were no bloody angel.'

Seth raised his hand to her but she stood her ground and glared at him, fiercely. 'The next time's the last time, Seth Lawless. You lay one finger on me and one night yer'll go ter sleep and not wake up. Yer'll end up where your Ezra is and it's my guess yer won't need a coat ter keep yer warm.'

Her threat had the desired effect. Evie wondered why Auntie Pauline would stay with such a man – after all they had no kids to worry about. Maybe Pauline could see the question in Evie's eyes.

'It's one of life's great mysteries, love,' she said, shaking her head. 'Why a woman puts up with a man. Get off ter work, Seth Lawless. I'll sort Evie out.'

Seth grunted and went out of the door. Pauline gave Evie another smile, which Evie returned this time. 'I know yer don't want ter be here, love, but we'll have ter make the best of a bad job. Yer mother were a good woman and I make no pretence I can replace her. All I can do is me best.'

'I was OK living with my sister,' Evie said.

'Aye, no doubt yer were. But we all have ter do what the bloody authorities say. I'll make sure yer see her as regular as yer like.'

'Thanks, Auntie Pauline. I'm supposed to be taking a test at school today.'

Pauline cackled. 'Test? I bloody hated tests. Well, yer've got out of that very nicely – so things haven't turned out so bad after all, have they?'

Evie saw no point in replying. The woman was pleasant but a bit stupid – she'd have to be to marry Seth Lawless. Evie knew one thing for certain: she wasn't going to live with these people.

Tommy enlisted the help of the only copper he knew, his old school pal, Alfie Bruce. They'd lost touch after Alfie went off to the Police Training College at Pannal, but Tommy had heard Evie talk about him and knew he worked at Millgarth, the same police station as Seth. They arranged to meet in the Horse and Trumpet on the Headrow.

'The Lawless sisters? Yes, course I know them,' Alfie said. 'Lola's a cracker, isn't she?'

'Er, yes,' conceded Tommy, reluctantly. He didn't really want anyone else thinking Lola was a cracker.

'You fancy her, don't you?' Alfie teased. 'Join the club, Tommy. If she hadn't got married I'd have been after her myself.'

Tommy gave Alfie a glance to check on whether his pal might make a serious rival. Was Alfie good-looking? He was tall and funny and athletic and he seemed to have more teeth than anyone else. It could well be that women found him attractive. He had always been a popular bloke at school. Tommy fingered his spectacles and wondered if Lola might find him a bit of a nerd.

'Well,' he said, 'she's free again, now.'

'Not free enough,' commented Alfie. 'She's got a dead husband to grieve for. I'm not getting in the way of that.'

'No, nor me,' said Tommy, quickly. 'So, how do we get Evie back for her?'

'No idea. It's all part of this – this stuff that's gets thrown at 'em. There's something weird going on.'

'You know about that, do you?'

'I have read your famous articles, Tommy. And I've been involved with them through work a couple of times. Lola was fined for something that should never have got to court and Evie was sent to a reformatory for losing her rag the day her mam was hanged for a murder she didn't commit.'

'And you're sure their mother didn't do it?' Tommy was testing him.

'Sure as I can be,' said Alfie. 'I believe Evie's story. That whole business stinks to high heaven.'

'Then Evie was set up with a shoplifting charge,' said Tommy. 'Then someone tried to abuse her, then someone tried to kill her. Nightmare. Now this. What's happening, Alfie?'

'Seth Lawless,' mused Alfie. 'He's the connection between her mam being hanged and this. I can feel it in my bones.'

'In what way?'

'Well, he's the murdered man's brother and he's always had a down on the girls because of the way they speak about their father, and now he's taken Evie off Lola.'

'Hmm, it's a fairly tenuous connection. Each of those factors is fairly understandable.'

'Come on,' said Alfie. 'Why would he want to take custody of Evie when he hates her so much?'

'Maybe he's genuine. Maybe he doesn't hate her. Maybe he just wants to put her back on the straight and narrow.'

'Hey,' protested Alfie, 'whose side are you on?'

'I'm playing devil's advocate.'

'I see – and how's the devil's advocate doing?'

'He's getting laughed out of court at the moment,' admitted Tommy. 'I don't believe a word I say. What about all the other stuff that's happened to the girls? What connection has he with that?'

Alfie shook his head. 'Don't know, but I do know that

Seth and Ezra once got promotions they didn't deserve, right out of the blue. That was really weird. They were a couple of complete thugs, scarcely a brain cell between them – especially Ezra. They'd both been in the army, which made it easier for them to join the police. Ex-servicemen always got preference.'

'Is it possible to find out why they were promoted?'

Alfie shrugged. 'The word is that someone with influence recommended them, and some crawler rubber-stamped it.'

'Is it possible to find out who the crawler is?'

Alfie shrugged. 'I'm a police constable, not a chief inspector. One of our sergeants started sniffing around and was told to keep his nose out.'

'Who by?'

'A chief inspector.'

'Name?'

Alfie grinned. Tommy was like a terrier, always had been. He'd been an awkward but enthusiastic left half for the school third eleven, all knees and elbows. When anyone took the ball off him he took it personally and would chase all over the pitch like a dog chasing a car, kicking anything and everything until he got the ball back. He'd been sent off more times than the rest of the team put together.

'Chief Inspector Merton,' Alfie told him. 'He's a bit of a bastard.'

'That can work both ways,' said Tommy. 'If he's a bastard he won't like seeing useless plods getting promotions they don't deserve. Why would someone with influence recommend them?'

'We should make a list of reasons,' suggested Alfie.

They both took several gulps of beer as they pondered things to put on the list.

'Maybe they've got a very influential relative?' suggested Alfie, lighting a Wild Woodbine. 'Smoke?'

'No thanks – nepotism, eh?' mused Tommy. He pulled a face and shook his head. 'Nah, it doesn't sound like a family where nepotism is rife. That would require an ancestor with a human brain.'

'True,' conceded Alfie. 'I think Seth and Ezra were the first Lawless generation to walk upright.' He took a thoughtful drag on his cigarette and popped out a string of smoke rings.

'Maybe,' he said, raising his eyebrows and waving a finger at Tommy to emphasize his suggestion, 'maybe someone owes them a very big favour. Maybe one of them saved our influential man's life in the army.' He turned his palms upwards awaiting Tommy to tell him he'd hit the nail on the head.

'Er, did they ever strike you as heroic types?'

Alfie conceded the point gracefully. 'Cross that one off the list.'

'Or maybe we're talking plain old blackmail.'

'Give that one a big tick and buy that man a big pint,' said Alfie, finishing his drink. 'Blackmail sounds right to me.'

'So,' summed up Tommy, 'we have a man with a lot of influence with the police who's being blackmailed by Seth and between them they're hell bent on making life hard for the Lawless girls. Does that sound feasible?'

'It sounds completely potty,' said Alfie, 'but I've got a feeling we're on the right track.'

'Why would they want to make life hard for the girls?' Tommy wondered. 'What harm can Evie and Lola do to anyone?'

They both fell into silence and sipped their drinks. This time an answer wasn't quite as forthcoming.

They stayed there until eleven o'clock closing time and left full of inebriated camaraderie and determination to rescue the Lawless girls from their misery. In the ensuing weeks they pooled their ideas and resources and energies to get to the bottom of the mystery.

And they got nowhere.

Christmas came and went and Seth barely acknowledged Evie's existence in the house. This was OK by her but she was seriously wondering what she was doing there. She was allowed one visit a week to see her sister and Danny, and she was threatened that if she abused this privilege it would be withdrawn. Auntie Pauline fussed over her and had been to the school to persuade them to allow her to take the test she'd missed. She passed with flying colours so, all in all, life wasn't as bad as it might have been. On each visit Lola had told her how Alfie and Tommy were working out a way to get her back.

She and Pauline ate their meals at a different time from

Seth, who preferred to eat alone, which suited Evie down to the ground. Her aunt and uncle's marriage seemed as empty as her mam and dad's, but without the violence. Evie guessed this was down to Auntie Pauline not being quite so much of a mouse as her mam.

'He used to knock me about,' Pauline once confided. 'But the day came when I'd had enough. I waited until he was asleep and beat him black and blue with his own truncheon. He were off work a week and scarcely dare go ter sleep after that.' She cackled at the memory. 'I told him if he did it again I'd wait 'til he were asleep then stab him through his eyes an' blame it on a burglar. I would an' all, and he knows it – which is why we sleep in different rooms.' She cackled again. 'He keeps his door locked – big bonus that. God, he snores an' farts all night long – it were like sleepin' with a bloody hippopotamus.'

'Why did you marry him?' Evie asked.

'I knew no better. Met him when we were seventeen, married at nineteen. I were pregnant, but I lost it two days after the bloody wedding. If it'd been two days before I wouldn't have wed the bugger.'

'Mam and Dad got married because of me,' said Evie.

'I know, love. Bringing a kiddie up without a husband's no bloody joke – even if the husband's a pile o' shit.'

'Is that what you thought my dad was?'

'Sorry, love. Didn't mean ter speak ill of the dead. He were no better, no worse than Seth. I should leave the bugger, but look at me. Who the hell'd have me?'

Evie looked at her and saw her point. Maybe being married to Seth had aged her but she looked a lot older than her years. Her fierce eyes were ringed with grey, her hair was lifeless, her skin was sallow, and her fingers heavily stained with nicotine. Evie rarely saw her without a cigarette in her mouth.

'You look OK to me,' she lied. 'If you left Uncle Seth I'd come with you.' It seemed an acceptable avenue of escape from Seth. Lola didn't seem to be coming up with anything.

'Now that's an offer worth thinkin' about, love. I can't leave him tonight, though. I'm off ter play bingo up in the Catholic church hall. You have ter get priorities right in this life. It's good fun is bingo, I reckon it might catch on.'

Twenty-Two

8 January 1957. 10.30 p.m.

Pauline wasn't a Catholic but neither was Mrs Rosenhead who went with her to the church bingo. The priest welcomed all denominations at his bingo and beetle-drive nights. Bingo had finished at ten o'clock and, as usual, Pauline went back to Mrs Rosenhead's for an hour or so for a cup of coffee and a natter.

Evie had finished her homework and was listening to Radio Luxembourg, 'Your Station of the Stars'. Barry Alldis was the compère of a new show called *The Top Twenty* and Evie was singing along to the new number one, Tommy Steele's 'Singing The Blues'. It had just taken over from Guy Mitchell who had been at number one for three weeks with the same song. Evie preferred Tommy's version.

Seth had finished his shift over three hours ago and had spent the intervening time in the Fforde Grene pub. By the time he got home he'd drunk ten pints of Tetley's bitter and had a need to release the sexual frustration that had built up inside him since he and Pauline had moved into separate bedrooms. Up until now he hadn't laid a finger on Evie.

She sensed, rather than heard, him coming up the street. Something was different about tonight and she didn't like it one bit. She turned the wireless off and went upstairs to the relative security of her bedroom.

Seth had heard the wireless from outside and decided it was reason enough to inflict severe punishment on his niece. Playing loud music and disturbing the neighbours at this time of night when she should be in bed. She heard him come to the bottom of the stairs and shout up.

'Evie, get yerself down here!'

She opened the bedroom door a crack and shouted down, 'What for, Uncle Seth?'

'Because I bloody say so, that's what for! Yer can come down here ter get yer arse tanned.' Even just saying it to her gave Seth a warped sexual frisson. 'Yer've had that wireless on loud enough ter wake half the bloody street up. Yer can come down here and get yer bare arse tanned.'

Adding the word 'bare' gave him an added thrill, as did ordering her to come to him, rather than him having to chase her. He wanted control over her. He wanted her to do his bidding. And he wanted a lot more than that.

Evie thought of getting out of the window but the drop was too great. Hanging on a peg at the back of the door was her coat. She knew she must put it on. It was all she knew. In her mind she had a vision of him coming up the stairs, even though she could still hear him shouting from the bottom.

'If I have ter come up there, it'll be ten times bloody worse!'

She had her coat on now but she made no move. Her heart was thumping violently as she listened at the back of the door. He had given up waiting and was coming for her. His heavy, thumping footsteps were ascending the stairs. There were fifteen altogether, she knew that. It was one of the things kids know – how many stairs they have in their house. She was counting and she could visualize exactly where he was at any given split second. She could see him as clearly as if there was no door to block her view. Seven, eight, nine, ten . . . She pushed the door open and saw his head rising above the balustrade. Eleven, twelve, thirteen . . . Evie took a couple of quick steps and took up a position at the top of the stairs. He was swaying with the drink and he lunged at her. She pushed him back. It wasn't a violent push, just enough to knock him off balance and send him tumbling downwards, cursing and yelling.

Evie followed him down and stepped over him as he lay at the bottom, semi-concussed. He suddenly retched and vomited all over the carpet. His wallet had fallen out of his pocket. Evie picked it up and took out all the notes – three pounds ten shillings. Then she dropped the wallet on his moaning body and walked out of the house. She was in trouble, but not as much trouble as she'd have been in had she stayed there.

She knew Lola's would be the first place they'd look for her so she caught a tram into town and got off outside the West Yorkshire Bus Station, where she boarded a bus that was just leaving for Keighley – wherever that was. It certainly sounded like a town where no one would look for her.

She sat on the top deck, right at the front, watching the passing landscape with little enthusiasm. One industrial town seemed to merge into another, with no countryside in between. At one bus stop she looked down at the street and read a newspaper placard saying Anthony Eden had resigned. It brought to mind the last placard that had taken her attention – the one telling the world of her mother's execution – and her spirits sank even lower. It had begun to snow and, lit by the bus's headlights, the snowflakes dashed towards the window like a mini blizzard. Evie wondered how she'd go on when she arrived in Keighley. Where would she stay? Who would look after her? Would she freeze to death in the snow? Somehow all these problems diminished into insignificance when set alongside the problem she'd just escaped. Seth was no better than his dead brother. Worse, probably. She dreaded to think what might have befallen her had she not escaped his clutches that night.

After an hour's journey the bus arrived at Keighley Bus Station. As she was getting off the conductress put a hand on her shoulder and asked, 'Are you all right, love?'

Evie lied, politely, 'Yes, thank you.'

To confess her predicament at this stage might have meant being delivered back into the clutches of Seth. The woman didn't seem convinced.

'I just wondered, that's all. Someone so young bein' out on her own at this time o' night.'

This forced Evie into elaborating on her lie. 'I've been to my auntie's in Leeds. I don't live far away.'

She desperately hoped the woman didn't ask her where she lived because she didn't know the name of a single street in Keighley.

'Well, I hope it's not far,' the conductress said. 'Pity yer mam didn't come ter meet yer.'

'I haven't got a mam.' This gave Evie the edge in the exchange.

'Oh, I'm sorry, love. It's just that, well, it's perishin' ternight. It were forecast ter get warmer, but I never believe these weather forecasts.'

Evie mumbled her agreement and walked away, quickly,

not having a clue where to go or what to do. The woman
was right; it was perishing. She buttoned her coat up to the
neck and turned up the collar. There was a road sign pointing
to Haworth; at least it was a place she'd heard of. She knew
it was where Charlotte Brontë and her sisters came from,
and she also knew it was supposed to be a bleak part of the
world. The wind was blowing from Haworth so Evie turned
her back to it, put her head down and walked the other way,
downhill through the settling snow. In her pocket was three
pounds ten shillings, probably enough for her to exist for
several days, if only she could find somewhere warm to
sleep.

A nearby factory clock told her it was ten past midnight. The
pubs had kicked out the last of the stragglers and shut their
doors an hour ago. Everywhere was closed. Few people were
about, which suited Evie. Maybe she could try a boarding house.

No, they'd ask questions of a kid trying to get into a
boarding house without grown-ups with her. Questions would
mean police, which meant she'd be sent back to Seth. She'd
rather die. Evie allowed herself a grim smile at that thought.
Maybe she'd have no option.

She crossed Aire Valley Road and headed east, simply to
have her back to the glacial wind, all the time keeping a
lookout for some sort of shelter for the night. Her hair was
thick with snow and her gloveless hands, thrust into her shallow
pockets, were beginning to become numb. Her feet were
freezing, and she wished she'd come out in her wellies, instead
of her school shoes, which weren't meant to cope with this
sort of weather. The temperature seemed to be falling by the
minute and tears of dejection were icicles on her cheeks. Even
her brain was becoming numb and the only thing she knew
for certain was that she couldn't take much more of this.

Then the snowflakes grew bigger and her size three shoes
were as big as men's boots. Without knowing why, she
turned down an alleyway that led down to the Leeds and
Liverpool canal. A row of barges were tied beside a towpath.
Evie trudged alongside them, trying to see if any might
provide her with the lifesaving shelter she desperately
needed; and somehow she knew she'd be OK. The utter
dejection left her, the cold was still there, the tears were
still frozen to her cheeks, but she knew she'd be all right.

'Bugger me, I thowt it were a walkin' bloody snowman! Are yer all right, lass?'

The voice came from a barge she'd just walked past. It was a friendly, unthreatening voice. Probably a woman's voice but Evie couldn't be sure about that. She turned and peered into the swirling snow.

Fifteen minutes later she was sitting on a wooden seat inside a barge, wrapped in a heavy woollen shawl, with her feet in a bowl of warm water, drinking a cup of cocoa. Facing her was Salome Ackroyd, better know to the canal dwellers as Owd Sal.

'Yer've run away, haven't yer?'

Evie nodded. She saw no profit in lying.

'I'll not ask why. Yer'll have your reasons, an' yer'll tell me when yer good an' ready. How old are yer?'

'Twelve and a half.'

'I'm fifty-seven and three eighths, I think – could be fifty-seven and a third. Never was good at sums.' Sal gave Evie a grin that displayed more gums than teeth. 'Which is most, a third or three eighths?'

'Three eighths,' said Evie, without having to think.

'Bugger me! Just like that. I knew actually – I were just testin' yer. I never thought anyone could work it out as quick as that. Bugger me, yer a sharp lass. Three eighths it is. One twenty-fourth is the difference, I bet yer knew that as well. There were a big argument about it in the Navigation Arms a couple o' weeks ago. We had to put pencil to paper to work it out – an' you fathomed it out in yer head. It's a bloody gift is that, an' no mistake.'

Evie sat there, assessing her sudden change in fortune. Just a quarter of an hour ago she'd been on the verge of freezing to death in a strange town in the middle of the night, and now she was a gifted child sitting with her feet in a bowl of warm water drinking cocoa.

'I've got a bit of money,' she said. 'I can pay for my keep – for a bit.'

'Pay for yer keep, eh? Fancy that? So, you're expectin' to stay, are yer?'

'I don't know what I'm expecting,' said Evie, truthfully. She knew she'd made a friend who wouldn't let her die on the streets any more than she'd turn her in to the police.

Evie knew that much. And it was a comforting thing to know.

Alfie had been quick to volunteer to call round and see if Evie was at her sister's. It wasn't a matter of great priority down at the station. There was even some amusement that Seth had been pushed down the stairs and had broken his ankle. It meant that Evie was in trouble, of course, but her arrest was being treated with no great urgency.

Lola smiled when she opened the door to Alfie. She had Danny in her arms. Her smile faded when she saw the serious look on Alfie's face.

'What is it?'

'Evie's done a bunk – I thought you might know something about it.'

Lola shook her head and frowned. 'When?'

'Last night. She pushed Seth down the stairs and ran away. He broke his ankle.'

'So, it's not all bad news then – I assume you think she's here?'

Alfie shrugged. 'I have to ask.'

'She's not.' Lola looked beyond him at the snow-covered street. 'God, is she out in this? I wish she had come here. I'd have hidden her away before letting that monster get his hands on her.'

'She apparently stole some money from his wallet, about five quid according to him.'

'Good for her – at least she won't starve.'

'If she gets in touch you will contact us, won't you?'

'No.'

'I'll rephrase that – get in touch with me.'

'Only if you promise not to tell your colleagues, which would be daft because it could get you into trouble.'

For the first time she realized she was attracted to him. His smile was genuine and his eyes sincere. Evie used to say he was handsome and maybe she had a point.

'Let me worry about that,' he said. 'Not many people down at the station think giving her back to Seth's a good idea. Problem is it's not up to us. Seth's going to be laid up for a few weeks, so he won't be giving her any trouble.'

'Any more trouble, you mean,' said Lola. 'Why would a twelve-year-old girl attack him and run away in the middle of the night in the middle of winter? I assume you'll be asking him that.'

'I'll mention your fears to my sergeant. They'll have to follow up on it.'

Lola closed her eyes as though a sudden pain had enveloped her. 'Are you all right?'

'Not really.'

She handed Danny to him just before she slumped to the floor in a dead faint. When she came to, Alfie was kneeling beside her, with Danny in one arm and the other cradling her. It felt good, to both of them. Alfie was concerned.

'I'll get you a drink of water.'

'I'm OK. It's just – it's just all the stuff that's happened. It gets a bit much at times.'

He helped her to her feet, still carrying Danny. 'Maybe a cup of tea, eh?'

'A double brandy would be better.' She gave a weak smile at the sudden concern on his face. 'It's all right, I'm joking. I haven't taken to the bottle just yet.'

I wouldn't blame you if you had, Alfie thought.

Lola sat cuddling Danny as Alfie busied himself making the tea. It was nice of him to try and help her, but what could he do? There seemed to be forces acting against her and Evie that a mere PC wouldn't be able to help her with. She called out to Alfie.

'Alfie?'

'Yeah?'

'Do you know the name of my MP?'

He came through with two cups of tea. 'It's a bloke called Clive Campion. Why, are you thinking of taking your troubles to him?'

'It wouldn't do any harm, would it?'

Alfie sat down. 'No, I don't suppose it would,' he said, 'but he is part of the government that's responsible for hanging your mother. He's also something to do with the Home Office.'

'It's his duty to help me, isn't it?'

'I guess so. Not too struck on politicians meself, but I'll make some enquiries. Find out the best way for you to get in touch with him.'

'Thanks, Alfie.'

Twenty-Three

E vie awoke to the smell of bacon frying in a miniscule galley at the front of the vessel. Her outer garments were hanging on a piece of rope stretched across the narrow cabin, which was heated by a two-bar electric fire that was powered by a hidden generator that Evie could hear rumbling away somewhere. It took her a few seconds to get her bearings, so soundly had she slept.

'I reckon yer'd have been in trouble had I not spotted yer last night.' Sal was standing beside her. 'It's all frozen over out there, even the canal. There'll be kids skatin' on it afore long.'

Evie sat up and gave a wide yawn as she tried to remember Sal's name. 'I'm ever so sorry, I've forgotten your name. I know you told me but I was—'

'It's Sal, some beggars call me Owd Sal. Sal – short for Salome what did the dance o' the seven veils so she could have the head of John the Baptist. It was her mother what put her up to it. Fancy doin' a trick like that. Some people, eh? Actually, me name's Hilda, but it didn't sound right when I were doin' me exotic dancin'. I've been Sal since I were nineteen. Started out as Young Sal and now I'm Owd Sal.'

Evie wasn't quite sure what an exotic dancer did but she couldn't imagine Sal doing any kind of dancing. She was a small, rotund woman who wore several layers of clothing so it was hard to discern just how fat she was. Cosmetically, the fifty-seven and three eighth years she'd spent on earth had not been kind to her. Her face was deeply lined, her skin weather-beaten beyond redemption and the hair that poked out from beneath her woollen hat was white and wiry and far from clean. But it was a face Evie felt she could trust. In her predicament she had little option.

'I've made you a bite o' breakfast, although it's nearer dinnertime.'

'Thank you.'

'Then we need ter fathom out what ter do wi' yer.'

'I see,' said Evie, who didn't really see.

'It's a good job it were me as saw yer, not some mucky owd feller. There's plenty o' them around here. Yer norra a bad lookin' lass, apart from yer wonky eye. Have they not done nowt about yer eye? Yer'd be a right bobby-dazzler if they could straighten that bugger out. They can work wonders nowadays yer know, bloody wonders.'

'They can do something when I'm older,' Evie said, vaguely. It was the total extent of the information she'd been given about her eye, which, like Evie, had good days and bad days. She looked at her drying clothes and realized she must have fallen asleep as she was talking to Sal. This got her wondering what had happened to her money. As if she could read the girl's mind, Sal tossed her her purse.

'Whatever was in there's still in there,' she said. 'I might look a rum un, but I'm norra a thief – at least I never steals off kids.'

'I never said you did.'

'If yer were a millionaire what had dropped his wallet yer might never see it again, but I'm guessin' yer norra millionaire.'

'No,' Evie confirmed, 'I'm not.'

Sal returned her attention to the frying breakfast and continued the conversation over her shoulder. 'Yer've no need to tell me who yer've run away from, no need at all, but yer never know, I might be able to help. I'm the type o' woman what knows stuff what other folk don't know, if yer get me drift.'

Evie got her drift all right. Sal was just plain nosey, but she seemed like a person who would listen. And Evie felt she needed someone like Owd Sal to listen to her right now. She told a potted version of her story as she got dressed:

'Two years ago my dad attacked my mam so I hit him with the iron and killed him and my mam got hanged because she said it was her who did it. It was in all the papers. My dad used to hit me and my sister, so he got what he deserved, but my mam didn't. Then I got sent to a home and my sister got married but they wouldn't let me go to the wedding so I absconded and got sent to another home.

'The day I was released from there my sister's husband picked me up to take me home to their house . . .' Evie rambled on, happy to unload her life story on to this stranger. '. . . Only a car ran us off the road and he was drowned – I got out.'

'Thank God fer that!'

'They wouldn't let me stay with my sister because she tipped a bucket of window-cleaner's water all over her mother-in-law's head, only she wasn't her mother-in-law then. Anyway they said she wasn't a fit person to look after me – which she is – but I had to stay with Uncle Seth who's my dad's brother and just as bad. I pushed him down the stairs and ran away.'

'I suppose you had good reason.'

'I think he was coming up to do . . . *stuff* to me.'

'Bugger me,' said Sal. 'Stuff, eh? Yer don't need to tell me. I had an Uncle Wally what did stuff to me. He stopped when I jabbed a penknife right up his arse – and I mean right up.'

'I never had a penknife.'

It seemed such a daft thing to say that Evie didn't quite know why she said it. Sal turned and stood with her head on one side, weighing Evie up.

'For all I know this could be a right cock and bull story. But people who make stories up generally don't make 'em up as fanciful as that.'

'If you don't believe me, a lot of it's been in the *Daily Herald.*'

Sal turned back to her frying pan. '*Daily Herald*? Well, I think I might just have to check on that. I've never heard nowt as fantastic in all me life. Anyroad, I know someone who reads the papers. I'll not tell him I know you, but there's nowt that's been in the papers these last ten years what he doesn't know about. What's yer full name?'

'Evie Lawless – my mother was Rachel Lawless, she was hanged on Friday the thirteenth of May 1955.'

'Lawless? Now there's a name what rings a bell. It's norra common name, so why should it ring a bell wi' me? Happen I've heard of yer. Maybe I've heard talk what I can't put me finger on. I remember 'em hangin' that Ruth Ellis girl – that were a bugger, that were. Nice lookin' lass like that.' Sal snapped her fingers. 'That's right, I remember 'em hangin' yer ma. Weren't your dad a copper or somethin'?'

'Yes – a sergeant.'

'Then yer ma had no chance. Yer've only got to give a copper a dirty look and yer get banged up. Yer go round tellin' 'em yer've killed one o' theirs an' they'll hang yer soon as look at yer. If your dad'd been a ragman yer ma would've have got off wi' a five-pound fine. No mistake about that.'

She turned around with a plate of egg, bacon, tomatoes and fried bread that had Evie's mouth watering, and placed it on the table, along with a silver knife and fork.

'Right, you get yerself outside o' this an' I'll go check on yer story. It's not that I doubt yer, only I've heard nowt so fantastic.'

'You won't tell anyone I'm here, will you?'

'Cross me heart, love.'

An hour later Sal was back, with Harry Buttershawe in tow. He looked closely at Evie and nodded.

'That's her.' He turned to Evie and added, 'You had yer picture in t'paper, didn't yer?'

Evie nodded, dismally. Why did everyone let her down? Sal had promised not to tell anyone. Sal explained her apparent treachery.

'I had to bring him back to confirm it were you,' she said. 'Because you never know.'

'Never know what?' Evie asked.

'Never know when someone's tryin' it on. In my business it's daft ter trust people yer don't know. Harry remembers readin' about yer, just like I said he would. But for all I know yer could be someone pretendin' ter be Evie Lawless for reasons best known to yerself.'

Evie couldn't think of any reason why someone should pretend to be her, but she didn't press the point. 'What is your business?' she asked.

Sal grinned at Harry. 'My business is ter get people what can afford it ter contribute ter me welfare.'

The glances her two adult companions were exchanging gave Evie cause of concern. 'Are you thieves?' she asked.

Sal laughed, Harry looked offended. 'Thief?' he said. 'Where d'yer get that from? I'm a flamin' winder cleaner.'

'Sorry.'

'And I'm a door-ter-door fortune-teller and concertina player,' said Sal, taking such an instrument off a shelf and playing a few notes that sounded good to Evie, although she didn't recognize the tune.

'Fortune-teller?' said Evie. 'You mean you can see into the future?'

'I can see what people want ter see.'

'Can you see into my future?'

Sal looked down at her, arms folded, her head on one side. 'I can see into yer past, girl, and what I see tells me yer need help. I suggest yer write to yer sister and tell her yer being looked after by a friend.'

'Is that what you are, my friend?'

'I'm someone yer can trust, girl. It strikes me yer need ter lay low fer a while.'

'That's pretty much what I thought,' Evie agreed, 'but I didn't know where. I just ran away. I suppose I'm lucky to have found you.'

'Serendipitous,' commented Sal, nodding to herself.

'What?'

'Just something I believe in. A girl like you could do with a bit of serendipity.'

Evie stayed with Owd Sal for a month, during which time she recovered her strength, her self-esteem and her faith in human nature. Sal would play her concertina and tell fortunes around the pubs and clubs of Keighley and district and Evie would accompany her where possible. Sometimes they'd travel on the barge if the venue was near the canal. All in all, Evie's life had taken a turn for the better, but she missed her sister, and she knew she should be going to school.

Sal made some remark about her studying at the University of Life but Evie had heard that before and it didn't wash. You didn't get 'O' Levels studying at the University of Life, and Evie needed 'O' Levels to pursue her career as a journalist, an ambition she'd caught from Tommy.

Twenty-Four

Dear Mr Campion,

I am writing to you because, frankly, I do not know where else to turn. Since my mother, Rachel Lawless, was hanged in 1955 for a murder it is becoming increasingly obvious she did not commit, both I and my sister have become victims of an anonymous campaign of vicious harassment from the authorities of this country, which has culminated in the murder of my husband, and my young sister, Evie, being taken from me and placed in the care of an uncle who quite openly hates her. Consequently she has run away.

    Please help me,

    Yours sincerely,

    Lola Lawless

The letter had been on Campion's desk for a week and it worried him. He had wanted his name kept out of this awful business. It was very bad that she had involved him, albeit without knowing how deeply he was involved already. In her mind his name was now associated with the deaths of her mother and her husband, and the more he allowed himself to become involved the stronger that association would become. How long would it be before his name was associated with the death of Kevin Weatherall?

He knew about Evie running away and cursed himself for thinking up the idea of her going into Seth's care. Seth was a blundering moron who had no sense of finesse when dealing with young girls. This whole thing could quite easily explode in his face. He read the letter for the tenth time before walking over to his window that looked down on Old Palace Yard. As he watched a queue of visitors at St Stephen's Entrance, waiting to be allowed into the Houses of Parliament, it crossed his mind that it wasn't beyond the realms of possibility that his next place of residence might have bars at the window and a view of the prison yard in Wormwood Scrubs as he awaited the hangman. He shuddered at the thought and he came to an immediate decision as he stared down at the heroic statue of Richard Coeur de Lion. The harassment was backfiring on him. All he had to do was stop it. He called in his secretary and dictated a letter:

Dear Miss Lawless,

I thank you for your letter of the 24th of January 1957. I have made enquiries regarding your situation and I am assured that you are most likely a victim of a series of unfortunate coincidences. However, if these 'coincidences' persist I will be happy for you to contact me again, at which point you can be assured that I will take the matter more seriously. In the meantime I will do what I can for your sister.

Yours sincerely,
Clive Campion MP

Campion knew she would have no cause to contact him ever again because he would end the harassment here and now. It was proving to be dangerously counterproductive. As soon as Evie surfaced he would arrange for her to be reunited with her sister and all would be well.

Unfortunately Seth didn't see things in quite the same light.

Seth eyed the ringing telephone with annoyance. Pauline had taken advantage of his incapacity and had left him to go and live with her widowed mother in Wakefield. He got back from the hospital to find a note on the table.

I have left you, Seth Lawless, because you're a complete shit. I don't know what possessed Evie to do what she did and run away but its my guess you got what you deserved.
Pauline

She had taken the time to clean out their bank account and most of the food from the pantry. The ambulance men returning him home had to alert the local WRVS to look after him until he was fit and well.

Heaving himself on to his crutches, he swung himself across the hall. The caller was Campion, who got straight to the point.

'I want to stop what's happening to the Lawless girls.'

'Do yer now? Well, I've got a broken ankle that thinks different.'

'We should leave them alone. This thing could blow up in our faces.'

'Well, I think it'll blow up in our faces if we do leave 'em alone,' Seth retorted. 'The wife's pissed off an' left me, did yer know that? Pissed off an' left me with a broken leg, courtesy of that evil little cross-eyed bitch. I'm gonna shut that little bitch up, once and for all.'

'You'll do no such thing. Do you want to move up through the ranks or not?' hissed an alarmed Campion.

'I'm not fussed,' said Seth, who knew he was struggling as a DC and didn't really fancy a detective sergeant's job. In any case, such a promotion would cause too many tongues to wag.

On the same day that she received the letter from Campion, Lola got one from Evie, much to her relief. It told her that her sister was alive and well. According to the postmark, it had been posted in Shipley, which was several miles from Keighley – a precaution Evie had taken on Sal's advice.

'Yer can never be too careful if there's coppers involved,' Sal had warned her. 'Coppers can intercept Her Majesty's mail without yer knowin'. They've got powers they shouldn't have.'

Seth's method of intercepting the mail wasn't officially sanctioned by the police. It was more to do with him knowing that Lola's postman had a criminal record for theft and deception that he hadn't revealed to his bosses.

'Any mail to her house comes ter me first. It's a police investigation, that's all yer need ter know. I'll ter yer what yer can deliver and what yer can't.'

Thus Lola's mail was always delivered a day late, although she never suspected it had been tampered with – such was Seth's expertise in opening and resealing letters. He saw the letter that Evie had posted in Shipley but it gave away no information that he could follow up. The one that came in three weeks later was what he'd been waiting for.

> Dear Lola,
> I am OK, but I am missing you and Danny loads. I would like to meet you and see how things are. We could meet under that clock in town where we met under when you took me shopping that time. How about Thursday at 7 p.m.? I'll be there anyway, even if you can't make it. If I do not see you I will write again.
> Yours sincerely,
> Your loving sister,
> Evie

Evie had underestimated the fame of Dyson's Clock on Lower Briggate. She thought she was being suitably cryptic.

Unfortunately, it was a clock that almost everyone in Leeds had met under at some time or other, even Seth. He was only guessing, but he was fairly sure he was guessing right.

He was now walking without crutches, although not yet back at work. His plan was simple. He would arrest the two girls at their rendezvous, drive them to the nearest secluded location where he would kill them both, quickly and efficiently. It wouldn't be too difficult, with neither of them suspecting his intentions. As far as they were concerned he was an officer of the law and it was in their best interests to do as they were told – just as young Kevin Weatherall had. Then he would drive the bodies out on to the moors and bury them. He knew a great spot where the ground was peat and therefore easy to dig a good deep hole. If you're going to top someone, make sure the body's never found. They'd made a mistake with the Weatherall boy and look what trouble that had caused. However, with these two troublemakers out of the picture that would no longer be a problem. But the job had to be done right.

He despaired of these amateur killers who buried their victims' bodies in rock hard ground with just a few inches covering them – if they were lucky. Any passing walker with a nosey dog would soon be ringing the police. Next stop the hangman. All because of laziness and bad planning.

Half an hour before Lola left home to meet Evie, young Danny exploded in a bout of violent croup that had Lola worried. Her babysitter arrived and advised her to place a kettle of boiling water by his cot so that the steam would ease the symptoms. It worked but it made Lola ten minutes late.

Seth sat in his car about fifty yards down Briggate from the famous clock. He angled his rear-view mirror to give him a good view of the waiting girl, then he looked at his watch. Two minutes past seven. Lola was late.

At five past, Evie walked up to the junction with Boar Lane and looked right towards the Corn Exchange, then left towards City Square to see if her sister was approaching. Then, to Seth's relief, she came back and resumed her position under the clock.

At eight minutes past Seth decided that the older sister wasn't coming and that it would be a good idea to take care

of the business with the sister who was already there, while
the road was relatively quiet. He got out of his car and
approached as she stood with her back to him. Evie gave a
start when he tapped her on her shoulder and grabbed her
upper arm. She struggled and Seth waved a finger at her.
'I'm not here as your uncle!' he snapped. 'I'm here as a
police officer and I'm placing you under arrest and taking
you into custody. The more you struggle the worse it'll be
for you.'

Evie stopped struggling and Seth looked around to check
if anyone was taking an interest. At that time on a Sunday
evening all the shops were closed and the street was almost
deserted. Evie went quietly as her uncle led her towards his
car. Evie hadn't recognized Seth's Standard Vanguard at first.
Had he not stopped she would have walked straight past it
without comment. Her mind was on other things. He was
holding her by her arm and putting the key in the door when
her mind came suddenly into focus. This was the car. This
was the car that had tried to run her down. The car that had
run Keith off the road. The car that had killed Keith! Uncle
Seth was behind everything. All the bad things that had been
happening. Staying in Uncle Seth's custody was very bad.
Very bad indeed. She knew she mustn't get into that car. She
could smell the sweat on him like the stink of a foul sewer.

His fat hand turned the key with all the threat and purpose
of a jailer opening the door to a cell. A condemned cell. With
every ounce of her strength she pulled herself away from him
and set off running down the road. Her youth and agility gave
her an instant advantage. Seth let out a roar of rage and he
raced after her, hampered by his limp. He was thirty yards
behind her as Evie arrived at Leeds Bridge and turned right
down stone steps leading to the River Aire.

Lola rounded the corner and spotted her sister running
down the road, away from her, and a large man in hot pursuit.
Even from behind, Seth's bulk, especially with his slight limp,
was unmistakeable. Lola was now in pursuit of both of them.

In her panicking haste Evie tripped on the top step and
fell headlong down the whole flight. She was sprawled at the
bottom, winded and semi-conscious when Seth arrived. His
plan was now completely awry. He was running on instinct
and the only instinct in his armoury was one of brutality.

He swung a heavy boot at her head and knocked her completely senseless.

Lola had arrived at the steps in time to see Seth pick up her sister and hurl her into the river. She screamed at him. Seth turned and gave her a grin. He indicated, with a beckoning hand, for her to come to him for some of the same. A barge came into view, causing him to change his plan. With his arrogant grin still in place he strode back up the steps, elbowing her out of the way. Lola ran down to the riverside, trying to work out where Evie had gone in. There was a dark shape just under the surface. She leapt in. The barge was slowing down. Someone on board was shouting. A man was on the bridge looking down at the drama unfolding below.

The river was dark and freezing cold. Lola was beneath the surface, feeling about with outstretched arms, trying to locate her sister. The shock of hitting the water had brought Evie to her senses. She drew in a lungful of water and immediately began to choke. Lola touched her arm then grabbed at her, pulling her to the surface. By now Evie had lost consciousness again. She had stopped breathing. Against the blackness of the river, in the evening twilight, her face looked deathly white as Lola pulled her to the river wall, which rose six feet above the river.

'Over here, love.'

The man from the bridge had run down to the riverside. The barge had stopped downriver and was now chugging backwards. Lola looked up at the man on the bank and hoped he might jump in to help but he was showing no signs of doing so. He was standing by an iron ladder running up the wall about twenty yards away. She didn't hear the splash from behind as a man from the barge dived in. Within seconds he had hold of Evie and was pulling her towards the ladder. Lola, exhausted, swam behind.

Seth walked, casually, back to his car, checking that he wasn't the object of anyone's attention. He could hear shouting coming from the bridge and he knew he might have to think fast to get out of this one. If he could enlist Campion's help, he wouldn't have much to worry about – and Campion just happened to be in Leeds. Friends in high places were not to be sneezed at – especially friends with secrets as dark as Campion's.

Between them the two men hoisted Evie out of the river.

Lola climbed up the ladder, unaided, to find the bargee giving Evie artificial respiration. Lola knelt beside her sister and stroked her face.

'Wake up, Evie. It's OK. Everything's OK. He's gone and he can't hurt us any more.'

The bargee pumped away at her chest, counting as he did so. But Evie lay still and pale. Lola's voice was becoming more urgent.

'Evie, don't leave me. Please, wake up, Evie!'

She pushed the man to one side and took over. A line of people had gathered on the bridge, some were coming down the steps. One of them was a nurse who had jumped off a passing tram on seeing the commotion. She knelt beside Evie and felt for her pulse as Lola was trying to pump her sister's heart back to life. The nurse let go of Evie's wrist and gave an almost imperceptible shake of her head, seen only by the bargee, who was of a similar opinion. Lola was sobbing as she pressed on her sister's chest. The nurse placed a hand on her shoulder.

'I'm a nurse, love. Let me have a go.'

'Can you bring her back to me? Please don't let her die. She's my baby sister.'

'I'll do what I can.'

The nurse's efforts were more professional. She was in her uniform, which met with the approval of the watchers on the bridge.

'She's a nurse. If anyone can bring the lass back ter life it's a nurse.'

There were some grunts of agreement but no one seemed too convinced. The bargee had got to his feet and was holding his hand over his mouth as if trying to suppress his worst fears. The nurse was working away, more for Lola's benefit than Evie's. She was fending off the moment when she had to give up and tell Lola the worst. There was a hush on the bridge as she placed her ear to Evie's chest. Then, without any comment she lifted the lifeless girl's wrist and felt for her pulse. Then she sat back on her haunches. It wasn't really a nurse's job to pronounce anyone dead but she knew someone had to do it.

'Has anyone rung for an ambulance?' she enquired.

It seemed that no one had. The bargee shouted up to the watchers above.

'Can someone get an ambulance, please?'

Lola was talking to Evie, kissing her forehead and stroking her sodden hair. 'It's going to be OK, Evie. They've sent for an ambulance. Please wake up, Evie.'

The nurse, herself in tears now, said, 'I don't think she's going to wake up, love.'

Lola turned her head and glared at her. 'Of course she's going to wake up!' Then to Evie, she said, 'Just you show her, Evie. Show her she's wrong.'

There was deathly silence on the bridge as the reality of the moment reached them. The man who had helped from the riverside took off his coat and placed at around Lola's shivering shoulders. He couldn't think of anything else to do.

Lola looked closely at her sister's face, examining every inch, and she wondered why Evie looked so perfect if she was dead. Dead people don't look perfect.

There was a lump on the side of her head just above her ear, but there wasn't a mark on her face. For the first time, she looked to have the inner peace that she had deserved all her life. Not that Lola realized it at such a time, but it would help whenever she remembered that moment, which was often. With the softest of fingers she closed her sister's eyes to permanently shut away the squint that Evie had always hated so much. The squint was worse than Lola had ever seen it. It had always got worse when Evie was stressed, and there's nothing more stressful than knowing you're going to die, especially when you're a kid. Dying when you're just a kid is no fun at all. But the stress was gone and now there was peace.

Lola cradled Evie's head in her arms and allowed her tears to drip down on to her younger sister's cheeks as she spoke to her. Evie's face was grey, her lips were blue, her hair was bedraggled, her flesh was cold, and she was quite dead. Life hadn't been great for either of them, but Evie had definitely had the worst of it, towards the end, anyway.

Lola stretched out on the ground, cheek to cheek with her sister, her shoulders now heaving beneath the man's coat. A woman on the bridge began to pray, others who knew the prayer joined in. The nurse, the bargee and the man stood back and allowed Lola her last moments with her dead sister.

'I should have looked after you better, kid. I should have done something to protect you and Mam from Ezra. Mam was never up to it, but I was, so we can't blame Mam, can we? You were

special, Evie . . .' Her voice rose with anger. 'And a fat lot of
bloody good it did you!' She allowed her anger to subside as
she stroked Evie's hair and kissed her forehead and her nose.
'Sorry about that, kid. Hey, just look at you – you were the
beautiful one, all the time. I might have got the looks but you
got all the beauty. You got the beauty and you got the gift and
the guts and the magic. Everybody said that about you. You had
the magic. Oh, Evie – look at you now. You didn't deserve this.

'I hope what you believe in is true, Evie – about God and
everlasting life, I mean. I really do hope that. Hey, of course
it's true; you knew it was true all the time.' She clasped her
hands together and prayed with intense sincerity. 'Please God,
I want it all to be true. Let Evie be there with Mam. Let her
be looking down at me and laughing for being so soft when
there's nothing to be soft about. It would be really great if
all that stuff were true.'

She sat back on her haunches as she prayed for the first
time in years. The people on the bridge heard her and prayed
along with her.

Seth was settled in front of his television set, watching *The
Makepeace Story*, when the familiar knock came on the door.
It was familiar insofar as he'd used the same knock a thousand times himself. It was a knock that said, 'Answer this
door and answer it quickly or else!'

He chose to shout rather than come to the door. Innocent
people couldn't care less who was at the door.

'Who is it?'

'Police.'

'Who?'

'Police.'

'Snap,' he called out. 'The door's open.'

DI Frank Foulds, from his station, and PC Alfie Bruce
entered the house. Seth had his injured foot up on a stool.

'I'm not due back in for a fortnight,' he grumbled, without
taking his eyes off the screen. 'Are they missing me?'

'DC Lawless,' said Foulds, 'where were you at seven o'clock
this evening?'

Seth continued to stare at the screen as if trying not to
miss the dialogue. A scene ended. Only then did he look up
at the inspector.

'What?'

'I said, where were you at seven o'clock this evening?'

'Where was I? Sorry, sir, but why d'yer want to know?'

Alfie was thinking that if Seth had killed Evie he was putting on a good show of knowing nothing about it. The detective inspector gave a throat-clearing cough and said, 'Your niece was drowned this evening and we've reason to suspect it was murder.'

'Evie? Our Evie, drowned, murdered? Oh my God!'

Seth got to his feet, wincing in false pain and exaggerating his limp. He turned the television off and gave the matter his full attention. Alfie was watching him, keenly. If he was lying, the acting was good.

'We need to know where you were at seven o'clock.'

'What? Oh, of course yer do, sir. Standard procedure. Close relatives are always the first suspects. No offence taken, by the way. I know it's the job. Good god! Poor little Evie.' He sat down again as if too overcome by the news to be able to stand up. Alfie just knew he'd have an alibi. He was playing the game too well not to have an alibi. Seth rubbed the back of his neck.

'Seven o'clock? What time is it now? Ten ter nine. I'll have been here. That's right. I was messing with the car earlier, then that Mr Campion came round. Jesus! I hope it was nothing ter do with that.'

'With what?' asked DI Foulds.

'With what he came round about. Jesus. What the hell's happening, sir?'

'I think it might be better if you told us. Who's Mr Campion? Is he a neighbour?'

Seth held his head in his hands. 'Look,' he said, 'it might be better if you asked Mr Campion.'

'This Mr Campion,' pressed the inspector, 'was he here around seven o'clock?'

Seth looked suitably confused – as confused as a man ought to be if he'd just been given the news of his niece's murder and was now being asked to verify the exact time of Mr Campion's visit.

'What? Oh, he were here quite a while. Yes, he were definitely here at seven o'clock – turned up right out of the blue, probably around half past six. Stayed a good hour. He was asking me about a letter he'd got from Lola – that's Evie's sister.'

'Letter?' said Alfie. 'Why would Lola write to him?'

'Because he's her MP.'

Alfie didn't notice the triumphant glint in Seth's eyes as he casually dropped in the priceless fact that Campion was Clive Campion MP. It was Alfie who had given her his address. If Campion verified this, Seth's alibi was cast iron.

Campion hadn't planned on going back to London that night; it just seemed a safe thing to do. If the police were going to question him it was better to be questioned on his home territory – the House of Commons. On top of which they'd have to follow him down from Leeds, which would give him ample time to compose himself and get his story straight. Although if that moron Lawless had messed things up and implicated him . . . it was a prospect not worth contemplating. He rang Seth from King's Cross station. It was one o'clock in the morning. Seth took some time to answer due to him having to get out of bed and come downstairs.

'What?' he said, cantankerously.

'It's me, how did you get on with the police?'

'Bloody hell! Why couldn't it wait until morning?'

Seth's annoyance gave Campion some comfort. He was more annoyed about being dragged out of his bed than worried about the police. On top of which he was still at home, not under lock and key. Campion was sufficiently relieved to apologize.

'Sorry, I just needed to know how you went on, in case the police get down here early to interview me.'

'I told 'em the truth. I told 'em yer came round at half past six to discuss that letter and yer didn't leave until around half seven. They told me Evie had been drowned in the river. Knocked me for six, that did.'

'What exactly did we discuss about the letter?'

'I didn't go into details,' Seth said. 'It's always best not ter go into details.'

'I may be asked to go into details,' said Campion. He took Lola's letter from his pocket. 'Listen to this, it's the letter Lola sent me. This is what we discussed.'

He read the letter, with Seth listening intently, then Campion added, 'I will tell the police that you and I discussed the possibility of her overreacting to a series of coincidences, but I said I'd look into it just in case she was right. All you need give them, if asked, is the general gist of our conversation,

do you understand, Seth? I'm laying my neck on the line for
you.'

'There are two necks on the line as far as I can see,' Seth
retorted. 'Just you stick ter your end of the story and we're
home and dry.'

'You mean you're home and dry.'

'We're in this together,' Seth reminded him.

'Are you absolutely sure no one saw you?'

'Absolutely sure. It were Sunday evening. It's very quiet
on a Sunday evening.'

Campion put the phone down. The problem had probably
been averted, but it hadn't gone away. In fact it was worse
now than ever. With Evie's death the situation was now ex-
acerbated. When Lola found out about Seth's alibi she would
know Campion was lying. Her word against his wouldn't be
enough to get a prosecution but she would know he and Seth
were behind her family's misery, and she would tell anyone
who would listen, including that damned newspaper reporter.
She needed to be silenced or completely disgraced. And
silencing her was too risky after this latest botched-up effort.

As he walked out of the station to the taxi rank his thoughts
went to Mrs Penfold. Did she still hate Lola as much as she
had after the bucket incident? Did she blame Lola for the death
of her son? There was a grandchild now. There was a jobless
widow with a child, with no family to support her and with a
criminal record, who had been there at the time of her sister's
death. In fact she was the only person there. And she'd blamed
a policeman for it. A policeman who was her uncle and guardian
and who could prove, without doubt, that he was nowhere near
the scene of the crime. A cruel and obviously false accusation.

He climbed into the taxi, nodding to himself. A plan was
unfurling in his sharp brain. He was smiling now. All he had
to do was keep Seth out of it.

Lola sat in an interview room opposite DI Foulds and Alfie,
who tried to offer her a reassuring smile.

'Mrs Penfold,' began the inspector, 'the story you told us
about events leading up to your sister's death have been
refuted by Seth Lawless.'

'He's hardly going to admit to it, is he?'

'It's not quite as simple as that, Mrs Penfold. You see,

Mr Lawless has an impeccable witness to verify his where-abouts at the time of your sister's death.'

'I've no doubt dear old Uncle Seth has impeccable witnesses coming out of his ears. From what I hear a lot of people owe him favours.' Most of the stories that she'd heard about Seth had come from Alfie, who was hoping she wouldn't involve him in this. 'It's common knowledge,' she said, scathingly, 'that Seth's as bent as nine-bob note. Surely someone must have seen him chasing Evie?'

'Plenty of people saw her being pulled out of the river,' said Alfie, almost apologetically, 'but we can't turn up anyone who saw her going in.'

'It appears that you're the sole witness to that,' added the inspector, accusingly.

'It is possible that someone might have recognized Seth and not wanted to get involved,' Alfie put in. 'There are some dodgy characters down that end of Leeds.'

The inspector shot him a glance that told him to stick to writing his notes and stop sticking up for her. Lola tried to think back to the incident, but she'd been so focused on Evie and Seth that she'd been oblivious to all else.

'All I can tell you is what happened,' Lola said. 'I saw Seth chasing Evie down Briggate. She ran down to the river. The next thing I saw was him lifting her up and throwing her in. I jumped in after her.'

'That will go in your favour,' said Foulds.

'My favour?'

The inspector nodded. 'There will be a full investigation into your sister's death. The fact that you risked your own life trying to save her should help to absolve you of responsibility.'

Lola shook her head in amazement. 'Responsibility? I've just told you that I saw Seth Lawless murder my sister and you're absolving me of responsibility? Well, that's ever so big of you – I'm simply overcome with gratitude!'

'Lola,' said Alfie, 'Seth's alibi's cast iron.'

'Whoever gave him it is lying,' Lola retorted.

'And why would a member of parliament lie about a thing like that?' said Foulds. 'At the time of your sister's death he was talking to a Mr Clive Campion, who had gone to his house to discuss a letter which you had sent to Mr Campion.'

Lola gaped.

'Mrs Penfold, you did send Mr Campion a letter?'

Lola looked from the inspector to Alfie. 'Well – yes.'

'And the content of this letter,' said Foulds, 'was about your family being persecuted by persons unknown?'

'But, it's true, isn't it, Alfie?'

Alfie gave a shrug. Foulds gave a frown. 'PC Bruce is here to take notes of the interview, not to pass comment. Mrs Penfold, your version of events is patently untrue. DC Lawless wasn't at the scene of the incident and the more you insist that he was, the worse it will be for you.'

'All I can tell you is what happened,' said Lola, firmly. She could feel anger rising within her. Her voice rose an octave. 'I've no doubt you're one of the people who think my mother was justifiably hanged and that my sister was treated fairly over the last few years of her life.' She tapped the side of her head. 'Think about it, Inspector. Think about how it all adds up to two and two making five. Do your bloody job, Inspector!' She got to her feet and went to the door. 'The only explanation is that Seth Lawless and Campion are in it together.' Then to Alfie, she added, 'Make sure you get that down, PC Bruce!'

For several minutes after Lola's departure the inspector and Alfie sat there, completely bemused. The silence was broken by Foulds.

'You know her, PC Bruce. What do you think?'

'I'm confused, sir. If Mr Campion hadn't backed him up I'd have taken Lola's word against Seth's any day of the week.'

'So, you think Seth's as bent as nine-bob note as well, do you?'

'He's not my favourite person, sir, nor was his brother.'

Foulds rubbed his chin. 'Hmm. Under normal circumstances I'd take a closer look at the witness. But how the hell do you take a closer look at a Home Office minister? And why on earth would a Home Office minister put his neck on the line for Seth bloody Lawless?'

'I don't know, sir – but there may be those who do.'

Foulds nodded, slowly. 'Trouble is, I can't ignore an accusation such as this, but I must tread very carefully.' He lit a cigarette and sat back in his chair. Then he looked at Alfie, as if trying to remember something. 'Haven't you applied for a transfer to CID?'

'Yes, sir. I applied some months ago, sir.'

'Then consider your transfer approved.'

'Oh, thank you, sir.'

Foulds waved away his thanks. 'Don't thank me; you may live to regret it. Among the other work we find for you I want you to follow this business up and report only to me. No one else, just me. I don't want our suspicions about Mr Campion to become common knowledge.'

'So, we do have our suspicions, do we, sir?'

'Let's say it's a mystery that needs solving. If what that woman has been saying is true, it's massive, with far-reaching implications. Oh, and if you say anything about this to Lola you'll be back in uniform before you know it. As far as you're concerned she's been giving us a complete pack of lies. I want DC Lawless, your new colleague, to be completely off his guard, him and Mr Campion both – that's if they've got anything to hide. We could be on a wild goose chase but we need to know the truth of the matter.'

'Very good, sir.'

Twenty-Five

March 1957

Evie had been dead a month now. How she would have loved to have celebrated Danny's first birthday. How she would have spoiled him and cuddled him. How Lola dearly wished Evie were here, if only to tell these people the truth. Such thoughts were going through her head as she watched her son waddle, unsteadily, towards Owd Sal, whom Lola had met at Evie's funeral. Danny had been walking just a week, but now he was on his feet there was no stopping him.

Her mind was out of kilter, as her mam would have said. She wasn't thinking straight. Alfie was there as well, as were

Theresa Tomelty, Tommy Pearson and Mr Jessop. Theresa had baked Danny a cake with his name on and a candle sticking out of the middle. They had sung 'Happy Birthday' and laughed as Tommy blew the candle out, pretending it was Danny who had done it. Lola felt like an onlooker from afar, like she was watching a theatre play from the gods.

All the voices seemed so distant and echoing and not in touch with her reality; the reality that had taken her sister and her mother away from her. Both unjustly killed. Only she knew the truth. They had all been so nice and condescending and so earnest in the attention they had paid when she had told of how Seth had killed Evie and how Clive Campion MP was one of those plotting against her. She had worked it all out. Campion was the one responsible for her mother being hanged. They had all nodded their agreement, but she could see in their eyes that they thought she was barmy, coming up with such an idea.

And there were times when she thought she was barmy as well. Had she got things mixed up? After all, it was she who had involved Campion in all this. He hadn't involved himself. She had written to him for help and then accused him of being one of her persecutors. People must think she's potty for making such an accusation. In fact, she was surrounded by people who probably thought she was potty, only they were too polite to say so.

'He's a lovely kid,' Sal said. 'He's a credit to you, under the circumstances.'

'Bringing up kids is no great mystery,' Lola said, defensively. 'All you need is common sense and a lot of love.'

Sal saw the wariness in Lola's eyes, brought on by Sal's 'under the circumstances' remark. Unwittingly, Alfie made things worse.

'With all that's happened to Lola it's a wonder she's kept her sanity.'

'There's nothing wrong with my sanity, thank you very much.'

'Lola,' said Mr Jessop, 'we know there isn't. Alfie was just saying that a lot of people wouldn't have handled things as well as you.'

'Really? So, how do you think I handled seeing Seth murder Evie and no one believing me? Not even my friends.' She rounded on Alfie, who dearly wished he could tell her what he truly thought. 'What about you, Alfie? Do you think I saw Seth murder Evie? Do you think Campion's in on it?'

Alfie looked around the room. As much as he knew these people all had Lola's best interests at heart he couldn't trust them not to blab if they knew Campion was being investigated. Especially Lola, who definitely wasn't herself. One word in the wrong ear would put Seth and Campion on their guard. He forced out his reluctant answer.

'I have to keep an open mind on it, Lola.'

Lola looked at him. Her sad, bereft beauty almost melted him into taking her into his arms and telling her that he was on her side and that he definitely believed her and he was on the case at that very moment.

'An open mind, is that what you call it? Alfie, you either believe me or you don't believe me.' Her gaze swept around the others. 'Come on, hands up everyone who believes Seth killed Evie and Campion's covering for him?'

No one put their hand up. Theresa knelt in front of her and took her hand. 'It's not that we don't believe you, Lola. It's just that we wonder if you might have made a mistake in the heat of the moment. Sometimes your mind plays tricks when you're under stress.'

'We all want to believe you, Lola,' added Tommy. 'It's certainly not beyond the bounds of possibility. But – what if you're wrong? What if you were having some sort of mental delusion – which would be perfectly understandable, don't get me wrong – but if that's the case then you could be bringing a lot of trouble down on yourself. We only want to protect you, Lola.'

Sal was cuddling Danny and suddenly Lola realized that if they thought she was too barmy to remember what had gone on the night Evie died they might well think she wasn't fit to look after Danny. They might take him away from her. She snatched her son from Sal's arms and backed into a corner of the room, screaming at them.

'I don't want you, any of you! You don't believe me! You think I'm barmy! So, go and don't come back!'

Alfie couldn't stand this. By now he was as convinced as Lola was that Seth had killed Evie. But if he revealed his hand to anyone it might jeopardize his investigation; an investigation that hadn't yet got off the ground. These things took time, sometimes a long time, before any progress was made. Could he wait until everyone had gone, then confide in her and her alone? That might give her some comfort – in the short term. Then Inspector Foulds' words came to mind. 'Say anything to Lola and you'll be back in uniform before you know it.'

As he looked at Lola he knew the inspector had good reason to say this. She wasn't thinking straight. Hard as it was for him to admit it to himself, she couldn't be completely trusted to keep her mouth shut. Better, in the long run, to leave her in the dark for now. As much as that hurt.

'Lola,' he said, 'honestly, I'm really on your side.'

'We all are, Lola,' said Tommy, not wishing to be outdone by the man he considered his rival for Lola's affections.

Danny began to cry and they all thought it best to make themselves scarce. Each of them was determined to call in on Lola when she was thinking straight.

They hadn't been gone five minutes when there was a knock at the door. It was a man from Raglan Road Properties wanting rent which Lola didn't have.

'I haven't got it.'

Such was her attitude that she might just as well have added, 'So what are you going to do about it?'

'There's three weeks due, Mrs Penfold – four pounds four shillings.'

'I'll pay it next week.'

'But—'

But Lola had closed the door. Evie's funeral had cleaned her out – that and Danny's birthday. She put Danny's hungry mouth to her breast. At least he'd be OK. That was the main thing.

There were always people who would lend money to people such as her, until things picked up. She'd never used a money-lender before, but needs must. Somehow she'd have to find work that suited a young mother, a young widow. In the meantime she still had tears to shed. Tears of bereavement and guilt. Somehow she had let Evie down. Lola was the big sister; it had been her job to look after Evie. She should have tried harder.

Knowing who had been doing her this damage made it harder. Up until then she had occasionally taken solace from the fact that, just maybe, it was all a horrible coincidence. But now she knew for certain that they had been out to get her and her family all along. They being Seth Lawless and Campion. Where Campion fitted in, she hadn't a clue.

Would they kill her next, just as they'd killed her mam and her husband and her sister? Why were they doing this? Surely it couldn't be because of the way Ezra had died.

She sat down and allowed Danny to suck away contentedly. Ezra's death had something to do with this – or maybe not. Maybe Ezra's life had something to do with it. She remembered something she'd once told Evie.

'I'm sure that Dad did something really bad the night I killed him, and not just to Mam.'

Could that have been it? She'd seen her dad that night. She'd smashed his cuckoo clock and he'd beaten her and thrown her out into the street. Lola tried to remember the look in Ezra's eyes. Was it the look of a man who had done something really bad? Then she remembered Seth coming to visit her just after Mam had been hanged. She'd told him that Ezra would be rotting in hell, 'and we both know why'.

Seth had blanched when she slammed the door on him. Why was that? What was she missing?

Her thoughts were disturbed by another knock. She took a reluctant Danny from her breast and placed him on the floor. There was a second, more urgent knock as she was adjusting her dress.

'I'm coming,' she shouted, irritably.

At the door was a woman in a nurse's uniform and two policemen. The nurse handed Lola a piece of paper, a bit like the one Mrs Pritchard had given her, prior to taking Evie away.

'What's this?'

'It's an authorization for us to take your son into foster care until such time as you're considered a proper person to look after him.'

With all that had gone before she might have expected this. She had shouted her accusations about Seth and Campion to anyone who would listen, most of all the police, but of course no one had believed her, and now Campion was taking his revenge. That much was obvious. Campion. She'd never even met the man, and he was doing all this to her.

'Why are they doing this?' she screamed. 'Why won't they leave me alone?'

'No one's doing anything to you, madam.' The nurse sounded overly officious. 'Our primary concern is your son's safety. His grandmother's volunteered to take him until such time as you're well enough to look after him.'

'Well enough? Who says I'm not well enough to look after my own son? That bloody witch'll be in cahoots with bastard Campion! I've already worked that one out. That's why they fined me twenty pounds for tipping a bucket of water over her head. He was behind that. It shouldn't even have got to court. I wish she'd bloody drowned!'

Danny toddled to her side, one of the policemen stepped quickly forward and picked him up. Lola hurled herself at him, punching him with all her might, but he turned his back on the blows. The other policeman grabbed Lola's flailing arm and pushed her back inside the house.

'Take the child to the car, please,' the nurse ordered. 'I'll wait here with Mrs Penfold.'

Lola was fighting the policeman, trying to get at her son when she passed out.

Twenty-Six

It was an effort to open her eyes and when she did she didn't recognize the flickering fluorescent tube in the ceiling above her. Lola was in a bed, but wherever this was she wasn't at home. She had only a vague recollection of what had happened to her that day. She ran her hands across her body and realized that someone had taken her clothes and dressed her in a sort of hospital gown.

The walls and ceiling were white, as were her bedclothes. The only thing that wasn't white was the dark green door, which was closed. She desperately wanted to know what was on the other side of the door but her limbs felt too heavy to move her from the bed, so she just lay there and closed her eyes. Two hours later she woke up again. This time the light had stopped flickering and she was able to push herself up on to her elbows. The dark green door was now open and beyond it was a woman in a pale green nurse's uniform sitting at a table, writing. Lola tried to call her but she had no voice. What the hell was happening?

Exhausted, she lay back down and began crying, only she didn't know what she was crying about. She knew there was something to cry about but she couldn't think what. Once again she fell asleep and when she awoke a man was standing over her. He had a short, white beard, a white coat and a stethoscope around his neck. There was just too much white about this place. He placed the stethoscope to Lola's chest and asked her to take a few deep breaths, but she didn't want to take deep breaths for this man. She wanted to know where she was.

'Where is this place?'

'You're in a hospital.'

'Hospital? Have I been in an accident? What happened to me?'

'Would you lie on your side, please, I want to listen to your back.'

Lola turned on her side and read a notice on the wall about hospital hygiene. It was headed Allerton Park Hospital.

'Excuse me,' she said. 'Is this Allerton Park Hospital?'

'Yes, it is,' replied the doctor, placing a thermometer in her mouth. Lola took it out.

'Which means I'm in a mental hospital,' she said. 'What am I doing in a mental hospital?'

The doctor gave her a patient smile. 'I wish I had a pound for every time I've been asked that question. I'm afraid you've had a form of mental breakdown. We've brought you here to get you well.'

'Bloody hell! You've drugged me, haven't you?' She tried to express her rage but couldn't. Her words were coming out in little more than a murmur.

'We've just given you something to calm you down. It'll wear off, then you and I can have a good talk about your treatment.'

'Treatment? I don't need treatment. Where's my boy?' She remembered her reason for crying now. Tears arrived in floods. 'They stole my boy off me. Please, I want my baby.'

'One thing at a time, Mrs Penfold. First we have to get you better.'

'Mrs Penfold? That's who's got him, isn't it?'

'I believe he's being looked after by his grandmother, yes.'

'She's stolen him. She'll have cooked this up with Campion.'

'You must try and calm down, Mrs Penfold. It's this irrational behaviour that's got you in here. No one's cooked anything up.'

Lola held him in her gaze. 'I'm sorry but you're wrong, doctor,' she said. 'Please don't treat me for something I haven't got. Please don't let them take my son away from me.'

He returned her gaze and said, patronizingly, 'Young lady, the first step in your treatment is to get you to accept that you're ill. Once you do that, the rest becomes easier.'

Lola didn't know how to answer this. She just closed her eyes and vowed to change her name from Penfold at the first opportunity. She would go back to being Lawless as a sign of respect for her mother and her sister, and she would stay Lawless until she had seen justice done for them both. Somehow it seemed appropriate. But her first job was to get out of this place and get her son back.

Mrs Sylvia Penfold had had her grandson's room ready for a week. A live-in nanny had been carefully selected from seven applicants, baby food had been bought and a complete range of toddler's clothing awaited him. Within days of his arrival she was making enquiries as to how she might change the infant's name from the very working-class Danny to something more suitable. She was currently favouring Marcus. The authorities told her that this could only happen if she legally adopted the boy. Mrs Penfold told them that it was only a question of time as the boy's mother was in a lunatic asylum and was unlikely ever to be regarded as a fit parent. If there was a problem she knew she could rely on her friend, Clive Campion MP, to move things along a bit. He'd done well for her so far.

Lola was sitting on a chair in the corner, gazing around the day room. One man was sitting, back to front, on a wooden

dining chair, trying to gallop it around the room like a
horse, with accompaning noises. Another was reading out
loud from a book, but it soon became obvious that the
written word had no connection with the spoken word. There
was easy-to-clean lino on the floor, magnolia gloss paint
on the walls and no pictures or ornaments for the patients
to break. All in all it was a dismal room that smelled of
Dettol and urine. In another corner was a crying woman
who, by the state of her, had just peed herself. A male nurse
was smoking and reading a newspaper. Lola called over
to him.

'That lady's had an accident, shouldn't someone be helping
her?'

The nurse looked up at Lola, then at the woman, then returned
his attention to the newspaper, as if Lola didn't exist. This
annoyed her.

'Excuse me, I'm talking to you. That lady needs help. What
do they pay you for?'

'Just behave yourself, Lola.'

'Since when was asking you to do your job classified as
misbehaving?'

The nurse wasn't used to any of the patients making sense;
he certainly wasn't used to any of them sounding more intelligent than he was. Perplexed, he got to his feet and went off
in search of a doctor – someone who could better deal with
Lola.

An old woman in a wheelchair was asking when she could
go home and a younger woman was shouting obscenities at
the wall. Lola had been there three days and no one had been
to discuss her problem with her. There were bars on the
windows and all external doors were locked. When she asked
why she was being kept locked up she was told it was for
her own safety. For two days she wept in fear and frustration. She wept for Danny and for Evie and for her mother
and for Keith. That morning she had woken up with the real-
ization that she was beginning to succumb to the insanity
that was surrounding her – which would be Campion's plan.
To make her think she was as potty as the other inmates. So
she stopped crying and began to think. She thought about
many things. The fact that Campion had verified Seth's alibi
told her everything she needed to know about the man who

was her representative in parliament. How the hell was she supposed to deal with him?

On the positive side she knew that at some stage she would have visitors. Alfie or Tommy or Theresa would come. Surely they couldn't stop people visiting her or suspicions would be aroused. How she wished she hadn't sent them all off with fleas in their ears on Danny's birthday.

What she didn't know was that Alfie had tracked her down via Mrs Penfold senior, who, to his amazement, was looking after Danny. She wasn't very forthcoming, apart from being eager to tell him that Lola had had a mental breakdown. He had already rung up the hospital and asked if he could call in for a visit, but had been told by an apologetic administrator that she didn't want to see anyone. This tallied with her attitude the last time Alfie had seen her so, with some regret, he passed the news on to the others.

'I've no doubt she'll see us when she's good and ready.'

He said it more to ease their worries than his own. There was something about all this he didn't like. He knew she'd been acting strange – he'd seen it first hand – but there was something about her going into a psychiatric hospital that he didn't understand. Who had taken her there? Had she gone there herself, realizing she wasn't thinking straight, seeking help? This didn't make sense. If you're sane enough to realize you're mad, then you can't be mad. You must be sane, much too sane to book yourself into a mad house. And surely there was no way she'd let her mother-in-law look after Danny. It didn't occur to him that the authorities would be anything other than scrupulous.

The hospital superintendent was most uncomfortable about the whole situation and had covered himself by sending a letter to the Health Ministry, setting out his fears. The man in the Health Ministry, who had given the hospital instructions regarding Lola, immediately rang Campion at the Home Office.

'I hope we're doing the right thing, sir, regarding the Penfold woman up in Leeds. We have her in our most secure unit and yet I'm not sure that she's a suitable case for treatment under the compulsory detention section of the Mental Health Act. We don't even have the appropriate paperwork to cover us.'

'I've cleared it at the highest level,' Campion assured him, brusquely. 'The woman is mentally unstable and poses a security risk.'

'The trouble is I'm not sure how she could be a security risk, sir.'

'Of course you aren't, it's not your business to know. Please don't discuss this with anyone. Just ensure that the woman is kept secure, it's for her own safety and for that of the country. It won't do your career prospects any harm either. I have the ear of Mr Wilcox, your departmental head, but I don't want you to embarrass him by discussing this with him.'

Campion was reading from a sheet of paper listing the hierarchy within the Health Ministry. He had picked out a name two rungs up the ladder from the man he was talking to. It had the desired effect.

'Mr Wilcox, really? Well, of course I wouldn't wish to embarrass him. Erm, how long shall we hold her for?'

The unspoken answer on Campion's lips was, *As long as it takes for her story about her sister's death to lose all credibility.*

'Just keep me posted as to her mental progress.'

'This could lead to her mental disintegration,' warned the man from the Health Ministry.

This brought a smile to Campion's lips. 'Oh, don't be so dramatic. I'm sure it won't come to that.'

He would rather it led to her complete disintegration, mentally and physically. He would like to have added the complete disintegration of Seth Lawless as well. These two people threatened his whole future. Would that he had the murderous tendencies of Lawless. With his authority and influence – and perhaps a little blackmail – he could doubtless summon the means of their demise. Maybe it would come to that. He hoped it wouldn't, but the alternative didn't bear thinking about.

He knew that power was the great corrupter of man. He knew that in all governments disgraceful things go on behind the scenes that are hidden beneath a cloak of secrecy. He knew of a certain country house party where a senior cabinet minister had eaten his food from a dog bowl, naked except for a mask. He knew of people who procured prostitutes for high-ranking government officials, and he knew of at least one person who had become a loose cannon, and who had died mysteriously.

Campion regarded himself as a major player in the government game, and as a major player he considered himself to be due certain privileges not accorded to the common man. Privileges such as getting away with murder.

They had given Lola a room of her own. She couldn't figure that one out. As far as she could tell she was the only patient with a room of her own. It had its own toilet and wash basin, which meant they could lock her in on a night without too much discomfort to her. Her only sources of contact were green-uniformed nurses and some other people who wore grey. The white-coated doctor she'd seen on her arrival hadn't been back to see her.

'Why do you lock me in on a night?' she had asked her question of a man who wore a grey uniform with some sort of badge on it.

'It's standard procedure for Category A patients. By the way, my name is Mr Frampton, you must always call me by my name when speaking to me, then I know who you're talking to.'

'What's a Category A patient, Mr Frampton?'

'You are, Lola.'

'Thank you.'

At first she had been given tablets to take, which she had refused.

'I don't take tablets, never have.'

'Maybe if you had, you wouldn't be in here.'

'What are they for?'

'To make you better.'

'I want to stay as I am, thank you very much.'

'Lola, if you stay as you are you'll stay where you are.'

Bernard Frampton was thirty-seven years old and a ward orderly. He had no qualifications. Finding people to do menial work in a mental hospital was hard enough without insisting on qualifications. His job was to lift, fetch, carry, restrain, and occasionally to administer medication, especially to reluctant patients whose tantrums took up too much time for the qualified staff to bother with.

Outside work, to the few people who listened to him, he

referred to himself as a doctor. A doctor was the job of his dreams, but he was neither intellectually nor psychologically up to such a job.

He had been at Allerton Park for just a month. It was the fourth mental hospital he'd worked at in his fifteen years in the job. Each of his previous transfers had been forced on him by hospital personnel departments who really wanted to sack him but found it easier to give him a threat and a sideways promotion, always accompanied by a reference that was just enough to give satisfaction but containing nothing that could be construed as a downright lie. Frampton carried with him a reputation for cleanliness and punctuality. Had anyone put the truth in his reference it would have mentioned that he was a creepy bastard who was suspected of interfering with patients. But, with the patients all being mentally ill they would make poor witnesses at any disciplinary hearing. It was always much easier to pass the problem on to someone else.

The very second that Frampton clapped eyes on Lola he made up his mind to have her. When she was so drugged up that she wouldn't put up a fight he would have her. The fact that Allerton Park knew nothing of his reputation helped enormously. He always had more fun during the first few months of a new job. He especially liked the fact that drugs were being administered to Lola covertly, hidden in her meals, which probably meant she wasn't a proper nutter, just someone who needed to be controlled, against her will, by the chemical cosh. He'd come across a few of those in his time.

Twenty-Seven

On her seventh day at the hospital Lola sat on her bed and tried to remember things. Her memories of Evie and Danny weren't as sharp as they should be. She knew she used to work in a shoe shop and yet she couldn't remember the name of the man she worked for. She tried to remember her mother. Her mother had always been in her thoughts. Lola remembered her mother always being in her thoughts. But she wasn't there now. Why was that? Why had her mother gone from her thoughts? Why did she struggle to tie her shoelaces?

In the top drawer of her bedside table was a Gideon Bible. She was staring at this when some tiny window in her mind allowed a beacon of light inside; enough to tell her this wasn't right. She knew what the book was because she could read the cover – Holy Bible Placed By The Gideons – but the words inside made no sense. She knew what the individual words said, but she couldn't connect them to make up sentences and, more importantly, she knew this wasn't right. She knew she could read. They were doing something to her to make her like this. She hadn't taken their tablets. Someone or something had told her right from the start that tablets were bad. It was the one thing she'd clung to. Tablets were bad. Don't take the tablets.

Had she still been able to read the Gideon Bible she'd have seen written on the page 3 index, scrawled in red crayon alongside the word 'Commandments', were the words 'Thou Shalt Not Take The Tablets', presumably written by another dissatisfied patient. She had read it on the first day and, at the time, it made complete sense. She had since forgotten where this commandment came from. But now she remembered it. She remembered this and she knew what she must do. They were beating her and she mustn't let them win.

Her food was always brought to her in her room. Everyone else ate in the dining room. Lola concentrated every molecule of her brain thinking this through. Tablets, the forbidden tablets would have to go into her mouth. That's how you take tablets. And she knew she wasn't taking them. She didn't know much but she knew that. The only other thing that went into her mouth was food. Her clouded logic told her this could mean only one thing: the tablets were in the food. She must stop eating. It was the only thing that made sense to her. The trouble was that the food was delicious. The only good thing about her life right now was the delicious food. It was lunchtime right now and she'd been sent to her room to await her meal. A key rattled in the door and Frampton brought in a wooden tray containing food that smelled mouth-watering.

Lola didn't know what it was, although she still recognized potatoes. Potatoes are hard things to forget. She also knew it smelled nice, and she knew it would taste nice.

The orderly placed it on a table along with a tin mug of tea, a plastic knife and fork and a large, linen napkin.

'Eat it all up, Lola.'

'Yes.'

'Yes, Mr Frampton. You haven't forgotten my name, have you, Lola?'

'No . . . Mr Frampton.'

He knew she had, which made her almost ready. Soon he'd be on night shifts; that's when he'd make his move. He gave her a smile that made her shudder and left, locking the door behind him. It would be opened again in an hour when Lola could go to the dayroom to sit and stare out of the window.

She sat on her bed and glared at the food. Suddenly she hated it. She took it through to the lavatory and flushed it away, including the mug of tea which came with every meal. She did the same with her evening meal and the following morning, despite the pangs of hunger, she flushed away her bacon and eggs, all the time smiling when the empty plates were taken away. By the following lunchtime she had gone twenty-four hours without food. The only thing that had passed her lips was water from the tap in her room. Her stomach was empty but her head was clearer than it had been since she arrived. It was clear enough for her to know for certain that her food was being drugged. It was also clear enough for her to act as though she were drugged up to the eyeballs.

For tea she was given two boiled eggs. She stared at them, long and hard, wondering how they could tamper with boiled eggs. How can you put drugs into an egg without breaking the shell? They could have injected the eggs with a syringe. She examined the shells, looking for a pinprick hole; there wasn't one. Maybe it wasn't the eggs, maybe it was the bread, or the mug of tea. She ate the eggs but threw away the tea and the bread. By lights out at nine o'clock she still felt OK. Still hungry, but her brain was almost back to normal – normal enough to figure out that they didn't have to drug everything they gave her. Maybe not even every meal. For her to get out of this place and get Danny back she'd have to be both mentally alert and physically strong. Figuring out what was drugged and what wasn't would be a simple process of elimination. She figured it would be harder to drug a potato or a sausage, or a rasher of bacon, than putting a drug in a drink. Drugged tea must be the hot favourite. The following morning she ate the whole of her breakfast, but didn't drink her mug of tea. At lunchtime she felt OK. She tested herself by reading a passage from the bible. When her midday meal came she drank the tea and threw away the meal. By teatime she couldn't read properly, so she threw away tea and ate the food. The following morning she was back to normal. The hot favourite had romped home. The only thing containing drugs was the tea. This told her two things: she was in the care of evil people; but none of them was an Einstein. None of them was as clever as Lola.

But regaining her senses came at a price. She now remembered Evie's death, she remembered what had happened to her mother and Keith and, worst of all, the deep hurt returned at the enforced absence of her son. An absence enforced by powerful people who had arranged her mother's hanging and her sister's and Keith's murders. What chance did she have? It made her cry continually. They assumed she was crying for no reason. Nutters have no reason to cry because nutters have no sense of reason.

'What are you crying for, Lola?'

'Nothing.'

'Nothing, Mr Frampton.'

'Nothing, Mr Frampton.'

She shook her head. Her grief was no business of his. He took her hand and stroked it. His flesh against hers felt revolting but she tried not to show it.

'There you are, you see. You don't know. If you don't know why you're crying, why bother? It's a waste of water.'

Out of all of them she disliked him the most. Some were actually quite nice. Maybe they meant well. Maybe they were only small cogs in a big wheel. Maybe they didn't know what they were doing was wrong. They were just obeying orders. She was sorely tempted to start drinking their tea again and make it all go away. In her weakened state she could think of no other way.

After two days of weeping she had the tea to her mouth. Tears were tumbling down her face and dripping into the cup. Just one sip gave her a feeling of self-loathing. She was letting Danny down, removing all chance of him ever escaping the clutches of that witch. She was also letting them get away with it.

She dried her tears, figuring they were mostly tears of self-pity. She must play them at their own game. She must pretend to be so gormless that her watchers would drop their guard. So she took up humming and scratching herself and smiling at nothing. Whenever a nurse, or Frampton, or anyone in authority, came into the room she would stare into the middle distance, and practise her humming and smiling and scratching. Very soon she became invisible. The superintendent sent a report back to Campion that his patient was quiet and subdued as per instructions. He was told to keep her this way until told otherwise. The superintendent knew that continual use of this drug would eventually do irreparable damage to her central nervous system. His other patients were weaned off it from time to time to see how they were doing. Mostly they did very badly. Very few of the weaners, as they were called, ever came off the drug permanently. In any case, no such weaning for Lola; the superintendent had a career to look after. You can't look after a patient and a career with equal dedication. Something has to give.

Most of the Category A patients were allowed out of the building to take a supervised walk around the block. On her sixteenth day Lola was allowed to join them. There were six other buildings in the grounds, all of them much less secure than Ward 4, which was in its own compound, surrounded by a high, chain-link fence.

As she trudged along in the muttering, mindless caterpillar, she bowed her head, as if in a dream world of her own, and as they turned a corner she carried on at a tangent and wandered towards the fence. She had her arms folded across her front and she frequently nodded her head as if in agreeable conversation with herself. From the edge of her eyes she surveyed the fence, which was too high to climb over but, in places, not impossible to squeeze under, where the ground fell away from the bottom wire. She noted the best spot and lined it up with a lamp post and a distant building. Even if she came here at night she could walk straight to it. A nurse called out to her.

'Lola, don't go wandering off.'

Lola looked upwards, as if wondering where the voice was coming from, then she twitched her head as if listening to hear it again. Gormless.

'Over here, Lola. Come back over here.'

Lola looked around and gave the shouting nurse her very best asinine smile, before walking back to join the shuffling line of Category A patients. She wondered what they had done to deserve this treatment. The trouble was that there was no way she could hold an intelligent conversation with any of them. The chemical cosh had done its work on them. Subdued them, just as Lola was supposed to be subdued. If she tried to engage any of them in intelligent conversation her pretence would be discovered. In any case, there would be no point in trying. No one in this ward could understand sense – and that appeared to include most of the nurses. How the hell could they believe they were doing the right thing, drugging the personalities out of the people who were in their care? If these people had tears to cry let them cry. If they had demons to chase, join in the chase, give them a helping hand. Wasn't that their job?

It must have been obvious to them that Lola wasn't beyond psychiatric help. Surely they could see she wasn't like the rest? How many of the patients had come in as disturbed people, requiring expert help and understanding, and become drugged-up zombies?

Her sense of loss was deep. Evie was dead and her son had been taken from her. She knew she would just have to mourn for Evie in the way that everyone has to mourn – in the way she mourned her mother. In the end the hurt would diminish. It had with her mother; it would with Evie. The dreadful memory would never go, but the hurt would diminish.

What she would never be able to handle was losing her darling son. He was alive but had been stolen from her. Stolen by that witch – with the help of Seth bloody Lawless and a government minister. Jesus! How much sense did that make? It didn't make sense, that's how much sense it made. None at all.

Whatever sense it didn't make didn't alter the facts. Seth

had lied and his lie had been backed up by The Right
Honourable Clive Campion MP. At the moment she had
neither the time nor the surplus energy to figure this out. All
her energy must be directed into getting Danny back. After
which she'd kick up the biggest stink of all time.

When she escaped it would do no harm to take a sample of
her drugged tea with her. Something to back up her story.
Now she was *compos mentis* she would memorize every detail
of her life in here until she got out. Not only what they were
doing to her, but what was happening to the other patients
as well. She would give all the information she had to Tommy,
who fancied her like mad. That hadn't escaped her notice.
Maybe he'd come through for her where Alfie had failed her.
That was another troubling aspect of her return to sanity. She
had over estimated Alfie, which was unusual for her. She was
usually pretty good at sizing people up. If her emotions hadn't
been in so much turmoil she would have realized just how
much being let down by Alfie had hurt her.

Twenty-Eight

'*I'm sure that Dad did something really bad the night I
killed him, and not just to Mam.*'
The memory of Evie's words came to Lola as she poured
the drugged tea into a vacuum flask she'd stolen from a kitchen
cupboard. She had gone in looking for a bottle but when she
saw the flask it seemed the very thing. Things were falling into
place for her. She had been hovering near the kitchen when the
cleaners had knocked on the front door to be let in. Frampton
had gone to the door and had patted his pockets for a key that
didn't seem to be there. He shouted through to the cleaners.

'Edna's got me key, I'll have to nip upstairs and get it.'
The reply was impatient. 'It'd be a lot quicker ter get the
one from the kitchen.'

'Oh, aye, forgot about that.'

Unseen, Lola followed Frampton to the kitchen and paused at the door long enough to see him open a drawer and take out a key. She smiled to herself. It wasn't exactly Alcatraz. With this level of incompetence a way to get out of her room on a night should soon present itself.

Escaping, along with her sanity, was only half the battle. She needed to find somewhere to go. Could she go back home? Doubtful. With her rent already well in arrears when she had been taken from her house the odds were that someone else would be living there now. What about her furniture and belongings? Probably sold off to pay the arrears. Oddly, she found answering her own questions to be a comfort. It meant she was thinking straight, and straight thinking was very important. That's what she told herself. OK, Miss Smarty-Pants, answer this. So, where do you go once you're out?

Miss Smarty-Pants came up with several suggestions. Mr Jessop would help, but it would be limited to maybe lending her a few quid. That strange woman who had befriended and helped Evie – Sal – she'd be ideal. Trouble was, Lola had no idea where to find her. She evidently lived on a boat in Keighley. Under normal circumstances Lola would contact Alfie, but he'd let her down once already, hadn't he? Well, he certainly hadn't gone out of his way to help her. Hadn't been to visit her once. Come to think of it, none of them had. Why was that? Theresa might help out, in the short term. But it was long-term help she needed.

She'd gone all around the houses, eliminating all options but one. The one she knew she'd end up with. Tommy. Tommy could help in many ways. He knew stuff. He knew people. And he wasn't scared of kicking up a stink. Maybe he'd even let her stay at his house until she got on her feet. She knew where he lived, which was a bonus. She also knew she would be taking advantage of his infatuation with her. Was that so wrong? Not if she didn't give him any false hope in exchange for his help. In any case, she didn't know herself how she felt about him. Maybe there was something there.

Another week went by and she was no nearer to finding a way out of her room on a night. The end of that week coincided with Frampton taking his turn on the night shift. It was his favourite shift. Had it not been liable to arouse too much suspicion he would have volunteered for permanent nights. Short of being a proper doctor, permanent nights in a nuthouse was his ideal job. He knew Lola was ripe for it. As he cycled to work the very thought of her lying helpless and naked beneath him gave him an erection that made cycling difficult. He had bought a packet of three French letters. One and ninepence from the barber's. He couldn't wait for the barber to rub Brilliantine on his finished haircut and ask him if he wanted something for the weekend.

'Oh aye, a packet of three, please,' Frampton had smirked.

Unlike most young men, who were embarrassed about such things, he had even enjoyed asking for them. It showed the barber he was really a bit of a lad, not short of female company.

Making a patient pregnant was a bad move. He'd made one pregnant in Menston Hospital and had been a prime suspect. He simply denied it and his victim was so confused that it didn't even merit a disciplinary hearing. There had been an abortion and he'd been moved on.

Lola was sound asleep when the key rattled in her lock. She turned over, with her back to him, as Frampton stripped off and climbed into her bed. His left hand slid under her nightdress and caressed her breasts, giving him an immediate erection that he pressed into her backside. Lola felt this and woke up, terrified. What the hell was happening? Then the hand moved down to her knickers and started to pull them down. She screamed and jumped out of bed. Her scream was heard by a nurse no more than thirty feet away. The nurse looked up, then returned her attention to her book. Screams in the night were normal in this place.

Lola recognized Frampton in the dim light coming through a gap in the curtains. All her hatred of Ezra and Seth and Campion returned and fuelled the rage she needed to deal with this situation. She picked up a bedside lamp, yanked its plug from the wall and, in the same movement, dealt Frampton a heavy blow to the head. It was the last thing he expected from this woman who was supposed to be helpless. He fell back on to the bed, unconscious. Lola stared at him. She was breathing heavily, wondering if she should call for help. She switched on a light and looked at him from a distance. He didn't seem to be breathing. To confirm this she'd have to take a closer look. Check his pulse, listen to his heart. No way. His erection was subsiding and she turned her eyes away from it and tried the door. It was open. The opportunity had presented itself in the form of a rapist – maybe even a dead rapist. He still wasn't moving. She had a vision of her moving towards him and checking to see if he was alive, and him springing to life and grabbing her. Finishing what he'd come to do. She'd seen such things happen at the pictures.

Watching him out of the corner of her eye Lola quickly dressed herself. She had the presence of mind to grab the thermos flask and stuff it in her pocket. Then, with one last look at the motionless form on her bed, she turned out her light, closed the door and moved, silently, along the corridor towards the kitchen. Please let the door key be in the drawer. It was. Thank God. There was a light coming from the half-open door to the office where the night duty nurse was reading her book. A floorboard creaked beneath her feet. The nurse called out, 'That you, Bernard?'

'Aye,' said Lola in a deep voice that wasn't so far off Frampton's. She hurried towards the main door, placed the key in the lock and held her breath as the levers clicked into place. She was outside now, pulling the door closed. Silently.

The night duty nurse was engrossed in her book and Frampton lay, unmoving, on Lola's bed. She couldn't get him out of her mind. Had she killed him? If so, what then? With her reputation she had no chance of being believed. They'd probably accuse her of luring him into her bed so she could steal the keys. Did this mean that escaping under these circum-stances was unwise? She could be found guilty of murder, just like her mother – and hanged. Like mother, like daughter, they'd say. Her blood ran cold at the thought. Should she go back and scream the place down? Cry rape?

Bit late now. The nurse would wonder who had spoken to her just now. It couldn't have been Frampton, nor did it sound like an hysterical rape victim. Lola ran across the grass towards the fence as fast as she could. Tears came, and tumbled uncontrollably down her face, so much so that she felt sick to death of crying. She felt angry at a world that was doing this to her. Making her life a misery. Making her cry. As she burrowed her way under the fence she stopped crying and made up her mind it would be someone else's turn next.

Twenty-Nine

It was five miles to Tommy's house. Lola arrived there around two in the morning, all the time listening for sounds of police cars combing the streets for a murderer on the loose. Luckily Tommy had a doorbell. She wouldn't have to wake up the whole street with her knocking. A bedroom window opened and he looked down.

'Lola?'

He didn't ask what she was doing there. It would be a stupid question. She was obviously distressed. Half a minute later he opened the door and she fell into his arms. The tears she had banished from her life less than two hours ago returned to prove how weak she was. Annoyed with herself she brushed them away with her sleeve and took the thermos flask from her pocket.

'What's this?' Tommy asked.

'It's tea, laced with whatever drug they kept me subdued with.'

'They?'

'The people at the nuthouse. No one came to visit me. Why?' Despite her distress her eyes flashed, angrily, at him.

'We were all told you were refusing visitors. After the way you spoke to us the last time we saw you it seemed believable – sorry.'

'I was taken there against my will.'

'Oh, no! We were told you'd checked yourself in.'

'Checked myself in? Tommy, my son was taken from me and I was locked in the serious nutter ward, drugged up to the eyeballs until I worked out what was happening to me.'

'You obviously did well to get out.'

'I think I did very well,' said Lola, 'except that I think I might have killed the man who tried to rape me.' She needed to unload this awful burden to a sympathetic ear.

'Bloody hell, Lola!'

'I know.'

She held her hands up to stop him telling her how serious this was. There are some things you just don't need telling. Then she sat down. There was dirt on her coat from where she'd crawled under the fence. There was a shout from upstairs.

'Everything OK, Tommy?'

'Yes, Mother, just a friend come to see me.'

Disgruntled mutterings came from above. A door closed. Then silence. Tommy forced out a smile and picked up a packet of Player's.

'You look in a hell of a state – here, take one of these.'

She accepted his offer, along with a light. 'I am in a hell of a state.'

'Someone tried to rape you?'

'A man called Mr Frampton.'

'Jesus, Lola! What was he – one of the patients?'

'No, one of the people who are supposed to look after us. I clonked him over the head. He wasn't moving when I left him.'

'Did you tell anyone?'

'No.'

'So, he could still be there – in need of medical attention?'

Lola hadn't thought of that. 'I suppose so.'

Tommy thought fast. 'In that case someone ought to ring them up – anonymously. Tell them exactly what happened.'

Lola nodded. It made sense.

'What ward were you in?'

'Ward 4 – I had a room of my own.'

Tommy picked up the phonebook and looked up the number of the local police station, then he placed a handkerchief over the mouthpiece and winked at her. 'This might look a bit melodramatic but it does work.' He dialled the number. Lola heard a man's voice answering.

'Just listen,' said Tommy. 'I'm not going to give you my name, just information. A man called Frampton who works at Allerton Park nuthouse tried to rape one of the patients,

Mrs Lola Penfold, tonight. Ward 4, she has a room of her own. He entered her room as she slept. She's been held in that bloody awful place against her will. They've been drugging her tea. She hit him over the head in self-defence and ran away. He might still be in her room, injured and requiring attention – not that he deserves any.'

He put the phone down and said, brightly, 'Right, that's put the cat among the pigeons. Fancy a cup of tea?'

The call was passed on to Foulds, who told DC Bruce to check it out himself and take a uniformed officer with him – and to ring for an ambulance to be on the safe side. Within ten minutes Alfie was banging on the door of Ward 4. The night duty nurse shouted through the door.

'Who is it?'

'Police.'

Impatiently, Alfie turned the handle and was surprised to find it unlocked. The two policemen stepped inside.

'I'm Detective Constable Bruce from Leeds CID. You have a patient in here called Mrs Penfold. Could you show me her room?'

The nurse looked, dumbly, at the door, wondering how he'd opened it without a key.

'Right now, if you please,' snapped Alfie. In the distance was the wail of an approaching ambulance.

'Of course, if you follow me.'

She led them to Lola's room and was about to knock when they brushed her aside and opened the door. Alfie found the light switch and turned it on. Frampton was on the bed, still naked. Alfie leaned over him, then glanced at his colleague. 'Fetch me some cold water, Reg.'

The nurse looked on in horror as the PC filled a cup from the tap and handed it to Alfie, who tossed the contents into Frampton's face. The nurse said, 'Oh dear,' and Alfie explained that it was police medical training.

Frampton opened his eyes, then moaned and clutched his head. There was blood matted in his hair and staining the pillow. Alfie gave him no time to collect his thoughts, or excuses. First rule of police interrogation: always kick a man when he's down.

'Why are you lying naked on a patient's bed?'

'What?'

'I asked you a simple question.'

Alfie turned to the nurse. 'Do you know of any reason why this man should be lying naked on a female patient's bed?'

'Er, no.'

Alfie returned his attention to Frampton. 'Explain why you're naked!' His fists were clenched and the uniformed constable was hoping his CID colleague wouldn't do anything silly.

'I didn't mean any harm,' whined Frampton.

'Any harm? You enter the room of a female patient, remove your clothes, and climb into bed with her while she's fast asleep and you don't mean any harm? What do you take me for, some sort of idiot? Do I look stupid, man?'

The PC drew Alfie's attention to a packet of condoms lying on the bedside table. Alfie looked at the nurse.

'Do you supply these to your patients, nurse?'

'Of course we don't.'

'Was Mrs Penfold likely to have these in her room?'

'Most certainly not!' she said indignantly.

Alfie looked down at Frampton. 'Then we can only conclude that these are yours. Presumably it was your intention to have sexual intercourse with the young lady. Sexual intercourse against her will. Do you know what that is? By the way, what's your name, you damned pervert?'

Frampton's mind was still too addled from the blow to dream up a believable denial. 'Bernard Frampton,' he mumbled.

Alfie looked at the nurse for her confirmation. She nodded. He returned his attention to Frampton, who cowered under his gaze.

'Well?' he thundered.

'What?' whimpered Frampton.

'Why are you in Mrs Penfold's bed, naked and with a packet of condoms?' He leaned down so that his face was an inch from Frampton's. 'Why?' Alfie was young and fresh-faced but the venom within him made up for his lack of years.

'You know why,' whined Frampton.

'I want you to damn well tell me! I want you to tell me right now, or things will get very bad for you, very bad indeed.'

Alfie was determined to get a confession in front of these two witnesses before he arrested him and read him his rights; the man might never be in such a weakened state again. The ambulance came to a noisy stop outside. Alfie placed his body between Frampton and the nurse. He grabbed the orderly's testicles and squeezed just hard enough to demonstrate what pain might follow were he to squeeze harder.

'Why were you in her bed?' Alfie's voice was low and controlled and full of menace. If Frampton had been aware that an ambulance had come for him he might have kept his mouth shut. His eyes were bulging. 'I just wanted sex,' he whined. 'I wasn't going to hurt her. It was only a shag. Anyway, I don't think I did owt. All I remember is touchin' her tits.'

'That's indecent assault and attempted rape.' Alfie released his grip and turned to the nurse and the constable. 'Did you both hear his confession?'

The PC nodded, the nurse said a disgusted, 'Yes.'

The ambulance men were in the hall, shouting, 'Hello?' Alfie told the nurse to bring them in. She left the bedroom as he was reading Frampton his rights.

Lola didn't sleep much that night. She sat drinking coffee, smoking for the first time in a month, listening for police sirens, listening to Tommy and occasionally dozing in an armchair. He'd offered her a bed in the spare room but, with her not being sure if she was a killer or not, she declined his offer.

'I'll check first thing in the morning,' he promised.

'If he's dead I want to handle it in my own time,' she said. 'I don't want to be dragged away kicking and screaming. I want to walk in to the police station and tell them exactly what happened.'

'If it comes to that I'll take you to a solicitor and make sure he guides you every step of the way. I know a good man.'

'Thanks, Tommy.'

As the time ticked by she had visions of her being held in the condemned cell, talking to the same two officers who had looked after her mam in her final days. Then being bound and taken next door to the execution suite. Hooded, then . . .?

At 7 a.m. Tommy opened the door to Alfie's knock. Lola heard him say, 'Alfie – are you here officially?'

'In a way – actually I'm not on duty – I er, I assume Lola's here?'

'How did you know?'

'Call it an educated guess.'

'How much trouble is she in?'

'Trouble? It's the bloke who tried to rape her who's in trouble. I need Lola to make a statement. Er, do you mind if I come in?'

Tommy stood to one side to let Alfie past. Lola came to the lounge door and asked, 'Is he OK?'

'She thinks she might have killed him,' Tommy explained.

'Frampton? No, he's alive and kicking. Won't be for long, though. Well, he'll be kicking his heels inside Armley Jail. He was still a bit groggy when I got there – too groggy to think up a good story to explain why he was in Lola's bed stark naked, complete with a packet of johnnies. We've got the pervert bang to rights on indecent assault and attempted rape. Are you OK, Lola?'

She was shaking with intense relief. Her legs buckled beneath her. Tommy caught her and took her back to her chair. Alfie felt a twinge of jealousy. He wanted to be the one doing that.

'He won't hurt you any more, Lola,' he promised. Tommy was in the kitchen getting a glass of water.

'Will I have to go back there?'

Alfie didn't know for certain – yes, he did, he decided.

'No.'

'Where will I live?'

'Here,' said Tommy, bringing her water through. 'You can stay here until you get yourself sorted.'

'I have no money for rent or anything.'

'Lola, there's at least one article in all this that'll pay your rent.' He looked at her, keenly. 'I think I'll get a mate of mine to take a decent publicity shot of you. It won't do any harm to let the readers know what you look like.'

She wasn't really listening. 'So, I definitely won't have to go back in a mental hospital?'

'Lola,' said Tommy, 'if anyone tries to dump you in a loony bin they'll have to deal with your solicitor.'

'Solicitor?' remarked Alfie, who had very mixed feelings about Lola living with Tommy and having photos taken of her and fixing her up with solicitors. It seemed to him that Lola could well owe Tommy a lot of favours.

'Just someone I know,' Tommy said. 'I'll fix up the spare room, Mum won't mind. Since my dad died she spends most of her time in bed.'

The mention of Tommy's mum was good news to Alfie. He'd forgotten that Tommy still lived with his mother.

'How is she?' he asked.

Tommy glanced up at the ceiling, beyond which his mother was trying to hear what was going on downstairs. 'Physically she's fine.' He tapped the side of his head. 'It's inside here that's the problem. She lived her life through Dad. When he went, he took a lot of her with him.'

'The loss of a good man'll do that to some women,' commented Lola, who still mourned her real dad.

'Well, it had a bad effect on Mum. Some days she's fine, other days . . .' his voice tailed off.

Alfie sat down opposite Lola. 'You know,' he said, 'this might be the break we need, to find out what's been going on. We can investigate this and extend things to check out why Lola was held there against her will.' He gave Lola an apologetic glance. 'I didn't know that, by the way. I was told you'd checked yourself in.'

Lola accepted his apology with a shrug. Then she brightened. 'So, you do believe me now? You do believe my version of how Evie was killed? You do believe Seth and Campion were lying?'

Alfie went quiet as both Lola and Tommy looked at him. Foulds had ordered him, in no uncertain terms, not to discuss this with Lola. The investigation was to be carried out with the utmost secrecy. But so far Alfie and his boss hadn't got very far. 'These things take time and patience,' Foulds had told him. 'We have to watch for the main chance. It'll come. We just have to be ready.'

In the meantime Lola had been suffering. Alfie felt the time had come to give the main chance a kick up the backside. 'Actually,' he said to her, 'I always believed you . . . sorry.'

'Why didn't you say?'

Alfie looked from Lola to Tommy and back. 'Because if I said I believed you you'd naturally assume we would investigate Campion.'

'Naturally,' agreed Lola.

Tommy could see where this was leading. 'And you were

ordered to say nothing about an investigation, with it being
Campion?'

Alfie nodded, contritely. 'And – because we think Seth's
involved – not even to anyone at the station. This is a two-
man investigation – not that we've got very far.'

'Two-man?' queried Lola.

Alfie smiled at her. 'My inspector would come down on
me like a ton of bricks if he knew we were having this conversation. He's on your side as well but he daren't let you know
it. It was him who sent me to Allerton Park. The last thing
he said as I came off shift this morning was to investigate
the hell out of this matter, but not to discuss the Campion
and Seth side of things with you.'

'He's scared I might blab, is that it?' said Lola.

'Yes,' Alfie admitted. 'Most people in your position
wouldn't be able to help themselves.' He looked at her,
steadily. 'I hope you're the exception or I'm out of a job. If
Campion gets a whiff of this he could do us all a lot of
damage.'

'He's got that much clout?' said Tommy.

'Apparently,' said Alfie. 'I'm not big on politics but I gather
he's in line to be Home Secretary. That's what my gaffer told
me this morning. He's been doing some checking over the
past few weeks. The only thing we've found out so far is that
Campion's got an unusual amount of sway with a lot of
people.'

'He sounds bent,' said Tommy.

'We know he's bent,' said Alfie, 'but he doesn't know we
know – that's the ace up our sleeve. That's why this mustn't
go out of this room.'

'I won't breathe a word,' promised Lola. For the first time
since Evie's murder she felt an element of optimism.

'Nor me,' said Tommy. 'Mind you, when the lid comes off
I want to be there.'

'It's going to be softly softly catchee monkey,' Alfie told
them. 'We've got Lola back, the next step is to get Danny
back. Then we'll sit back and wait for Campion's reaction.'

His remark earned him the reward he'd hoped for. Lola
gave him a bear hug; she also gave Tommy one and said, 'I
love you two boys.'

Tommy's mother, listening at the top of the stairs, went

back to her room. She'd voted for Campion, and what her son was doing wasn't right. It also occurred to her that she might lose her darling son to this woman, whoever she was. She'd already lost one of her men; she couldn't stand to lose the other.

Thirty

It was Lola who came up with an idea to get Danny back. It was a pretty basic idea but, as she said, basic ideas had fewer things to go wrong. It involved just her and Tommy. Alfie was back on shift and busy hounding the staff at Allerton Park Mental Hospital. Tommy was telling her about his dad dying.

'He was only forty-three. Cancer of the lung. Smoked like a chimney. I reckon it was the fags that did it.'

'I've heard that as well,' Lola said. 'When I get Danny back I'm going to give them up.'

'You still haven't told me how you plan on doing it.' Tommy had a 1948 Morris Eight that had belonged to his dad, who had died three years before. He was driving her to Keith's mother's house.

'It's a very subtle plan,' Lola told him. 'It all revolves around psychology – only a mother would understand.'

'I see,' said Tommy, who didn't see at all. He pulled up outside Mrs Penfold's house. It was early evening.

'She's probably just got Danny ready for bed,' Lola guessed, getting out of the car.

'What do you want me to do?'

'Just keep the engine running.'

'Lola, you can't—'

Lola hurried up the driveway and walked straight in through the side door. There was radio music coming from one of the downstairs rooms. She took a deep breath and walked in.

Danny was sitting in a playpen, shaking a rattle. He caught sight of his mother and gave her a delighted smile. His grandmother was in an armchair reading a newspaper. She looked up in surprise at Lola who was sweeping Danny up in her arms and hugging him to her.

'How dare you come into my home uninvited!'

'Don't be silly. How else was I to collect my son?'

Mrs Penfold got to her feet and took a couple of paces across the room, but Lola's fierce expression prevented her going any nearer.

'Put my grandson down,' she demanded, 'or I'll call the police!'

'Do you honestly think there's any way you can stop me taking my own son away from your clutches, you evil old woman? The only reason I might put him down is to flatten you!'

'You have no damned right!'

'I have every right.'

Lola walked out of the room with Danny, calling out over her shoulder. 'If you have any objections, you'll have to go through my solicitor.'

She walked to the door and down the drive, with the older woman following close on her heels. Lola handed the boy to Tommy, then turned to face his grandmother, who was now screaming at her.

'Give me back my grandson or I'll call the police!'

'The police already know,' lied Lola. 'And it could be that you end up in jail for this.'

Mrs Penfold was taken aback. Her anger abated. 'For what, might I ask?'

'I think you already know. For being party to my unlawful abduction and imprisonment, just so you could get your hands on my son. The police are investigating it all right now. One man's already been arrested. If you don't believe me, read the papers.'

The older woman blanched. She'd just been reading in the *Yorkshire Evening Post* about an incident at Allerton Park mental hospital where a member of staff had been arrested for what had been described as a 'serious offence against a patient'. It gained Lola enough time to get in the car and instruct Tommy to drive.

He drove in silence for a couple of minutes, then said, 'Lola, at what point did the subtlety and psychology come into play?'

'At the last minute I swapped subtlety for smash and grab,' Lola explained.

'What about the psychology?'

'She knew she had no right to my son, which gave me the moral high ground. It's always an uphill struggle when you know you're in the wrong. She screamed and shouted, but it was all a bit half-hearted.'

'Really? Will she try to get him back?'

'Possibly, but this time I'll be ready for her. Could you arrange for me to see this solicitor pal of yours tomorrow?'

'Of course.'

As they drove, Lola began humming to her son. So much had been taken away from her and now, for the first time, she'd got something back. A thought struck her. 'Did you see her face when I mentioned her part in my unlawful abduction?'

'Not really, I was too busy with Danny.'

'She was worried. I must tell Alfie to check her story out. She could be part of the whole thing – and no, I'm not getting paranoid.'

'Phew, I might be!' said Tommy, wafting his hand in front of his face. 'Just how much preparation did you put into this caper?'

'Not enough, obviously,' grinned Lola, who didn't mind the pong one bit. 'You'd better take me to a chemist.' Danny looked up at his mum and smiled, happily. Lola's heart lightened.

Tommy's mother was posting a letter to Clive Campion MP, c/o The House of Commons, London. The envelope was marked Private and Confidential.

Melvyn Jackman, the superintendent of Allerton Park mental hospital, sat opposite Alfie. He was a fat man whose belly forced him to sit well back from his desk. Alfie wondered how he managed to work at a desk. He had discussed the attack on Lola without any condemnation of the hospital. The attacker had been a rotten apple, Alfie had conceded, there's one of those in every barrel. Jackman had settled back in his chair, at ease, when Alfie asked him his killer question.

'Just one last thing, Mr Jackman – Lola Penfold was brought here against her will and for no reason she can understand. I wonder if you could let me see the paperwork that gave you the authority to do this?'

Jackman frowned. 'What?'

'I assume there is some paperwork?'

'Sorry,' said the superintendent. 'That, er, that would be abusing, er, doctor–patient confidentiality.'

'Suppose the patient waives that confidentiality?' asked Alfie, brightly.

'It's a two-way thing – doctor and patient.'

Alfie nodded and tapped his fingers on the desk. 'I could get a court order,' he said.

'It would be denied you. You'd need a hell of a good reason to set a precedent like that.' Jackman was making it up as he went along. Alfie knew this.

'Fair point, but I think you're wrong.' Alfie got to his feet. 'I was hoping to clear this up today but, to be honest with you, Mr Jackman, you being obstructive makes me think you're hiding something. I'm afraid this investigation will continue until we get to the truth.'

The superintendent failed to disguise his alarm. 'I'm sorry you think that way, Detective Constable. I can assure you I'm not hiding anything.'

Alfie paused at the door. 'I think you might get a lot sorrier before much longer, Mr Jackman. I know you're hiding some-thing. Our next interview will be down at the station. I'll let you know when.'

'But—' said Jackman.

But Alfie had gone.

Campion was in his constituency office when the call came through from Jackman. He assumed he was about to be given an update on Lola's condition.

'Mr, Jackman, nice to hear from you. How's our mutual friend?'

There was a pause that unsettled the MP. 'Mr Jackman?' he said.

'There's been some trouble, Mr Campion.'

Campion's pulse rate began to climb. 'Trouble? What kind of trouble?'

'She was attacked by one of our staff. She ran away and now we're being investigated.'

'Ran away? How could she run away? I thought she was in a secure ward.'

'I don't know how she did it, but she did.'

'So, she's no longer in your care? This isn't good enough. You must get her back.'

'I doubt very much if we can get her back. One of my staff has been arrested for attempted rape, among other things. He's apparently held up his hands to it but the police are asking me very awkward questions as to why she was in here in the first place. Questions I can't answer without involving you. I've stalled them for the time being, but they're going to take me to the station for questioning.'

Campion began to bluster. 'But you must claim professional immunity and refuse to cooperate.'

'I've, er, I've sort of done that.'

'Have you . . .? Right, in that case I'll see what I can do from this end.'

An hour later Foulds was called into Detective Chief Inspector Merton's office. The senior officer was well dressed, well groomed, ten years Foulds' junior and the epitome of a career policeman.

'We've had a complaint from the superintendent of Allerton Park mental hospital. Claims one of our officers is harassing him.'

'Tough,' said Foulds. 'I asked DC Bruce to do a thorough investigation of that place.'

'Why's that?'

Foulds thought if he brought Campion into it at this stage he would be severely warned off, especially with the MP due an imminent promotion – which everyone in the force seemed to know about.

'The victim claims she's not the only one being abused, sir. I thought it merited a closer look.'

The DCI walked to the window and spoke with his back

to Foulds. 'The victim being Lola Penfold, formerly Lola Lawless, who has already falsely accused one of our officers of murdering his own niece.'

'Did Mr Jackman complain directly to you, sir?'

The DCI swung round to face him. 'Not directly, no. If you must know he went through the chief constable.'

'Don't you find that a bit odd, sir?'

'I think it's odd that you're pursuing a case and spending police resources purely on the word of a known liar.'

'I don't think she's a liar, sir.'

'Just drop it.'

'Yes, sir.'

Lola flew into a rage when Alfie went to Tommy's and told her what had happened. 'So, what the police are saying is that just because I'm Lola Lawless my word isn't to be believed?'

'Something like that,' admitted Alfie. 'The chief inspector caught my boss on the hop. He had to give a good reason for me giving Jackman the third degree.'

'I'd have backed his story up,' Lola said. 'I think there is bad stuff going on there. It's a damn good job you got a confession out of Frampton or he'd have got away with assaulting me. My word against his, what chance would I have had?'

'There's enough here for me to write an article, stir things up a bit,' chipped in Tommy, 'make a few quid as well. These Lawless articles are always good for a hundred quid or so.'

'I guess I owe you that much,' Lola conceded, 'with me having no money for my keep.'

'Hey! I didn't mean it like that.'

'An article might put Seth and Campion on their guard,' warned Alfie. 'We need them to think they're bulletproof.'

The three of them sat in deep thought for a while, then Lola got to her feet. 'I've got an idea.'

'What?' asked Alfie.

'Haven't thought it through yet, but I need to strike while the iron's hot.'

'You haven't thought it through?' said Tommy. 'Does it involve subtlety and psychology?'

'It involves you giving me a lift to the superintendent's house.'

'Does it involve me?' enquired Alfie.

'Yes – you can look after Danny.'

Lola had never clapped eyes on Jackman, and he only knew her through newspaper photographs. He was amazed at how stunning she was as she sat in the chair that Alfie had occupied just a few hours before.

'You're looking remarkably well, considering.'

'You mean considering I was kidnapped, drugged and then brought here and sexually assaulted by one of your hand-picked staff?'

'I admit there was an unfortunate side to your stay here.'

'Unfortunate? It would have been a damned sight more unfortunate if I hadn't stopped taking those drugs you hid in my tea. How do you think that's going to look in the papers, Mr Jackman?'

'I think it's something you'd have to prove.'

'I've got a flask full of that special tea of yours, ready to be sent for analysis. The flask has got Allerton Park Hospital stamped on the side.'

'That's not conclusive.'

'It's good enough for a newspaper article. In newspaper terms we Lawlesses are good copy. An article on what happened to me here would open a very big can of worms. It also might force your hand to tell the police who's behind all this.'

'I don't know what you mean.'

'In that case you've got nothing to worry about. If the article's untrue you can always sue for libel.'

He went quiet as he ran the implications of her threat over in his mind. Then he looked up at the determination on her gorgeous face and decided these threats weren't idle. He'd probably be pretty pissed off himself had the same thing happened to him.

'So, what is it you want?'

'I want a hundred pounds in cash – and I want it tomorrow.'

Jackman gave an awkward laugh. 'A hundred pounds? That's three months' wages for one of our nurses. Why would I give you a hundred pounds?'

'For that you get me completely off your back. The alternative is that you deny the true story that'll be in the papers within forty-eight hours. I reckon at best you'll lose your job, at worst you'll end up in jail with whoever else was involved.'

'This is blackmail.'

'It's compensation for suffering caused.'

He gave a wincing smile. 'How do I know you'll keep your word?'

'That's a risk you'll have to take. The one thing you should know for certain is that I will take this story to the papers if you don't give me the money.'

'Where am I supposed to get a hundred pounds at such short notice?'

'I suggest you ask your friend, Mr Campion.' She was fishing, but his eyes told her he'd taken the bait. 'You might also ask him to leave me alone from now on. If he pays up and leaves me alone I'll call it quits.'

Campion was 200 miles away in London. When Jackman rang him his immediate reaction to Lola's demand for a hundred pounds was one of derision.

'She mentioned your name,' Jackman told him.

'Did she now? What did she say?'

Campion knew she would have wondered why he'd confirmed Seth's alibi. She would strongly suspect that he had much to do with her problems. Was this a bad thing – her knowing he had this sort of power over her?

'She told me to ask you to leave her alone. She said if you pay up and leave her alone she'll call it quits.'

This interested him. 'Call it quits, eh? Did the police mention my name when they came?'

'No – look I don't know what's gone on between you two, but as far as Lola Penfold's concerned I got the strong impression that she'll definitely be out of your hair if you pay her off.'

The more Campion thought about it, the more he was tempted to pay her. She was a persistent bitch and if the price for getting her off his back for good was a hundred pounds it might be money well spent. He didn't want any scandal to deprive him of a seat on the front bench.

'Give me the number of your bank account, I'll transfer the money first thing in the morning.'

*   *   *

The following evening Lola picked up a hundred pounds in cash. 'I assume this is Campion's money?' she said.

Jackman shrugged, noncommittally, but his eyes told her she was right. She smiled.

'I thought so.'

Alfie wasn't sure Lola had done the right thing in taking Campion's money. 'At least it won't stop Frampton being banged up,' he remarked.

'Exactly,' said Lola. 'My attacker goes to jail and I get a hundred quid to tide me over.'

'If you'd mentioned it to me I'd have told you to ask for a thousand,' said Tommy. 'You could have set yourself up very nicely with a thousand.'

Lola flashed him an angry look 'I'm not an extortionist. I'm after justice for Mam and Evie and Keith,' she looked away than added, 'Even if I have to do it myself.'

'Steady on, Lola,' said Alfie.

'No, I won't steady on. When someone's done something like that to you, you can't live a normal life unless you get suitable retribution.'

'What sort of retribution?' enquired Tommy.

'Well, if you could point me in the direction of the nearest snake pit, that might do it. I could have them thrown in and maybe toss a dozen rabid dogs in after them. It'd be less than they deserve, but beggars can't be choosers.'

Thirty-One

Dear Mr Campion,
I feel it my bounden duty to write to you, as both I and my late husband voted for you in the election. My husband said you are a man who gets things done . . .

Campion was on the point of screwing the letter up and tossing it in the waste paper basket when his eye picked out the name Lola further down the page. He continued to read.

> . . . My son Thomas has got this girlfriend called Lola who has just escaped from a mental home. I think she is a bad lot. Tommy writes for newspapers and I think he might be writing a story about you, with this Lola woman's help. I think my Tommy is being led astray by a pretty face. I know my late husband would turn in his grave if he could have heard our son talking like that. Tommy won't take any notice of me but I thought if I warned you you might be able to have a word with him and tell him not to have anything to do with this woman or he might end up in jail. I would hate for him to get into trouble. He is all I have. If you wish to telephone me my number is Leeds 60326.
>
> Yours sincerely
> Mrs Edith Pearson

She had written it with a Parker pen on pale blue Basildon Bond, which she hoped would impress the MP.

Campion picked up the phone and rang Seth's house. There was no reply. He rang three times that day before Seth answered.

'Where the hell have you been?' Campion snapped. 'I've been trying to get hold of you all day.'

'I've been at work. What the hell's eating you, anyway?'

'The bloody Lawless girl.'

He hadn't spoken to Seth since before Lola had been taken to Allerton Park. The less he had to do with the idiot copper the better.

'I thought yer'd had her banged up good and tight in the nuthouse?' grumbled Seth. 'What went wrong?'

'Some prat who couldn't keep it in his trousers. Thought it was OK to go round sticking it in the patients – that's what went wrong. She's out now and gunning for me. And the reason she's gunning for me is because I had to back up your bloody alibi! She knows full well we were both lying in our teeth.'

Seth gave this some thought. 'Everyone down at the station thinks she's a flake,' he said. 'No one's investigating us.'

'Are you sure?'

'Course I'm sure. If there was someone investigating me I think I'd know. I'm not that bloody thick.'

Seth's belligerent confidence was reassuring. Campion heaved out a heavy sigh of relief. The conversation that Tommy's mother had overheard would have taken place before he'd given her the hundred pounds. Jackman had told him she'd be out of his hair if he paid her off. If she had been telling the truth maybe that was the best way out of it.

'The first hint you get that there's something not right you tell me.'

'Then what?'

'Then we take extreme measures. You do to the Lawless woman what you did to her husband and her sister, only you do it with a bit more finesse. You don't leave a body for anyone to find.'

'I see. Well, that's me taking an extreme measure, what extreme measures will you be taking?'

'What are you talking about?' grumbled Campion.

'I'm talking,' retorted Seth, 'about you saying "then we take extreme measures". What you mean is, I take all the risks and do all the dirty work while you sit on your fat arse.'

'It's a last resort,' said Campion. 'It probably won't come to it. If you must know I've already paid her off. The deal is that she gets out of our hair.'

'Our hair, not just your hair?'

'Everybody's hair. If she doesn't, it's over to you.'

'How much did you give her?'

'A hundred pounds. The story is that it was an out-of-court settlement by the hospital.'

'Jesus!'

'So you see,' said Campion, 'I am doing my bit.' He put the phone down and rang another number. 'Arthur, get me what you can on a freelance reporter called Tommy Pearson. He's done pieces in the *Herald* on the Lawless family.'

An hour later he dialled Mrs Pearson's number. Tommy answered.

'Tommy Pearson.'

Campion put on his charming voice. 'Hello, Tommy, nice to put a voice to the name.'

'Who's speaking?'

'My name is Campion, Clive Campion. I'm MP for—'

'I know who you are, Mr Campion,' said Tommy, coldly.

'Good, well I've just received a letter from your mother. She's very concerned about you; thinks you're going to write some defamatory article about me that might get you into trouble. I trust that isn't the case.'

Right at that moment Tommy could have throttled his mother. 'I don't know where she's got that from,' was all he could think to say. Campion continued in an avuncular fashion that Tommy found annoyingly disarming.

'I suspect it's because I was asked to back up DC Lawless's story about where he was when his niece died. I understand you have a particular interest in the Lawless family and have written some fine articles on their plight.'

Tommy could see where this was going. His mother must have been earwigging on his conversation with Lola and Alfie. 'And you're worried I might write an article exposing you for what you are – is that it, Mr Campion?'

'Tommy,' said Campion, evenly, 'if you submit a defamatory article about me, any newspaper worth its salt will check the facts thoroughly before they go to print, lest they be sued. If you have absolute proof then go ahead; if not, and you do find some sleazy newspaper to print your article, then prepare for bankruptcy and the end of your career in journalism.'

Tommy remained silent, listening. The politician continued. His tone was matter-of-fact; neither harsh nor threatening.

'I was telling the truth about Seth Lawless. Can you think of any reason why I shouldn't? I scarcely know the man, but at the time of his niece's death I had called round to his house to discuss a letter that your friend Lola had sent me. If you doubt my word speak to her. Prior to that I'd never clapped eyes on him. The next thing I know I'm having to confirm DC Lawless's whereabouts because his niece, Lola's sister, has been murdered. As far as I'm concerned the only way he could have done it is if someone got the times wrong. This whole thing is getting too bizarre.'

'No one got the times wrong, Mr Campion,' Tommy said, lamely. Once again, Lola's version of events didn't make sense. Campion sounded quite a decent bloke. Why would a decent bloke who was about to be made Home Secretary get involved in something as sordid as this?

'In that case,' said Campion, 'either Seth Lawless is being framed or someone's made an honest mistake.'

'Lola wouldn't frame him, she's not like that.'

'OK, we'll call it an honest mistake. Mistaken identity; seeing things that weren't there; Seth Lawless has a double – your guess is as good as mine. All I know is what I saw. The only solution I can come up with is that someone viciously attacked Evie, and Lola went into a state of shock causing her, in her weakened state of mind, to substitute the attacker for Seth Lawless – a man she hates. Maybe she has good reason to hate him – I didn't much like the man myself. But I do know that odd things happen to you when you're in a state of shock – hallucinations, all sorts of things. Why do you think she was taken into a mental hospital?'

'I don't know, you tell me.'

'Well, I have looked into that matter but I can only tell you in the strictest confidence. Can I do that?'

'You can.'

'She was taken in because professionals involved in her health, and the post-natal care of her child, became worried about her state of mind after her sister had been murdered, and their fears were acted upon in the interests of mother and child.'

'Professionals? You mean her doctor and her child welfare nurse?'

'I don't know the details, and I've already told you more that I should have, trusting you won't mention it to anyone, particularly Lola. Do that and she'll lose complete trust in the medical people around her. She's got little enough reason to trust them as it is, with what happened to her in there. If the man is found guilty, as seems likely considering he's already confessed, he will be dealt with very strictly, you can be sure of that.'

'She was in quite a state at the time, I must admit that,' said Tommy, remembering how Lola had kicked them all out of her house.

'Look, all I know,' said Campion, who was smiling as he spoke, self-satisfied that he was winning the battle of Tommy's mind, 'is that her state of mind at that time is now backfiring on me and I don't like it, Tommy. I don't like it one bit.'

'I suppose it's all very possible,' conceded Tommy. Campion sounded so very plausible. Surely Lola was wrong

about him. 'So, you think she was in a state of shock and
saw things that weren't there?'

'It's one theory,' Campion said. 'Anyway, whatever the
reason, my press office has sent word around the newspapers
that a woman with a grudge is trying to persuade a gullible
reporter called Tommy Pearson to write an untrue article about
me. They will all be advised to check the facts and contact
my office before printing a word, and you, young man, would
be well advised to take heed of your mother if you want a
career in journalism. You get a reputation as a crank reporter
and your career's over before it's started.'

When he put the phone down Tommy felt as if he'd been
caned by the headmaster. He desperately wanted to believe
Lola, but was this just infatuation getting in the way of
common sense? He needed to think this through and put aside
his feelings for her. If possible.

Within a day Lola sensed Tommy's doubt of her. Whenever
she broached the subject of Seth and Campion he steered the
conversation away. He decided not to tell her about Campion's
phone call – not yet, anyway. Alfie called, full of enthusiasm,
Foulds still didn't know he'd told her and Tommy, but Alfie
figured he could trust them. 'Foulds thinks it's fishy that
we've been told to drop the investigation into the activities
at Allerton Park,' he said. 'Seems that the order came from
on high.'

'I wouldn't have thought there was much left to investigate,' said Tommy.

'It might have given us a lead into Lola's case,' Alfie pointed
out. 'Allerton Park's somehow tied in with Campion.'

'How do you know?' Tommy asked.

'I know,' Lola said. 'I could see it in Jackman's eyes when
he gave me the cash. I told him I assumed it was Campion's
money and he didn't give me an argument.'

'It's a bit flimsy, if you don't mind me saying so,' said
Tommy.

'As a matter of fact, I do mind you saying so, Tommy,'
said Lola, heatedly. 'Just whose side are you on?'

'I'm on your side, Lola. It's just that you're jumping to
conclusions without much to back them up.'

Lola coloured. Alfie placed a hand on his pal's shoulder

and defended him. 'He's just being cautious, that's it, isn't it, Tommy? Devil's advocate and all that.'

'Something like that,' said Tommy. 'You do need to be cautious, Lola.'

Tommy hated not being as sure as Lola was about Seth and Campion. The MP had been so convincing. He wished he hadn't. He couldn't think of any reason why Campion should lie. This doubt, in turn, cast doubt upon Evie's theory that Seth had killed Keith, and that Seth and Campion had been the cause of all the Lawless family's troubles, dating right back to Rachel being hanged.

He didn't quite know how, but he felt that by talking to Seth he might get a more balanced picture of the situation.

Seth was surprised to see him. He looked into the street beyond where Tommy was standing, to see if he'd brought anyone with him, such as a photographer. A visit such as this was cause for concern to Seth. This bloke was here to pry.

'You're that reporter bloke, aren't yer?'

'Er, yes.'

'Yer a friend of Lola. I saw yer at her husband's funeral.'

'Really?' said Tommy. 'I didn't realize you were there.'

'I went ter pay me respects, but I kept me distance. I know where I'm not wanted.'

'It's, er, it's Lola I've come to talk to you about.'

Seth turned instantly belligerent. 'In that case, I think the best thing yer can do, lad, is piss off. She's caused me no end of grief, has that lass.'

'I'm not here to cause you grief, Mr Lawless. I'm just here to get at the truth. If you've got nothing to hide I'll be doing you a favour.'

'Doing me a favour? Is that what yer think? Well, I like them that do me favours. Yer'd best come inside, lad.'

Tommy followed the big man inside the house. It was the house of a man unused to having no wife around. As he passed, Tommy glanced inside the kitchen and saw pots piled up in the sink. There were clothes strewn on the stairs and a musty smell throughout. On the living room table was a plate bearing the remains of egg and beans, an HP sauce bottle, half a loaf and a jar of jam. Seth made no apology for the untidiness.

The two of them sat down on opposite chairs. Seth lit a cigarette and sat back. 'Right, lad,' he said, 'do me a favour.'

Tommy thought it might be a good ploy to shake this unpleasant man's complacency.

'Lola insists you killed her sister,' he said. 'Why would she say a thing like that?' He examined Seth's face for signs of guilt, or perhaps a twinge of nervousness, but Seth gave nothing away. He tapped his temple.

'Your guess is as good as mine, lad. That lass's not right in her head. I make no wonder, with what's been happenin' to her, but I'm not best pleased she's takin' it out on me.'

Tommy noticed that Seth hadn't immediately jumped in with his cast-iron alibi. Surely a guilty man would have trotted this out straight away? For his part Seth knew that Tommy would be aware of the alibi, so he held it in reserve. He was no longer complacent. He was confident. This lad had nothing on him. He was here on a fishing expedition.

'I gather you were talking to Mr Campion at the time of Evie's murder.'

'No one's sure it were murder, lad. We've only Lola's word fer that, and she says it was me who did it.'

'What do you think happened to Evie, Mr Lawless?'

'How the hell am I supposed ter know?' Seth took on a pained expression. 'Yer know she were me dead brother's lass, livin' wi' me and my missis?'

'Of course I know that, Mr Lawless.'

'Of course yer do. But I bet yer didn't give me credit for feelin' a loss. I bet yer didn't think for a minute that I'd grieve over the lass?' He said this in the form of a question, and Tommy was lost for a reply.

'I didn't think so,' said Seth. 'Well I did grieve. She never liked me, didn't the lass. Maybe I wasn't the ideal uncle. I'm not a likeable man ter many people, but I still have feelings. I lost me only livin' blood relative an' no one gave me credit fer grievin' over her. Not only that, but I'm accused of killin' her.'

'Lola's been through a lot,' Tommy said. 'It's bound to have had an effect on her.' He mentally kicked himself for admitting that Lola had behaved irrationally. Getting to his feet to leave he wondered if he was any wiser. The answer was a grudging yes. He was probably more convinced that

Lola was wrong about Seth and Campion. He hadn't seen a flicker of guilt in Seth. He didn't like the man, and if he'd been harmed by Lola's accusations, then tough.

Thirty-Two

L ola was sitting on a wall with her eyes fixed on Seth's front door. Danny was asleep in his pushchair and passing men smiled and tipped their hats to her, even men who weren't normally quite so courteous. Such was Lola's beauty.

The spring sun warmed her face but she felt cold within. From the top deck of a bus she had spotted Tommy's car parked outside Seth's house. She knew it was his by the dent in the wing and the first three letters of the number plate – PUB. She had alighted from the bus out of a mixture of curiosity and disappointment. What the hell was Tommy doing in that house with that man?

She had been sitting there just five minutes when Tommy came out. Seth had seen him to the door; there was a polite smile on Tommy's face, which meant they had parted on good terms. How on earth could he part on good terms with that monster? He was about to get into his car when she called out to him.

'Tommy.'

He looked up. His embarrassment was obvious.

'Lola, what are you doing here?'

'I was about to ask you the same question.'

She made no move towards him. She just sat there, gently rocking the pushchair on its springs. Tommy waited for a gap in the traffic before he strolled, as casually as he could, across the road. His brain was moving a lot faster than his feet. He knew her questions would be direct. He knew she wouldn't beat about the bush. She didn't disappoint him.

'Why have you been visiting the man who murdered my sister? From where I'm sitting you seemed quite friendly towards him.'

He sat down on the wall beside her and allowed himself to collect his thoughts. 'Lola, I just needed to see him to get to the truth.'

'The truth about what?'

'About what's been happening to you.'

She turned to him. Her face was consumed with accusation. The anger within her gave her a glow that seemed to illuminate her beauty from within. Tommy had never seen such beauty. He was tempted to lie to her; to tell her that he was completely on her side; to say that he'd just heard a string of lies from Seth that had totally convinced him that he was guilty of Evie's murder and a lot more besides. He looked away and pulled himself together.

'Lola,' he said, his eyes following a passing cyclist, 'I wouldn't hurt you for the world, you know that.'

'You've hurt me by going to seek the truth from Seth. The truth? Tell me, Tommy, what do Seth Lawless and the truth have in common?'

She sounded so wounded. Tommy couldn't think of a thing to say that would placate her. He loved her, there was no doubt about that. He wanted to take her in his arms and hold her and make everything right for her. Maybe if he told her.

'Would it help if I told you I love you?' he said, still watching the cyclist. He winced as he awaited her reaction. What a daft time to tell her.

'Tommy, that's a very odd thing to say, under the circumstances.'

He sighed. He had envisaged telling her in a far more romantic situation. In a classy restaurant with a bottle of expensive wine on the table, flowers and piano music in the background.

'I know,' he said, 'but it's true.'

Lola ran her hand through her hair. She hadn't expected this. It was very flattering but she could think of no reason why it should alter what she had to ask him.

'I told you about Seth killing Evie,' she said. 'Do you believe me? And, Tommy,' she added, gently, 'don't let your – your love for me get in the way of your answer.'

He rested his elbows on his knees and sank his face into his hands. Then he got to his feet.

'I want to believe you Lola,' he told her. 'I'd run through a wall for you.'

'But?' she said.

'Oh, hell, Lola. What can I say? I've talked to Campion and he seems OK. He told me you'd written to him and he was talking to Seth about your problem around the time Evie died.' He studied her face and asked, 'Did you write to him?'

'What if I did? Me writing to Campion doesn't give Seth an alibi.'

'I know, love, but I've now talked to Seth. He's an odious bastard but that doesn't make him a killer. I also know that seeing your sister die so soon after your husband and your mother could well have done things to your mind. Caused you to focus your rage on the man you hate the most, the man who took Evie from you.'

Lola nodded, slowly. 'What you say makes sense, Tommy. Apart from one thing.'

'What's that?'

'I saw Seth kill her. I was shocked. I was in a state. I was scared. But I saw exactly what happened. I was as close to him as I am to you. I smelled the stink of his breath as he passed me. I saw him do it, Tommy.'

'In that case, I believe you.'

She shook her head, sadly. 'No, you don't, Tommy. My story doesn't make sense to you. Why would Seth kill her? Why would an MP give him an alibi?'

Tommy stared at her for a long time. 'You're not sure yourself, are you, Lola?'

'What?'

For a brief moment a seed of doubt was planted in Lola's mind. Here was a kind, genuine, intelligent man; a man who said he was in love with her; a man who would run through a wall for her. Was it possible that the shock of the moment had made her mind play tricks on her?

Then a shudder ran through her whole body as her mind conjured up a pin sharp picture of Seth picking up Evie and hurling her into the river. And that seed of doubt disintegrated. She heard herself screaming and she saw Seth scowling at her. He was running up the steps towards her, elbowing her out of the way. Now she was at the edge of the water trying to see her sister. And there she was, just a dark shape floating beneath the surface. She was in the water herself

now. Freezing water. There was Evie's arm. She was pulling
at her, bringing her to the surface, taking her to the man who
was shouting, 'Over here, love.' The rest was a blur. The bit
where Evie died was blurred. It was nature's way of anaes-
thetizing the pain. She had gone into shock just after Evie
died, but not before. She remembered the events leading up
to it with absolute clarity.

'Tommy, I've never been so sure of anything in my life.'

'Lola, maybe if I—'

But she stopped him. 'I'm really grateful to you for being
there for me and for putting me up when I had nowhere to go.'

She blinked back tears. She wanted to tell him she needed
someone who believed in her, but you can't force people to
believe. Keith would have believed in her. He was never the
man of her dreams but, oh god, how he had loved her. To
Keith she could do no wrong. Keith had placed her on a
pedestal, above everything and everybody, even his own
mother. If she needed anyone right now, it was Keith.

'I'll move out as soon as I find somewhere.'

'There's no need.'

'I think there is.'

'Can I give you a ride home?'

'No, thanks. I need a bit of time to reflect on things,' she
said. 'By the way, I don't think you love me.'

'You're wrong, Lola.'

She shook her head and gave him a sad smile. 'Tommy,
when you love someone, you also have blind faith in them.
You won't be able to help yourself.'

'How do you know?'

'I just do.'

Alfie took the news about Lola moving out of Tommy's house
with mixed feelings. He had never liked her living with
Tommy, who was a nice bloke whom a vulnerable woman
might well fall for; but the reasons for her moving out meant
that she might well be feeling a bit badly done to, and he
was relying on her keeping her mouth shut about the investigation into Campion and Seth.

He would go and visit her in her new home, as soon as he
found out where she was. In the meantime he'd just have to
hope she kept quiet. He was wondering if the old adage 'Hell

hath no fury like a woman scorned' applied to women whose word wasn't believed. If so, he was in trouble with DI Foulds. On balance he thought it best to come clean to his boss.

'You bloody idiot! Why do you think I told you to keep this to yourself? We're ploughing a bloody lonely furrow on this one. If the people upstairs get to hear of it, it'll cost us both our jobs. The man's just been made Home bloody Secretary, or hadn't you heard?'

Alfie mentioned that he had heard. 'What shall we do?' he asked, miserably. 'Shall we drop it?'

Foulds thought about this. 'Do you honestly think she'll blab about us being on the case?'

'I wouldn't have thought so. She said she wouldn't.'

'Not good enough,' said Foulds. He paced up and down his office, then his face brightened. 'The best thing to do is to give her nothing to blab about.'

'Sir?'

'I want you to go and see her. I want you to tell her that the investigation is now closed. Tell her that as far as the police are concerned, Campion and Seth have committed no crimes.'

'She'll be upset,' warned Alfie.

'She can be as upset as she bloody well likes,' said Foulds. 'If she thinks the case is closed she'll have nothing to blab about – nothing that'll worry us, anyway.'

'OK, sir. I need to find out where she's living first.'

'And after you've told her, I don't want you to see her until this investigation is over. Do I make myself clear, DC Bruce?'

'Perfectly, sir.'

Thirty-Three

Danny was on the floor playing with a Dinky car when Lola heard a loud knock. She checked her hair in a mirror and opened the door.

'Alfie, how did you know where I live?'

'It's something to do with me being a detective.'

He'd made her smile. She was pleased to see him. Alfie had always believed her. He had never doubted her like the rest of them. His only problem was that he'd also been able to see things from Tommy's point of view.

'I must look a right mess.'

Alfie grinned. 'Come off it, you could never look a mess, Lola. Aren't you going to invite me in?'

'Oh, sorry, yes.'

He went inside and knelt down beside Danny, who was genuinely pleased to see him. The boy handed Alfie his toy car, which was examined with exaggerated admiration. This delighted Danny.

'He's missed you,' Lola said.

'I missed him – I bet Tommy does too. He saw a lot more of him than I did.'

Lola hadn't thought about this. Had she been selfish with Tommy? 'It was time for me to stand on my own two feet,' she said. 'Tommy can come and visit whenever he wants.'

Alfie looked around. The house had been let furnished. This meant the furniture was pretty basic and none of it was Lola's. But she'd added her own touch to it.

'You got it looking OK,' he remarked.

'It's habitable and nothing more.'

'Am I right in thinking you've spent a lot of your hundred quid?'

'Some of it.'

'What will you do when it runs out?'

Under other circumstances she might have told him to mind his own business, but she knew he only had her welfare at heart.

'I've got Family Allowance and widow's pension that just about pays for Danny, after that I suspect I might have to go on the dole – either that or get a job which I can work around Danny. Maybe find some work I can do at home.'

'If I can help you only have to ask.'

'I know that, Alfie – thanks.'

She sat in an armchair and watched him playing with her son; and she liked what she saw. They exchanged small talk about the weather and a film he'd just been to see and she told him about Danny's latest escapade when she'd caught him halfway up the stairs.

Alfie made her feel as Keith never had, or as Tommy never had. He made her feel good inside. She liked Alfie being here more than she cared to admit to herself. But for reasons she couldn't explain to herself she felt that being emotionally tied to someone was a weakness she couldn't afford right now. With so much going on. With so much to resolve in her life. First things first. First sort out Seth and Campion. First avenge her mother and sister and husband. If she fell in love, all this hatred might disappear. She needed to keep that hatred alive. It mustn't die.

'Is this purely a social visit?' she asked.

Alfie answered without looking up from his game with Danny.

'Business and pleasure.'

He hated what he had to say to her. For a split second he almost blurted out what Foulds had instructed him to say, whilst telling her it was only to fool her into keeping quiet and that he was with her all the way and would never let her down. But without Foulds the odds were that Seth and Campion would never be brought to justice. Foulds knew what he was talking about. When it was all over Lola would thank him.

'Tell me about the business side,' Lola said, quietly.

He looked up at her now. Danny was tugging at him, wanting the car back. Alfie smiled and gave it to him, then he got to his feet.

'I er, I went in to see Frank Foulds this morning.'

The expression on his face told Lola she wasn't going to like this.

'And . . .?'

Alfie winced. 'And he's called off the investigation into Seth and Campion.'

Her eyes narrowed. 'Called it off? How do you mean, called it off?'

'I mean they've closed the file on it. They've exhausted their enquiries.'

'I thought there was only you and Inspector Foulds making any enquiries?'

'That's right, but Foulds is the boss. I'm only a foot soldier.'

'Alfie, if you believed in me you wouldn't do this to me.'

'Lola, it's not that I don't believe in you.'

But she was already opening the front door. Her eyes were swimming with tears of disappointment and anger.

'Just go, Alfie. I don't want to raise my voice in front of Danny.'

'Please, Lola—'

'Go!'

Danny looked up as his mother's voice rose several decibels. Alfie left, dismally, wondering if he could have handled it better.

Thirty-Four

'Alfie lad, don't often get to see you down here in the dungeons.'

'I try and avoid this place, Dicksy. Didn't this used to be the old cells?'

'Aye, when Queen Victoria were a lass. We've had closed files piling up down here fer thirty years ter my knowledge. What can I do for you?'

'Well,' said Alfie, 'it's kind of unofficial.'

PC Dicks, who was in his early fifties, grinned. 'About half the people who come down here are on unofficial business. Everybody's trying to get the edge on some other bugger.'

'No,' said Alfie, 'it's not like that. I'm not trying to get the edge on anyone. I'd just appreciate it if you didn't mention to anyone what I was looking for.'

'My lips are sealed, Alfie lad. What is it you're looking for?'

'It's a file on a girl called Eve Lawless.'

Dicksy nodded. 'That's a fairly thick file, lad.' He disappeared down an avenue of shelves and came back within seconds. He placed Evie's file in front of Alfie, almost with reverence.

'Eve Marie Lawless, poor lass,' said Dicksy, reading off the cover. 'Born 17 July 1944, died 24 February 1957. Personally I wouldn't have regarded this as a closed file, but there were them who said it was, and it's not my job to question it.'

'Who brought it down?' enquired Alfie, as casually as he could.

'The lass's uncle, Seth Lawless. He said the thought of it being stuck in a drawer, for everyone to gawp at, depressed the hell out of him.'

By the look on Dicksy's face he obviously didn't believe a word of this.

'Well, Seth's a very sensitive soul, as we all know,' said Alfie, opening the file. 'Can I take it away?''

'Sorry,' said Dicksy. 'After Seth had brought it down I checked with Inspector Foulds to see if keeping it down here was in order. He just said to keep it extra safe – cheeky sod – as if I don't keep everything down here extra safe.'

Alfie could have mentioned that Foulds wouldn't mind him taking it away, but that might have prompted unwanted questions. He took the file to a corner where he sat on a chair and turned to the pages recording Evie's arrest for shoplifting. He remembered something she'd said about this and wanted to confirm a suspicion.

He came to a witness statement made in August 1955 by a store detective in Lewis's department store:

> . . . I was approached by a male customer who said he had seen a girl stealing a watch. I accompanied the witness to the teenage fashions section where he identified the girl I now know as Eve Lawless. Eve Lawless was subsequently searched and a watch was found on her person. She had no receipt for the watch and it was later found to have come from our jewellery department. She denied taking the watch.

The store detective had both signed and printed his name – Barry Firth. Alfie looked up at PC Dicks.

'Dicksy, you wouldn't happen to have a photo of Seth down here, would you?'

'I've got mugshots of every villain that ever passed through this nick.'

'What about the coppers?'

'I was including the coppers,' grinned Dicksy. 'I've even got one of you before you started shaving. It must be at least a year old.'

Alfie ignored his jibe. 'Do you have one of Seth?'

'I reckon I have, lad. Bring it straight back, mind, and don't tell anyone I gave it to you. It's bound to be against the rules. Everything's against the rules, nowadays.'

Barry Firth was a on a tea break in Lewis's staff canteen when Alfie called in to see him.

'DC Bruce from Leeds City Police.' Firth was a small man with a mean face and Alfie guessed he enjoyed his work. 'I'm doing some background work on a girl who was drowned in February of this year.'

'Right,' said Firth, munching a biscuit. 'What's it got to do wi' me?'

'Well,' said Alfie, 'she spent some time in a reformatory after being caught in this store for shoplifting back in August 1955. I understand it was you who caught her.'

Firth shrugged. 'What was her name?'

'Eve Lawless.'

He nodded, 'Yeah, I remember her.'

'Apparently it was a member of the public who told you about her.'

Firth popped the remainder of his biscuit into his mouth and rubbed the crumbs off his hands. 'As it happens I remember the bugger. Big feller, used to see him about town when he were in uniform.'

'Uniform?'

'Yeah, he were a bobby. I come into contact with bobbies quite a lot in this job.'

'So, you knew him?'

'Well, not as such. I used to see him on traffic duty on Briggate.'

'Did you take his name at the time?'

'I don't think I had the chance. If I remember rightly, as soon as he'd pointed the girl out, he made himself scarce – probably didn't want to get involved in all the fuss, a lot don't. We didn't need him, as it happened. The magistrate saw straight through the girl's lies.'

Alfie took Seth's photo from his pocket and showed it to the store detective. 'Is this the man we're talking about?' The photo was of Seth in his uniform days. Firth munched and nodded.

'That's him. What did you say his name was?'

'PC Lawless.'

'PC Lawless? Poor name for a copper, same name as the girl. Were they related?'

'He was her uncle.'

Firth burst out laughing. 'Her uncle? Some bloody uncle!'

'I might need to talk to you again,' said Alfie.

Lola counted her money, which was all in fivers apart from the loose change and two ten shilling notes. She checked the amount against her list of expenditures.

According to her list she had spent exactly seventy-two pounds and six and sixpence out of her hundred pounds. This represented five pounds to Tommy for board and lodging – which he'd taken under protest; twelve pounds to Mr Murgatroyd, her landlord, for four weeks' rent plus a four-pound security deposit; eleven pounds for new bedding for her and Danny; nine pounds ten and six for a new cot; twenty-one pounds on new clothes for the two of them; two pounds ten on food and seven pounds on sundries. This left her with twenty-seven pounds nineteen and six which would last three weeks if they lived frugally. After that? Her meagre widow's pension wouldn't go far.

Three weeks later she pushed Danny's pushchair into the main office of the Department of Health and Social Security on Eastgate. Above one desk hung a sign saying 'Enquiries'. She made towards it.

She was a week behind with the rent. She had pawned her engagement ring and her watch. What money she had coming in was being spent on food and there wasn't much of that left.

A woman at the enquiry desk gave her a form to fill in and she took the lift up to room 17 on the second floor. It was crowded. She handed her form in at reception and a man in a uniform told to wait until she was called.

There was a smell of body odour, last night's beer and cigarettes. Lola wondered how these people could still afford to smoke. She couldn't afford them at one and nine for twenty. It was over an hour before a man called out from an adjacent desk.

'Mrs Dolores Penfold?'

'Yes,' said Lola, getting to her feet.

'If you'd like to take a seat, Mrs Penfold.'

'Thank you.'

'Mrs Penfold,' said the man, 'according to our records you were recently forcibly confined in Allerton Park Hospital under section twelve of the Mental Health Act.'

'Shanghaied is the word I'd use,' Lola told him. 'While I was in there I was assaulted by one of the staff. He was arrested and charged with sexual assault. I assume that's in there as well.'

'Er, no – well, it wouldn't be.' He looked up at her. 'We also have no record of you being discharged.'

Lola felt her anger rising again. 'I discharged myself.'

'But you can't do that when you've been forcibly confined. According to your records you were suffering severe mental impairment.'

'The records are a lie. For that to have been the case I would have had to be assessed by a doctor – I wasn't assessed by anyone. I discharged myself just after the man tried to rape me.'

The interviewees at the desks on either side were listening to her story, which seemed even less plausible than their own works of fiction. Lola felt suddenly drained. She got to her feet before they sent for the men in white coats.

'Tell you what, why don't we forget about it? You're not going to give me any money anyway.'

She put Danny back into his pushchair and, fighting back the tears, she walked out.

Alfie closed the door behind him as he entered Fould's office. He sat down without being invited.

'Seth set Evie Lawless up on a shoplifting charge,' he said.

Foulds sat back in his chair. 'Tell me more.'

'I've been to see the store detective who caught Evie with a stolen watch on her. She always maintained it must have been planted on her by a man who bumped into her. I must admit even I thought that was a bit far-fetched. Anyway I

took a look at the case file. This store detective made a statement saying a male customer had seen Evie steal a watch.'

'And this male customer was Seth?'

'Yes, sir.'

'Are you sure?'

'He identified Seth from a photo I showed him.'

'Hmm, case file, photo. Do I detect Dicksy's involvement
in this?'

'He doesn't know about the investigation and I'm sure he'll
keep his mouth shut,' Alfie assured his boss. 'He was surprised
Evie's file had been sent down to him so quickly – said he'd
checked with you.'

Foulds thought about it then remembered. 'He did – it was
Seth Lawless who took the file down, wasn't it?'

'Yes, sir – said he couldn't bear the thought of the file
being in the office for everyone to gawp at.'

'Out of sight, out of mind, more like,' said Foulds. 'No
one gawps at files. What a bloody stupid thing to say!' He
shook his head and let out a long breath. 'Well, it's something – and it's nothing. It confirms in my mind that Seth's
a wrong 'un, but it's circumstantial. There's no reason why
he shouldn't shop his own niece. And if he did, it's quite
feasible that he wouldn't want anyone knowing it was him
who did it. If I ask him about it he'll dream up some excuse,
but it'll put him on his guard. We don't want that.'

'Right, sir,' said Alfie, who pretty much expected this.

'I've been going through a few files myself,' Foulds
mentioned, sitting back in his chair. 'On the night Ezra
Lawless died a youth called Kevin Weatherall went missing.'

'I remember it, sir. He turned up in the river a few weeks
later. Seth was put in charge of the investigation. Surprised
a lot of people, that.'

'I know,' Foulds said. 'I was specifically asked by the DCI
to put him on it.'

'What, Mr Merton, sir?'

Foulds nodded. 'It apparently came from higher up still –
very much higher up by the sound of it. I didn't give it much
thought at the time. We get these odd requests now and again.
The first thing Seth did was to arrest an innocent man. By
the time the poor beggar had managed to prove himself innocent the case was clap cold.'

'But the case is still open, sir?'

Foulds nodded, then said, 'There's a connection to the Lawless brothers.'

Alfie leaned forward in his chair. 'What sort of connection?'

'The place from where the youth went missing was on their beat that very night.'

'Was there any evidence of the youth being assaulted, sir?'

'By the time we found him all evidence of that nature had been lost to us,' said Foulds. 'Eight weeks underwater can do that to a body, especially in a river as polluted as the Aire. In fact we don't know for sure whether it was murder or suicide, although the odds are heavily in favour of it being a murder, with it having a heavy chain wrapped around it. I must say it would be a novel way to commit suicide.'

'I should think the odds are heavily in favour of Seth and Ezra having something to do with it,' said Alfie.

Foulds looked at Alfie, then shook his head. 'DC Bruce, that's a serious allegation to make without proof, especially about a police officer. I don't want to hear you making that accusation again until we have absolute proof.'

'No, sir.'

Foulds went on. 'They'd been patrolling the Crown Point beat that night. Had anyone else been put on the investigation that would have been one of the first things they'd check back on: to see who was on that beat that night and note their observations, if any, in the crime file. It's one of the reasons bobbies keep notebooks. There's no mention of any such check in the file.'

'If you asked Seth, sir, he'd say he didn't need to check it with him being on the beat with Ezra and them not seeing anything.'

Foulds smiled. 'You're a sharp lad, DC Bruce – that's exactly what he would say. But the beat officer's observations that night should have been in the file. It's only checking back through the duty rosters that I found out who was on shift that night.'

'No doubt with PC Dicks' help, sir.'

Foulds smiled. 'I sometimes think Dicksy will be here 'til he's ninety. No one dare get rid of him.'

Foulds took out his pipe, Alfie lit a cigarette. They gave the matter some thought as the room filled up with smoke.

'Seth and Ezra were well-known faces on that beat, sir,' said Alfie, after a while. 'The pros hated them both.'

'Coppers aren't there to be liked by prostitutes,' Foulds said.

'No, but if any of them noticed anything untoward that night it would stick in their minds, even after all this time. Maybe I should go down there and have a word.'

'Maybe you should, DC Bruce. Try not to ask specific questions about Seth and Ezra. Let them think it's purely about the dead youth.'

It was early June and the nights were light. Alfie stepped over a drunk sitting on the pavement with his back against a wall and a bottle clutched in his hand. There was a spreading pool of urine beneath him. Alfie would normally have stopped at a police box and ordered a van to come and take the drunk into custody, but he had other things on his mind.

'Yer not gonna leave him there, are yer?' called out a familiar voice from across the road.

'Evening Marlene,' Alfie called back. 'Can I have a word?'

'What sort of word?'

He crossed the street. 'It's about a youth who was found in the river a couple of years ago.'

'I remember, what about him?'

'I was just wondering if you've heard anything that might help? If you knew anyone who was about that night?'

Marlene shrugged. 'Bloody hell, that were over two year ago. I've no idea where I was that night. If yer asked me where I was this time last week, I couldn't tell yer.' She had a cigarette in her mouth, which clung, tenaciously, to her lower lip as she spoke.

'This time last week you'll probably have been here,' countered Alfie. 'This time last year you'll probably have been here – in fact the odds are that you'll have been here that night. Marlene, do you want to keep on the right side of me or not? I'm not asking for freebies or backhanders, I just want to catch the lowlife who threw the lad into the river. I thought you might have wanted to help.'

'He was thrown in, was he?'

'Probably,' Alfie said. 'Probably assaulted first.'

'I'd help if I could,' Marlene muttered, 'but I know nowt.' She hurried away, leaving Alfie staring at her back, wondering if she knew more than she was saying. But why would she not want to help him catch a lad's murderer? Was she scared? Seth had that effect on people.

Thirty-Five

Not even Danny could cheer her up now. She had stopped breastfeeding him. If she wasn't eating properly she wasn't producing. It stood to reason. She could afford baby food but she'd cut down drastically on her own rations. She'd stopped smoking, stopped the paper delivery and told the milkman just to deliver a pint every two days. Her staple diet was bread, potatoes and tea, which was low in nutrition but it filled her up and stopped her feeling hungry. She scarcely knew her neighbours, so she could hardly turn to them for help. Anyway, she didn't need anyone's charity, she would help herself. It was the only way.

The one thing she knew for certain was that her boy would be taken from her if she couldn't look after him properly. Money was everything in this life and, in her circumstances, how she got it was immaterial. Needs must, when the devil drives.

There was a loneliness and an emptiness inside her that had swallowed up her conscience. It had devoured her dignity, her sense of decency, any self-worth she might have had left, and her sense of morality. In her experience, life itself was immoral. Good people didn't prosper, she knew that much. Good people fell by the wayside to make way for the bad people. She'd tried being good.

She watched Danny in his playpen as she waited for the babysitter. He paused in his play, looked up at her with those big, trusting eyes of his and gave her a heart-melting smile. She loved him so much it caused an ache inside her. She had to do whatever it took to keep him healthy and safe. It was half past seven. A neighbour's girl was due here any minute. Lola had promised her two shillings an hour and told her she'd be back by eleven o'clock at the latest. She told her she was going to the Odeon to see *The Bridge on the River Kwai*. Although the weather was warm, to avoid any funny looks from the babysitter, she put a light raincoat on over the skirt she had drastically shortened. It now came halfway up her thighs, ending just below what she had heard boys call the giggling strip, the strip of flesh between the top of the stockings and the knickers – get past that and you're laughing.

The babysitter duly turned up but she would have been reluctant to stay had she known that Lola had just a shilling bus fare in her pocket. It was all the money she had in the world. If things went well she'd have a few pounds when she got back. She'd heard about girls who earned as much as five pounds a night. Money like that would soon put her back on her feet. The only thing she didn't know was, could she do it? Why the hell not? Men had tried to take it from her often enough, why not make them pay for it?

Lola had walked the streets previously to give her a general feel of the place; she didn't want it to come as a shock when the day arrived. Then she had dressed like an old school ma'am so as not to give the wrong idea. Most of the clients drove cars, which pretty much put them in the higher income bracket. And she was amazed at how many clients there were. Many more clients than pros, she worked out.

The bus fare into town took up half of her worldly wealth. It was a bright June evening as she strode passed the Quarry Hill flats, sensing that a thousand eyes were on her. Five hundred people looking through their windows, saying, 'I know what you are and where you're going.'

A train thundered over the railway arches as she walked beneath them, past the Smith's Arms, past the Palace, which was advertising a skiffle group and cheap beer that night, and past the Leeds Parish Church, before swinging left into The Calls. Her reconnaissance had told that this was the place where such business was carried out.

She still hadn't taken off her raincoat, which would identify her as a street girl, and not just any street girl at that. She was trying to concentrate her mind on the injustices that had been done to her – injustices that would justify what she was doing. She thought about her mother and Evie and Keith and what the hell did her self-esteem and dignity matter against what they'd had to suffer? All she had to do was to have sex with a stranger, for which she'd be paid two pounds – she certainly wasn't going to do this for any less. If Lola had any problems, self-awareness wasn't one of them. Two pounds was a good day's pay for most girls.

There were five girls there already. Each standing alone. Each with her own patch. One was completely brazen, with her skirt right up to her knickers, one was weary-looking, a couple of them much too old for the job and one much too young.

Lola selected a stretch of unoccupied street, removed her raincoat and folded it beneath her arm. Within a minute she was getting jealous looks from other girls, who realized they didn't stand a chance while this new girl was around. A car pulled up within a few feet of where Lola was standing. A young woman got out and scowled at her.

'Hey you, go find yer own bleedin' pitch!'

'You tell 'er, Lucy,' shouted one of the other girls. 'Cheeky bloody mare.'

Lola moved to another unoccupied stretch and avoided eye contact with the other girls. Two minutes later a car appeared.

It cruised straight past the two brazen prostitutes and pulled up alongside Lola. Her heart began to bounce around inside her; her breathing quickened; a man wound down his car window. Middle-aged, moustache, balding – probably harmless.

'How much for the, er, the full thing?' he asked, almost bashfully. 'I've, er, I've got me own place.'

Lola was dumbstruck. This was it. She tried to compose herself by controlling her breathing.

'Are you all right, love?' enquired the man.

Lola nodded and managed to say, 'Two pounds.'

'Two pounds? You're new at this, aren't you?' said the man.

The brazen girl called out, 'Yer can have me fer half that money, mister – an' I'm norra bloody beginner like her.'

'Take no notice of her, mister,' called out another girl, 'it's like shovin' a sausage up a chimney.'

As far as Lola was concerned the banter fell on deaf ears. Her heart was making far too much noise.

'Two pounds it is, then,' said the man.

He leaned over and opened the passenger door, a signal for her to jump in. She walked around the front of the car, under the hostile gaze of the watching girls. Heavy footsteps clattered along the cobbles. A voice shouted, 'Police!'

Lola froze. Her heart plummeted to the bottom of her stomach. This was her worst nightmare. The other girls scattered amazing quickly in their high heels and tight skirts. The man in the car slammed the door shut and drove off, leaving Lola to face this on her own. Jesus! What sort of trouble was she in now? Arrested for soliciting. They'd take Danny off her for sure. She couldn't turn to face the oncoming copper. She stood there, immersed in shame, with her head bowed, no lie or excuse ready, waiting for the heavy hand on her shoulder.

'Lola?' said Alfie.

She was looking at her feet when she recognized his voice. Still she didn't look up. Her fear and despair turned to shame at what she was doing. He put his arm around her and escorted her off the road to the pavement. She neither spoke to, nor looked at him, such was her shame. Shame compounded by the fact that it was him, Alfie. If there was anyone in the world whom she didn't want to know about this, it was Alfie. She had kicked him out of her house for not believing in her, but that hadn't diminished her feelings for him.

'Lola, look at me.'

She couldn't. He crooked a finger under her chin and forced her head up. 'Why, Lola?' he asked.

She found her voice, and sufficient anger at this stupid question to balance her shame.

'Maybe it's because I've gone nuts again. We nutters do strange things, or hadn't you heard?'

'People who are desperate for money do strange things as well.'

She broke down in tears and almost collapsed. He half carried her along the footpath until he found a low wall she could sit on. Some prostitutes were returning. Many eyes

were on them, including passers-by. Lola's skirt had ridden
right up to the tops of her thighs.

'I, er, I should put your coat on, Lola,' Alfie advised.

Silently she did as he asked then managed to walk alongside him trying to get her thoughts in order. She felt he
deserved an explanation. 'I'm totally skint,' she told him. 'The
dole office treated me like a leper – which shouldn't have
surprised me considering my track record with officialdom.'

'It wouldn't surprise me if Seth and Campion weren't
behind that as well,' Alfie commented. 'Anyway, I'll help you
until you get back on your feet – no strings. You can pay me
back as and when you can afford it and not before.'

There was light coming back into her world now. She felt
herself smiling with relief. Alfie had never judged her. She'd
jumped down his throat a couple of times because he had
opinions that clashed with hers, but he had never judged
her.

'What on earth have Seth and Campion got to do with the
dole office?' she asked him.

'Well, probably nothing – for a change – but I think Seth's
behind a lot of things – including murdering a young man
not far from here a couple of years ago.'

'What?'

'I've got no real proof, but I'm sure he and Ezra were
involved. It happened the night Ezra died.'

'The night Ezra died?'

'He also set Evie up on the shoplifting thing. He followed
her into Lewis's, planted a stolen watch in her pocket then
reported her to a store detective.'

'Really?'

'Well, I can't prove the stolen watch bit – but it was him
who followed her and reported her.'

She took Alfie's hand. 'You lied to me, didn't you, Alfie
Bruce? You haven't dropped the investigation into Seth and
Campion.'

Alfie squeezed her hand and gave an embarrassed grin.
'OK, I'm really sorry about that, but Foulds is scared to death
that we'll be found out investigating the Home Secretary
without permission. On top of which, if Seth and Ezra are
found to be as bent as it seems they are – or were in Ezra's
case – it'll put a stigma on the whole force that'll take some

wiping out. This business is as delicate as hell, Lola. Even if we're successful I reckon it might end both our careers.'

'So, why are you doing it?'

'I thinks Foulds is doing it because he's old-fashioned and he can't stand bent cops.'

'What about you?'

'If you must know, I'm doing it for Evie and for your mother. Even if they kick me off the force it'll have been worth it if I can help put that right. There's not just me and Inspector Foulds on the force who think your mam was badly done by.'

'So, what do you think happened to Evie?' Lola was testing him here.

'Lola, we both know what happened to Evie,' Alfie said. 'Seth murdered her. When it gets to court, you'll be the star witness.'

They walked on for a while, now approaching Leeds Bus Station. Alfie obviously had something on his mind.

'Lola, were you really that desperate? I mean, turning to pr—?'

She interrupted him. 'Alfie, I'll never know if I'd have got into that car with him, but yes, I was very desperate.'

He smiled. 'My guess is that you could never have gone through with it. Anyway, I'm taking you home where you'll stay and look after your son. You will also keep your mouth very shut about this investigation. Foulds will have to be told. Under the circumstances I doubt if he'll bite my head off this time.'

Thirty-Six

Campion sighed when he heard Seth's voice on the phone. He had allowed the call to be put through much against his better judgement. It had been against his better judgement to give Seth the number to his secure line, but the truth

was that Seth was becoming an arrogant loose cannon who
needed appeasing from time to time.

Seth spoke a little too loudly for Campion's liking. 'I've
got a nice little job for you, Mr Home Secretary.'

The insolence in Seth's manner set Campion's teeth on
edge, but he controlled his deep annoyance. 'Seth, I know I'm
two hundred miles away but you don't have to shout.' He
walked over to his office door, which was slightly ajar, and
eased it shut. 'What's this about?'

'Well,' said Seth, 'they've evidently found out I was the
one who shopped our Evie in that shoplifting job.'

'Shopping your own niece isn't a hanging offence, Seth,'
said Campion. 'Just tell me what you know.'

'What I know is that one of our lads has been to interview
the store detective, asking questions about me. He even
showed him a photo of me for identification. I want this
stopped, and I want it bloody stopped now!'

'How do you know all this?' said Campion irritably.

'How do I know? Because the bloody store detective rang
me up, that's how I know. The cheeky sod asked me if it
were really me who'd shopped me own niece. I could do
without cheeky sods like that ringin' me up, Mr Home bloody
Secretary.' Campion felt like saying he knew the feeling, as
Seth went on, 'I could hear people laughin' in the background. Bastards! They thought it were a bloody big joke.
Like I said – I want this stopped.'

'Give me the details,' sighed Campion. 'If there's an investigation I'll see what I can do to forestall it.'

The DCI was facing his window when Foulds entered his
office in answer to a summons.

'Inspector Foulds, are you carrying out an investigation
into DC Lawless? If so, why haven't I been informed?'

Foulds wasn't ready for this. 'An investigation, sir?'

'An investigation, Inspector Foulds. DC Bruce took a photograph of DC Lawless and showed it to some store detective,
for what purpose I can't imagine. Could you enlighten me,
Inspector Foulds?'

Foulds thought quickly. He had to give some sort of reason
and he certainly couldn't deny all knowledge.

'I didn't want to tell you before I had absolute proof, sir, but I have reason to doubt DC Lawless's integrity. Unless I satisfy myself that I'm wrong I'll find it difficult to trust him.'

The DCI turned to him and sighed. 'Inspector Foulds, I not only doubt DC Lawless's integrity but I also doubt the man's sanity.'

'Then why has he been forced on me, sir?'

'Forced on *us*, Inspector Foulds. I don't know the ins and outs of it, but it came from high above. It doesn't make any more sense to me than it does to you. Questions on this particular subject are apparently taboo. But when secretive orders come from on high we have to trust that our superiors know what they're doing.' He looked, keenly, at Foulds. 'You have a very large bee in your bonnet about something, Inspector Foulds. I want you to either tell me all about it now or drop the matter completely. And, as I say, this isn't me talking to you, this comes from the very highest level. You appear to be ruffling some very important feathers.'

Foulds knew exactly whose feathers he was ruffling, but he also knew he couldn't tell his boss anything. It was either all or nothing. The truth was that they didn't really have anything. So it was nothing.

'I'll drop the matter completely, sir.'

'Good.' He turned back to the window. 'You also have my permission not to trust DC Lawless. I suggest you give him permanent desk work and get him so bored he goes back to uniform of his own accord.'

'Yes, sir.'

'And, Inspector.'

'Yes, sir?'

'Remember, whatever it is, drop it. I won't warn you again.'

'Sorry, Alfie, I'm dropping it – and this time I'm deadly serious. I get the impression that even if we get a result, we'll still get hammered. I also get the impression that there's something big going on that we're not party to. It sometimes happens in the job. Some investigation going on in another part of the service that's so bloody hush-hush they'd rather keep us guessing than blow their cover.'

Alfie tried to read Inspector Fould's face. 'Something that Campion's involved in, sir?'

'Possibly, but it's most likely something he's involved in quite legitimately.'

'I don't understand it, sir.'

'Neither do I, Alfie. So, let's just get on with the job we're paid to do. God knows there's plenty of work for us without us making even more.'

Alfie couldn't think of a way to tell Lola this. He wasn't going to tell her Campion was legit because he didn't believe it himself. So he bit the bullet and told her the truth about Foulds dropping the case, adding, 'If I get caught meddling, it'll cost me my job.'

'Best not meddle, then,' said Lola.

'Best not get caught, more like.'

Thirty-Seven

L oud knocks always made Lola suspicious. It was eight in the morning and she was feeding Danny.

'Who is it?'

'Post, love.'

'Oh.'

She put her son down and opened the door. The postman handed her an envelope then held out a pen and a clipboard.

'It's registered, love. Could you print your name here and sign where the cross is?'

As she signed she looked up and recognized him as being the postman who had delivered to her previous house. This prompted a question that had been at the back of her mind ever since Evie had died. She made to hand him his pen back, but kept a grip on her end as she asked him her question.

'You delivered to my old house, didn't you?'

'Er, I think so, yeah.'

'In February I got a letter that I think someone must have opened, is that possible?'

An innocent man would have said a resentful 'No' without any hesitation. But this man was taken aback, there was guilt written all over his face. Lola decided to jump in with both feet before he had time to collect his thoughts.

'It was from my sister. She died soon after it was delivered.'

'Did she? I'm sorry to hear that.'

She fixed him with an accusing stare that he couldn't meet. He dropped his eyes as she spoke. 'Did you show my letters to Seth Lawless before you delivered them to me?'

He stood there, dumbfounded and worried at the mention of Seth's name. Lola pressed on. She was now angry with this man, who had obviously been party to her sister's death.

'My sister was murdered because Seth Lawless read that letter. He knew exactly where she'd be at the time she was murdered, and there's no way he could have known, other than him reading my post. He was the one who murdered her. I know this, because I saw him do it.'

Her voice was rising as her anger mounted. They each held one end of the pen. The man was plummeting into deep shock. A few seconds ago he'd been an innocent postman; now he was accused of being an accessory to murder. He knew who Lola was, and he knew her sister had drowned some months ago, but he didn't know Seth Lawless had anything to do with it. It now struck him that, around the time of Evie's death, Seth had stopped wanting to intercept Lola's letters. Bloody hell!

He let go of his end of the pen and backed away, gulping and sweating. Then he turned and hurried on his way. Lola watched until he was out of her sight, wondering if she should run after him and apprehend him. Make him take his confession to the police. What confession? He hadn't confessed to anything. She would tell Alfie, let him make an official approach to the postman. She let out a long sigh and opened the envelope. It contained seven pounds ten shillings, and it was from Tommy.

Dear Lola,
This isn't charity. It's some residual money I owe Evie from the articles I wrote about her.
Tommy
PS. If you ever need any help you know where I am.

She didn't know what residual money was, but she put the money in her pocket alongside the postman's pen. All in all, this had been a very productive few minutes.

The postman didn't finish his round that morning. He went straight home, dumped his bag in the hallway and slumped in a chair. His wife couldn't get a word of sense out of him, except that things weren't too good at work and he might lose his job. At lunchtime he went to the pub and stayed there until he'd drunk sufficient pints to make sense of everything. The woman could well have been talking a load of bollocks. In his experience women tended to talk bollocks. Trouble was, if she was telling the truth not only would his job be up the spout, but his freedom as well. His freedom, his wife, his family and his pension.

He must go to see Seth, tell him what had happened, confront him, find out the truth. There were ten pints of Bentley's swilling around inside him when he rang Seth that afternoon. He explained what had happened as best he could.

'Are you pissed?' said Seth, trying to make sense of the man's drunken garble.

'I've had a few. I needed ter get things straight in me head. Is it right that you killed that lass?'

'Keep your bloody voice down,' Seth hissed. 'Of course I didn't kill her. Who else have you been talking to?'

'No one.'

'What about your wife?'

'I'm hardly gonna tell her, am I? Nor nobody at work, neither. If they find out I've been letting yer open that lass's post I'm in deep shit – 'speshly if it were you what topped her sister.'

Seth thought swiftly. This thing could spiral out of control if he didn't act quickly.

'Tell you what, we'll meet and I'll explain things. You've nothing to worry about. Just don't talk to anyone.'

'Are yer sure, Mr Lawless? I wouldn't trouble yer, but it's me job—'

'Don't worry.'

Seth arranged to pick the man up on a street corner which

was ten minutes' walk from the pub. He told him to set off straight away. He didn't want him to have time to hang around the pub shooting his drunken mouth off.

He drove the postman along Harrogate Road out of Leeds to the north, talking to him all the time, reassuring him, explaining how Lola had had it in for him ever since her mother had been hanged. He told him how she had been in a mental hospital and that she should be back in there, making accusations like this. He had intercepted the letters on unofficial police business and if the postman was at all worried he could check with Seth's boss, Inspector Foulds. By the time they reached Harewood he had settled the postman's mind. Seth had him laughing at a joke he'd just heard about a talking frog, and the postman was remarking on how Lola was a nice bit o' skirt, pity she was a nutter.

Then Seth turned off the main road and drove along deserted side roads, between high hedgerows and beneath trees which were fully laden with leaves. It was a fine afternoon with swallows swooping across the sky and summer sunshine bouncing off the bonnet of the car, and they exchanged remarks about the beauty of the countryside compared to the dirty city. The postman asked if he could stop for a pee.

Seth cheerfully obliged, saying, 'After the amount you've had to drink I'm surprised you've lasted this long. As a matter of fact I might join you, the old bladder's not what it used to be.'

'It's your age,' grinned the postman. He got out of the car, unzipped his fly, and proceeded to pee into a roadside ditch

'Bentley's bitter in your case,' called out Seth as he walked around the car and bludgeoned the peeing postman to death with a lump hammer he'd brought along for that purpose. He kicked the body into the ditch and drove away, congratulating himself on how swiftly and efficiently he'd dealt with the problem. But he knew there was a more threatening problem. Get rid of Lola in an equally efficient manner and he was home and dry. Seth was grinning at the thought. He knew he'd enjoy doing this.

Thirty-Eight

Campion wasn't grinning when he read the article Tommy had sold to the *Daily Mirror*. The item of news that had triggered it was the discovery of a postman's body in a country lane near Wetherby.

Alfie had already told Tommy about a postman whom Lola suspected of handing her mail over to Seth before delivering it to her. At first Tommy had tried not to be sceptical about this, especially as Alfie was taking it seriously. Then the postman's body was found. Apparently it had been lying in a ditch for over a week before it had been discovered by two boys out cycling, and it had taken another day for him to be identified as a Leeds postman. This had pricked Alfie's curiosity, and his curiosity had turned to deep suspicion when he worked out that the postman was the very one Lola had been talking to, and he had gone missing on that same day.

When the news reached Tommy it completely changed his mind about Lola. He now believed her, and to prove it he put his neck on the line with an article detailing her trials and tribulations.

He told the story of how she had reported her confrontation with the dead postman to the police on the day he went missing. Of how she had witnessed her sister's murder but hadn't been believed and had subsequently been locked up in a mental hospital where she had been sexually assaulted by a member of staff called Frampton, who was now in prison awaiting trial.

Throughout the article Seth had been referred to as Mr X, which left the newspaper in the clear as far as libel was concerned, but left the reader craving to know his identity. The article also referred to a senior politician called Mr Y, who attracted even more curiosity. The article covered Keith's mysterious death after being driven off the road, and the highly controversial execution of Lola's mother.

It was the stark truth of the parts of the article where libel wasn't an issue that gave it its credibility. That and a photograph of Lola looking her most beautiful, one that Tommy's photographer pal had taken while she was staying with him.

The news that the postman had been found dead shocked Lola. She knew that she was somehow responsible. She knew that had she not challenged him about her opened letters he might still be alive. She knew that Seth must have got to him, just the same as he'd got to Keith and Evie. And she knew she had to be next on his list.

Alfie had promised to do whatever he could to protect her. He told her how everyone at the station knew exactly who Mr X was – he had discreetly made sure of that – and Seth suspected that everyone knew. Alfie had brought up the subject when he bumped into Seth at work:

'By heck, Seth – that niece of yours is really worried about that Mr X.'

'She's no niece of mine, never was.'

'No, but she's related by adoption through your Ezra. Don't you feel any sort of responsibility towards her? Don't you feel protective?'

Alfie was pushing things but he knew Seth had to play along with his game.

'If I can help the girl in any way, I will.'

'That's good, Seth . . . and just so's you're not on your own the rest of us will be watching out for her as well. That should be a comfort to you.'

It troubled Campion that it was Tommy Pearson who had written the article. Tommy and the *Daily Mirror* had covered themselves against any libel by not naming names but the conversation he'd had with that snotty bloody reporter had obviously not got through the lad's thick head. He pondered over what to do to bring Tommy to heel.

Seth had also read the article and he wasn't pondering over anything. He knew exactly what to do, it was just a case of

how and when and where. That prat Alfie and his veiled
threats meant nothing to Seth. The girl would die a mysterious death and they could shove their suspicions where the
monkey shoves its nuts.

Lola was sitting in Tommy's front room when she read the
article. He had been round the previous evening to tell her
about it, and to warn her of the inevitable herd of reporters
who would be knocking at her door.

'Shouldn't you have mentioned that to me before you did
the article – so that I could have a choice in the matter?'

'Hmm, possibly – call it a flaw in my character. You and
Danny can come back to my place until the fuss dies down,'
he added, hopefully.

'How long will that be, do you think?'

He shrugged. 'About a week, I reckon.'

'Will it be OK with your mum? I'm not sure she likes me.'

'She has mood swings and memory lapses. I'll tell her she
likes you.'

Lola pondered her options, which seemed to be limited.
'In that case I don't think you've left me much choice, Tommy.
By the way, how much did they pay you for this?'

'A hundred and fifty quid – actually I didn't do it for the
money. I did it for you—'

She interrupted him. 'I need money and I think half of
that's mine.'

'You can have it all.'

'Half's fair. I can pay most of my debts with it.'

The next day the *Mirror* rang Tommy to say a model agency
had left a number for him to ring.

'I don't imagine it's me they're after,' he guessed.

'You're a sharp man,' said the girl from the paper.

It was a London number and it was answered by a man
called Darren. Tommy introduced himself.

'Please, please,' said Darren, 'tell me that photo in the
Mirror isn't twenty years old.'

'Er, didn't you read the article?' said Tommy, irritated.
'The girl herself is only twenty.'

'And she really looks like that?'

'No, it doesn't really do her justice.'

'Oh, you mustn't!' Darren squealed. 'What's the rest of her like?'

'Her body puts her face to shame.'

'Oh dear, I'm drooling. Do you know if she's with an agency at the moment?'

'No, I, er, I think she's freelance.'

Darren sounded relieved. 'I want to see her in my studio, right now.'

'She's hiding from the press right now.'

'Oh, buttons to them. Tell her to go out and face the buggers. Let them see her. Let them plaster her face all over their papers. Then whisk her down to me straight away.'

'I think you might have to whisk yourself up here, mate,' said Tommy. 'She's got a lot on her plate right now.'

'Oh dear, I really don't travel too well. Is it very cold up there?'

Tommy was grinning. 'Up here? This is Yorkshire, not the flaming Yukon. It's July, shirt sleeve weather, God's own county, home of cricket and the best beer in the world. It's not all flat caps and stew – well, it is in Bradford, but this is Leeds.'

'I'll arrange for a local photographer to call round,' decided Darren, who didn't seem entirely convinced about the merits of Yorkshire. 'Tell her this is the Dorothy Graham International. If she knows anything about model agencies she'll know about us.'

Tommy remained noncommittal about Lola's knowledge of model agencies. The only thing he knew was that models earned good money, and money was what Lola needed right now. He ended the call and walked into the living room, where Lola was reading the morning paper and Mrs Pearson was knitting and listening to *Workers' Playtime* on the wireless.

'That was about you,' he told Lola.

'Blast! They've tracked me here, have they?'

'Not really. It was a model agency. They saw your picture in the paper. I think they might want to offer you work.'

Lola snorted. 'They want to cash in on my short-lived notoriety, you mean.'

'Sounds to me like they want to cash in on your ugly mush. I told the man you had an equally ugly figure, but he wouldn't believe me. He's sending a photographer round to take some snaps.'

'You never know, you might make a few quid doing catalogue work,' said Mrs Pearson, unexpectedly. 'You've got nice hands, you need nice hands for the knitting catalogues.'

Lola looked at her hands then smiled at Tommy's mother. 'I don't suppose it'll do any harm,' she said, returning her attention to the paper. 'I need to earn something, and Tommy . . .' She looked up at him.

'What?'

'I'm very scared.'

He wanted to put his arm around her and tell her that he'd protect her, but in truth he didn't quite know how he could manage this – short of whisking her somewhere far away, out of Seth's reach.

'Maybe you should go away somewhere.'

'Scarborough's nice this time of year,' Mrs Pearson said, clicking away. 'The Grand Hotel, lovely view of the bay. Ask for a sea view, or they'll fob you off with anything.'

Tommy's suggestion now sounded so lame and defeatist. He knew what she'd say.

'Tommy, I've been a bit numb since I heard about the postman. Seth must have done it, surely. I'm not running away. This thing needs sorting out, once and for all.'

'If it's any consolation, I doubt if he'll come for you,' Tommy commented 'Not after the article I've just written. Everyone's eyes are on him. Even Seth's not that stupid.'

'I wouldn't bank on it,' murmured Lola. The danger she was in had sharpened her mind and made her realize that if she were to live she also had to think and act quickly. 'Tommy,' she said, after a while, 'would you pay Mrs Penfold a visit for me?'

Mrs Penfold's lounge was pretty much what Tommy had expected. Plush and pristine with an expensive looking three-piece suite in showroom condition, a seventeen-inch television set in a walnut cabinet, a light oak, roll-top writing desk and a matching sideboard on which stood a cut-glass tantalus, the type you only ever got as a wedding present from a wealthy relative who was trying to outdo everyone else. The room was decorated with summer flowers perfectly arranged in gleaming, cut-glass vases. Even the Persian cat, fast asleep on the deep pile carpet, was beautifully arranged. It was a room in which it was hard to relax.

'Please take a seat, Mr Pearson.'

She had taken Tommy by surprise by allowing him inside her house on the strength of his self-introduction and a polite smile.

'Thank you.'

Tommy sat down, wishing he'd changed the trousers he'd cut the lawn in that morning. He had already glanced at the carpet to see if he'd trailed any dirt in on his shoes. None was evident. He took a copy of his article from his pocket and handed it to Mrs Penfold.

'It might be as well if you read this – it's my article in the *Mirror*.'

She waved it away. 'I've read it – obviously, I've read it – it concerns my son. It's the only reason I've allowed you over my doorstep – to explain yourself.'

'Mrs Penfold, it concerns many people, including your son.'

Her face hardened. 'Just who are this Mr X and Mr Y?' There was a strong element of cynicism in her voice. 'Did you just make them up? If you did, you want locking up. Playing on the emotions of people such as me just to sell a story.'

'They're real people,' said Tommy, evenly. He kept his eyes on her face. 'Mr X is Seth Lawless.'

'I know of him. But I gather you have no proof of this, or you would have named him in your article.'

'Lola was a witness to him murdering her sister – that's proof enough for me.'

'And you believe that, do you?'

'In the article I also say that Mr X murdered your son, Mrs Penfold. His intended victim was Evie.'

She bit her lip and frowned. On reading the article she had convinced herself that it was rubbish. Now she wasn't so sure. 'I know what you said in your damned article, Mr Pearson.'

'I didn't write it with the intention of hurting you, Mrs Penfold.'

Her emotions were now collapsing. In her mind, what had

killed her son was him getting mixed up with that family. But it wasn't Lola who had killed him. It wasn't she who had run him off the road into the river. According to Tommy it was Seth Lawless. She was wondering if her friend, now the Home Secretary, might be able to help throw some light on the matter, some light and some justice. He'd helped her in the past.

'Who's this Mr Y – the politician?'

Tommy was more hesitant to answer this one. 'Mr Y is the man who gave Seth an alibi for the time he was actually murdering Evie. He also gave Lola a hundred pounds to keep her mouth shut about what happened to her in Allerton Park mental hospital. He's the man who rang me up and warned me not to write any articles about him.'

'And does this man have a name?'

Tommy nodded, slowly. 'Yes, Mrs Penfold, he has a name. I believe he's the man we think helped you get care of your grandson on the day Lola was forcibly taken to Allerton Park.'

Her eyes widened with shock as the implication of his words hit her.

'Mrs Penfold,' said Tommy, 'we both know who I'm talking about, don't we?'

'Someone did ring me, yes,' she admitted. 'But you can't possibly be talking about the same man. The person who helped me was—'

'Clive Campion?'

He knew from her expression that he'd hit the nail on the head. She looked utterly shocked.

'No, no . . . Now, this really is ridiculous!' she snorted, getting to her feet. 'Look, I want you to go, Mr Pearson.'

Tommy got to his feet. 'So, you're saying it wasn't Clive Campion who helped you get custody of Danny?'

'No, I'm – look, I, I don't want to say anything.'

'You've said enough, Mrs Penfold. I just wanted to verify that fact.'

'For God's sake, he's the Home Secretary! Why would he get mixed up in anything like this?'

'I've no idea, Mrs Penfold, but I'm fairly sure he was largely responsible for the wrongful execution of Rachel Lawless, and indirectly involved in the murder of your son, among other people.'

'My son? Oh my god! What have I been thinking of?' She sat down again. Tommy did the same. He reached across and took her hand, which was shaking. She began to weep. 'I didn't know. I just wanted the best for my Keith.'

'I haven't come to judge you, Mrs Penfold. How could you know? You didn't want your only son to get mixed up with the family of a murderer. You wanted something better for him.'

'That's all I ever wanted.'

'Only Rachel Lawless wasn't a murderer.'

She got to her feet again and walked around the room, clasping and unclasping her hands. Then she came and stood in front of him, like an errant child.

'What do you want me to do?'

Tommy stood up and placed his hands on her shoulders to calm her down. 'Just tell me about your relationship with Campion,' he said, gently.

She shook her head, vigorously. 'Relationship? I wouldn't call it a relationship. He first rang me just after I'd had that run-in with Lola in the shoe shop. He told me I should press charges. I did – and the court was very hard on her.'

'Did you think he had anything to do with the court being hard on her?' Tommy asked.

'I'm absolutely sure he did. He rang me up later, and told me. Oh my God! She was my son's wife – and I did that to her.'

'Campion did that to her,' said Tommy. 'I think he was behind every bad thing that happened to Lola's family.'

'What about this . . . this Seth Lawless?'

'I suppose he's what you might call the hit man. He uses his police authority to get up to all sorts of stuff, including murdering that poor postman.'

'And my poor boy.'

'Yes, I'm sorry. Look, Mrs Penfold, I only came here to verify what Lola and I already suspected. Because of who Campion is we've got to tread very carefully. I've told you what I know because I feel you have that right – with Keith being a victim in all this. But it would be as well if you didn't breathe a word to anyone.'

'No, I won't. You seem to know what you're doing. Are the police doing anything?'

'If they were, it would be a copper coming to talk to you, not me.'

'I suppose it would, yes.'

Before he left, Tommy had a final thought. 'Mrs Penfold, in view of what we've just talked about, do you still hold a grudge against Lola?'

She gave this some thought. 'I was wrong to object to her marrying Keith – I had no right to do that and I bitterly regret it. I also regret any pain I might have caused the girl.' Then she thought back to the ignominy she'd suffered when Lola had plonked the window cleaner's bucket on her head. 'But there are some things it's really hard to forgive.'

'I wish you'd try, Mrs Penfold.'

Thirty-Nine

Lola knew if she had told Tommy where she was going he'd have forcibly stopped her – so would Alfie, come to think of it. In fact, so would Evie had she been alive to do it. The constant memory of Evie's death was more than enough to spur Lola on.

Alfie had told her about his chat with Marlene and how he thought she knew more than she was telling. Maybe Marlene wouldn't talk to Alfie, but she might talk to Lola. And there was only one place to find Marlene.

She had washed off all her make-up, covered her head with a headscarf and put on the raincoat she'd worn on the day she'd made her fortunately failed debut as a prostitute. Attention was the last thing she needed this evening, especially the attention of a certain police officer.

Luckily there was drizzle in the air which justified her wearing the raincoat. On top of which, when it's drizzling most people look down. It was something she noticed as she made her way to The Calls.

Lucy was there, along with two others, neither of whom

fitted what Lola knew about Marlene, who was apparently very tarty looking and in her late thirties with a pneumatic chest. All three of these girls were in their twenties at most, perhaps even still in their teens. It was a job that put years on you.

'Is Marlene about?'

She asked the question of Lucy, whom, Lola figured, would probably know most of the other girls.

'Who wants ter bleedin' know?'

'I bleedin' do,' said Lola, taking a step forward and matching the girl's aggression. Lucy didn't recognize Lola as the girl who had recently tried to muscle in on her patch.

Lucy took her time lighting a Sobranie. 'She's just gone off wi' a punter. I think it's only a ten bob hand job. She'll be back in a few minutes.'

It was fifteen minutes before Marlene appeared. Her face was bruised and her lip was bleeding.

'Bloody 'ell, Marl!' exclaimed Lucy. 'What happened? Did he smack yer one?'

'What's it look like?' grumbled Marlene. 'The bastard took me bloody money as well. Stuck his hand down me clouts and grabbed the lot. Two pound bloody ten – an' that were after I'd given him his ten bob's worth. Nearly sprained me wrist doin' that.' She looked at Lola. 'Who's she?'

Lola was concerned that her name might ring a bell. It was an unusual name around Leeds and it had been in the papers from time to time. 'My name's Dolores. I'm a pal of Alfie Bruce. I want to talk to you.'

Lucy sniggered. 'She hasn't got time for talk, love. She's got overtime ter do ternight. She's two and a half quid down already.'

Marlene corrected her. 'Three quid – the bastard never paid. It's not all glamour, isn't this job.'

'I'll give you five pounds for a short chat,' said Lola. 'Maybe we could go for a coffee somewhere.'

Marlene stared at her, remembering the last conversation she'd had with Alfie. 'Is it about that lad what got drowned?'

'Yes,' said Lola. 'As a matter of fact, it is.'

There was a long pause, then, 'Why are you so interested?'

'I'm related. I need to know what happened.'

'Related? . . . Oh, I see.'

It had been on Marlene's mind ever since Alfie had mentioned it. In fact it had been on her mind ever since the night it happened, over two years ago. 'Five pounds?' she said. 'Yer don't look as if yer've gorra tanner ter scratch yer arse.'

Lola took a five-pound note from her purse and held it out to Marlene, who took it and stuck it down her brassiere. 'We'll go t' Kardomah on Briggate,' she said. 'I'll treat yer to a coffee.'

'You'll have to,' said Lola. 'I'm skint, now, apart from my bus fare.'

Marlene laughed and linked arms with her. 'Come on, Dolores. What do yer pals call yer? Don't tell me, I bet it's Dolly.'

'It'll do,' said Lola.

They were halfway down their coffees and still Lola hadn't broached the subject. She didn't want Marlene to think she was being pressured. It was Marlene who, eventually, brought it up.

'It's been on my mind ever since it happened.'

'You mean the lad who was drowned?'

Marlene nodded; Lola still didn't press her. She obviously wanted to get something off her considerable chest.

'I know I should've said summat, but with it bein' them two bastards . . .'

'What two bastards?'

'They'd have done ter me what they did to him without battin' a bloody eye.'

Lola was trying to make sense of what she was hearing without asking what might have seemed like daft questions. She made an educated guess.

'I assume we're talking about Ezra and Seth Lawless.'

A look of surprise crossed Marlene's face as she sipped her coffee. 'Bloody hell, Dolly! Yer know about it, don't yer?'

'Not the details. I don't know the details.'

With Lola looking on, patiently, Marlene finished her coffee as she mentally put the events of that night into a story she could tell. She eventually stared into her empty cup.

'There were three of them, did yer know that?'

Lola thought for a second. 'I thought there might have been. I wasn't sure.'

'Ezra and Seth and a bloke in a suit. I nearly threw up, I tell yer. It were bloody sickenin' what they did ter that young lad.'

'What? You mean you saw it?' said Lola.

Marlene nodded and took out a packet of Woodbines. She lit two and gave one to Lola without asking if she smoked.

'I were with one of me regulars down by t' river. We'd finished doin' business and we were havin' a quiet fag, when we heard 'em. They couldn't see us. We were in a snicket I sometimes use – very private. But we could see 'em all right. Clear as day. It must have been a full moon or summat.'

'What did you see?'

Marlene shook her head at the memory. Tears came to her eyes. Tears of guilt maybe.

'Yer know, Dolly, I still think ter this day I should've done summat. But I didn't – neither of us did. I suppose me punter didn't want his wife findin' out what he'd been up ter. I were just shit scared o' Seth an' Ezra.'

Lola took her hand. There was a buzz of conversation around them that would drown what Marlene had to tell her.

'Marlene, what did you see?'

Marlene wiped away a tear, smudging her mascara. The bruise on her face was now quite livid and her lip had swollen. She took a compact out of her tiny handbag and looked at herself. 'Christ, I look a right mess.'

'What did you see, Marlene?'

The prostitute leaned forward so that no one could possibly hear but Lola. 'I'll tell yer what I saw. I saw Ezra knock this lad around, then he made him strip off. The lad were scared ter death, cryin' his eyes out – it were middle o' winter, freezin' bloody cold, and he were standin' there starkers.'

Marlene paused, Lola prompted, 'Then what happened?'

'That's when he turned up.'

'Who turned up?'

'This feller in an overcoat, Seth brought him. He sounded posh – too posh for what he did.'

'What did he do, Marlene?'

Marlene took a long drag on her cigarette. 'Ezra knocked the lad senseless. He were spark out on the ground an' this posh feller took his coat off and . . .' her voice tailed off as she screwed up her face in disgust. She looked up at Lola. 'Yer don't need me ter spell it out, do yer?'

'You mean this posh feller raped the lad while he was unconscious?'

'Yeah – that's exactly what he did. Bloody hell, it were sickening, Dolly, lass.'

Marlene's hands were shaking as she put her cigarette to her mouth. 'He were sixteen – six-bloody-teen years old and the bastard did that to him!' Tears were running freely now. Lola waited until they stopped.

'Then the other feller went off,' she said, eventually. 'Calm as yer like. He just put his coat on an' buggered off.'

'While the lad was still alive?'

A nod and a deep frown.

'Then what happened?'

Marlene looked at her. Her face was now a disaster area. 'You say he was a relative? Yer might not want to hear this.'

Lola held her in her gaze and said in a controlled, low voice, 'Marlene, I'm not a relative of the lad. Ezra Lawless was my stepfather. My sister killed him that night and our mother was hanged for it.'

'What? Jesus, Dolly – I know yer, now.'

'Well, I'm not called Dolly. I used to be Lola Lawless – Marlene, I need to know what happened that night. I need to put Seth away for good. He killed my sister and my husband – and he'll kill me next.'

Marlene stared at Lola for a full minute, as she took in all the implications of what she was about to say.

'He might kill me after you.'

'Not if we get him first.'

There was courage in Lola's face that Marlene wanted to share. For once in her life she needed to do something courageous. It might make her feel good about herself again.

'They tied a chain around him and threw him in the river – then they walked off, as if nowt had happened. I'll swear ter that in court if yer want me to.'

'You'll swear to that in court?' Lola took Marlene's hand and squeezed it tight. This was it. This was the breakthrough she'd wanted. This could solve everything. This could even get her mam a posthumous pardon. 'Please don't say that unless you mean it, Marlene.'

'I mean it, love. When yer've seen summat happen like that an' yer've done nowt about it, well it tears away at yer insides.'

'I saw him murder my sister,' Lola said, 'but no one believes me. Now the police have got two witnesses to two murders – he won't get out of this. Besides, there's all sorts of other stuff.'

'I've got summat else as well.'

'What?' asked Lola.

'I've got the name of me punter – and I know where he works.'

'You do – will he help?'

'He might not have any option – anyway, you can always ask.'

Eric Smith had a barber's shop on North Street and he wasn't a happy man. The business was doing OK but his private life was crap. His wife had left him two years previously. She had taken their only daughter with her and gone to live with her parents in Wigan. He didn't miss his wife, she'd been frigid and humourless, but he did miss his daughter, who had been poisoned against him – and just because he'd been going to prostitutes to compensate for his wife's lack of passion. She'd made him out to be some sort of sex beast. Better men than he had resorted to a lot worse than going to prostitutes. He knew that for certain.

Marlene and Lola came into his shop together. It was the day after they'd talked in the Kardomah.

'How's it going, Eric?' greeted Marlene, who was a blatant walking, talking advert for her profession. 'Long time, no see.'

'Marlene, what the hell are you doing in here?' He didn't sound very welcoming.

'I've come for a haircut. Have I come to the right place?' She sat in a vacant barber's chair and spun herself round. A bearded man, whose hair Eric was cutting, looked at her reflection in a mirror, then he looked up at Eric's reflection.

'Are you branching out a bit, Eric?' he grinned. 'I've heard of you fellers asking if we want something for the weekend, but I think this is taking things a step too far.'

Lola sat in a chair in the waiting area beside a man reading a *Reader's Digest*. The man looked up from his reading and smirked at the banter. This annoyed Lola.

'We want a chat, Eric,' Marlene said. 'About what happened the last time we met.'

'Is that what they call it nowadays, a chat?' sniggered the bearded customer.

'A private chat.'

The customer laughed loudly. 'Well, you don't want to be doing it in public like a pair of mongrels. You get locked up for that.'

Marlene picked up a pair of scissors from the counter and snipped off most of the customer's beard before Eric could stop her.

The man whipped the cloth from around his neck, swore at Marlene and stormed out of the shop. The customer sitting beside Lola ran out as Marlene approached him, snipping the scissors.

'Now look what you've bloody done,' wailed Eric. 'As if I haven't got enough to worry about.'

Marlene went to the door, locked it, and turned over the Open/Closed sign. 'Now we can have our private chat,' she said.

'I don't want a private chat. That night were something I've been trying to forget about.'

'But you haven't forgotten about it, have you?'

'No,' Eric admitted, 'it's hardly something you forget in a hurry.'

'No, and you never will – Eric, this is Lola, she used to be Lola Lawless – recognize the name?'

Eric sat down in one of the barber's chairs, with his back to them, talking to their reflections. 'Well, I'm hardly gonna forget the name Lawless,' he said. 'It's a name that bloody haunts me.'

'And me,' Marlene said. 'But now we can do something about it.'

Eric looked at Lola's reflection. The marked difference between the two women didn't escape him. 'What relation are you to them bastards?' he asked.

'Ezra was my stepfather.'

'And Seth's been up to his old tricks, Eric,' added Marlene.

'If we'd come forward when we should have, there'd be people alive today who aren't. Lola's husband and sister, for a start.'

'And my mother,' added Lola.

'Your mother?' Eric nodded as he remembered. 'Right . . . she'll be the one who . . .'

'She was hanged for the murder of Ezra, only she didn't do it. My sister killed him because he was attacking Mam.'

'It needs sorting, once and for all, Eric,' Marlene said. 'I'm going to the police – it's up to you what you do.'

'Police? Will you tell them I was with you?'

'I'll have no choice.'

Eric spun round in his chair to face them. 'Then what option do I have?'

Lola sensed he was relieved that things had come to a head. 'Will we get into bother for not coming forward sooner?' he asked.

'No idea,' said Lola, who wasn't pleased with them for hiding such a secret for all this time. But she could understand their fear. 'You'll just have to hope for the best.'

Eric got to his feet and tidied up the counter as he thought about the situation. The women watched his face in the mirror.

'I, er, I know something else that might be of interest,' he said, almost reluctantly.

'What's that?' asked Lola.

'I think I know who the feller was; the one who did – yer know – to the lad.' He gave a dry laugh. 'In fact, I definitely know who he was.'

'You never said at the time,' said Marlene.

'I don't think I said anything at the time – neither of us did. It wasn't a time for chit-chat. But I recognized him – and you'll never guess in a million years.'

'I seem to remember 'em callin' him Mr Green,' Marlene said.

Eric nodded. 'That threw me a bit – but his name definitely wasn't Green.'

'It was Clive Campion,' said Lola.

'Bloody hell!' Eric gasped. 'How the hell did you know?'

'Well, it's a long story,' Lola said, 'but he'll be going down as well as Seth.'

'Clive Campion?' said Marlene. 'Isn't he an MP or summat?'

'He's now the Home bloody Secretary,' Eric told her. 'I

knew I should have said summat, but who's gonna believe me? You didn't know who he was, did you?'

Marlene shrugged. 'Hadn't a clue. Look, Eric, we both should have said summat. We've let this thing go on too long. Now Seth's goin' round bumpin' people off, ten to the dozen.'

Forty

Detective Chief Inspector Merton looked at Foulds and shook his head.

'What you're telling me, Frank, is that we've got the word of a prostitute and her punter that they saw the Home Secretary raping a young man, assisted by two of our uniformed officers. All this happened after dark, down by the river where there's no lighting, and they've suddenly turned up with the story two and a half years later.'

Foulds said nothing. Merton had all the facts laid out in front of him; the ball was in his court now. The DCI sighed and rubbed his chin, aggressively.

'There's too much for us to ignore, sir,' Foulds said, eventually.

'I'll tell you what there is here, Frank. There's enough to knacker the career of the Home Secretary, purely working on the "no smoke without fire" theory. But, if it's not enough to hold up in court, it'll knacker our careers as well.'

'I think we have enough, sir. We certainly have enough to arrest DC Lawless on two charges of murder.'

'If we arrest DC Lawless we have to arrest Campion. How the hell do you arrest a Home Secretary on this evidence? Christ! How do you arrest a Home Secretary on any evidence? It's too patchy, Frank. In this case it needs to be an absolutely cast-iron, twenty-four carat, one hundred per cent certainty. What we've got is a barber of dubious morals, a prostitute with a string of convictions and a woman with a criminal record and a history of mental instability.'

'No doctor ever declared Lola mentally unstable,' Foulds pointed out. 'Campion brought pressure to bear, the same as he did with us to give Seth a CID job.'

'Which is an indication of how much power he's got.'

'It's power that should be taken away, sir. Perhaps you should let the super handle it.'

'If I take this upstairs, Frank, it'll keep getting passed further and further up until it either stays up there or it comes tumbling right back down here. Right back down to me and you – even if we get convictions. We've already just had one Prime Minister resign recently, this could bring the whole government down – and when governments tumble there's a lot of collateral damage. Scapegoats are sought. That's you and me, Frank – scapegoats.'

'You seem to know a lot about Campion, sir.'

'I once fell foul of him, Frank, so I made it my business to keep tabs on him. If you repeat what I say I'll deny it. Campion's a man with a lot of money, which he uses to buy power and influence – the sort of power and influence that comes from keeping your eyes and ears open on the way up. If he can't buy you he'll blackmail you. Coppers, judges, politicians, businessmen. He has things on all sorts of people. It's the way things are sometimes done in politics. Campion's a master of the bloody art.'

'Are you telling me he's got something on you, sir?'

Merton gave a wry smile and shook his head. 'Not since I got divorced he hasn't. He somehow found out about an indiscretion and tried to use it against me. I settled for divorce instead – it was on the cards.'

Foulds was impressed with Merton's dedication to the job. He would probably go right to the top – if he could keep his nose clean on the way up, which was what this conversation was about.

'Sir, I've got these people ready to come in and make statements. What do you want me to do?'

Merton drummed his fingers on his desk. 'I want you to do nothing, Frank. I need to have a quiet word in a few ears.'

'But—'

'No buts, Frank.'

'So long as it's properly dealt with, sir.'

'Don't threaten me, Frank.'

Foulds sat there in silence for a few seconds, then got up and left the office without another word.

Alfie was waiting for Foulds in his office when he got back. He got to his feet. 'Well, shall I wheel them in, boss?'

Marlene and Eric were waiting in reception.

'He's scared of his own shadow!' Foulds spat the words out with disgust. He kicked a waste paper basket right across the office, spilling its contents all over the floor.

'He's probably right to be scared, boss,' Alfie pointed out. 'It'd certainly affect his promotion prospects if things went belly-up. What's happening, then?'

'What's happening? I'll tell you what's happening, Alfie – Mr Merton wants to have a quiet word in a few ears.'

'And what does that mean, exactly?'

'It means, Alfie, that words will be spoken, and deals would be struck. Campion may or may not resign, depending on who's got the most to lose if he shoots his mouth off. People in high places will be worried about going down with him.'

'What about Seth?'

'Seth will be their big worry. Best thing all round would be if he disappeared without trace.'

'What? Do you really think that might happen, boss?'

Foulds sat down and shook his head. 'Things happen in the higher echelons of government that are rarely spoken about. It's rumoured that there's a department within the security service that deals with such matters. It's a department that doesn't exist – if you know what I mean. And when something doesn't exist it can't be held to account.'

'Blimey!' said Alfie. 'They wouldn't do that, would they?'

'You tell me. One alternative is to pension him off, complete with dire threat to keep his nose clean and his mouth shut – not much of an alternative if you ask me. To be honest, I don't know what they'll do with him.'

'Another alternative is to tell the truth,' Alfie said. 'What are they going to do about me? How do they keep my mouth shut? I'm a serving police officer and I have a duty to report crime.'

Foulds looked at Alfie and smiled, as if Alfie's question was one he'd been hoping for.

'Do you have any great career ambitions?'

Alfie shrugged. 'I'm not a high-flyer, boss. I'd like to think I'd make it to inspector one day – but I'm in no hurry. I certainly wouldn't put my job before something like this. In fact I don't think I'd want to stay in the job if this is the price I have to pay.'

Foulds placed a hand on Alfie's shoulder. 'No, Alfie, neither would I – but I've got a lot more time in than you. I've got more to lose.'

'There's Lola as well, boss. She won't sit back and let them cover things up. She can be a real pain in the arse when she wants to be.'

'I bet she can,' agreed Foulds, 'but Lola shouldn't really know what's going on, Alfie. And if you do tell her, it's without my authority. You must make that clear to her.'

'I'll make it as clear as I possibly can, boss.'

Forty-One

T wo days later, on a Wednesday evening in mid-July 1957, six people were sitting around the table in the offices of the *Daily Mirror* in Fleet Street – Lola, Marlene, Eric and Tommy – each of whom had told their own part of the story. Also there were Cecil King, the MD of the newspaper, and Hugh Cudlipp the managing editor.

On the table were sworn affidavits from Mrs Penfold; Mr Jackman, the superintendent of Allerton Park; Miss Pritchard, the juvenile liaison officer who had, on instruction, placed Evie into Seth's care; and Barry Firth, the store detective.

The newspapermen looked at each other. This was too big and convincing to ignore. They knew if the *Mirror* didn't run it another paper probably would.

'It all boils down to one thing, Hugh,' Cecil King was saying. 'Are we absolutely convinced that it's true?'

All eyes turned to Hugh Cudlipp, who was thumbing

through Tommy's article. 'I don't see how it can't be true,' he said. 'We have murders, an awful rape, an unjust execution, a bent Home Secretary – whom we already know to be bent – witnesses, affidavits. What on earth are the police scared of?'

'Losing their jobs?' suggested Tommy.

'I'll tell you what convinces me,' said King. 'Above all these good people here, and above all these affidavits, what convinces me is my own memory of that poor woman being hanged. It was the most unexpected and shocking thing I've known in a long time. Everyone expected her to get her sentence commuted to life. There was never any explanation as to why not, and now we know why not. Pressure was applied from Campion.'

King looked around the table at the four 'guests' and smiled at the rapt expressions on their faces.

'To look at Campion,' he went on, 'you'd think butter wouldn't melt in his mouth, but he's the most back-stabbing, Machiavellian, devious individual in government. I reckon he only got this job because he had something on the PM – I wish I knew what.'

'So,' said Cudlipp, 'what do we do?'

King thought for a moment, then looked at Tommy. 'This Inspector Foulds. Would he be prepared to verify this – unofficially.'

'Try him – he's expecting your call.'

Tommy knew for certain that he would, unofficially. Five minutes later, at his home in Leeds, Foulds answered his telephone. King came on the line. 'Good evening, Inspector Foulds, Cecil King of the *Mirror*.'

'Good evening, Mr King.'

'Inspector Foulds, I'll be brief, because I expect you're a busy man – have you read the draft of Pearson's article?'

'I have.'

'In your opinion, is it accurate?'

'In my opinion, yes.'

'Thank you, Inspector.'

King put the phone down. 'That's it. We run the article on Friday.'

'Publish and be damned, eh?' smiled Cudlipp.

'Wasn't that the Duke of Wellington?' said Tommy.

'No, it was Cudlipp and King,' said Cecil. 'And this could be our Waterloo . . .'

The taxi was passing the end of Lola's street. It seemed daft not to take the opportunity and call in to check that everything was all right. They were returning from London. She had told the driver to drop her off here. Tommy wasn't happy.

'Lola, it's one in the morning.'

'I know. I just want to call in to check everything's OK. I'll walk back to your house – it's only fifteen minutes.'

'Oh no you won't! I'm coming with you.'

'Tommy, if you must know – after all that's gone on – I just want a bit of time on my own. I like walking at night, always have.'

'What if Seth's out walking the streets?'

'Now you're getting paranoid.'

'I don't like it.'

'Tommy, you go on. I'll be back in half an hour.'

It was just time on her own that she needed. Some time in her own space. In her room at Tommy's house Danny would hopefully be asleep, but requiring her awareness. You must always be aware of your children, even when you're asleep, she knew that much. She couldn't remember the last time she'd had a moment entirely to herself. In Allerton Park she'd been aware of the proximity of the nurses, of the fact that she had no say in whether or not they came into her room and turned the light on to check her.

She went into her front room, sat down in her chair and lit a cigarette. She glanced around to check that she hadn't been burgled or anything. She sniffed for a gas leak and listened for a dripping tap. But there was nothing, only glorious silence. It was true what they said about silence being golden. And she knew that the opposite of golden silence isn't loud noise. The opposite of golden silence is fear.

She had lived with fear and worry all her life – well, ever since Ezra had entered it. Ezra then Seth. Was it soon to be over? Or was this too good to be true?

Next week she was due to go to London to see Darren at the Dorothy Graham International model agency. He had been delighted with her photographs and was promising her the moon. But Lola thought he sounded like someone who would

promise anyone the moon, so she wasn't counting any
chickens. It would be a nice trip for Danny, who would enjoy
a ride on the train if nothing else. Theresa was coming too,
at the agency's expense.

Lola thought about Tommy, whom she now knew was in
love with her, just as Keith had been. Keith had been an
exceptionally good man and would have given her a good
life, but she had never truly loved him, which made her feel
enormously guilty. She hadn't loved him any more than she
loved Tommy.

The circumstance of her life had clouded her judgement
about whom she loved and whom she liked. But poking his
smiling face through that cloud was lovely Alfie. Over and
above her recent feelings of misery and fear and dejection
and anger she also had strong feelings for Alfie. Love? She
didn't know for sure. It was a feeling she'd tried to stifle.
Why? Maybe, with her life as it was, loving someone was
simply an indulgence she couldn't afford.

In any case, did Alfie love her? He had never told her so.
Let's face it, she'd never let him near enough to her, emotionally, for the subject to be broached. What would her mam
have advised? How her mam would have loved to have been
around to have given such advice to her daughter – part of
being a mam. And what about Evie? What advice would she
have given? Evie had liked Alfie. She had preferred him to
Keith – at first, anyway. Then after he died Evie had nothing
but praise for Keith. If Evie was to be believed Keith was
the greatest and bravest person ever to walk the face of the
earth.

Seth had been driving past Lola's house at regular intervals
ever since Tommy's Mr X article had appeared. He knew she
wouldn't stay away for ever. He'd driven past three times a
day and twice a night, watching for signs of life. It was half
past one when he noticed a downstairs light on. He grinned
to himself and muttered, 'Bloody Bingo!'

He parked in the next street and walked back. The house
was now in complete darkness and, just for a second, he
wondered if he'd been looking at the right one. Then he saw
her come out of the front door. She turned to lock it. Seth
jumped over the low wall into the tiny front garden. He

brought her down with a rugby tackle, choked off her scream with one hand and put the other around her throat. He didn't make a sound, but Lola had no doubt who it was.

Seth was devising his plan as he throttled her. He would put her body back in the house, then lock the door. She would be found, maybe tomorrow, maybe next week. Whenever. The longer she lay there the harder it would be to ascertain her time of death. It was him taking time to allow himself these thoughts, instead of concentrating on the job in hand, that gave Lola an extra few seconds to try and save her life.

Beside the door was a lump of ornamental stone, beneath which the previous occupants had left the key for one other. Lola's hand closed around it and, with all her diminishing strength, she hit him on the side of the head, twice. His hands came off her throat and mouth. She let out a piercing scream, got to her feet and ran away.

Seth lay there, stunned. Windows opened in response to the scream. People could see a man lying there, motionless, and someone running away. Twenty minutes later Lola was sitting in Tommy's house, shivering with fright as Tommy rang the police.

Forty-Two

At eighty thirty that morning the cell door opened and Alfie walked in with a mug of tea.

'It's a cock-up, Lola,' he muttered. 'Can't say too much, but it's a cock-up. I've rung Foulds, he's on his way in.'

'I've been arrested for assault on Seth – for God's sake, Alfie, he was trying to strangle me.'

'I know – Tommy told me. According to Seth you rang him up and asked him to call round. Then, when he turned up, you hit him with a stone. With him being one of our own we have to give his story some credence whether we like it or not.'

'Why the hell would I do something as stupid as that?'

Alfie grimaced. 'That's the problem. It's public knowledge that you've got every reason to hate him. Look, I know it's all stupid. I'll sort it out as soon as Inspector Foulds gets here.'

'Do I have to stay in this cell?'

Alfie felt lousy about the whole thing. 'It won't be for long, Lola. I promise you.'

'Alfie, will this affect what we're doing – you know, with the papers?'

This hadn't occurred to Alfie. No doubt the news would be picked up by the press before long. Would it put the wind up the *Mirror*? He'd no idea.

'I don't see why it should,' he lied, miserably.

When Foulds arrived he was immediately summoned to Merton's office. 'Our case against Seth Lawless and our Home Secretary is diminishing before our eyes,' Merton told him. 'It seems these Lawless women have a thing for hitting people over the heads with blunt instruments.'

'Seth attacked her,' Foulds retorted.

'So she says. She arrives home at one in the morning – not having lived there for quite some time – and, lo and behold, at that very moment, Lawless turns up to attack her. Sounds flimsy.'

Forty-Three

A t 10 a.m. Hugh Cudlipp was in his office at the *Daily Mirror*, scrutinizing Tommy's article and weighing up the colossal impact it was going to have. It was a hell of a story, but did he have a duty to give the Home Secretary the right to respond before the story was printed? He'd just had word that Lola had been arrested for an attack on Seth – which didn't help matters. Once the story was in black and white it was a fait accompli, whether or not Campion had a genuine rebuttal. He allowed himself a reluctant nod. In fairness, the Home Secretary surely had that right. It might kill the story dead, but the man had a right to give his side of a story that would ruin his life. Cudlipp picked up the telephone.

Clive Campion was at his home in the Berkshire countryside when the call came through. He feigned outrage at such an accusation and told Cudlipp his newspaper would be closed down if such libel were ever printed.

'Just so I get things straight, Mr Campion. You're saying you never met Ezra Lawless?'

'Of course I didn't. I believe I met his brother once.'

'So you did, Mr Campion. It was you who gave him his cast-iron alibi when he was accused of murdering his niece. That was a very fortuitous meeting as far as Seth was concerned.'

'Mr Cudlipp, if you value your career you'll kill this ludicrous story dead.'

'I'll certainly let you know our decision regarding publication, Mr Campion. Tell me, why did you telephone Mrs Penfold, the mother of Lola's husband?'

'I've never heard of the woman.'

'I see, and did you ever speak to Mr Jackman, the superintendent of Allerton Park mental hospital, around the time Lola was being held there?'

'Look,' protested Campion, 'this is getting bloody ridiculous! I've much more important things to be getting on with than speaking to the likes of you. Good day to you, sir.'

Forty-Four

At 1 p.m. Alfie brought Lola some lunch and assured her that everything possible was being done to free her, but she could sense the doubt in his voice.

'There's something going on, Alfie. What is it?'

Alfie looked at her and sighed. He scratched his head and sat down beside her. 'Look, I only know what Inspector Foulds is telling me and I'm not supposed to tell you that.'

'I'm listening.'

'The DCI seems to believe Seth's version of events.'

'*What?*'

'I know. Beats me how anyone can believe that slimy bastard. I reckon it's maybe more convenient for Merton to believe Seth that believe you.'

'So, where does that leave me?'

Seth couldn't wait to be discharged from the Leeds Infirmary and get down to the station to do a bit of gloating. It was three in the afternoon when the slot in her cell door slid open and Seth's eyes leered through.

'Assaulting a policeman with a deadly weapon . . . could get ten years for that, but I'm told you'll probably get off with five. Lucky you, eh?'

She turned her face away from him. His words dripped through the door like poisonous treacle.

'And who's gonna believe a word you say in the future, eh? Who's gonna believe your bloody lies about me? When you get out, all you'll be fit for is whoring. I'll look forward ter that – watchin' you out whoring. Might even help meself to a freebie.'

Lola was now in tears, which made him laugh out loud. She heard the door being unlocked and she tensed herself. He was coming inside. To hurt her again. How could they allow him to do that? The same as they'd allowed him and Campion to hurt her and her family all these years. She didn't look up but she knew the door was open. This time she heard Alfie's voice.

'OK, Lola?'

She looked up to see Alfie and Seth standing side by side in the doorway, and just for a second they looked to be in cahoots – her worst nightmare.

'What—?' she began.

Alfie gave her a broad smile. 'You're free to go, Lola. It's all been sorted out.'

He then stepped behind Seth and slapped handcuffs on him before he had a chance to react.

'Seth Lawless, I'm arresting you for the murder of Kevin Weatherall. You do not have to say anything, but anything you do say may be taken down and used in evidence . . .'

'What the hell are yer playin' at?'

'There'll doubtless be other murder charges to follow,' the voice belonged to Foulds, 'including that of Evie Lawless.'

Lola sat there, mesmerized by the dramatic change in her fortunes.

'*What?*' screamed Seth. 'The Home bleedin' Secretary gave me an alibi for that one!'

'Sadly for you, the Home Secretary blew his brains out three hours ago,' Foulds told him, calmly. 'And luckily for us, he left a note, the contents of which were sent through to us with some urgency, as it mentioned one of our officers, namely you, in a very bad light. If there's one thing to be said for suicides, they do like to get everything off their chest before they go. You can read all about it in the *Daily Mirror* tomorrow. We'll get you a special copy.'

Lola savoured the moment as all the venom and strength drained out of Seth. His legs collapsed beneath him as he was pushed past her, on to the bed she'd just vacated. He began to blubber.

'Come on, fellers, play the game, I'm a copper. I'm one of you.'

'You never were one of us, Lawless,' said Alfie.

Seth's lip began to quiver. 'But . . . surely they'll take me bein' a copper into consideration – I'm a good copper.'

'If you're lucky,' whispered Foulds, into his ear, 'you'll get away with just being hanged. By rights you should be drawn and quartered.'

Epilogue

HMP Strangeways, Manchester, Friday, February 7 1958. 8.58 a.m.

With him being a copper, Seth knew the procedure. He knew that the noose, which awaited him, would now be just a few feet away from his cell. He had pleaded guilty in the hope that it might save him from the gallows and he'd almost passed out when the judge placed the black cap on his head and pronounced sentence.

Seth's guilty plea removed any grounds for appeal. His only hope was that the sentence might be commuted to life, but it was a forlorn hope. He'd killed four people and in the eyes of the public and the judiciary, justice must be seen to be done. Hanging was the ultimate deterrent.

The two prison officers, who had kept vigil with him throughout his last few hours, got to their feet as they heard footsteps approaching. Seth lay on his bed with his back to them, intermittently sobbing and talking to the wall. The officers looked at one another and knew this wasn't going to be easy.

'It's time, Seth.'

'What?'

'It's time, lad.'

He had curled himself into the foetal position and was shaking, violently. The footsteps stopped and the door rattled open. Two more officers came in and helped their colleagues to hoist the blubbering prisoner to his feet and strap his hands behind his back. The governor, the hangman's assistant and the prison chaplain stood by the door. Seth was now weeping, uncontrollably, and pleading with them not to do this to him. The officers steeled themselves against his pleas and carried him, upright, through to where Harry Allen, the hangman, was waiting in the execution suite next door. Allen gave the

condemned man a most unexpected smile that calmed Seth
long enough for his feet to be strapped together and a white,
cotton hood placed over his head.

'Now take it steady, lad, we don't want you hurting yourself, do we.'

'No,' sobbed Seth, gratefully, allowing himself to be positioned on the trap door. What he couldn't see was that the two
officers on either side of him were standing on planks spanning
the trap door opening; each officer had one hand holding on to
a strap dangling from above and the other hand steadying Seth.

It took Harry Allen just an instant to check that all was as it
should be before he pulled the lever that sent Seth to his death.

Tommy stood outside the prison, mingling with the crowd.
There were the customary anti-hanging protesters, but not as
many as usual. Most people had other things to think about.
Manchester was in deep shock due to the plane crash in Munich
the previous day, which had killed so many of the Manchester
United team and left the lives of others in danger.

A man came through the gates and pinned up a notice to
confirm that the execution of Seth Lawless had been carried
out at 9 a.m. Some people began to sing 'Abide With Me',
but they were outnumbered by the ones who let out a loud
cheer as the news was passed around. Tommy asked a few
questions of people on either side of the capital punishment
fence, but he couldn't get Lola from his thoughts.

His article would tell the whole story of the Lawless brothers
and Clive Campion; and how Rachel Lawless's conviction for
murder had been quashed, albeit posthumously; and how her
body had been taken from the prison grounds and buried beside
her daughter, Evie, in a well attended and very moving ceremony. It was an article that would get him a job in Fleet Street.

As the crowd dispersed Tommy looked up and caught sight
of Lola in the distance, smiling at him as she often did nowadays. The trouble was, she smiled at everyone nowadays. He
took an airmail letter from his pocket. It had arrived the day
before. He read it for the tenth time.

Dear Tommy,
I want to be as far away as possible on the day they
hang Seth, so I've managed to get myself a modelling

assignment here in Milan. The agency couldn't be more helpful. Keith's mum's looking after Danny. We're talking now, although I doubt if we'll ever be the best of friends. I'll never get Mam or Evie or Keith back, but I have got my own life back, Tommy, thanks, in no small measure, to you. I'll always be grateful to you for everything you've done.

I love you dearly,
Lola

Tommy allowed himself a wry smile as he put the letter back in his pocket. Loving someone dearly was a million miles from being 'in love' with them. He knew this because Alfie had received a similar letter – she loved him dearly as well. In fact, Tommy had an idea that she loved Alfie a bit more dearly than she loved him. But what Lola loved more was the life she had ahead of her, and neither Tommy nor Alfie begrudged her that. He looked up at her face again and returned her dazzling smile.

'Have a great life, Lola.'

She was looking down on him from a hoarding, advertising Silvikrin shampoo. Over the past few weeks she'd smiled at him from newspapers, magazine covers and from the sides of buses.

They were nice photos but, to Tommy's mind, they didn't do her justice.

Lola was standing in the Piazza del Duomo in Milan, trying not to think about the time – just as she'd tried to avoid looking at the clock on the day of her mam's hanging. The whole city seemed to be revolving around her as she posed for the clicking camera. Behind her was Milan Cathedral, looking fabulous beneath a clear blue sky. The only cloud was Seth's cloud, the one that had hung over her since Ezra's death. Geoff, the photographer, called out to her.

'Eyes and teeth, Lola.'

A distant clock chimed out the hour and, try as she might, Lola couldn't help but count the bongs – ten o'clock. Seth will have been dead for an hour. She thought she'd feel different – relieved, somehow. But why should she? She hadn't felt any relief when she'd heard that Ezra or Campion were dead. So, was this it? Was she to live with the black cloud of their memory floating around her for the rest of her life? She tried to smile, but struggled. Geoff knew all about it, but he'd kept her busy all morning. Never given her a moment to think. Good old Geoff.

'OK,' he said, 'we'll try wistful and work up to that smile.'

So she thought about Alfie. Such thoughts usually made her smile. If she'd had to choose between Alfie and Tommy she'd probably have chosen Alfie, but she didn't have to choose. They were both lovely men, but neither was the one. Maybe it was a shame, but that was that. She felt a sudden shudder, like an electric shock, vibrating through her body, but causing no pain. Geoff's grin turned to a look of concern.

'Are you OK, Lola?'

'As a matter of fact I am – I feel good.'

'You look great.'

She laughed out loud and, for the first time since she was seven, she felt as free as the pigeons fluttering overhead. Free as a bird – just like her mam and Evie, up there in their heaven. The black cloud had gone.

She looked into the camera lens and saw Evie smiling at her as clearly as if she were standing right in front of her. Lola smiled back, the camera clicked several times – Geoff never missed the chance of a good shot.

She knew for sure that Seth had gone to a place where he could harm no one. She also knew that Evie was happy, and so was Mam. She knew it was all over, she knew that for certain. But there was something she didn't quite understand. Why now? What was so special about right now?

'Geoff, what time is it in England?'

He glanced at his watch as he swapped lenses on his camera. 'Erm . . . just turned nine o'clock.'

'And we're an hour ahead here?'

'Yeah, why, forgot to adjust your watch?'

'Not really. I just forgot I'd adjusted it. I'm not thinking straight at the moment.'

He looked up, suddenly realizing the significance of the time. A fleeting but disturbing vision of a hanged man crossed his thoughts.

'Ah, is this the time when, erm—?'

She gave him the smile he'd been waiting for and said, 'It's finished.'

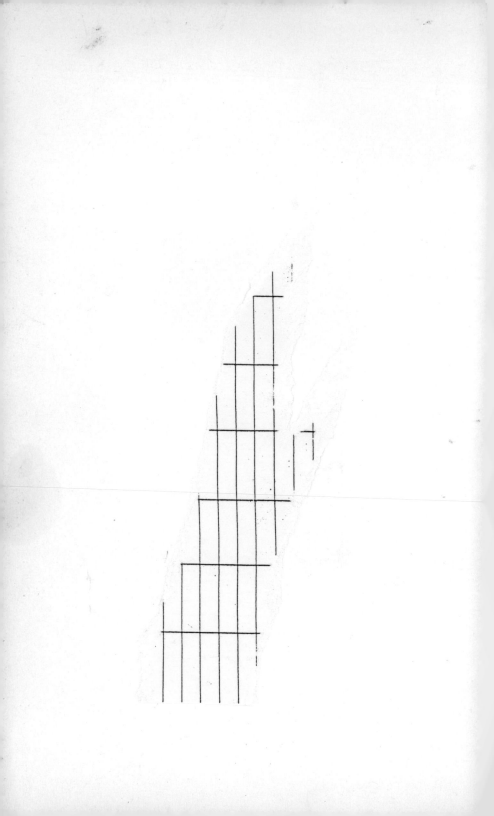